I0718111

One Knight's Return

CLAIRE DELACROIX

NEW YORK TIMES BESTSELLING AUTHOR

Copyright © 2019 Deborah A. Cooke.

All rights reserved.

ISBN-13: 978-1-989367-23-0

Books by Claire Delacroix

Time Travel Romances
ONCE UPON A KISS
THE LAST HIGHLANDER
THE MOONSTONE
LOVE POTION #9

Medieval Romances
ROMANCE OF THE ROSE
HONEYED LIES
UNICORN BRIDE
THE SORCERESS
ROARKE'S FOLLY
PEARL BEYOND PRICE
THE MAGICIAN'S QUEST
UNICORN VENGEANCE
MY LADY'S CHAMPION
ENCHANTED
MY LADY'S DESIRE

The Bride Quest
THE PRINCESS
THE DAMSEL
THE HEIRESS
THE COUNTESS
THE BEAUTY
THE TEMPTRESS

The Rogues of Ravensmuir
THE ROGUE
THE SCOUNDREL
THE WARRIOR

The Jewels of Kinfairlie
THE BEAUTY BRIDE
THE ROSE RED BRIDE
THE SNOW WHITE BRIDE
The Ballad of Rosamunde

The True Love Brides
THE RENEGADE'S HEART
THE HIGHLANDER'S CURSE
THE FROST MAIDEN'S KISS

THE WARRIOR'S PRIZE

Dear Reader;

One Knight's Return is a medieval romance about the arranged marriage of Quinn de Sayerne and Melissande d'Annossy. This is an enemies-to-lovers story that is set in my fictional realm of Tulley. Quinn has been summoned home from crusade by the Lord de Tulley, who is the overlord of his father who saw to Quinn's training as a knight. Quinn's wicked father, Jerome, has died, and Tulley wishes Quinn to take over the holding. Quinn is thrilled by this opportunity especially since he left Sayerne as a boy. Much to his surprise, Tulley has conditions upon the granting of the lordship—he insists that Quinn marry the daughter of a neighboring estate, Melissane d'Annossy. Melissande is even less enamored of this idea than Quinn, but they have little choice if they want to retain their respective holdings. Sparks fly between the pair from the beginning, for Melissande is outspoken about her disapproval of Tulley's plan. Quinn resolves to win his lady's loyalty and her heart, though he knows it won't be an easy task. I love this pair and the energy between them, as well as how complementary their skills prove to be. Once they begin to work together, they are a formidable team!

A version of this story was originally published under the title **My Lady's Champion**. When I began to update the file for republication, I realized that I wanted to make some major changes to the story. I've done that—the second half of the book is almost entirely new—so have published this new version with a different title to distinguish it from the older version.

One Knight's Return is the second book in a series of medieval romances featuring a company of knights who fought together in the First Crusade and who call themselves *Rogues & Angels*. All eight of these knights will have their stories told and find their HEAs back in Europe. Each knight has received a gift which will feature in his story. The gifts are a bit enigmatic and challenge the knights' various expectations. In addition to the changes made in the evolution of the romance, I also included new scenes with the company of knights who served with Quinn in Palestine.

There are also connections between the knights of this company and my other medieval romance series: many of them are the forebears of later protagonists, and I'll tell you more about those links as they unfold. On my website, these stories are all under the *Sayerne* tab, because that's the world they share.

The next story in the series will be **One Knight's Desire**, which is Niall and Heloise's story and an entirely new work. Heloise is Tulley's niece and likely his heir, while Niall is a charming rogue who never intends to be bound to a single woman. When he loses his heart to Heloise, things become interesting. Can he convince Heloise of his merit as a suitor? What about Lord de Tulley?

I hope you enjoy this new version of Quinn and Melissande's story, and also the companion knights of the *Rogues & Angels* series.

All my best
Claire
http://delacroix.net

One Knight's Return

PROLOGUE

February 1102

uinn de Sayerne was home.

He sighed with satisfaction as he surveyed the mountains that rose on either side of the familiar valley. Their silhouette was etched in his memory, yet to see them again was a gift.

His party had ridden past the keep of the Lord de Tulley earlier in the day and he had noticed his companions stare in wonder at that fortification. Tulley's keep perched on the top of the steep hill, commanding the valley in each direction. Quinn had found it impressive as a boy, but now, he saw its strategic advantage and appreciated the expense of its construction. A high and broad wall encircled the base of the hill, with the keep at its summit. The road wound upward from gates to keep, the village perched on the hillsides. Tulley was a marvel, but Quinn yearned for Sayerne's simpler structure. They continued past his overlord's holding in Quinn's haste, though he knew he would shortly return to pay his respects.

The party rode hard to the east until they reached the bridge that he knew as well as the lines on his own hand. He turned left once across the river, leading his fellows onward to the keep of

Sayerne.

In the twenty years since Quinn's departure, there had been moments when he wondered if he would ever return to the holding where he had been born and raised. His heart pounded in anticipation of a dream achieved as his destrier, Fortitude, raced through the deep snow.

When he crested the last rise and the Sayerne's fortress came into sight, his heart leaped. No column of smoke rose from the château, and indeed, the keep looked to be abandoned. Another man might have been daunted by the changes, but Quinn saw only home.

"Here it is!" he exclaimed to his companions, then looked again upon his legacy.

The keep itself was built of stone, a single low tower surrounded by a curtain wall and moat. The village clustered on either side of the road, outside the gates but near the moat. Quinn could see the lines of the furrows in the fields surrounding the village, their dimensions evident even when buried in snow. The sky was a fierce clear blue overhead and the wind was crisp; the mountains looked down on Sayerne as always they had and he could not believe his good fortune.

He would be Lord de Sayerne.

When no one spoke, Quinn glanced back. Bayard appeared to be skeptical, but even his companion knight's expression could not diminish Quinn's pleasure.

He had always feared that somehow his father would contrive to deny him his legacy. It would have suited the old man well, but Dame Fortune had smiled upon Quinn. After all these years, beloved Sayerne would be his. The Lord de Tulley had written to tell him so, thus it was true.

Quinn spurred his destrier forward, refusing to note that the river had frozen over. The mill was outside the keep's walls, the race fed by the same stream that was diverted to fill the moat. The mill wheel was lodged in heavy ice and Quinn could not remember it ever being so, even in winter. He told himself that the property must be well managed for all the wheat to be made to flour already. For so long, Sayerne had been a dream that buoyed his spirits, a touchstone that gave him hope for the future. He had come too far on that dream to readily surrender it.

Still, he wondered as he rode closer to the village. There was no sound of children playing, or any voices at all. The wind whistled through the village, which appeared to be empty. Not a single face peeked out from the darkened doorways. Quinn's dismay grew as a straw roof tumbled to the ground, even as he passed.

Undoubtedly, it was too cold to stir, even for a neighbor.

Some disrepair was to be expected in a land without an active lord.

Perhaps the villagers had moved within the walls for the winter.

Quinn was determined to maintain the euphoria of homecoming until he stood within the keep itself. Then and only then would he assess the damage done to the estate. They made their way through the silent village to the gates in those great walls. Quinn reined in his steed and stared, hearing Bayard and the four squires do the same behind him.

The gates of Château Sayerne stood open, undefended.

That was a sign of abandonment that he could not deny. Quinn stared without comprehension as one gate swung in the wind, its hinges creaking.

How could this be?

Where had everyone gone? And why?

"It seems that the rumor of your boots' stench has preceded you," Bayard commented. The squires laughed, their voices falling silent when Quinn did not join in their merriment.

It was the hand of his father that Quinn saw at work. He had the estate, but his bitter sire had ensured that he had naught else. It seemed that he had granted Jerome less credit for vindictiveness than was the old man's due.

Quinn straightened with newfound determination. He would claim his legacy, in whatever condition it might be, and rebuild the majesty of Sayerne.

In the center of the bailey was a magical place that Quinn had loved as a child. The bailey rose there, in a hill that was a small echo of that at Tulley. From the back of a horse, one could see over the walls to the land beyond. With the low tower at one's back, on a day so clear as this, Quinn would be able to look down the valley, all the way to Tulley. He rode directly there, ignoring the depth of the snow. His heart thundered in his chest as he turned Fortitude in place and looked upon his home.

Far beyond the walls of Sayerne, the land rose to mountain peaks on either side of the valley of the river Helva, and those peaks touched the crisp blue of the winter sky. The snow reflected the sunlight with a brightness that hurt the eyes. He could see Tulley in the distance and imagined he could see the red banner snapping in the wind at its summit. The tower of the keep behind him cast a stark shadow across the snow and the wind whistled slightly. His father's neglect could not destroy Quinn's own memories or the beauty of the land itself.

He was home, despite the odds, and that alone was cause to celebrate.

"Good day!" he called toward the stables. He knew that no one would answer, yet the silence made him wince. He stared up at the silent tower of the keep, noting its dark windows. It looked mean and humble to his eyes now, as well as abandoned. The snow had blown into deep drifts in the bailey and even the way to the stables was not cleared.

No one had been at Sayerne in a while.

It was cursed cold. Would there be fuel for a fire? Any morsel to eat? And what of the horses? Would there be fodder and bedding for them? Quinn feared not.

He refused to be daunted. He *would* rebuild.

"I had no notion that our destination would be abandoned," Bayard commented.

"Nor I, but it is. It is no less mine for all of that." Quinn raised his voice, letting it ring out across the bailey. "I am Lord de Sayerne, and I stake my claim on my ancestral holdings!"

He leaped from his saddle and abruptly found himself hip-deep in snow. Fortitude snorted and stamped, tossing his dark head and prancing to one side. Of course, Quinn should have anticipated that the snow would rise over the tops of his boots for it fairly reached Fortitude's belly.

Bayard, curse him, laughed aloud.

Quinn felt the snow slide its icy fingers into his boots and noticed the squires' surprised expressions. He scowled at his old companion, hoping to reassure the boys with a jest.

"Laugh while you may, for this snow is wicked cold in the boots."

"That I can see from here," Bayard said.

"Perhaps you should confirm how cold it is within one's tunic." Quinn lunged toward his fellow with a fistful of snow before Bayard could guess his intent.

His weight threw the other knight off balance in his saddle and landed the two of them in the deep snow. They tussled, laughing and shoving handfuls of snow into each other's garments by turn. The young squires laughed then cheered for one knight or the other.

"Woho! It is indeed cold in the tunic!" Bayard roared. "How does it fare within the chausses?"

Quinn shouted in dismay as Bayard shoved a handful of snow into his chausses. He spun and pelted his chuckling companion with snowballs. They chased each other, dodged and feinted, until Quinn leapt and landed solidly atop his friend.

Bayard's dark hair was already dusted with snow but Quinn still pushed him headfirst into a drift. The knight gained the surface again with a roar that sent the horses stepping sideways, then attacked Quinn.

When they halted, breathless and covered in snow, Quinn could not help but laugh. "Your hair," he managed to say. Bayard's dark hair stood up on one side, snow shoved into it. "You could be a demon defending this place."

Bayard made a menacing face and the squires retreated. One slipped from his saddle and made a snowball. "Take this, demon!" he cried and his missile hit Bayard in the middle of the chest, splattering on his green tabard. The snowball fight commenced again, this time with all six of them at odds, three of the boys yet astride their palfreys.

"Perhaps it was you who frightened everyone away," Quinn teased.

Bayard grinned. "Are you certain that no one sent one of your boots in advance to terrify those in residence here?"

"Not me, though I would not put such a feat past you."

"Me?" Bayard shook his head in mock disappointment. "Sadly, the thought did not occur to me in time. I could have dispatched a warning with that courier from your lord if my wits had been about me. He would have had a memorable journey, riding all the way from Palestine with that boot."

They laughed together at that.

"As your wits desert you, so Sayerne's villeins have deserted me," Quinn said, his smile fading as he considered the implications of that.

"Perhaps we should both check our boots," Bayard whispered, giving him a nudge.

Quinn was glad of his comrade's presence. Bayard could always find a bright light and together, they would see all restored to rights. "If the villeins were so dismayed at the prospect of a new lord, it is better that they left," Quinn concluded.

"Aye," Bayard agreed. "There will be challenges enough without doubt in the ranks."

Quinn beckoned to the squires and indicated the stables. "See whether you can make your way there and tend to our steeds. They have traveled far this day and are in sore need of rest."

"Aye, my lord." The youngest boy, Michel, eight summers old, jumped from his palfrey's back with enthusiasm.

He disappeared into a drift of snow.

"Nay!" Quinn shouted.

Bayard choked on a laugh.

Quinn trudged through the drift that rose as high as his own chest and reached into the hole left by Michel's passing. He gripped the back of a tabard, then hauled the boy above the surface of the snow and gave him a shake.

Michel sneezed.

Bayard chuckled and Quinn might have smiled himself, but little Michel from the sunny south had been granted a surprise he would not soon forget. Quinn lifted Michel to his shoulders and spoke to the other boys. "Make a pathway with your steeds before you dismount," he suggested. "Use my destrier and Bayard's first, for they will cut a larger path. Fortitude and Caligo are accustomed to the snow."

All three boys nodded in hasty agreement.

"Perhaps Michel could help us in the hall," Bayard suggested.

"That was my thought exactly," Quinn agreed. He waded back to the central rise where the snow was less deep. He set Michel on his feet and determined that the boy was no worse for wear. Michel had been born in the Holy Land and Quinn had kept a watchful eye on the boy as they traveled north. He had feared for the boy's welfare when they rode through the Beauvoir pass, for the wind had been fiercely cold. Michel could not be said to lack in resolve, for he continued in defiance of any obstacle. Quinn feared his determination would lead him too far one day, for he was small of stature.

Bayard eyed the tower, his gaze lingering on the line of the roof, and his doubts clear. "It might not be any warmer inside."

"There must be wood and tinder left behind."

"Must there?" Bayard mused but Quinn ignored him.

Surely his father would have left him enough for a blaze? Quinn was less certain than he would have liked to be. Michel rushed ahead of the knights, undaunted by his experience with the snow, and the pair followed the boy.

The hall was dark and musty. Only a single shaft of light drifted into the lower hall from the open portal, but the winter sunlight was bright enough to reveal that the room was barren, save for the dust that stirred as Quinn crossed the hall.

The fire screen he remembered was gone, as were the poker and pail. The spit from the great fireplace had disappeared, as had his mother's beautiful tapestries which had covered the walls. They had been part of her dowry and he wondered at their fate. As a boy, he had been enthralled when she told him the tales depicted upon them.

Even the trestle tables and benches had been removed. Tufts of abandoned herbs had blown into the corners but otherwise there was not even a candle stub remaining in the great hall. A glance into the kitchens revealed that every pot and knife was gone. A lantern with an increment of oil was clearly too much to expect.

The solar proved to be similarly empty, with a large hole in the roof and a snowdrift beneath it.

Quinn's characteristic optimism faltered then.

"Betrayed again," Bayard muttered.

"Nay," Quinn said with quiet resolve. "You cannot be betrayed by one you do not trust."

Someone—and Quinn knew who—had made certain that there would be naught to aid him here. From his death bed, his father had probably ordered the villeins to clear out Sayerne.

It was as cold as a tomb within the hall and Quinn shivered. Of course, there was not a stick of wood to be seen.

Curse his father! Quinn kicked at the few stale rushes in frustration. A squeal made him jump, followed by the sound of little feet scratching against the flagstones.

"Fetch that, boy!" Bayard bade Michel with a terseness that commanded obedience. Michel leaped to do the knight's bidding, then halted at his next words. "We shall need a morsel for our supper!"

The boy turned, his horrified expression enough to make Quinn smile. Bayard maintained a serious expression by some strength of will.

"My lord?" Michel asked tentatively.

"Do not worry," Quinn counseled him. "We have not even checked the storerooms yet."

"And they will be bountifully stocked?" Bayard responded with rare impatience. "We cannot remain here, Quinn, not even for one night. It is good that you have inherited an estate, but we cannot sustain ourselves on snow and the occasional rat. We must seek shelter elsewhere. What of your neighbors?"

"I have not gained my inheritance only to abandon it!" Quinn replied. "The château is solid and well built..."

"That roof," Bayard said but Quinn continued.

"The property is extensive enough to support many more than we six. It will take work, I admit, but the power to return Sayerne to its former glory lies within our own hands."

"Quinn, I see the advantages and I do not suggest that you walk away." Bayard's voice dropped. "I only suggest that we return in the spring, when we will not freeze to death while we sleep. Coin will not solve this alone, my friend, unless there is someone selling what you need."

"I will stay with you, my lord Quinn, even should the others decide to go," Michel said steadfastly and came to stand beside them.

Quinn smiled for the boy and ruffled his fair hair. He knew Bayard was right, but leaving so quickly after his return felt like a concession and one he should not be quick to make.

A man cleared his throat in the portal at that moment. A short, spare man stood there, watching Quinn. The new arrival was attired in Tulley's livery of red with four silver stars.

They must have been spotted when they passed Tulley and followed up the valley. A messenger from the liege lord who had summoned Quinn could only bring good tidings. Perhaps the Lord de Tulley had a plan to help Quinn remain here. Perhaps he sent provisions.

"Quinn de Sayerne?" the man asked.

Quinn nodded. "Aye, that is my name."

The man surveyed Quinn and a frown lodged between his brows. Quinn realized the state of his appearance and brushed some of the snow from his hair. He would have liked to have had a cleaner tabard, even to greet his liege lord's clerk, and to have polished his old boots, but there was naught for it now.

"I have a message for you from the Lord de Tulley. I am to await your reply." The clerk bowed and offered a scroll of parchment.

Quinn accepted it and stepped back outside into the sunlight. He lingered for a moment, eying his own name written across the parchment and the weight of Tulley's embossed seal. He ran his finger across both, for he had never received such a fine missive before.

"How did you know I had arrived?" Quinn asked, delaying the moment of breaking the seal.

"Your passage at Tulley was noted this morning, and of course, my lord had word of you resting at Beauvoir."

"Of course." Quinn knew that Tulley missed little that

happened within his holding.

"My lord knew that you would return once the missive regarding your father's demise had been delivered to your hand."

"I appreciated Lord de Tulley taking the time and trouble to inform me," Quinn responded in an echo of the man's formal tone. "It cannot have been easy to seek me out in the Holy Land."

"The Lord de Tulley is most fastidious about ensuring the line of succession is maintained appropriately."

"Still I appreciate his efforts," Quinn said with a smile.

The servant nodded brusquely. "I shall inform him of such, sir."

Quinn broke the seal and unfurled the parchment. He read it, then glanced up to meet Bayard's gaze.

"I am summoned to the lord's hall, with my party," he confessed. His investiture awaited him, he was certain.

"That splendid keep? On the mount?" Bayard asked.

"The very one."

"That is a fine invitation, indeed." Bayard turned and laid his hand on Michel's shoulder. His expression so sober that Quinn knew he meant to tease the boy. "Do not worry about the rat tonight," he advised the squire. "We will leave him for our return. The Lord de Tulley will probably offer finer fare, and the rat will be fatter by our return."

"Rat?" the messenger repeated with distaste. He peered into the shadows of the hall once more and his complexion paled. "There are rats in the hall?" He grimaced and his gaze flicked between the two knights. "And you planned to dine upon them?"

"It would have been a cold meal, as there is no fuel to be found here for the fire." Bayard leaned closer to the messenger and his voice dropped. "To my view, rats are not so good raw, for they tend to writhe on the way down." He made a gesture with one hand meant to clarify his meaning.

The messenger stepped away from Bayard, his horror clear.

"Perhaps you would like to try one?" the other knight suggested. He snapped his fingers at Michel and the boy ducked back into the hall, as if to catch a treat for the clerk.

That man turned and hastened back to his steed, calling the

remainder of the message over his shoulder. "Lord de Tulley expects you at the board as soon as you might see fit to present yourself."

"It is too far to ride all the way to Tulley this day," Quinn said. "The sun will set early at this time of year…"

"Aye, Lord de Tulley is aware of your progress. He has charged us to leave provisions for you at the barn used to store grain on the border of Sayerne. It is simple accommodation, but there is no grain this year and at least there is a roof." He spared a glance at the roof of Sayerne's keep and shook his head slightly in disapproval.

It was somewhat startling to Quinn that Tulley knew so much of his doings, and the state of Sayerne, but he was glad of the suggestion. "I thank you!" he said and bowed to the clerk. "That would be most welcome." His spirits were restored by both the missive and the promise of a warm meal.

The messenger was already in the saddle and rode out of the bailey with a speed better suited to fleeing the dogs of hell. Quinn could see the clerk's accompanying party awaiting him in the distance, near the specified barn on Sayerne's borders.

"Do you imagine he could run any faster?" Bayard asked. "And over the rumor of a rat. How soft the men are in these parts." He snorted. "We could tell him tales that would keep him sleepless for a fortnight."

"But it is better that many of those tales are left untold, my friend," Quinn said. "We will start anew here, you and I, should you be inclined to remain."

"I have no other place to go, as you well know. A younger son must make his fortune where he finds it." Bayard turned to Quinn. "Perhaps it is fortunate that Niall and Amaury fell ill in Venice and Lothair remained to tend them. Lord de Tulley might not have been so glad to host twice our company."

"Or you might not have had sufficient to eat," Quinn teased and Bayard laughed.

"Oh, I am well and truly prepared to enjoy a feast," he said. "And a hot bath. Not to mention a thick palette by a fire."

"The others will arrive in due time, though, and I would hope to have Sayerne fit to welcome them."

"They will all arrive in May, as agreed," Bayard said, surveying the keep once more. He shook his head. "There is a great deal to be done, Quinn, and you have no villeins."

"Aye." Quinn clasped his companion's shoulder. "But Sayerne is mine, Bayard, and Lord de Tulley must mean to aid my success."

"At what price?" the other knight asked.

"I do not care," Quinn replied. "I will pay it, without hesitation."

Bayard eyed him for a moment, as if keeping some comment to himself.

Then Michel appeared in the doorway to the hall. "My lord, I could not find the rat."

Bayard's gaze trailed to the gate, but the clerk was already out of sight. "It seems that the lord's messenger lost his appetite."

"Or perhaps he knows more about the bounty of the lord's board than we do," Quinn commented.

"Woho! Now there is a thought!" Bayard's brows rose at the promise of food. "Let's hasten to this barn to take our ease, and thence to Tulley in the morning." He, too, ruffled Michel's hair and the boy's eyes lit in anticipation.

"If I did not know better, I might think you had only accompanied me to have food in your belly," Quinn accused as they turned toward the stables.

Bayard laughed. "I anticipate more than that pleasure now that we are home. Do you think Tulley has a pretty daughter?"

"He has a niece, as I recall, but expect her to be well-defended from the likes of you."

Bayard grinned. "Any pretty maid will suit me, it must be said. A cook's daughter perhaps, or a miller's daughter. A maid from the kitchens."

"A woman who will see you fed."

"Among other pleasures." Bayard's dark eyes twinkled. "I would see her well-pleased, to be sure." He sobered as he glanced over the ailing estate again. "Trust you to find a haven for us that will require solid labor from our hands."

"Such work will be good for you," Quinn said. "You become

too old to earn your way with a blade."

"Too old to fight? But not too old to work like a peasant?"

"You do not have to stay."

"First I am old, now I am not sufficiently robust to move millstones. This *is* a sorry day for my pride." Bayard poked Quinn on the shoulder. "Do not imagine that you will shake me from your side in this adventure," he said, his voice gruff. "You may believe you owe me a debt, but to have a home would be the greatest gift a man might give to another. Should anyone be able to rebuild this place, it will be you, Quinn. I have never raised a blade beside a man of such will."

Quinn smiled, knowing the words came from the heart. "Then consider yourself at home, my friend. We have battled alongside each other for too long to part company now."

The two knights paused in the middle of the snow-filled bailey and shook hands under the bright winter sun. Then they hastened through the snow to their squires and steeds.

The grain barn, with its warmth, fodder and food, was more than sufficient to entice them on this night.

CHAPTER ONE

elissande was not pleased to be summoned to Tulley so early. Indeed, the messenger must have left that keep at first light, or even before. She had received word of another raid upon Annossy while breaking her fast, this time at the mill on the border, and had been conferring with her Captain of the Guard when the messenger arrived.

Did Tulley himself know of it already? She would not be surprised if he did. Her overlord seemed to know every detail first of events in his holding.

Her every attempt to see to her own concerns had been denied by the messenger, and she was commanded to escort him to Tulley immediately. Berthe had packed a few necessities—including a kirtle sufficiently fine to be suitable for a meal at her liege lord's table—and the two women had left Annossy with the messenger and the one warrior who accompanied him. Gaultier, Annossy's Captain of the Guard, had remained behind to learn more detail of the raid.

Melissande did not like to be ordered to do any deed, and her mood was not improved by the presence of another larger party upon the road. They looked to be ruffians and followed behind, making her keenly aware that her own party was smaller and less well defended.

In what peril was the world that a noblewoman could not feel safe upon the short stretch of road between her holding and that of her overlord?

Perhaps these men were the brigands responsible for the attack on the mill.

Melissande yearned to know, but she had not the confidence to confront them. They did not seem to be in a hurry and did not catch up to Melissande's party before reaching Tulley itself.

Lord de Tulley's niece, Heloise, rushed to meet Melissande at the gates. Perhaps Melissande had been summoned because the younger woman was in need of companionship. She knew Heloise had come to Tulley at Yuletide, after the death of her parents, and could well imagine that the other woman found little to amuse herself. She also knew that Tulley doted upon his niece and would do whatsoever was necessary to ensure her happiness. Tulley had neither spouse nor child himself. Melissande had met Heloise several times over the years and knew the maiden enjoyed the hunt. The snow this winter was likely sufficient to limit that pleasure and the girl must be vexed to be trapped indoors, even at Tulley.

Was Heloise's boredom the reason for Tulley's imperious summons? It was vexing to be considered no more than entertainment for a maiden with naught to do, but Melissande smiled for Heloise. She was a pretty and cheerful maiden. Melissande liked her and would not have wanted to be alone in Tulley's hall herself.

But she had scarce greeted Heloise than the Lord de Tulley's châtelain urged her toward the small chamber where Tulley conducted his business. Heloise was left in the hall with Berthe. Melissande found herself alone with her liege lord, and that so quickly that she scarce had removed her gloves. She had time to fear that something was sorely amiss, then he spoke.

Tulley, at least, was not inclined to be evasive.

"It is past time for you to wed, Melissande," he said crisply. "And you will do as much this very day."

Melissande was shocked by his blunt declaration but he held her gaze with resolve.

"Indeed, sir?"

"Indeed." Tulley seemed to have aged since she had last seen him the previous fall. Though his blue eyes were bright, the lines were etched more deeply in his brow. He looked smaller than he had, but no less determined than ever.

Melissande knew it was Tulley's right to choose her spouse since her father was dead. She supposed she had been foolish to hope that he had forgotten his obligation since he had not insisted on her taking a spouse sooner.

Tulley forgot naught.

He sat then in his great chair, his tidings delivered, and eyed her when she remained silent. "I thought you might have more to say of this matter, Melissande. You have never been reluctant to share your opinion before." He seemed amused by this, which irked her.

"I did not realize Arnaud de Privas had come to Tulley as well," she said.

Her lord snorted in a manner that was a reply in itself. "I have already told you to forget that whimsy of a betrothal."

Melissande stood taller. "A pledge is not whimsy, sir."

Tulley held Melissande's gaze. "If your sire were alive, he would have seen that pledge dismissed long before now. You were but a child! There is more at stake here than you might guess."

The implication that she could not understand the repercussions of her choice annoyed Melissande as little else could have done. Her tone was less temperate when she replied. "My word is at stake and that, sir, is of immeasurable value to me."

"My borders are imperiled by your lack of spouse," Tulley countered. "You will wed."

Melissande straightened. "My lord, when my father died, you promised me the opportunity to administer Annossy alone and prove my abilities. I am grateful for your trust. I had hoped that you might have invested me with the seal of my father's estate by now."

"I cannot entrust you with the seal. You are but a woman!"

Melissande kept her tone even with an effort. "I am my father's daughter, trained in Annossy's administration from the moment I could read."

"And yet a woman still."

"My mother held the seal while my father rode to war and administered the holding in his stead."

"On the assumption that he would return, and he did. If he had not done so, I would have ensured she wed another. The compromises made in the instance of war cannot be construed as permanent solutions, Melissande."

"My mother was an excellent administrator..."

"And you have taken a lesson from her, for which I am glad. But these recent attacks upon Annossy show that the holding is vulnerable!" Tulley spoke with heat. "The marauders know the holding is governed by a woman. You know as well as I that their actions reflect their perception of weakness."

"I am not weak!" Melissande protested. "The villeins are satisfied and the tithes have been beyond expectation. Annossy is well-ruled..."

Tulley interrupted her. "But not sufficiently well-defended."

"I could hire more men-at-arms," she began but Tulley waved off her suggestion.

"They will follow a man, and you know that as well as I do." He leaned forward and his tone softened slightly. "I hold these lands for the emperor by grant of the Count of Arles. Should any of them be lost, my own position would be compromised. You know that I cannot risk that. The attacks upon Annossy compel me to make a choice, Melissande. I have let you temporarily administer your family holdings, but I will not invest you with the seal."

Melissande glimpsed the warrior that the Lord de Tulley had once been, and appreciated anew his reputation as a man who would see his will done against all obstacles.

If she had been a man, she would have openly defied him. If she had been a man, there would have been no criticism of her administration. If she had been a man, she would have chosen her own spouse freely. Or taken none at all.

She could not remain silent. "I will choose..."

"Nay, Melissande," Tulley said with impatience. "You will wed and, as befits my right as your liege lord, I have decided to whom."

"It would please me to keep my pledge to wed Arnaud de Privas, my lord." That was an understatement in the extreme. Melissande's word was her bond, a habit taught by her beloved father, and a source of pride. "When he returns from winning his fortune..."

"He will not return," Tulley said briskly. "At any rate, the gaining of his fortune ensures that he cannot wed you."

"I do not understand, sir."

"Do you think, child, that after all these years I would ignore what I know to be important to you?" he demanded. "I did seek out that rogue Arnaud and I found him."

Melissande's heart leapt even as she noted that the lord's tone was disparaging.

"That rogue has taken a wife himself."

"A wife?" Melissande echoed.

"A wife. A rich wife." Tulley nodded. "It would appear that your loyalty has been misplaced."

This could not be. She and Arnaud had been sworn to each other as children. Though Privas had fallen upon hard times after the death of Arnaud's father, still the match had been the wish of all four parents, and Melissande could not simply ignore what had been promised.

She doubted that Arnaud would have done as much either. It was true that she did not know him well—she scarce remembered the boy who had taken her hand in his on that long-ago afternoon and repeated the words of the priest—for he had left soon after their betrothal to train for his spurs with a distant uncle. By the time he had been knighted, Privas had been desolate, and Arnaud had sent word that he would seek his fortune then return for her.

Melissande had waited, refusing all suitors for the man her father had chosen.

What if Tulley was trying to remove her objection, even with a falsehood, so that she cede to his plan? He did not approve of Arnaud, she knew it well, although she could not understand why.

"That must be untrue," she said before she could consider the wisdom of her words.

Tulley's gaze turned cold. "The source was reliable beyond

doubt," he said. "Arnaud wed Marie de Perricault a year past."

"Marie!" Although Melissande had not seen the older woman in years, she remembered her testy manner. Perricault was over the mountains and to the north of Annossy, closer to the court of the French king. "Arnaud would not break his word to me!"

"I regret to tell you that he did just that."

"Might your source be deceived in this?"

Tulley gave her a warning look.

Melissande took a steadying breath. She had to speak her thoughts aloud. "All these years, you have treated me with respect and honesty. Please do not abandon that path now, my lord."

Tulley's expression remained impassive.

"Tell me that you did not find Arnaud," she dared to continue. "Tell me that you refuse to seek him out for whatever reason; tell me what flaws you find in his nature or why you find our fathers' scheme to be a poor one, but do not lie to me about his fate. I know that I must do as you dictate. Do you think that deception will reconcile me to your will?"

"If you do not wed my choice, you will lose all this very day."

Melissande was startled. "I shall see your word tested, sir. I shall appeal to the emperor himself!"

"Whose authority is thin this far from his court," Tulley responded. "Do you think that he will strain his relations with me over the pleas of a landless noblewoman, however beauteous she might be? Annossy is mine to grant as I see fit. I could easily make an argument that your refusal to wed threatens the security of my borders." The lord settled back in his chair again. "Do you truly imagine that he would take your side?"

Melissande stared at her shoes. "I made a vow at my father's behest."

"And now you will make another." Tulley's gaze was resolute.

Melissande would be wed, regardless of her own will.

Soon.

And likely to a man whom she did not know.

Melissande could imagine no worse fate than this. She had been tutored by both her parents to administer Annossy, due to their lack of a son, and she knew she excelled at the task. It was unfair for her abilities to be discarded, simply because of her gender, and her blood simmered at the injustice of her situation.

"At least, you have seen the wisdom of holding your tongue," Tulley muttered.

Melissande took three deep breaths before she trusted herself to speak. "Who would you insist I wed, my lord?"

A rap at the door to the lord's office interrupted whatever Tulley might have replied. The lord smiled, his expression prompting Melissande to glance toward the portal.

A knight filled its frame.

Nay, not a knight but a renegade.

Foreboding touched Melissande's heart. Not a ruffian. Surely Tulley would not wed her to a man far beneath her social status. She said a silent prayer as the room, which had seemed too warm just a moment past, felt suddenly chilly.

Was this one of the men in that ragged party they had glimpsed on the road? Nay, it could not be. They had ridden in the same direction and there were several holdings east of Annossy, as well as abandoned Sayerne and high mountain passes blocked with snow.

Nay, her first impulse had to be wrong. This had to be some man-at-arms in Tulley's employ. A messenger or a mercenary. His arrival at this moment was naught but a coincidence. He brought a message, no more than that.

But still Melissande looked.

He was tall and broad of shoulder, though his travel-stained garb made him look rough and disreputable. His mail glinted in the candlelight, half-hidden beneath a tabard with a torn hem. A well-worn cloak was tossed over his shoulders, its hem dirty, and his thick leather gloves were scuffed from years of heavy wear. His boots were worn and dirty. His armor was not grand and it was not for appearances only.

He was a warrior, one who had meted death and confronted it.

Melissande shivered, intrigued despite herself.

He carried his helmet and ran one hand through the length of his untrimmed hair as she surveyed him, as if he sought to groom himself. It was an ineffective effort. His hair was wavy but clearly unclean, falling to his shoulders. There was stubble on his chin and a streak of mud across his cheek. His eyes were the most remarkable hue of amber and they lit with appreciation after his gaze swept over her.

Indeed, the corner of his mouth lifted, as if he might smile, and the expression was more beguiling than it had any right to be.

Melissande told herself that he must be plagued with lice, and took a step back.

Perhaps he had sought out Tulley to pledge his blade to that lord's service.

But the châtelain would never have shown him into this chamber while she conferred with Tulley, if that had been the case. The vagabond would have been left to wait in the hall.

God in heaven, *nay*.

"My lord," intoned Tulley's châtelain. "Quinn de Sayerne, son of Jerome de Sayerne, as you requested."

Son of Jerome de Sayerne! Melissande regarded the arrival with new horror as the truth proved to be even worse than her suspicions. Jerome de Sayerne was finally dead, but his son arrived to plague her anew. That lecherous serpent could only have spawned a son of no greater merit than himself.

Melissande had believed Annossy's troubles over when Jerome died. Though it was not difficult to believe Jerome's son might sell his blade as a mercenary. The thievery Jerome had initiated against her family's holdings had nearly destroyed Annossy.

Now the son would finish what the father had begun.

Indeed, if sire and son were cut from the same cloth, it was not unlikely that this man *was* behind the recent raids on Annossy.

Surely, Tulley would not compel her to wed him.

But her overlord's resolute expression left no doubt that he would do exactly that.

Quinn de Sayerne would be Melissande's husband and, if she did not miss her guess, their vows would be exchanged without delay.

She and Annossy were lost forever, and worse, there was naught she could do about it.

☙❧

It was troubling to see such a beautiful woman displeased, and worse to recognize that Quinn himself was the source of her dismay.

The noblewoman in Tulley's office had long fair hair, although it was twisted and braided so that its golden glory was difficult to see. She frowned at Quinn when he entered the chamber, her expression making him well aware that Tulley had granted him no opportunity to bathe before the meeting. He had been troubled enough about that fact, but the châtelain had insisted he bend his knee first, and so Quinn had complied.

Even the lady's foul mood did not deter from the beauty of her heart-shaped face and slender form. Her green eyes were tipped upward at their corners and heavily lashed despite her fair coloring. They snapped with fury as she glanced toward him, as if he were guilty of some crime. Her very presence made Quinn aware of how long he had lived in the company of men. It seemed that she, too, had been rushed to this chamber, for a fine dark cloak lined with fur still hung over her shoulders and her gloves were yet in her hand.

She must have been in the small party that rode down the valley ahead of his own.

Quinn was not certain what to say to her or if he should speak to her at all. In all honesty, he recalled few of the niceties of polite society. The company of noble ladies was a distant recollection for him and he had never possessed the easy charm of a knight like his comrades Amaury or Niall.

He considered his own garb and knew he would have to improve his wardrobe before he sought a bride.

"Lord de Tulley?" he said, knowing his voice dropped lower in his effort to appear composed. The lord's smile seemed genuine and Quinn dared to hope that all was not lost.

"Aye, Quinn. I suspect that you barely recall our last meeting." The lord rose from his chair and rounded the desk to shake Quinn's hand. "You were only a boy, then. You have grown tall these twenty years."

"Aye, sir. And I thank you for your support." Quinn regarded the older man with surprise at his unexpected familiarity. He recalled those bright blue eyes and the relentless set to the older man's lips. He also recalled Tulley being stern and uncompromising. Although the thick mane of white hair was new, there was a vigor in the lord's grasp that recalled a long-ago summer afternoon to Quinn's mind.

"It was you who sent me to earn my spurs and bade me seek my fortune," he said.

The lord nodded as he released his hand. "Aye. I always knew that you would grow up straight and true, despite the challenges laid at your door." He looked Quinn in the eye again. "How are matters at Sayerne?"

Quinn flicked a glance to the silent lady, disliking that he had to confess the truth before her.

Although, it seemed impossible that she could think less of him.

"Neglected," he admitted.

The lady sniffed at his admission and averted her face. Obviously, she thought the fault was his and Quinn immediately longed to defend himself. That she evidently thought little of him was something he should not find troubling. Bayard had warned him often enough of the fickleness of noblewomen for Quinn to let such a judgment concern him.

He fired a hostile glance in her direction when the lord turned away. She held his gaze boldly and something sparked between them, something that put a flush in her pale cheeks and a fire in his own blood. She averted her gaze again, tossing her head like a filly objecting to the bridle.

Tulley paced behind his desk. "You appear undaunted by Sayerne's state," the older man mused. His manner was much that of a cat toying with a mouse and Quinn eyed him before he responded.

Surely the lord did not intend to grant Sayerne to another? Quinn realized suddenly that the missive had only summoned him here. It had not mentioned his investiture, although he had assumed...

Quinn resolved to learn the truth in short order.

"Sayerne is my inheritance," he said with care. "And there is naught wrong with the holding that hard work will not put right."

The lady folded her arms across her chest. "And who will do this work, now that your abused villeins have fled?"

"It is only natural that villeins would leave an estate without a lord," Quinn countered. "I am convinced that they will return when they hear that I have arrived and intend to rebuild."

"You?" The lady scoffed. "Surely the arrival of the son of Jerome de Sayerne will have no appeal for his tenants!"

That he should be accused by a stranger of being like his father prompted Quinn's anger as naught else could. He had never abused another. He had never cruelly taken whatever he desired and ignored the repercussions. He was as different from his father as a man could be, and he was different by choice.

"If the villeins cannot be troubled to learn the manner of man I truly am, then I shall rebuild without such fools in my service," he retorted. "Should I be obliged to do so, my lady, you may rest assured that *I* will rebuild Sayerne, stone by very stone, with the labor of my own hands."

Her eyes narrowed as she regarded him, but clearly her opinion did not change. Their gazes locked and held, that strange awareness crackling between them, and Quinn knew he had been without a woman's touch too long.

Why else would this maiden of ice so stir his blood?

Tulley cleared his throat. Quinn spun to face the older man, heat rising on his neck that he had forgotten that man's presence. Out of the corner of his eye, he saw that the lady's cheeks tinged a brighter hue of pink.

How unexpected that they had something in common.

Perhaps she was not made of stone, as she might have him believe.

Quinn realized then that he did not know who she was. He scolded himself silently for neglecting his manners. He was certain that the lady had noted his error and would remind him of it, if she were ever given the chance.

"An assumption is being made," Tulley said. His bright gaze flicked between Quinn and the lady. "Sayerne has not yet been invested upon anyone."

Could the lord intend to grant Sayerne to this forthright lady?

Why else would Quinn have been admitted to the lord's offices in her presence? He slanted a glance in her direction, somewhat reassured that she looked as surprised as he felt.

"My lord?" Quinn asked.

Tulley smiled. "Do not worry, Quinn, my intention is still that you will hold Sayerne. However, times demand that I place a condition upon your investiture."

This was no good tiding. "A condition, my lord?"

"I would see you married."

"Married?" Quinn blinked.

"Aye, the line of Sayerne must be assured and I cannot let you take the reins of the estate without some succession—if it is not secured, then it should be in the process of being so."

Quinn faltered, for he had not planned to take a wife so soon. "But I have no betrothed, no fortune..."

"Surely, Quinn, you intend to wed?"

"Aye, my lord," he said with haste. "It is only the timing that is of concern. Sayerne is in need of repair and I would not expect any lady to endure such circumstances." His voice gained assurance as he made his argument. "Grant me but a year, my lord, that my home might be fitting for a bride and then I will welcome your counsel."

To his disappointment, Tulley frowned.

"Nay, Quinn, a year will not do. The matter must be resolved immediately or I cannot invest you with the estate."

Quinn was shocked to have his fear so calmly presented as a possibility. Was he only to glimpse Sayerne then be denied it? He cast his thoughts back to Tulley's missive, the one summoning him home, and realized the older man had promised naught.

He had simply notified Quinn of Jerome's death and urged him to return to Sayerne.

Quinn felt as if a cold hand seized his innards.

Tulley seated himself and frowned. "Your marriage will solve more than you know." The lord darted a glance to the lady. "Will it not, Melissande?"

The lady caught her breath in obvious disapproval. Quinn noted that she was even more affronted by the suggestion than he.

Indeed, she could not hold her tongue. She stepped toward Tulley and appealed to him. "Sir! Spare me your praise of this vagabond!" she said. "It is more than enough that some son of Jerome has come to claim that cursed family's holding, without you greeting him as a saint!"

Quinn felt obliged to argue. "I may be no saint, my lady, but do not call my family cursed."

The lady turned upon him with flashing eyes. "Whyever not?" she demanded. "They might as well have been cursed, as a result of your father's choices."

"I cannot answer for my father..."

"Tell me then why villeins fled your father's land at every opportunity. Tell me why no less than two dozen of his bastards born of serving wenches populate the countryside, each and every one denied the bounty of his hall. The women themselves were cast to the winds when their condition became evident. Explain to me, if you will, why every year until this one I have been obliged to argue with that foul man over the boundaries between Sayerne and Annossy. Perhaps you can tell me the fate of the grain that was stolen out of my warehouses every winter."

Her lips tightened as her gaze swept over him and he found himself stirred by her fury. She was no ice maiden, but a dragon filled with fire and fury. Her eyes flashed and Quinn was entranced.

"Jerome de Sayerne was a dreadful neighbor and it is difficult to expect any better from his son!" She lifted her chin and glared directly into Quinn's eyes. "Perhaps you, mercenary that you are, might explain to me who raids my estates even now." She pointed her finger toward his chest and he noted how small and fine it was. "I would not put such a deed past the get of Jerome de Sayerne. One way or the other, he pledged to merge Annossy with Sayerne. Know this, sir, that I pledged to stop him from realizing that dream, no matter the cost."

Annossy. She was the Lady of Annossy. Quinn remembered that the estate bordered upon Sayerne, before he resolved to set matters to rights with his neighbor.

When she made to enunciate her last point with another jab of her finger, Quinn snatched her hand out of the air. Her skin was surprisingly soft. She was so startled that her eyes widened slightly. She made to step back, but Quinn did not release her hand.

"And I tell you, my lady, that my sire and I parted ways twenty years past because of our differences," he said in a low growl. "I am as unlike him as oil to water."

Her fine eyes narrowed. "Your father was also deceptive, when it suited him."

"I am not," Quinn growled. No one called him a liar, even a beauty such as this.

"We shall see," she replied, undaunted. She squared her shoulders and tried to tug her hand from his. Quinn held fast. "Mercenaries plague my borders," she said through gritted teeth. "And you appear to be a mercenary." She met his gaze in silent challenge. "I do not need such a man as a neighbor."

"If Tulley wills it, you will have one all the same."

"How much do you know about the raids on Annossy, Quinn de Sayerne?" she asked.

"Naught," Quinn replied, admiring her spirit. "I have returned from the Holy Land this very week, my lady. You see not a mercenary before you, but a knight in sore need of a bath." He smiled slowly, but the lady stared at him. She seemed disarmed by his jest and he savored the fact that he had surprised her.

He suspected it did not occur often.

Her gaze flicked from his smile to his eyes, then over his clothing. "You can be no knight," she whispered. Her voice faltered and he did not doubt she was recalling the reference to his spurs.

"But I am."

"He speaks the truth, Melissande," Tulley interjected. "I sent for him upon Jerome's death. Quinn speaks the truth, as he always did."

At Tulley's endorsement, Quinn's smile broadened. He was surprised to see that rosy flush staining the lady's cheeks again as she watched him. Indeed, her cheeks were afire, and she looked more alluring by the moment. She flicked a significant glance to her hand trapped within his and tried again to pull it free.

Quinn loosed his grasp upon her hand, then brushed his lips across its back.

She shivered at the touch of his lips and her eyes widened, their hue brilliant emerald before she dropped her gaze to hide her reaction.

But Quinn had seen it.

And he was intrigued.

"I beg your pardon for my appearance, my lady," he said. "It is my pleasure to make the acquaintance of a neighbor."

The lady's lips tightened and she stood taller, that beguiling fire in her eyes once again.

Tulley cleared his throat and Quinn reluctantly turned his attention from the lady to his lord.

"Melissande d'Annossy will be far more than your neighbor, Quinn," Tulley said. "She will be your wife."

Too late, Quinn realized where this conversation had been directed all along. He felt like a fool for not guessing the truth sooner, and wondered if Melissande's understanding had been responsible for her vehemence.

"My lord, nay!" she protested.

"You would refuse to wed me, despite the lord's command?" he asked her.

Her sidelong glance was filled with disdain. "I would refuse to wed any man of your father's seed."

"And I would protest wedding a woman who fails to obey her feudal lord."

She spun to face him, propping her hands upon her hips. "I am the one who understands how to administer a holding so that it prospers."

"And I am the one who understands how to defend a border," Quinn retorted, echoing her posture. "If Annossy is subject to raids, you should be glad of a spouse like me."

"I am not!"

"Then you are a fool as well as a beauty," Quinn said shortly. She gasped in outrage and he wondered if she would strike him.

Then her gaze flicked to Tulley and she fell silent with an obvious effort.

"Neither of your protests have any meaning at all," Tulley said mildly. "For I have decided. You will be wed this very day."

"This very day?" the lady echoed.

"Today?" Quinn repeated, thinking of his dirty garb.

"Today," Tulley agreed. "Might I remind you, Quinn, that you are not invested yet with your estates. Should you not do my bidding, as any obedient vassal should, I will be obliged to find another to whom I might entrust Sayerne."

Quinn dropped to one knee and bowed his head, but Tulley was not done.

"I have arrived at a solution that will serve the needs of you both. I charge you, Quinn, to eliminate the raids on Annossy as your first responsibility."

It appeared that Tulley had a list of tasks. Quinn did not argue, but listened. Marriage first, brigands second. He hoped at some point, the seal of Sayerne would land within his grasp.

He bowed over Tulley's hand. "As this is your condition, my lord, I will make this marriage in good faith."

The lady hesitated before she spoke. Tulley cleared his throat and she spoke, her tone filled with resignation. "As will I."

Quinn felt his eyes narrow. He was not that foul a choice of spouse.

Tulley's gaze flicked between the two of them. "It seems that there is a lack of enthusiasm for this match. Perhaps even now one or both of you harbor plans of annulment."

No one denied the accusation.

Tulley leaned forward, his manner intent. "Understand me well: there will be no annulment. Do not expect otherwise, for I will demand proof of consummation at first light tomorrow morning."

"My lord!" the lady protested.

"It is only good sense," Tulley concluded.

Quinn could not look at the lady after such a deliberate mention of intimate matters. Indeed, he felt a warmth spread through him, and he recalled his first impression of her beauty. It might not be all bad to consummate this match.

Should she allow it. He would not force her, to be sure.

"Perhaps I named the wrong man barbarian," she muttered, as

though she could not restrain herself from comment.

Quinn's gaze flew to Tulley, certain she would be chastised for her rudeness, but the older man only smiled.

"Since I have known you so long, Melissande, and understand the strain of this situation, I will let your audacity pass." He stood and brushed at his tabard before smiling at them both. "Shall we say within the hour?"

Quinn nodded. He saw the lady do the same, with reluctance.

Tulley smiled. "I should think that commitment to wed would be sealed with a kiss."

The lady's cheeks blazed crimson. Quinn swallowed and felt clumsy. It had been so long since he had touched a woman, and the lady's manner was less than encouraging.

But Tulley watched and waited. Quinn had little choice.

All hung in the balance.

He would meet her in good faith.

The lady did not aid in the endeavor. She stood motionless, waiting, fists clenched at her sides. Quinn knew that he would have to initiate this embrace. He stepped closer and the softness of her scent caught him by surprise. Did she wear perfume? He had forgotten such feminine charms. Something tightened within him, but she did not so much as meet his gaze.

Curse her! They were both beholden to Tulley and it would be simpler if she met him halfway. Riding into battle was less of a challenge than this. Quinn hoped that she mustered some enthusiasm for his touch by the time they met abed.

In truth, it mattered little.

He would not sacrifice his inheritance.

He took a step closer and heard her catch her breath. Still, she stared fixedly ahead. He lifted his hand and gently touched two fingers beneath her chin. She shivered, but did not otherwise move. He coaxed her chin upward so that he might meet her gaze, but she closed her eyes. No doubt she wanted to leave him ignorant of her thoughts.

Would she defy him in every matter, every day? He began to suspect as much.

Would she vex him with such vigor for the rest of his life?

Quinn already wondered.

But he would not be deterred. Quinn bent and brushed his lips across hers. He felt the lady shiver again, though there was no other change in her posture.

It was after his hand had dropped away that he saw her single tear. It shimmered as it slipped through her lashes then over her cheek and she did not wipe it away.

Quinn felt like a knave, although he did not truly understand her response. Surely one light kiss could not be so burdensome as to cause a tear?

Tulley cleared his throat. By the time Quinn glanced to his overlord and back to the lady, that tear might never have been. Melissande exhaled shakily and opened her eyes.

Still she did not so much as glance at him.

What manner of woman had Quinn agreed to marry? A maiden of ice or one of unexpected fire? A woman who dared to challenge him, and to vex him, yet one who stirred his blood as never before. A woman of keen wits, to be sure, and one with the tongue of a viper; one who believed naught good of him at all.

He wondered how he would survive this match.

He wondered if he could win her, with time. It would be a challenge, to be sure, but to have this lady fight on his side, by his side, would be an achievement of merit. It could be the kind of marriage his mother had told him about, when she had shared those old tales of chivalry, the kind she had urged him to seek for himself.

Quinn was skeptical of his success with this lady as his wife, but he was determined to try.

"I would suggest you both summon some enthusiasm in short order," Tulley said, then left the chamber. His boots sounded in the corridor and Quinn heard him call for his châtelain.

Perhaps in this moment, he and Melissande could reach a detente.

CHAPTER TWO

elissande was humiliated. Not only was her pledge ignored but she was compelled to wed Jerome's son within the hour. Worse, Tulley himself would check the linens in the morning for evidence of the match's consummation. Her agreement was not sufficient to appease him and that irked her beyond all.

If only Jerome's son had not returned with such haste, she might have found Arnaud herself. She did not believe that he had betrayed their vow and wed Marie instead. Why else would Tulley insist upon both haste and blood on the linens? Obviously, he feared that Melissande would learn the truth and demand an annulment. Tulley had a plan and meant to see it brought to fruition before either she or this warrior could choose otherwise. Once their match was consummated, they would be compelled to remain wed.

Until death did so part them.

It said much for her frustration that she wondered how soon that moment might arrive.

"This is your fault!" she said, turning her frustration upon Jerome's son. "Could you not have remained abroad? Or lingered in some city to delay your return?"

"Me?" he echoed. "What man would not make haste to claim his inheritance?" He lifted a brow. "And truly, it has taken a year to ride from Palestine. I could not be expected to linger more than that, lest Tulley change his mind." He pushed a hand through his hair. "I already feared I might come too late."

It seemed he did know Tulley sufficiently well to recognize that their liege lord could be changeable. "Aye, why not hasten home, when you gain Annossy in the bargain?"

His eyes narrowed slightly as he surveyed her. "I came for Sayerne."

"And you are welcome to it."

"It is a fine holding."

"It is a ruin." Melissande folded her arms across her chest, feeling that the chamber was too small with this large and masculine man beside her. She was aware of his attention and his mood, and even of the heat of his skin. "Sayerne is neglected beyond hope of repair and you are a fool to even imagine it can be rebuilt in a lifetime."

He smiled, ever so slightly, and the sight made her heart skip. The expression softened his features and weakened her resistance with dangerous ease. "Perhaps I am a fool when it comes to matters of holdings and administration. Perhaps I have need of your counsel."

"No woman finds it alluring to be considered useful."

Quinn's smile broadened and her heart skipped again. "That is a harsh summary, my lady. Do you not think a man and wife should confer together to decide what is best for their holdings?"

How could Jerome's son know about a good marriage and how it might work?

"I do not think that the affluence of Annossy should be used to pay for the rebuilding of Sayerne." There, she had said it aloud.

His expression turned thoughtful and she wondered if she had given him an idea. "When we are joined in marriage, the holdings will become one."

Melissande closed her eyes at that prospect.

"And be administered as one," he continued.

"Just as your father desired."

"Perhaps. Of greater import is Tulley's desire in this matter."

Tulley. Melissande gritted her teeth in vexation.

Quinn took a step closer and lifted her hand in his, unfurling her fingers with a stroke of his finger. God in heaven, it was persuasive for such a powerful man to touch her so gently. "My lady, I think we have little choice but to cede to Tulley in this, and endeavor to make the best of a match neither of us anticipated." His tone was yet more persuasive.

"Or desired," she added.

"But it must be so. And perhaps there is advantage to be found in our union." His words were compelling and his voice low. Melissande had a difficult time catching her breath. Quinn de Sayerne had a charm about him, to be certain. Having that amber gaze fixed upon her disturbed her more than she would have liked to admit, never mind having her fingers caught in the warmth of his hand. Her gaze lifted to the firm outline of his lips, but she glanced away before he could make more of her reaction than was justified.

Quinn de Sayerne had accepted her hand only to obtain his inheritance.

He needed Annossy's wealth to restore Sayerne.

And what would be left of Annossy when he was done? Both she and her parents before her had labored too hard to lose everything at Tulley's whim.

She tugged her hand from Quinn's grasp. To her surprise, he released her fingers without a fight.

Melissande shuddered to think that Jerome had triumphed after all.

"Surely you cannot find my presence so loathsome as that?" Quinn asked. "We scarce know each other."

"But I know your goal. How do you imagine that you will make Sayerne prosper again?" she asked. "The estate has been mismanaged for as long as I can recall. Where will you find the coin to do it? Do you have any notion of the cost? You would be better off to pledge your blade elsewhere and move on. You do not even have a villein to call your own."

Color rose on Quinn's neck. Melissande wondered whether she

had pushed him too far, although she had done no more than state the truth. What was this man like when he was furious? She had a strange desire to know, to see his composure shattered, to know the truth of him in a temper.

She wished she could see his worst before they wed. That was the truth of it. Then she would know better what to expect.

"Undoubtedly because they have all moved to the richer abodes," he replied more harshly than he had thus far. His gaze bored into hers and Melissande took a step backward in trepidation. "Might I guess that some of them have moved no farther than Annossy?"

Melissande flushed. "I did not steal them, nor did I tempt them away. A villein of good sense will seek out a place where he might see his belly filled and his family sheltered. Your father ensured that most on his lands spent their nights in hunger."

"Is it not an offense to harbor the villeins of another estate?"

He knew the law, against her expectation, and Melissande realized she would be a fool to underestimate him. "It is, but I merely showed charity to those in need of it."

"Charity?" Quinn echoed and she felt her flush deepen.

"They were being abused. How could I turn them away?"

"And so your compassion was shown and appreciated. And now that they are no longer in peril, I will expect their return."

Melissande caught her breath. "They are my villeins now."

He arched a brow. "Will Tulley take your side in this, if I appeal to his court?"

"To what will they return? Ruined homes and empty larders, fields left fallow too long and no seed to plant? You must think beyond your own ambitions to their welfare. *That* is the task of a responsible baron."

"I would ensure their welfare."

"They would have to see it to believe as much of Jerome's son. They are not fools, to be sure."

Quinn folded his arms across his chest as he considered her, that slight smile tugging at the corner of his mouth.

Wretched man. She could not even think coherently when he looked at her thus.

She tingled.

"Perhaps I must ride to Annossy and make an appeal in your court, my lady. I wager you would like to see me kneel before you, as Lady of Annossy and source of justice there."

The suggestion was surprisingly provocative and Melissande found herself at a loss for words. Quinn took another step closer, pressing his advantage, his gaze locked with hers. Melissande could not take a breath. She could feel his heat. She was snared by his intent gaze and she yearned for something she could not name.

Quinn could name it. Melissande would wager upon that.

"Do you mock the notion of me as judge?" she asked. "Or do you mock the notion of a woman as administrator?" She lifted her chin. "If so, I invite you to compare the state of Sayerne and Annossy, to see who fares better at this task."

He raised a hand to her shoulder, resting its weight there as if he would draw her into his embrace. Melissande recognized the hunger within herself and knew that this would be war. They would battle for supremacy and, to her dismay, Quinn already had her body upon his side. She felt the shiver that rolled through her body, the heat that emanated from the weight of his hand upon her shoulder, and she knew that if he kissed her again, she would be lost.

She raised her hand to remove his. "We are not wed yet, sir," she said with heat, knowing it was a feeble excuse.

He caught at her wrist and pulled her closer. "Nay, not yet," he whispered, his voice so low and his tone so intimate that her knees were weakened. His gaze heated as he bent toward her and she felt a desire beyond what she had experienced before. Melissande was stretched to her toes, her breasts tantalizingly close to his chest. His proximity fanned the flames kindled by his earlier kiss, but Melissande would have died rather than confess this truth.

How could she be surprised that a barbarian knew best how to awaken her base urges?

Quinn bent and his lips were against her hair, his breath in her ear, and Melissande was shaken by the power of his touch. She averted her face in an attempt to hide her reaction, knowing it was only a matter of time before he had all he desired of her.

And then what? She would be discarded, like one of Jerome's women, and left to fend for herself—without Annossy.

Her heart tore at the truth of it.

"Do not imagine, my lady, that you will compel me to defy Tulley," Quinn whispered. There was steel in his tone and she heard the truth of his resolve. "I will not lose Sayerne. On this night, we must make our match and we must consummate it, by Tulley's command. It need not be an ordeal, though you can make it so."

Melissande twisted away from his whisper but glanced up. She was trapped then by the determination in his eyes. Despite herself, she recalled the brush of his lips over hers. Would he be gentle with her? Or did he seek only to disarm her? Her blood simmered, as if she was no better than a harlot.

"Scoundrel," she whispered, hating how readily he fed such urges within her. "You care for only your own ends. I can see clearly that you are your father's son."

Quinn's eyes flashed like lightning, but his grip did not tighten and his voice did not rise. Again, she glimpsed the power of his restraint and had to admire it. "My sire and I had naught in common," he insisted. "You, my lady, will be the first to learn the truth of that." Their gazes held for a long moment and Melissande knew she had engaged an opponent who would not readily retreat.

His gaze dropped to her mouth. He smiled that slow smile again, the one that undermined her belief in all she knew to be true, and she could scarce draw a breath.

"Perhaps we should seal our pledge anew," he suggested, a rogue to his marrow. The mischievous glint in his eyes was so beguiling that Melissande did not move away in time.

Then Quinn bent and his mouth slanted across hers.

His kiss was firm, his lips coaxing, the strength of his hand on the back of her waist before she guessed what he was about. He did not claim, he did not possess: he invited, and that so astonished her that Melissande did not even consider making a protest.

Indeed, she surrendered and it was bliss. Quinn's kiss was gentle and intimate, yet tempting all the same. It hinted of greater pleasures to come and made her heart race. He smelled of sun and leather and horses, but beneath it all was the heady scent of his own skin. He made a sound of surrender that pleased her greatly, then locked his arm around her waist, drawing her to her toes. Her breasts were crushed against his chest and his mouth opened, claiming her more boldly.

Nay, he feasted upon her, coaxing her response, and she let him.

Melissande was overwhelmed and awed—and more desirous of his touch than she could have believed possible. She guessed that this was not the first time for Quinn to kiss like this, that he knew she was innocent in such matters and tempered his own desire for her, but that awareness still did not check her response.

When he deepened his kiss, that warmth spread within her, destroying her ability to deny him and feeding her own desire. Melissande was aware of every fiber of her being; she tingled from head to toe; she burned for more of whatever he might give. She found herself pressing herself against his strength, her eyes closed in pleasure. His fingers fanned out against the back of her waist, holding her captive to the pleasure he was determined to give. When her own fingers slid into his hair, pulling him closer, she realized her folly.

He was trying to disarm her.

He succeeded with great haste.

She would be valued for her beauty and her womb, for her ability to give him sons—if indeed she could—while her wits and skill would be ignored.

He would train her, claim all she possessed, and discard her.

Then he would sacrifice Annossy to Sayerne.

"Nay!" Melissande tore her lips from Quinn's and laid her hands flat on his chest to push him away.

He obediently retreated, though he watched her closely.

"We are not wed yet, sir," she repeated, hearing the tremble in her voice. She felt rumpled and flustered as she never had before. Her skin was flushed and she knew that her cheeks were stained crimson. Her lips throbbed and she felt a new heat in the depths of her belly.

"Yet I find more promise in our union than earlier," he replied, his voice a low rumble. His eyes glinted and again, she was treacherously close to be being beguiled.

Melissande shook her head, her fear rising. How could she forget what she knew of his kin? She wagged one finger at him. "You will beat me, as your father beat his women."

Quinn shook his head with reassuring resolve and propped his hands on his hips. "I told you that we two were different," he said with such conviction that even she was tempted to believe him. There was something about this man that made his pledges weighty. "I will never lay a hand upon you in violence. I will never compel you to welcome me to your bed."

Did he speak the truth, or was she a fool to give his words any credit at all?

He was resolute, to be sure.

What did she know for certain? That he loved Sayerne as much as she loved Annossy. And in that was the trouble. Melissande did not wager that Quinn's objectives would be readily put aside, for any reason.

"Even if I deny you this night?"

"I hope you will not," he said solemnly, his gaze locked with hers. "For it will cost us both dearly."

Melissande exhaled at the truth in that.

Then he smiled crookedly and reached to brush a finger gently across her cheek. "Be warned, my lady. I reserve the right to attempt to convince you to welcome me."

Again, there was a playfulness in his manner, one that disarmed her for its unexpectedness. And that intimate rumble of his voice when he murmured. God in Heaven, the sound heated her to her toes! Melissande struggled against the sense that she could rely upon Quinn, knowing full well that he was manipulating her.

And with ease.

She was a fool. Surely she could not abandon her suspicions that he was behind the raids on Annossy as readily as that? She would not have put it past Jerome to have arranged such attacks in order to see his goal achieved.

What of his son?

A year's ride from Palestine? What if he had been returned for a month or two, yet had not declared his presence before?

"Nay, you will not," she said. "Indeed, I must have your pledge before we wed this day."

"What pledge?" he asked warily.

"I may be compelled to marry you, and I may be compelled to welcome you this night, but after this night, you will come to my bed only if you are invited. You said yourself that you would not force yourself upon me."

Quinn's voice dropped and already Melissande knew him well enough to be warned that his temper was thinning. "I do not intend to lose my estate," he said. "Remember that Annossy also hangs in the balance, my lady."

"I have already agreed to the consummation of our match, but that will be the sum of our intimacy, until I so choose."

"Ever after you would deny me?"

"Aye."

"You know Tulley will desire that we produce a son."

"Then you had best make haste to win my trust, sir." She shrugged. "Or perhaps that son will be conceived this very night."

"Why?"

Melissande flung out her hands. "I know naught of you, sir, and what I suspect is not encouraging. I will not be reduced to chattel without a fight."

Quinn eyed her for a moment, then stepped closer. Melissande retreated from the resolve in his gaze, but Quinn did not halt. He closed the distance until Melissande found herself backed into the wall. Then he leaned over her and she closed her eyes that he might not see how keenly aware of his proximity she was.

"I offer that pledge, my lady, and I take your wager," he whispered. "We both have need of a son and I intend to be...persuasive." His lips brushed her cheek again and Melissande held herself taut.

Curse Tulley! Had she been a man, she would never have been in this position. Curse all men for their need to lord their power over women.

Curse Quinn for making her want to surrender.

The thought was so clear and the truth of it so resonant that Melissande clenched her fists.

"I will not be readily convinced," she managed to say.

"I think otherwise," he whispered, his breath fanning her cheek. Melissande kept her eyes closed, knowing that if he was smiling slightly, she would be lost. "I shall make you shiver," Quinn vowed softly and she knew it was true. She felt his lips touch her cheek, as gentle as a butterfly, and it took all within her to keep from turning her head for another kiss. "I shall make you moan and I shall make you beg me to touch you. You will not invite me to your bed; you will entreat me. And we will conceive a son." He kissed her ear and she found her back arching toward him, her hunger for his touch making her burn. "And then, we shall conceive another."

His lips touched her jaw, his kiss leaving a trail of fire that made Melissande gasp with need.

His power over her was terrifying.

She had to stop his assault, no matter what it took.

"Never!" she said with vehemence. "I will never yield willingly to your embrace and I will never *entreat* you, sir!"

Quinn, of course, smiled that wretched smile.

"I shall take this as a challenge, my lady," he murmured. His gaze swept over her features, his eyes glowing with such heat that he did, in fact, make her shiver.

He leaned closer and Melissande knew his intent. Desperate to escape his kiss, she ducked beneath his arm and fled for the door.

"You were not invited," she whispered and saw his eyes flash. She lunged for the doorway, certain that Quinn would catch her and take his vengeance.

To her relief, she safely gained the portal. She flung herself into the corridor without a backward glance, then ran down its length. What had she done? What was in her mind to taunt him? Within hours, they would be alone, and he would beat her, just as Jerome had beaten his women.

She might not see the morning.

Melissande's heart nigh stopped when Quinn bellowed from behind her. "My lady! You would test the patience of a saint—and I have already told you, *I am no saint!*"

She had finally prompted him to lose his temper.

And it was as fearsome as she had thought.

She ran.

It was only once Melissande had raced up the stairs to her assigned chamber, and locked the door behind herself, that she dared to halt and catch her breath. She listened, but no one pursued her.

Was it possible that Quinn's fury only made him shout?

Or did he restrain himself until they were alone?

Melissande's hands were shaking. She sat on a stool opposite the door and struggled to compose herself. In that moment, she realized that she had not thought once of Arnaud after Quinn had walked into Tulley's chamber.

How fickle was she? One kiss and her word was worthless. Nay, one look and her vow was forgotten. At Quinn's touch, she had forgotten her own reserve and even her dignity.

Much of what she valued was lost already—and their nuptial vows had not even been exchanged. Quinn de Sayerne would be the ruin of all she held dear.

Worse, Melissande was powerless to halt what Tulley had begun.

Quinn stormed into the bathing chamber near the stables, kicking open the heavy wooden door then slamming it behind himself. Three unfamiliar servants, as well as Michel, jumped and turned to regard him in surprise.

Ye gods, but Melissande d'Annossy could set his blood to boiling as never it had before! He had never been so infuriated— and that within a heartbeat of being so consumed with desire. Quinn felt vexed and challenged and ardent, all at the same time. It was a most confusing combination and one that left him riled beyond all.

And he had barely made the lady's acquaintance. If she had been welcoming, this fire in his blood could have bode well for their match. As it was, he feared that he would yearn every day and night of his life, and she would ignore him.

But Tulley could not be denied. Quinn had to wed Melissande

and he had to bed her, and he had to convince her to make their marriage one of merit.

He simply did not believe in this moment that it could be done.

She had granted him one night to conceive an heir. Oh, he would have to ensure that her pleasure was complete. Quinn shoved a hand through his hair in frustration. If only he had possessed an increment of Niall's charm, or a measure of Amaury's confidence with women. Quinn knew he was an unpolished suitor and Melissande's refinement made him more keenly aware of his lack.

Surely this marriage could not cost him all?

Bayard was yet bathing, characteristically taking his leisure in the hot water. The room was filled with steam and the smell of wet cloth. A fire blazing within a brazier was the only source of light, but none of this tranquility soothed Quinn in the least. He paced the width of the chamber and back, ignoring the watchfulness of the others.

Could he successfully seduce Melissande?

Could he win her favor?

Michel approached him cautiously, the boy's manner proof that Quinn's bout of temper showed. "Would you bathe, my lord?"

"Aye." Quinn bit out the word.

"Then we will need more hot water." Michel gestured to one of Tulley's servants, who hesitated. When Quinn glared, the man bowed hastily and fled the chamber, bucket in hand. Bayard laughed but Quinn did not so much as smile. He eyed the other servants who followed their comrade with haste.

"And what did the Lord de Tulley say that vexed you so mightily?" Bayard asked.

"It was not Tulley who vexed me," Quinn admitted. "Though he struck the tinder."

The other knight's dark eyes gleamed with curiosity. "Bad tidings?"

"Bad enough." Quinn shed his cloak and unbuckled his belt, aware of the filth layering his skin. He had to court Melissande and win her favor—though he doubted the extent of his charm and he felt the press of time.

Could the feat be done?

Or was Sayerne already lost?

"I do not think I have ever seen you in such a foul mood," Bayard commented.

Quinn knew the look he tossed his comrade was a dark one.

Bayard chuckled. "Aye, foul indeed."

"If you wish to see a foul mood, then come to my wedding," Quinn replied. "I will take a wife in less than an hour."

Michel froze in the midst of folding Quinn's tabard to stare.

"Wedding?" Bayard laughed again. "You are to be married? On this very day?"

"Aye, or else Sayerne will not be mine." Quinn sighed. "Lord de Tulley has set the terms and there is little to find amusing in the situation."

"Married!" Bayard repeated. "And so quick as that! Do they fear she will flee?"

"She might."

Bayard leaned back in the bath, his eyes dancing. "Quinn wed. There is a marvel I had not thought to see it so soon."

"And if you continue to comment, then it will be a marvel you will not see."

"How so?"

"I shall ban you from the festivities for your comments."

Bayard, untroubled, laughed and laughed.

Quinn did not join his merriment. Even though his annoyance had faded, still he felt disgruntled. The lady Melissande certainly possessed a gift for irking a man.

Or perhaps for irking him.

He sighed and confided the worst of it. "The Lord de Tulley has even been so courteous as to choose the bride."

Bayard's eye lit. "Who is she?" he asked. "What is she like? I might wager that she does not see the appeal of the match, given your mood."

"She does not."

"How fascinating." The other knight showed no inclination to abandon the tub. Quinn felt the chill against his bare skin, although the room was warmer than most. He gave his companion a quelling look, but Bayard only smiled as he settled deeper into the steaming water.

The selfish cur showed no sign of ending his bath.

"Have you not soaked the flesh from your bones by now?" Quinn demanded. "I would not catch my death this day."

"Then she cannot be so unpleasant," Bayard said. "Although, one must wonder at her looks for Lord de Tulley to be so anxious to see her match made. In such a rush, as well." He clicked his tongue. "Is she a termagant?"

Quinn chose not to reply.

"Or perhaps he meant to give you no opportunity to reconsider. Tell me more of her."

"She is heiress of a neighboring holding, Annossy."

"Wealthy." Bayard's brows rose. "Is she old?"

"Nay."

"Pretty?"

Quinn did not reply.

"A young heiress, likely fine of feature, given your attitude," Bayard concluded. "That sounds like fine fortune indeed. What precisely is your objection?"

"The objection is the lady's."

Bayard chuckled. "Those boots of yours," he teased, just as Tulley's servants returned into the chamber with steaming buckets of water. The châtelain himself supervised them, directing them to retrieve a second wooden tub from a shadowed corner. They rolled it out to the middle of the room as more water was fetched to fill it and the châtelain snapped his fingers to hasten them.

Two tubs? Quinn's eyes widened slightly. It had been a long time since he had visited any hall blessed with such luxury. In fact, Quinn and Bayard had shared bathwater on so many occasions that who would indulge first was an ongoing jest.

"This is a well-equipped keep, Quinn," Bayard commented, evidently seeing the direction of his gaze. "And your reward for leading us here is no small one, for you will not have to be second after me into the bath on this night. Better yet, I will not have to emerge any time soon. I have waited long for this bath and I will savor it."

Quinn smiled despite himself at his comrade's satisfaction.

"Especially as I now have a wedding to attend." Bayard leaned back in his tub, beckoning to the servant for more hot water. "By the saints above, it will take me a week to soak this filth from my hide." He sighed and closed his eyes as his water was warmed, then sank beneath the surface for a moment.

Quinn waited until he broke the surface again. "If you are as dirty as you say, then the second tub is a blessing indeed and I am glad of it." He might have hoped the matter of his bride to be closed, but he knew his comrade better than that. Bayard was cursed curious and never left a matter rest until he understood all of it.

Even now that knight watched Quinn, as if he could glean the truth from his manner. Quinn turned his back upon Bayard, purportedly to climb into the second tub, but truly to hide his thoughts from his perceptive friend.

Bayard waited until the châtelain and Tulley's servants had departed. Only Michel remained when Quinn settled into the water and closed his eyes at the luxury of the hot water.

"It cannot be a bad sign for this lady to have you so troubled after only one short interview," Bayard said. Quinn tried not to wince. "You will make the best of this match in the end, Quinn, if it begins with such passion."

"This match can have no best!" he replied with a vehemence that made Bayard's brows rise. He tempered his tone with an effort. "She is as frosty as the winter wind, and there is no reasoning with her." He frowned. "Unless, of course, she is furious and so articulate that a man can scarce utter a word in protest."

Bayard said naught, the silence stretching long between them.

"It is unlike you to be so troubled about *any* matter," he finally noted. "I will guess that she meets with your approval but the opposite situation is not true."

Quinn flung out his hands in frustration and water flew in all directions. "It is unlike me to be accused of being a mercenary, a brigand, and the echo of my sire in one interview! The lady has no shortage of criticisms to make, all unfounded."

"A brigand?"

"There are raids upon her holding, which has prompted Tulley's hand."

"Because she has no lord husband."

"But evidently she fears I am like my father. I see in her eyes that she wonders whether I lead the brigands. Her skepticism would match yours in magnitude." With that, Quinn fell silent.

Bayard propped his elbows on the sides of the wooden tub and sat up, a glint in his eye. "Is she foul to look upon?"

His comrade's curiosity troubled Quinn, which both surprised and annoyed him anew.

"Nay," he admitted.

Bayard's chuckle did naught to ease his mood. Quinn was grateful for the relative darkness of this place, for he felt color rising on the back of his neck.

"Dare I suggest that this is a matter of pride, Quinn?" that knight asked. "A pretty lady has spurned you, and not without cause, given your appearance upon arrival here. Are you insulted?"

"Of course not." Quinn spoke gruffly. "But a man's merit is not his garb."

"What manner of lady would she have been if she had swooned before you? No woman you would welcome to wife, of that I can be certain."

"Such a woman might be perceptive."

"Such a woman might be undiscriminating," Bayard replied. "As whores are like to be." He took the brush and scrubbed his nails. "I would be pleased if a pretty lady, never mind one I was commanded to wed, confessed the truth to me without hesitation. Such a deed would show her merit as one who is honest, and her trust in me that she might confide her thoughts. I should have thought you would be the same."

There was unwelcome truth in that.

"I do not think she trusts me."

"You have only just met her, and not looking your best." Bayard nodded. "She likely had some whimsy of wedding a man she chose, not one thrust upon her. Women put much credence in matches based upon love."

"Do they?"

"Aye. It is the task of the husband to convince the lady to come to love him." Bayard smiled. "I should think even you might manage that feat in time."

"I thank you for your confidence in my talents."

"What talents you possess, my friend, have naught to do with the seduction of reluctant maidens." Bayard blinked. "Is she a widow?"

"I do not know," Quinn confessed. "I do not think so."

"Then she will be a maiden and rendering the marital debt will be a new obligation for her. Be gentle this night, Quinn, and that may gain you much."

"Do you think as much?"

"Many women fear the first time, because of the pain."

Quinn recalled that tear. If Melissande thought little of his father, she might know of Jerome's violence. Had she not recoiled as if in fear that he might strike her? Aye, if she knew his father, she might well dread this night.

He might not have Bayard's skill in such matters of intimacy, but he could see to her pleasure.

"And still you scowl, as I would not if I anticipated the seduction of a beauteous woman after making her my wife."

"I had no thought of taking wife at this time," Quinn said. "The timing is inopportune. No woman—let alone this one—would enjoy living at Sayerne before all is right once more. It is not seemly to expect a woman to endure it."

"And that is your sole objection?"

"Aye."

"Ha."

Quinn ignored his friend. He closed his eyes and leaned his head back against the rim, considering how he might tempt Melissande's pleasure. She had softened to his kiss, so perhaps his skills would be sufficient...

"Perhaps *I* could coax a response from your bride," Bayard mused. "Would you like me to try?"

Quinn sat up and glared at his friend.

Bayard appeared to be oblivious to Quinn's response. "Perhaps we could share her charms..."

Quinn knew Bayard sought to provoke him, and he felt no satisfaction at that man's success. "You will not touch my wife!" he said, pointing at Bayard with a dripping finger. "If naught else, my sire showed me the results of faithlessness in marriage and I will tolerate none of it in mine!" There was silence in the bathing chamber and Quinn took a steadying breath. "Make no mistake in this, Bayard, should you test me in this matter, it will be you who pays the price."

With that, Quinn sank into the bathwater again, his mood as foul as when he had arrived.

Bayard splashed in the water, clearly unoffended. "It does seem that this matter concerns you greatly and I take warning. But you are certain that you have no interest in this lady for her own charms? You did say that she was fair to look upon."

"I never said..." Quinn fell silent when he saw his friend's grin.

The man was cursedly observant.

"Although she is fair," Quinn admitted.

"Only fair?"

"Lovely," Quinn said, his voice husky. "And blessed with the tongue of a viper."

Bayard laughed aloud. "I cannot wait to meet her."

"I make this alliance to ensure my inheritance."

"Ah. And to see her borders defended." Bayard rose from the bath, and a pair of squires brought him heavy linens to dry himself. "So, it is of no relevance that in all the years we have traveled together and fought together, despite all the foes and trials we have faced, I have never seen you agitated about any detail, save this lady and her disapproval of you as her intended spouse." He shook a finger at Quinn. "Even when our demise at Acre seemed inevitable, you were calm, but not on this day, when you are to take a lovely heiress as your wife." He raised his brows, inviting an explanation for a situation that did not seem to require one.

Quinn could not hold his friend's gaze. "It is the unexpectedness of the situation."

Bayard smiled and shook his head. "Quinn, you are the most temperate man I have ever known, and the one knight blessed with a serenity that would astound the very angels."

Quinn did not feel serene.

"It is Sayerne at root," he insisted. "That place is too close to my heart. It is the possibility of losing my inheritance after waiting so long that unsettles me."

"Is it?" Bayard asked, his tone indicating that he expected no answer. He wrapped a length of linen about his waist with a flourish. "Then might I assume that you have no interest in what you wear to take your vows?" He picked up Quinn's tunic, which Quinn realized was looking even more disreputable than he had realized. Bayard held it high, then sniffed at it with disdain. "Your travel garments will do well enough, if this wedding is only a formality to be endured. A man's merit is not his garb, after all." He met Quinn's gaze with all the innocence of a new babe.

Curse the man.

Quinn could not attend his own nuptials in such worn clothing, with his hair untended and his jaw unshaved. The lady already thought him a ruffian and Quinn wanted naught more than to prove her wrong.

"You speak aright," he said. "The institution of marriage must be respected, if naught else, regardless of the reason for the match."

He turned to Michel and deliberately ignored Bayard's grin. "Go, Michel, and see if Lord de Tulley might lend me suitable garb for this occasion." The boy bowed and would have raced immediately to the door. "But bring my knife first, for I am in need of a shave. Perhaps you could lay hands on some shears, as well, for my hair is in dire need of a trim."

Michel grinned as he produced Quinn's dagger and the shears from behind his back. "Bayard said you would be needing these. I sharpened the blades, sir."

"I thank you, Michel." Quinn glanced toward his companion.

Bayard waved into the air and narrowed his eyes, as though he spied something elusive in the distance. "My dame often said I should have been a seer."

Quinn threw the soap at him and hit him square in the chest. Bayard jumped in surprise, not having seen the missile coming. Quinn laughed at his friend's surprise, his customary mood restored, at least for the moment.

He could win Melissande, and he would—for Sayerne.

CHAPTER THREE

erthe had gone to the kitchens, as was her wont at Tulley, and taken her mending. Lady Heloise had no obligation to entertain her, and truly, that lady seemed to wish to confer with her own maid. Berthe preferred to remain in the kitchen, working quietly, while she gathered gossip for her lady. She always listened and spoke little but, as her mother would have said, she kept her eyes open.

She noted the arrival of a rough company shortly after her lady had been summoned to Tulley's chamber. Two of them were men, and the others were but boys, though all were dirty and their clothing worn. They were fighting men, she could tell at a glimpse, and wondered if Tulley had hired more men-at-arms. They were greeted with courtesy, though, and clearly had been expected. Berthe saw the crosses on the tabards of the two men and wondered if they were crusading knights. Only one entered the kitchens and the châtelain was quick to usher him away. They would have been the party riding behind her lady's own small group and Berthe was curious as to their reason for being at Tulley.

The whispers began immediately.

"So, he is the one," said a maid. "I should not turn him aside."

The scullery maids laughed together. "He needs a bath."

"I would scrub his back."

"I would scrub more than that." There was another gale of laughter, and the cook's quelling glance made no difference.

"Quinn has improved mightily with the years," said one woman who had been at Tulley for as long as Berthe could recall. Her name was Rose and she had to be twice Berthe's age. "I recall when he was no more than a lean boy. Truly, Tulley saw his promise early."

"I would entertain him this night if the lady refuses him," jested one maid and there was a chorus of agreement.

"Ensure you are near their door," advised another. "In case she casts him out."

"Only a fool would deny such a man."

Berthe felt her color rise, but she kept her attention on her mending. She had been taught to keep her thighs together, but she knew that many of the woman who served at Tulley did not think similarly.

So, Lord de Tulley had plans for this man, whether he be knight or mercenary. Berthe listened. What had they said his name was? Quinn. Berthe wondered where he had been summoned from. It was curious that they had ridden behind the party from Annossy, so they might have come from another holding sworn to Tulley. Perhaps they had made their way over a difficult pass. She supposed the lady who would wed this Quinn must be Heloise and wondered if Tulley's niece guessed her fate.

Perhaps she should have stayed and listened to the conversation between Heloise and her maid.

"I hope Lady Melissande likes the look of him," said one of the girls.

Berthe almost dropped her needle.

"What she thinks is of no import," Rose countered. "She will wed him this day and bed him this night regardless of her view of the matter."

"But..."

"Lord de Tulley has no qualms in taking away what he has given," Rose said, her manner arch.

Berthe blinked in astonishment at this. Would Tulley seize

Annossy if her lady did not wed this stranger? One of the younger kitchen maids sat down beside her, her manner friendly but watchful. "Will your lady welcome him to her bed?" she asked with a smile that was not entirely pleasant. "It is said that Lady Melissande d'Annossy is made of ice, but perhaps she needs a man to thaw her." Her expression turned lewd as the other maids laughed.

"My lady is reserved, to be sure, for she was taught to conduct herself with dignity."

"Dignity will not aid her this night," Rose said. "Fighting men always understand their advantage."

"That is what you like about them," charged one of the maids and they laughed again.

"What Tulley demands is what occurs in this keep," agreed the cook. "The lady would be wise to cede rather than fight his command." He gave Berthe a look. "You might want to encourage her in that."

"But surely Lord de Tulley will not demand that my lady wed a stranger?"

"Her legal husband will not be a stranger," Rose said. "For long."

There was laughter at this.

"I thought you meant he was summoned to wed Lady Heloise," Berthe protested and Rose smiled.

"There is not a man alive good enough for that one, at least to Lord de Tulley's thinking." Rose shook her head. "Indeed, I feel sorry for any man who grants her a glance, let alone the one she weds."

"It is the raids on Annossy's borders that concern Tulley, no more and no less," the cook informed her. "Your lady will see that it is best for there to be a man in charge at Annossy."

Berthe was not certain Lady Melissande would agree. She did not share the detail that there had been another such raid the night before.

Did Quinn and his party know something of that?

Indeed, this was her opportunity to learn more for her lady. "Who is this Quinn?" she asked. "From whence did he come?"

"He is Quinn de Sayerne, of course, and is returned from the Holy Land at Tulley's summons to claim his father's holding," Rose supplied.

Berthe was surprised and not entirely pleased. "Jerome had a son?"

"Aye, but Tulley took Quinn under his own care some twenty years ago and sent him away."

There had never been a lady at Sayerne in Berthe's memory.

"Lord de Tulley sponsored Quinn to train for his spurs, then encouraged him to join the crusade," Rose continued. "He saw him trained to be his minion and awaited only the death of Jerome."

Those in the kitchen crossed themselves.

"It is always Tulley's scheme to plan for the future," the cook agreed.

"But this Quinn and his fellows could not have come from the Holy Land so quickly as that," Berthe said.

"It was a year at Christmas that Tulley sent a messenger to find Quinn, and word came last summer that he had been found," Rose informed her. "Quinn did not sail for home, though, but rode over land. It is farther and takes longer, but knights will cater to their steeds when possible."

"I have never known a horse to like a ship, to be sure."

"That will be his companion, Bayard de Neuville, who arrived with him, along with their squires," Rose said.

"Then they are knights?" Berthe asked. She had been uncertain, based on Quinn's appearance, but found this detail reassuring.

"Aye, Bayard and Quinn are," Rose confirmed.

"But here is the greater question," said one of the maids. "Is it true that Quinn's eyes are golden? Are they the hue of honey or of amber?"

"Which of us shall discover the truth?" The women began to chatter and laugh again, and Berthe kept her head bent over her mending.

A young man burst into the kitchens. "We have need of hot water aplenty," he said. "The newly arrived party have brushed down their horses and desire to bathe."

"The fire is stirred up and the cauldron is simmering," the cook said. "We started to heat the water as soon as we heard they would be arriving."

"You knew before they arrived at the gates?" Berthe asked.

The cook laughed. "Tulley has spies in every corner. He knew when they halted at Beauvoir Pass, and when they stayed in a tavern two nights ago. He sent a party after them to Sayerne yesterday with provisions. He likely knows more than that."

There was laughter and agreement to that. Berthe could not believe that Tulley would sponsor a man who was less than deserving of his trust. Twenty years before Tulley had sent this Quinn to gain his spurs, at Tulley's own expense. He must have seen merit in him young. Berthe found Tulley brusque and domineering, but he was fair.

There must be more to Quinn than met the eye, and she was inclined to think well of him for being both knight and crusader.

If she had doubts about the wedding, they were to be dismissed. No sooner had the boys taken water to the stables than the châtelain hastened into the kitchens with purpose. "There will be a feast this night," he declared, clearly agitated, and the cook nodded agreement. "We have a wedding to celebrate! We will have the rest of the venison and bring wine from the cellars...."

"Who is to be married?" Berthe had to be certain.

The châtelain fixed her with a bright look. "Lady Melissande will wed Quinn de Sayerne. If you have not brought suitable garb for your lady, then you might speak with the maid of Lady Heloise with all haste. She is with her mistress in the hall."

"Aye, sir," Berthe said and gathered her mending. There were times when she was glad to be a simple country lass and a servant besides, and this day had to be one of them. To think that her lady would be compelled to wed a stranger and was commanded to do as much immediately!

Lady Melissande would be devastated. What of her old pledge to Arnaud de Privas? Berthe understood, though, that there would be no choice. Tulley was never to be denied.

She halted abruptly when a man marched toward her, the same man who had followed Tulley's summons. He fairly filled the portal and Berthe had little choice but to stand aside. He looked to be riled, and she doubted he had noticed her. His golden eyes blazed with fury and his lips were drawn to a grim line. He barely granted her a nod as he passed her, then strode through the kitchens to the bailey beyond.

The maids stared after him in silence.

"Gold," whispered one.

"Honey," asserted another, then sighed.

"Amber," declared a third.

"There will be need for more water!" the cook said and sent them hurrying.

Berthe was intrigued that the bridegroom was no less enamored of this match than she guessed the bride would be. But whyever not? His reaction pricked Berthe's pride. Her lady was lovely, young, and the heiress of Annossy. Any man should be glad to wed her!

This night, though, would not be easy for Lady Melissande. Berthe loved her lady dearly and did not wish to see her unhappy in any way. What could she do to assist? If naught else, she could ensure that her lady looked her best. Indeed, Lady Melissande's beauty might melt the coldest heart.

And Berthe could bolster her lady's confidence. Aye, Tulley always had good wine and plenty of it. Berthe took a pitcher of it and some spices from the open bowl. Such was the affluence of Tulley that a few sticks of cinnamon would not be missed, and her lady was both guest and bride.

Even Tulley's châtelain could not take issue with her choice.

Melissande unlocked the door to the chamber she had been assigned to find Berthe in the corridor. It was the same chamber she had been granted before at Tulley and familiar for that. Berthe lit a brazier and began to mull wine. There were lanterns lit and the chamber soon was both warm and filled with welcoming light. Melissande went to the window and folded her arms across her chest, staring at the distant tower of Annossy, its pennant waving from the summit. Her heart was so cold that it might have been wrought of lead.

She would wed the son of Jerome before the sun set.

It was outrageous.

Worse, there was naught she could do about it. Tulley was adamant and she knew that pressing him further would only vex him. She could do without Tulley being annoyed with her, given that he had pledged her to Jerome's son when he was pleased.

Berthe began to chatter, as was her wont. "My lady, you look to have had a shock of the worst order. And you are too cold." The maid pressed Melissande's hands between hers for a moment, then tutted under her breath. "Come over here and sit yourself down by the fire. I have stirred up the blaze in the brazier and it will warm you through to your toes."

"I fear it will not," Melissande said, though she did as she was bidden.

Berthe urged a stoneware mug into her hands. It was warm. Melissande glanced down to its ruddy contents, the smell of cinnamon teasing her nostrils. "A cup of spiced wine is what you need, my lady, for that will warm you through and through. It encourages the blood to race and heats you from the very core." She stood back and sighed. "You will need sustenance, I fear."

Melissande sipped the soothing brew and eyed her maid. "What have you heard?"

"Is it true that you are to wed Jerome's son?"

Melissande nodded and watched Berthe's expression change to echo her own mood.

"Irksome man! How is it that Lord de Tulley can forget your pledge to Arnaud de Privas? How can he command you to wed?"

"He can and he has," Melissande said grimly.

"At least Lord Quinn is not old. Or lamed."

"It is the character of my husband that concerns me more than his appearance."

"Aye," Berthe agreed, then her eyes widened. "And that is fine, is it not? He is a warrior, to be sure, and Annossy will be blessed by his presence."

"Will it?"

"Of course, my lady!" Berthe's eyes sparkled with mischief, which surprised Melissande. "All of the women in the kitchen declare they would be glad to bed Quinn de Sayerne in your stead."

"Do they?" Melissande admitted he had an appeal, in a rough way.

"Aye, Dame Fortune has smiled upon you, my lady, for that rogue Tulley—pardon any disrespect, my lady, but he is one who sees to his own interests first—could have seen you wed to the first man who came along, and not waited for a fine specimen such as he."

"You have seen him then?" Melissande indulged in a sip of wine so seldom that this heady brew of Berthe's was having a strong effect upon her.

"Aye! He passed me twice, and once he stood directly before me. He is tall and broad, my lady, a man who can swing a sword and one who will defend both you and Annossy."

"You cannot know that, Berthe."

"Tulley has sponsored him for twenty years," Berthe replied. "Because of his honorable nature, Tulley ensured that he trained for his spurs, and suggested that he ride to Palestine on crusade, *and* sent a messenger to find him and summon him back when Jerome died. He is Tulley's man, to be certain, my lady, and that cannot be a bad alliance for you." Berthe added a little more wine to the cup. "What did you think when first you saw him, my lady? You must have been aware that he is a *man*."

"I feared he had lice," Melissande admitted and Berthe laughed before she covered her mouth with one hand.

"You did not, my lady."

"I did."

"And what did you think next?" the maid asked, her eyes sparkling.

Melissande dropped her gaze. She had thought Quinn alluring. He was disheveled, poorly garbed, and less than clean, but did have the most wonderfully warm gaze—when he wasn't angry, of course.

"You must tell me, my lady, are his eyes truly golden? They seemed to be lit with fire when I saw him."

Melissande felt a jolt that Berthe's question should so closely echo her own thoughts, but the girl continued. "Aye, they are gold, and most uncommon for that."

"Are they the shade of honey or of a deeper hue, like that of amber?" Berthe asked. "There is great dissent in the kitchens over this and I—for the sake of accuracy, of course—would like to be the one to set the matter straight." The maid paused, her expression expectant, and regarded Melissande.

Melissande cleared her throat. It was easy to recall the precise shade of Quinn's eyes, and the way they changed when his temper flared. Although she was not one to encourage talk among servants, it seemed that the gossip mill was at work already on this matter.

"It depends upon his mood," she admitted, hoping against hope that her cheeks were warm because of Berthe's brew.

"His mood," Berthe breathed. "How so, my lady?"

"When he is angered, they flash like gold in sunlight, but when he is...intent, they darken like wildflower honey." Melissande was certain her own cheeks were on fire.

Berthe's eyes were round. "Intent?"

"Aye," Melissande agreed and took another sip of wine. "Intent."

"Intent." Berthe clasped her hands together, sighed, then spun across the room. "I was thinking, my lady, that you might wish to wear something special, seeing as it is your wedding, and also that you would wish to look your best." She cast a quick smile over her shoulder. "I am so glad I thought to bring your new kirtle made of the samite we purchased from that trader from the East. That green shade is most alluring, for it makes your eyes shine like emeralds and your hair look like spun gold." Berthe stroked the kirtle as Melissande watched. "With the gold embroidery upon it and your red slippers, it is fitting enough for a royal bride. I have borrowed some red ribbons and pearls from Heloise's maid, that I might dress your hair." She smiled. "My lady, you will look beautiful."

Beautiful. For a match she did not wish to make.

Melissande frowned. She hoped that her finery was not destroyed by the brute in his consummation of their match. Would she have time to disrobe? Or would her kirtle be torn in Quinn's desire to claim his marital due? Although Melissande did not intend to lose Annossy, still she dreaded the inevitable.

Too late, she wished she knew more of these delicate matters.

She eyed Berthe but knew she could not possibly ask her maid.

She held out her cup to Berthe, knowing that boldness would come from wine. It had already made great strides in settling her fears.

"I am still chilled," she lied, and Berthe's expression turned sympathetic.

"Oh, my lady, I have ensured there would be plenty," the maid said and hastened to fill the cup again.

By the time Melissande descended the stairs to the hall in all her finery, she was warm through and through. Two cups of Berthe's spiced wine brew had almost dismissed every bit of her trepidation. Indeed, she felt a little unsteady on her feet. She stumbled on the bottom step but a strong hand caught her elbow.

Melissande glanced up to thank her benefactor, but fell silent when she met Quinn's steady gaze.

At least, she thought it was Quinn. He had shaved and she saw the strong outline of his features for the first time. His hair was trimmed, his garments fine. His eyes alone remained the same. Melissande swallowed and found she could not look away.

How could she have questioned whether the man was handsome? In this moment, he looked every measure the noble knight.

A smile slowly curved his lips and Melissande knew for certain that she had drunk too much wine. Why else would it be so difficult to catch her breath?

Why else did she want to reach up and touch him with a fingertip?

"My lady, you are a vision," he said. "That hue suits you most well." His voice was low, his complement for her ears alone. That they exchanged a confidence, even over such an inconsequential matter, seemed intimate beyond belief.

It reminded Melissande of precisely how intimate matters would be between them before the night was through. At that thought, her knees weakened, but Quinn's grip on her elbow was resolute.

"I thank you," she said. "You, also, have managed to look reputable."

There was an understatement. Quinn's hair was combed to order and she could see that it was thick. The torchlight in the hall picked out coppery tones within it and it shone with good health. His shaved jaw was squared and determined, his nose straight and aquiline.

And still there were the attributes she had noted before. The green brocade tabard, though simple in pattern and cut, emphasized the breadth of his shoulders. The wool chausses of darker hue merely accentuated the lean strength of his legs.

"One glimpse and I feel I am to wed a queen," he confessed, still smiling slightly. She sensed that he invited her to match his mood, but Melissande could not.

"My dowry might be as rich as that of a queen," she said. "Annossy is a rare prize."

Quinn's eyes narrowed slightly. Melissande caught her breath as he leaned toward her and her gaze dropped to his hand. He was neither small nor weak, yet his touch was gentle. She stared at his tanned fingers, noting the few calluses. He was a man who swung a blade to earn his way. He was a man, too, and would have a man's appetites. Melissande tingled in sudden awareness of him.

"My lady," he whispered against her hair. Melissande kept her gaze locked on his hand. "Surely we might call a truce for the duration of our wedding night, at least."

The way he murmured "our" with such ease made Melissande's heart skip a beat.

But she would not show him her weakness. She summoned a smile, took a deep breath and lifted her head to meet his gaze.

"It would only be civilized," she said with a resolve she was far from feeling. "Shall we see the deed done?"

"That is hardly in the spirit I intended," he said. Melissande felt bereft when he turned away, his lips set in a hard line instead of the smile she found so beguiling. "But it shall be your way, my lady. The worst may as well be done sooner rather than later." He offered his elbow with deliberate politeness and Melissande slipped her hand into it.

The worst? By her accounting, he made the better bargain. Melissande lifted her chin, determined not to show Quinn how he had pricked her pride, and walked into the chapel with him. Tulley awaited them at the altar, along with his priest. Heloise already smiled through tears that she would witness their union. It was clear that she yearned for her own wedding day, and Melissande could only hope that Tulley chose better for her. Another knight stood on the groom's side of the chapel, and she could only assume that he was a comrade of her husband. He had dark hair and dark eyes and looked confident in his own allure.

Quinn said naught. He did not look left or right, nor did he hesitate in leading her directly to the priest.

He wanted Annossy and Sayerne united, just like his father before him. He wanted her, but only as a means to his end. She did not doubt that matters would proceed from bad to worse.

Melissande might be forced to wed this man, but she would grant him no more than necessary.

On this night or any other.

Tulley looked satisfied when Quinn and Melissande entered the chapel.

Quinn was not surprised. The old lord was as fond of getting his own way as Quinn recalled.

Neither was he surprised that his intended looked as reluctant as earlier. He suspected that she and Tulley shared a determination for shaping their circumstances. In a way, Quinn marveled that Melissande would have such an expectation, for few women of his acquaintance would have been accustomed to make their own choices.

What was her history? How long had she been alone at Annossy? He had assumed that her parents had recently died, but now he wondered. It was clear that she resented the loss of command over her family holding, but why had she expected it to remain hers to administer?

Quinn had a hundred questions but doubted she would confide

in him.

If he had hoped for his intended to approve of the change in his appearance and be more welcoming as a result, Quinn was to be disappointed. She took his arm as if she could not bear to touch him and Quinn's annoyance rose. He saw Bayard note the lady's reluctance and did not doubt his comrade would have advice for him on the morrow. He was irked and marveled again that this lady should have the power to so rile him when he was known for his temperance.

She did not appreciate his assets and that was the sum of it.

Quinn was not so foul to look upon, and he was a knight. He would hold Sayerne, though it had no wealth in this moment, but he was resolved to rebuild it. He was prepared to labor for his goals and to treat his lady wife with the respect such a woman deserved. But it was evident that Melissande had condemned him.

Was her hatred of his father so profound as that? If so, they shared that view. One would think they might be able to build upon that common ground.

Of course, they could only do as much if his wife spoke to him.

He had to wonder what precisely she knew of his father's deeds. Was her attitude the result of some old crime? Or did she simply look down upon all who were not of the line of Annossy? It could well be that such a lady had been raised to believe that no man was deserving of her charms.

Quinn did not know whether to take reassurance from the possibility that her dislike of him was not personal.

Indeed, there was something about this lady that annoyed Quinn, yet at the same time, he felt an uncommon desire for her. It was dangerous for a woman to have such power over him, and he could only hope that it diminished in time.

Perhaps their wedding night would see his characteristic calm restored. Her beauty made him keenly aware that he had been celibate for the entirety of his journey on crusade. Was that the reason for his annoyance? That he was more than ready to celebrate their match and she was not? Was it merely pride?

Ye gods, what if she denied him this night? What if there was no evidence of consummation to show Tulley in the morning?

Should he feign it, by shedding his own blood on the sheets?

He was caught to be sure, between the lady's desire and that of Tulley. Tulley, however, could exact the higher cost.

Quinn led his bride to the altar, wondering if he made a dreadful a mistake in taking this frosty lady to wife at all. Would he rue this day for the rest of his life? The priest began to bless the match with the familiar words.

In truth, Quinn had no choice. The dream of Sayerne had sustained him for years. He supposed it was no surprise that Tulley had guessed the truth.

Those attacks upon Annossy's borders must vex the old lord more than Quinn had realized. Tulley must believe his holdings were at risk, which made Quinn and Melissande pawns in the older man's game.

If Melissande did not thaw this night, Quinn resolved, he would avoid her. He would cut his own finger to give Tulley the sign he desired, then Quinn and the lady would separate. Between their two estates and the work required to rebuild Sayerne, it should be simple to do.

There was an old saying: wed once for duty and thence for love. Perhaps his next match would be one of the heart. He found himself thinking of his mother, and his heart filling with sadness as the priest blessed them.

If naught else, Quinn could do better than his own father.

"And the ring?" the priest invited.

Quinn realized he had not planned for this exchange, but then he had been given little opportunity to do as much. He looked down at the golden ring on his smallest finger and resolved to offer it in the spirit of a joined future. "It was my mother's," he said quietly to Melissande, then removed it from his hand. He held it over her left hand, over each finger in succession. "In the name of the Father, of the Son and of the Holy Spirit." Then he pushed the ring onto her middle finger, the same finger his mother had worn it upon.

"Is it your sole token of her?" she asked, looking down at the ring.

Quinn could not read her mood. "Aye. She surrendered it to

me as a token when I left."

Melissande nodded and eyed the ring, her thoughts hidden from Quinn. Something in her seemed to have softened at the mention of his mother.

"You may seal your pledge with a kiss of peace," the priest said.

Quinn glanced down to find Melissande watching him intently. Her eyes flashed, though he could not have said whether it was fear or desire. Then she dropped her gaze, hiding her thoughts from him once more.

But she had responded to his touch before. Could there be promise in this match?

A man could only try.

"Aye," he replied to the priest. "One must adhere to tradition."

Melissande inhaled sharply. Did she dread his kiss or her own reaction to it?

There was only one way to know for certain.

Quinn touched a fingertip beneath Melissande's chin. Her gaze rose to his and she turned to him, both of them taking a step closer in the same moment. Quinn liked how they moved instinctively together and chose to see promise in that. He moved slowly, determined to reassure whatever fears she might have. Her eyes closed when he cupped her face between his hands, but Quinn did not intend to let her hide from him so easily.

"Open your eyes, my lady," he whispered. "I would have you certain of which man you wed."

She did as he requested and he glimpsed uncertainty in those magnificent eyes. Had she been abused in the past? Or was she innocent and unaware of what must come between them? Either way, her response launched a protective urge within him. Quinn smiled at her, his heart leaping when she tentatively smiled back.

She might meet him halfway, after all.

"To the future," he murmured then bent to brush his lips across hers.

Melissande quivered, then sighed. She tasted like wine and cinnamon and her kiss filled Quinn with the same sweet warmth as earlier that day. Well aware that they were watched, he slanted his mouth across hers to demand a little more while they were in company. She hesitated, then leaned against him, her hands upon his chest and her lips parting in unexpected invitation. Quinn's hand slid to her nape and he lifted her closer, deepening his kiss with satisfaction. The lady froze, then responded with an ardor that made Quinn's heart thunder.

It was only with the greatest effort that he recalled their place and put her aside. To his pleasure, the lady's eyes were shining when he lifted his head. She smiled at him, her expression more welcoming than it had been thus far. Quinn was tempted to toss her over his shoulder and make for a private chamber before this moment passed, but the priest cleared his throat.

"Is it not wonderful?" the other noblewoman said with a sigh. Her eyes were shining. She was fair, like Melissande, but younger.

"My niece," Tulley said gruffly. "Heloise von Idelstein."

Quinn bowed over the lady's hand and she smiled at him and Melissande. "I love weddings," she confessed. "I cannot wait for my own."

That comment, Quinn noted, banished his lady's smile. Melissande sobered, regal again, and slipped her hand into his elbow. They might have been strangers and he saw Bayard's brows rise as that man noticed the change, as well.

"Yet wait you shall," Tulley said to Heloise. He adroitly steered his niece to his side, ensuring that she was distant from Bayard, whose eyes gleamed with mischief. "The cook has assembled a wedding feast on short notice," he continued. "Let us proceed to the hall and savor the results of his efforts."

Disappointment at the change rose within Quinn until he recalled that Melissande had not smiled during their first encounter. He made progress in easing the lady's concerns already and would take each victory as it came.

Perhaps she feared the night ahead. Any maiden would. He would have to ensure that their mating was enjoyable—for a fine wedding night would set the right tone not just for their shared future but their happiness.

Clearly what Melissande needed was a goodly quantity of wine to dismiss her reservations.

Quinn would ensure that she had it.

CHAPTER FOUR

If the wedding feast had been a war, Melissande would have lost before the first foray.

It was clear that Quinn launched an assault against her senses, and it was one she could neither deny nor evade. He had the experience in this endeavor, which left Melissande susceptible to his every assault. He was seated beside her, on her right, with Tulley on her left. Quinn's comrade, Bayard, was on Quinn's right, and Melissande guessed that to be a choice by Tulley intended to keep his niece Heloise at the greatest distance from that knight. Heloise was on Tulley's left.

She had seen at first glance that Bayard had a twinkle in his eye and more than a measure of good looks. Heloise was already casting glances at the two knights, which Tulley either blocked or ignored. Melissande had seen him glare at Bayard once and that knight seemed to have taken a warning. He flirted with Berthe, who appeared to take umbrage from his attention, a reaction that prompted him to tease her yet more. If Bayard thought to make an easy conquest there, he would have to think again. Berthe would never indulge him.

Caught between Tulley and Quinn, Melissande felt surrounded by those who desired her match to be a success, and worse, who cared little for her own view.

She was snared, and by the time the night was through and the match consummated, she would be secured as Quinn's prize.

The meat was good, the wine was better, and the occasional brush of Quinn's elbow against hers was enough to keep her tingling from head to toe. The marriage vows had been exchanged before witnesses and she was bound to respect them. She felt the weight of his ring upon her hand, an unfamiliar burden. The gold had been warm when he granted her the ring and she had seen the grief light his eyes when he spoke of his mother. How and when had Jerome's wife died? Melissande did not recall exactly, and wished she had paid more attention. She had been young. She knew Jerome had had a daughter but not met Annelise, for she had been sent to a convent as a young girl and had only returned briefly to Sayerne. Was that of import? How Melissande hated that she did not know. She could feel the heat of Quinn's thigh close beside her own and was well aware of the hard strength of him. She heard his low voice at close proximity—indeed, she felt it as a vibration deep within her. The sensation was not unwelcome.

It might have been the wine and not the allure of her new spouse.

In fact, Melissande was certain her cup was enchanted. No matter how much wine she drank, there was always another sip remaining. It was most curious and a puzzle well beyond her current capabilities to explain. Had she ever consumed so much wine in one evening? She could not recall ever drinking more than a cup or two, but on this night, she had no reliable tally.

Two from Berthe in her chamber, then this cup which seemed to have no bottom. Why, there was yet another mouthful within it! Melissande drank the wine and when next she looked, the cup was full again.

Worse than the muddle of the wine—or perhaps because of it—Quinn could not be ignored. He placed his hand upon the back of her waist when he leaned forward to confer with Tulley and the weight of it felt both proprietary and thrilling. He offered her the best parts of the meat—indeed, he even fed morsels to her, his eyes twinkling with an admiration that had to be feigned. He laughed at Bayard's comments and told Heloise about Palestine's wonders and captivated all at the board. He neither provoked her nor ignored her, but seemed to approve of whatever she chose to do. The man sought to beguile her and Melissande was shocked by his success.

Indeed, she found herself intrigued by her spouse, even though she knew that curiosity was treacherous. It was but a step from curiosity to concern and she knew it well. But still, she wondered.

Why had Quinn gone on crusade? Had it been merely Tulley's suggestion or was there more to that tale?

Where had he earned his spurs?

What were his other alliances?

Why did Tulley hold him in such affection? Was it simply because Quinn was a man and a knight, or was there more of a bond between the two?

If he had left twenty years before, then she had been very young, too young to even know of him. What had her father known of him?

How did Quinn imagine he might rebuild Sayerne? She knew how much labor it would be and that it was nigh impossible, given the lack of coin and villeins at that holding. Did he have no real idea of what lay before him or was he simply optimistic? She could not imagine that he was a fool.

Would Melissande have thought differently of Quinn if she had first encountered him as he appeared on this night? She did not wish to be one whose opinion was governed by appearances, but she had to admit that she would have given this Quinn more credit. Aye, he was cursedly handsome, the man who had taken her to wife. Now that he was clean, it was impossible to ignore his allure. Yet he was not one to court the affection of every woman in the hall. She could not fail to note that. He was attentive to her, granting that dangerous smile to her alone, as should be.

How could he be Jerome's son and share so little of that man's wicked nature?

Or was Quinn simply better at disguising his truth than Jerome had been?

Melissande could not decide. Clearly, it was to his advantage to win her approval. Perhaps once she had surrendered to him, his charm would vanish.

As the evening continued, despite her doubts, Melissande found that sweet and unfamiliar hum of awareness building within her. It was a spell that Quinn had cast and even knowing that, Melissande enjoyed the sensation. She watched Quinn's deft handling of his knife, admiring the grace of his hands. She smelled the heat of his skin and felt his warmth. Her heart nigh stopped when he pressed the length of his thigh to hers and did not move it away again.

Indeed, she could not take a breath, she was so shocked.

Tulley talked about the merits of barley as opposed to rye. Quinn leaned forward, apparently intent upon Tulley's counsel. His hand was on her back again and Melissande felt her very blood simmer. She sipped her wine, seeing that her hands trembled when she placed the cup on the board. Quinn's hand moved on her back, a lazy stroke of his thumb along her spine that melted her bones. He did not glance her way, as if he were unaware of the contact. Melissande was flustered beyond all. She did not move away, but found it impossible to follow the conversation.

"You planted barley at Annossy last season, did you not?" Tulley invited.

"Aye." Melissande nodded, smiled, and seized her cup.

"And it fared well?" Quinn asked, almost whispering in her ear.

"Aye," Melissande ceded, unable to summon a more authoritative response. She sipped from her cup again, relieved when Tulley abandoned his efforts to include her in the discussion. He turned to explain to Heloise the various kinds of grain that prospered locally and their merits.

Quinn's thumb never halted. Now, he made circles on her back, enticing little circles that made her mouth go dry even as that heat spread further.

She realized that she wanted to touch him. She wanted to slip her hand beneath the table and place it on his thigh. She wanted to feel how different his body was from her own. She wanted to explore him, and that curiosity shocked Melissande truly. Did marriage make a woman wanton? Quinn laughed at a comment from his comrade Bayard and she decided she liked the hearty sound of his laughter.

"My lady?" Berthe said from behind her.

Melissande saw that the meal had been removed from the board.

It was time.

Melissande drained her cup and this time, it remained empty. Quinn's hand closed upon her elbow to support her as she stood and she was aware of how much she needed that assistance.

"Do not trip, my lady," he advised, his voice pitched low. Melissande felt a tide of terror that the moment was nigh upon her. Quinn gave her elbow a little squeeze and she found him smiling at her. He kissed the back of her hand, his gaze glowing. "I shall be along shortly," he murmured, as if that was promise not threat.

Melissande stared into his eyes, astonished that she was soothed by his words.

"Aye, husband," she managed to whisper. His quick smile sent a jolt through her. She turned hastily and the room spun. Quinn's grip tightened on her one elbow and Berthe caught the other so that Melissande regained her balance.

How much wine had she drunk?

"Come along, my lady," Berthe said.

"Do you need my assistance?" Quinn asked.

"Nay, nay, nay," Melissande said, her panic rising anew. "Stay and enjoy the minstrels." She turned quickly and stumbled anew.

Bayard had stood and he quickly steadied her. "Whoa!" he declared, then gave her an engaging smile.

"I thank you." Melissande was surprised to find that she felt no reaction to his touch.

There was a puzzle, for Bayard was not hard upon the eyes. He had a charming smile and a confidence that many a maid might find alluring.

But not Melissande.

She turned and crossed the hall hoping her fear did not show.

"My lady, let me aid you on the stairs," Berthe said.

Melissande felt Quinn's gaze upon her but did not look back. The stairs required every measure of her attention. It was curious how they shifted and moved. Melissande knew that they had not acted in such a manner before, but this was yet another puzzle best left for later.

She conquered them with Berthe's aid, as well as the hall above, which seemed to have developed a markedly uneven floor. Finally, they reached the chamber and Melissande sighed with relief. A fire burned brightly in the brazier and there were four lanterns lit, as well. The bed linens had been changed and turned down. The import of that could not be mistaken.

It would be soon.

And there was no escape.

"Come along, my lady," Berthe urged. "We do not want to keep your lord husband waiting. You have fared well in this match, my lady."

"I think not," Melissande managed to say.

"Aye?" Berthe's cheer sounded forced to Melissande. "He is young and unmarred. He is handsome and strong, a knight no less, and an heir in his own right. You could have been wedded to an old friend of Tulley's, a cripple of good lineage, or a man much enamored of his ale." Melissande might have fought to remain in her garments, but she was helpless against Berthe's efficiency. The maid turned her around and removed her clothing quickly. Even the hope of remaining in her chemise was overcome. "You might have been bound to widower with a houseful of children, all determined to despise you because you are not their mother. You might have been…"

All too soon, Melissande was nude and bathed and being hustled toward the bed.

"I thank you, Berthe," she said as she climbed into the bed. At least the linens would offer some modesty. "I shall count myself fortunate, with your counsel."

"You do not sound convinced, my lady."

"I suspect you are sufficiently convinced for both of us."

Berthe scoffed, then kneeled on the bed. She unbraided Melissande's hair and combed it out. "Do not concern yourself with this night's task, my lady," she said. "Your lord husband is a kind man, any woman could see that, and I am certain that you have naught to fear on this night."

He was Jerome's son.

She had no notion of whether his nature was deceitful or not.

And they would be alone together all the night long.

Melissande gripped the linens in dread. The sound of men's voices came from outside the door and her heart skipped. Any effect from the wine seemed to be dismissed, leaving her both cold and uncertain. The men fell into silence outside the door, then a knock resonated through the quiet room.

It sounded imperious to Melissande. Commanding. Would Quinn command all her choices from this day forth, as was his right?

"Good evening," Berthe called.

"Good evening, my lady," roared one who might have been Bayard. "We found a gift for you in the hall!"

"Wretch," Berthe whispered, fighting a smile, and rose to open the door. She did not reach it, though before it burst open. Quinn was shoved into the chamber, laughing and protesting. He clutched his tabard in one hand and his chemise was torn open. Laughter carried from the men outside the chamber. Melissande flushed as rude jests were made, knowing they would be seeking a glimpse of her.

"Spare the lady's gentle ears!" Quinn insisted, but he was ignored.

Melissande could not look away from the skin revealed by Quinn's gaping chemise. His skin was bronzed, no doubt from the sun in the East, and there was a dark patch of hair upon his chest. His sleeves were pushed up and she could see his forearms. She blinked and stared, even as Berthe made a quiet hum of approval.

A lady should have no interest in her husband's physical charms. Melissande burrowed beneath the covers, feeling the weight of every curious male eye upon her.

"Come, Quinn," Bayard said. "It is time to put you to bed with your bride."

He might have followed his comrade into the chamber, but Berthe blocked his progress. His eyes twinkled as he surveyed the maid, but she held her ground. Indeed, she braced her hands on her hips. "You will do no such deed, sir," she said, though she did not seem like a formidable obstacle to the knight.

"Do you deny me, wench?" Bayard said.

"Aye, I deny you and all your kind," Berthe said, making a shooing motion with her hands. "Away with you, all of you rogues and knaves!"

"But we must put Quinn to bed," Bayard said with a grin.

Berthe swatted his shoulder and he blinked in surprise. "You will not!"

"I can manage the feat alone," Quinn interjected. There was determination in his tone and he moved to stand beside Berthe.

"But..." Bayard protested.

"It is time that you were leaving, sir rogue," Berthe said.

"Sir Rogue!" the other men echoed, then laughed.

Berthe did not smile. "My lady welcomes only one man to her chamber and it is a finer man than you."

"But it is tradition!" Bayard argued. He yelped when Berthe reached up and grasped his ear. Evidently, she was not gentle. The other men erupted into gales of laughter as she tugged Bayard toward the door.

"But naught," she said. "Out with you, Sir Rogue. It should be clear to even the most dim-witted soul that a man and a woman need their privacy at this moment. How much of a fool are you that you cannot see the truth?" Berthe hauled him into the corridor by his ear, much to the delight of the other men.

They chanted "Sir Rogue" as they followed, laughing.

"I am no fool," Bayard argued. "And I am no rogue."

"And how would I know?" Berthe demanded. "I might have expected finer behavior from a knight, especially one who has taken up the cross and gone to the Holy Land, but it is clear that I have overestimated you..."

Berthe continued her lecture, Bayard continued to object and the other men kept chanting.

Quinn flicked the door closed with his fingertips. He dropped the latch, then turned to face Melissande. She watched him over the linens, her palms damp.

"Alone," he said softly.

"Aye."

The fire crackled and Quinn slowly smiled. That smile would be Melissande's undoing, she knew it well.

"Hail, my lady wife," he said softly. "Well met."

Perhaps it would be his low murmur that tumbled her defenses forever.

Melissande swallowed. "Hail, husband," she replied in a whisper.

The moment of their consummation was upon her and the wine had abandoned her to her fate.

She supposed it was too late to pray.

His wife resembled nothing more than a cornered and terrified rabbit. Quinn laid his tabard aside, moving slowly that he might not frighten her even more.

She peeked over the linens and her gaze was locked upon him. Her eyes were wide and of a darker emerald in her uncertainty. Quinn knew then that this consummation would not be achieved as easily as he had hoped.

Sayerne hung in the balance. That was both a sobering and a fortifying thought. The certainty that Tulley would rap on the door with the very dawn in search of his evidence did little to help.

The deed must be done, though the lady was afraid.

Perhaps she knew little of what must transpire. Perhaps she had been told dire tales.

Either way, it was his responsibility to gain her trust in this. He must prove himself different than whatever she feared he would be.

"Ah, that Bayard is such a rogue!" he said, ensuring his tone was light. He considered his torn chemise and shook his head. "He never misses an opportunity for some jest or another. Mercifully, your maid treated him as he deserved. Sir Rogue," he said and shook his head, laughing. "It is an apt title for him."

Melissande remained silent but Quinn would not be so readily discouraged.

"What is her name? She looks to be a loyal one."

"Berthe."

A single word but it was more than before. "Was that not a fine meal?" he asked. "I could scarce believe Tulley's cook concocted such a feast with such little notice. Tell me, are all cooks hereabout so talented, or is Tulley particularly fortunate?"

Melissande cleared her throat. Quinn did not look toward her, but removed his belt and set it aside.

"Tulley's cook is particularly gifted even among those in the region. He has been here long." Melissande spoke slowly and with care and Quinn imagined that she was still feeling some effect of the wine. He could see her lips now, above the barrier of the linens.

"Then I shall have to ensure I do not become plump, now that I am home," he said amiably. Quinn heard a soft rush of his wife's breath that might almost have passed for a laugh.

"I doubt that will transpire," she said, with some of her earlier fire.

"Nay?"

"Given those raids, you will have labor aplenty defending Annossy's borders."

"Excellent. I have no desire to be idle. A knight should use his skills to good end, lest his abilities fade." Quinn pulled off his shirt, unable to keep from glancing over his shoulder to see her reaction. Melissande hastily averted her gaze, but there was new color in her cheeks.

The evening showed more promise than just moments past.

Quinn strode over to the bed and sat on its edge, leaving on his chausses. Melissande put distance between them. She lay on her back, clutching the linens before herself like a shield.

She did not flee, though. Quinn took his time removing his boots before he turned to her anew. He leaned on the mattress, easing closer to her, and her eyes widened. She did not retreat, though.

"Do you think that I am too plump now?" he asked. Melissande did not seem able to keep her glance from darting over his bare chest.

"I think you are vain," she replied, but her voice was breathless.

Quinn grinned as he leaned closer.

"Are you plump?" he asked.

"You know I am not."

"Are you vain?"

"If you think I will display myself to you like a whore, you are doomed to disappointment, sir."

So much for the effect of the wine. Her eyes were flashing with vigor.

"What needs to be done cannot be done with the linens between us."

She glared at him. "Perhaps it need not be done. Perhaps an annulment would suit us both better."

Quinn touched the tip of her nose with his finger. "Then you can greet Tulley in the morning and confess that truth to him."

She smiled with obvious reluctance. "Do not tell me that a knight and crusader of your repute fears Tulley."

"Of course, I fear him. He holds all that I desire in his grasp." Quinn sighed. "If we do not consummate the match, I will put my own blood on the linens to ensure that Sayerne is not lost."

She sat up abruptly then, forgetting the linens. "You would not!" The sheet slipped lower, revealing the softness of her throat and shoulders. He could see the gleam of her hair, but strove to hide his body's reaction to her beauty.

Instead, he spoke deliberately. "I am willing to meet you abed. I am willing to do as Tulley decrees. I am not willing to lose my family holding. Are you?"

She exhaled. "Of course, you are willing," she said with impatience. "You will have no pain."

"Is that it?"

She held his gaze and nodded. "I am told it hurts."

"Ah." Quinn reclined beside her, apparently at ease, even as his thoughts flew. "I am given to understand that it is only the first time that hurts, and that only if there is haste."

"I will not linger over this obligation," she said through her teeth. "If it must be done, I would have it done and over and..."

"Oh, but I will linger," Quinn vowed softly. He saw her inhale and reached out to touch a fingertip to her arm. He felt her go taut, then she compelled herself to relax. "Indeed, I would savor." He let his finger wander toward her shoulder and the softness of her skin fairly made him dizzy with desire.

"Your eyes grow darker."

"That is not the sole change, my lady."

Her gaze swept over him and her eyes widened. "Close your eyes and I will cast away the sheet. Then we might put the ordeal behind us and sleep."

Quinn chuckled. "Close my eyes? Never!"

"But..."

He rolled closer, letting his fingertip rise to her cheek. As before, his gentle touch seemed to disarm her or at least halt her protests. She stared at him, her eyes wide. He let his finger trail down her throat and surveyed her, liking that the line of her lips had softened slightly. "If I am to be condemned to only one night of lovemaking for the rest of my days, then be assured, my lady, I shall not keep my eyes closed." He leaned closer and touched his lips briefly to hers. "And I pledge to do my utmost to ensure that it is not an ordeal."

"After this, you will await an invitation," she said, breathless.

"Then you cannot fault my scheme to be persuasive."

Melissande pulled away. "I know that you will not sleep in a cold bed, even if mine is forbidden to you."

Quinn sat back in surprise. "On our nuptial night, you are convinced that I will be unfaithful to you?"

"Like sire, like son," she said. "Your father seldom slept alone, should the number of his bastards be any indication."

"I have already told you that my father and I have naught in common. I left Sayerne because he and I did not agree. On that day, I vowed that I would not return while he drew breath and so it has been."

Her lips worked as if she would ask a question of him but did not have the courage. He knew what question it must be, yet he did not have the urge to speak of his father's crimes in this moment. "You offer only sweet words to see the deed done. Once you have had your way and your possession of your holding is secured, you will not be so sweet."

His father had left a long shadow, indeed.

"Nay, Melissande," he whispered, willing her to believe him.

"That is not so. I will always treat you with dignity and honor, but I can only do as much if you grant me the opportunity."

"If I surrender." She bit out the words, her opinion of that most clear.

"If you meet me halfway," Quinn countered and she met his gaze anew. "This is our wedding night. You cannot in fairness ask me to close my eyes. You cannot accuse me of infidelity before our match is even made. All I ask of you, Melissande, is a chance."

She said naught.

He leaned toward her and she closed her eyes.

"If this is to be the only time we couple," he murmured. "I would make the mating sweet. And I would look upon your beauty, if only this once."

Melissande swallowed.

"I do not mean to hurt you." Quinn lifted her fingers from the linens and took her hand within his. Her fingers were cold. "But you know that this task cannot be avoided on this night."

She took a deep breath then she nodded, a decision clearly made. "You speak the truth," she said. "Come to bed, husband, and do your deed."

With that, Melissande flung back the linens and lay back against the sheets. She closed her eyes and placed her hands at her sides, her hands locked into fists.

She might have been a corpse.

Quinn's astonishment was not enough to keep him from noting either her slender perfection or the ripe curve of her breasts.

It was certainly not sufficient to keep him from being insulted. A man of merit did not inflict his desire upon his wife—and he had told her that he would not. Quinn shoved to his feet and paced the width of the chamber.

"You do this apurpose," he accused, shoving a hand through his hair.

"Apurpose?" she echoed, then sat up. Her eyes were bright with indignation. "Of course, I submit apurpose!"

Quinn found her vehemence reassuring. He understood her better when she was annoyed.

"Is that not what Tulley and now you want of me? I simply do your bidding from this day forward, like any dutiful wife." This last was spat with a vigor that Quinn might have heeded under other circumstances.

"A *dutiful* wife!" he replied instead. "Now there is something I am not destined to enjoy!"

"Oh!" Melissande bounded from the bed to shake a finger beneath his nose. "If obedience in every matter is what you desire of me, then you should forgo Tulley's test and let the match be annulled! I submit to this deed, sir, but I will not surrender every measure..."

Quinn barely heard her words, so transfixed was he by the cloud of gold that followed her leap from the bed. Melissande's hair hung loose to her hips, fair gold with the sheen of the finest silk. It shimmered as she moved as though it possessed a life of its own, and in that moment, Quinn could think only of touching it.

He had never seen the like. Since he had left the Continent fifteen years past, Quinn had not glimpsed any sight so fine.

"What ails you, husband?" she asked, halting before him.

"Your hair," he whispered in awe.

"You are not listening to my words."

"I am too enchanted for mere words."

Melissande folded her arms across her chest and retreated. "It is simply hair," she said, but Quinn knew that she was flattered.

"There is naught simple about such beauty, my lady," Quinn said. "It is like spun gold." He reached out a hand. "May I touch it?"

Something of his wonder must have shown in his expression, for Melissande considered him for only a heartbeat before she nodded agreement. She turned slightly and Quinn stared at the majesty of the golden tresses cascading down her back. Her hair gleamed in the firelight and bounced slightly as she moved.

He took a step closer and was surprised to find a tightness lodged in his chest. Quinn reached out, noting how rough and heavy his hand looked in contrast to his lady's splendor.

He hesitated, but he could not deny himself the temptation.

Her hair ran over his hand like a golden waterfall and slipped over his fingers as though it possessed a will of its own. It was soft beyond soft, silky and smooth. Quinn lifted a gleaming handful to his gaze and the sweet scent of his wife rose to tease his nostrils.

His body responded with a healthy vigor that caught him by surprise. He looked to his bride, but she kept her face studiously averted, her hands folded before her like a Madonna. Quinn glanced down and saw the rosy curve of her buttocks.

Then he could not help but look. He lifted her hair away, loving the feel of it as it spilled over his fingers.

She was splendid. Her skin was fair and smooth, her curves delicate and feminine. Her flared hips led his eye to the indent of her waist and thence to the curve of her breasts, her nipples ruddy and beaded in the cool air of the room. Her neck was long, her chin held high.

Quinn had never imagined he would find such a bride, let alone be cast such a prize by fortune's lot alone. Their argument was dismissed from his thoughts and he could not imagine why he might have even been irritated with a woman of such sweet beauty.

"Melissande," he murmured, hearing the reverence in his low tone. She turned slightly. "You are beyond beautiful," he said, feeling again like a rough warrior in her presence. In this moment, he could wish to be a courtier, with the right words on the tip of his tongue.

Her lips quirked in amusement. "You say that only to gain my surrender this night," she accused, though her voice had lost its earlier sting.

It was clear that his touching her hair had managed to disarm them both.

"Nay," Quinn said with resolve. "I say that because it is true. Deny me now and I will step away." He smiled at her. "I would even close my eyes, should you command it now, but I am honored that you have permitted me to see you." He let her hair slip over his fingers again, then moved his hand away.

Surprise flickered in Melissande's eyes and, for a moment, she seemed uncertain what to say. They stood close to each other in the golden light, the chamber silent save for the crackle of the fire and the slight sound of the lady's breath. Quinn could hear his heart thundering in his ears as their gazes held once more. He saw her gaze darken and her cheeks flush and knew she softened toward him once again.

Quinn did not intend to let such an opportunity pass.

He took the step that brought them toe to toe. She did not flee, but only watched him, and he was certain she held her breath. He lowered his head slowly, encouraged when she only waited, then captured her lips with his. To his delight, Melissande hesitated only a moment before she placed her hand on his chest and leaned into his embrace.

It was precious little, but that was all the encouragement Quinn needed to deepen his kiss.

Melissande might have been determined to deny her reaction to her husband's touch, but Quinn's admiration undermined her plan. His caress interfered with her power to protest and left her hungry for more. His words, his appeal, his smile, all combined to dismiss her resistance. All her life, her wits had been seen as her greatest asset, but when Quinn caressed her, it seemed that only pleasure was of import.

Surely it was no crime if she enjoyed her husband's skillful touch just this one night?

Surely she had no ability to do otherwise.

Melissande was seduced and she knew it well.

Indeed, she was already attuned to Quinn's touch. His hand cupped her nape and the heat of his palm there weakened her knees. He was so powerful, and yet he was so tender with her. Melissande felt cherished. The wonder in Quinn's expression when he touched her hair had startled her. He had shown a weakness, if only for her hair, and Melissande found herself suddenly more willing to surrender.

To experience all that Quinn could show her of this new pleasure.

It was clear that lovemaking was not new to Quinn. If they were compelled to mate this one and only time, she should make the most of the opportunity.

Unable to resist temptation, she spread out her fingers, exploring. His skin was warm yet unyielding, and she felt the pulse of his heart beneath her hand. It quickened its pace, right below her fingers. The sign that he was affected by their embrace encouraged her and Melissande dared to lean closer.

What if she could stir him as he stirred her? That was a most intriguing notion.

She moved closer, ever closer, even as she parted her lips for his kiss. He made a sound of pleasure that reminded her of a growl, then his other arm wound around her waist. Her breasts brushed against his chest and that touch made her nipples tighten. She slid her hand into his hair, opening her mouth to his kiss, and gripped the hair at his nape.

Quinn bent and swept her off her feet, swinging her into his arms. He spun around, never breaking his kiss, and Melissande found herself on the bed. He loomed over her, his lips on her cheek, her jaw, her earlobe and trailing down her neck. She gripped his shoulders, liking how the hard strength of him fit beneath her hands. Quinn trailed a row of burning kisses along her collarbone, across the swell of her breast, then captured her nipple within his lips.

Melissande gasped in surprise. She clutched at his hair as he teased her with his lips and tongue. She felt something new fire to wakefulness within her, something marvelous.

Quinn's hand slid lower and Melissande caught her breath as his fingers slipped between her thighs and she felt their warmth. She gasped but Quinn lifted his head and smiled slowly, the intent in his eyes nigh stopping her heart.

"Leave this matter to me, my lady," he whispered. "I swear upon my very soul that this will not hurt."

Melissande did not even think to question her trust in his word. She had lain back for only a moment before his fingers sent pleasure flooding through her. She parted her thighs, wanting only more of what he could give. Quinn chuckled but then his fingers continued their sweet assault and Melissande was lost to sensation. She closed her eyes as Quinn kissed her other breast. Heat rose beneath her skin and she marveled that she had not known of such desire.

And that she had tried to avoid it.

Quinn touched her with increasing boldness, his caress making her writhe on the fine bed. It was too hot in the room and there was too much tension beneath her flesh, yet there was no escape from the pleasure he was determined to give. She both wanted immediate release and wished the sweet torment would last forever. Her very blood simmered with newfound need.

Melissande grasped Quinn's hair and drew him back for her kiss, her embrace demanding as it had not been before. She felt her own kiss turn fiery and her own hands caress him boldly. She slipped her tongue into his mouth and explored him with abandon.

Melissande felt his hardness nudge against her hip and felt a sense of triumph that Quinn was aroused as well, even though she was just learning how they could please each other. Though she had not looked upon a man before, there were horses bred at Annossy and she had watched.

Quinn's fingers were relentless, just as his kiss demanded even more. Melissande arched against him, rubbing herself against his chest like a wanton. She was too aware of him, of every sensation, of the velvet of the coverlet beneath her back, of the soft mattress beneath them, of the strength of the warrior who claimed her as his wife.

"Drift with the tide, my lady," he whispered. "Do not fight it."

The fan of his breath made Melissande shudder from head to toe, then he dragged his teeth across her tight nipple. The heat radiated through her and still it grew hotter. She tangled her legs about Quinn until they were entwined, his strength only feeding her pleasure, and wanted some release she could not name.

"Follow it, follow it," he urged. "Trust it."

Melissande did. She rode the pleasure and let it take her wherever it would; she let Quinn do with her whatever he would, trusting that she would find satisfaction beneath his touch. It was a wondrous surrender, a moment in which she realized the cost she had borne in managing every detail herself, in administering Annossy alone, in having complete responsibility for all matters herself. She surrendered to her husband, believing he knew best, letting pleasure take its due.

And she was rewarded.

A mere heartbeat later, Melissande felt Quinn's fingers brush against her with greater force. She cried out as pleasure thundered through her and gripped his shoulders in the tumult. She was both free and sheltered in Quinn's protective embrace, and she could imagine no better place to be.

Then there was only Quinn angled over her, the steady rhythm of his heart against her own, a gleam of satisfaction in his golden eyes.

It was more than sufficient. She stared at him, filled with awe, and he smiled slowly.

To be sure, it had not hurt.

He had kept his pledge and she should see him rewarded.

But for the moment, Melissande was spent. She curled against his chest, sighed, and dozed against his warmth, content.

CHAPTER FIVE

uinn propped himself on his elbows and studied his new wife. The fingers that had dug into his shoulders rested on his upper arms. Her eyes were closed, her lashes delicate on her cheeks. Her lips were parted and her cheeks flushed. The glorious golden tangle of her hair spread itself across the linens beneath her, glinting in the light. Quinn could feel its silkiness wrapped about his fingers. He wanted to kiss her to wakefulness again, but let her doze instead.

The scent of Melissande's release was intoxicating. Quinn was glad that she had been pleased—and against her every expectation.

Indeed, it had even been against his own.

She stirred and her lips parted, and Quinn could resist temptation no longer. He bent and brushed his lips across hers. Melissande's eyes flew open and he feared what she might say.

To his relief, she smiled. "That did not hurt," she whispered and stroked his upper arms. He liked that she seemed to want to explore him and smiled back at her. "You kept your vow."

"As is my inclination in all matters."

"But it is not done, is it?" There was a wistfulness in her tone.

Quinn shook his head. "Nay, my lady, we have only half done the deed."

She nodded, though her smile was less confident than it had

been. "I do not know what to do next." He recognized that she had braced herself for the inevitable and wished he could ensure that it did not hurt, even the once.

"Fear not, my lady, for I do."

Her smile was fleeting but she did not recoil.

Quinn eased his weight over her, glad that she parted her thighs for him. "I shall try to be gentle." He caught his breath and closed his eyes at the promise of their union, willing himself to proceed with caution.

It had been so very long.

Melissande's grip tightened on his arms and he heard her breath catch.

Quinn leaned lower, crossing his arms beneath her and cupping her shoulders within his hands. He smiled down at her and kissed her again, feeling some of the tension ease from her. He must proceed slowly, regardless of how long he had been alone, regardless of how much he wanted to hasten. He had to be slow and careful, so that Melissande might taste the pleasure mating could bring.

Quinn closed his eyes in pleasure as he eased inside her. She was warm, like satin left in the sun, and unbearably soft. He moved and heard her gasp.

He froze, his eyes flying open.

Melissande smiled. "Just a twinge," she whispered and he was glad that she wanted to reassure him.

Quinn eased deeper, watching her closely, and she inhaled sharply. Her gaze was unswerving, though, and her eyes began to sparkle with newfound confidence.

"It is not so bad as that," she confessed, to his relief. Her smile turned impish. "I want more, husband."

Her demand thrilled Quinn, though he still moved slowly.

Her smile broadened and she lifted her knees, welcoming him as he had never expected. Quinn froze.

"You like that," she murmured.

Quinn could only nod.

"Tell me how to please you, husband," she whispered. "It is only fair that we each have some pleasure this night."

Quinn could not find the words.

Evidently, his silence tempted his bride to guess.

Melissande arched against him, pressing her breasts against his chest. She rubbed them there, a move that she clearly found pleasurable, then ran her hands over his shoulders and chest with proprietary ease. She explored him more boldly and Quinn welcomed her touch.

"Does that please you?" she whispered. She tightened her legs around him. "And this?"

Quinn's pulse pounded in his ears, his chest was tight and still she coaxed him further.

"Melissande... I..." Quinn could not form a coherent thought to save his life.

"This?" Melissande stretched up and kissed his ear. The gentle touch of her tongue, the sensation of her breath there, the brush of her lips, all combined to make his blood nearly boil. She ran a line of kisses down to his nipple, then teased it as he had teased hers. Quinn was on fire. He ran his hands down her back, locked his hands around her waist, and moved deeply inside her.

She smiled, a siren with her gleaming hair beneath her and a thousand promises in her eyes. Quinn gripped her hips and claimed her with a trio of strokes, each deeper than the last.

Melissande drove him onward, rising against him with a passion he had not dared to share. Her legs tightened around his waist, her arms locked around his neck. Quinn was trapped within her, captured by her, enfolded and encircled by her warmth. She urged him to a frenzy with a determination that stole his breath away.

His eyes flew open as her nails dug into his shoulders once more. Quinn realized that she was reaching the crest again. Her eyes were glittering and he nearly laughed aloud that they should find such harmony unexpected.

Melissande was his bride and partner for all time. She was his and his alone—and Quinn would pleasure her until his dying day.

At that realization, Quinn's release swept through him in a torrent and he roared with satisfaction. He moved against her, ensuring that she would find her pleasure, and smiled as she gasped in wonder again. They clung together then fell to the mattress, still entangled in each other, still breathing heavily.

Quinn lifted a hand and pushed a stray tendril of hair back from Melissande's cheek. It twined around his finger, as if to hold him fast to his lady's side, and he kissed it.

"Melissande," he whispered, awed that she was his wife. "My lady Melissande."

She opened her eyes and granted him a sleepy smile that warmed him through to his soul. She curled against him and slept, even as he marveled at his good fortune.

He had feared this mating might be a trial.

He could not have been more wrong, and he was glad of it. This was a sign that their future was bright together. They might have started badly, but all would improve from this night onward. They would have sons and rebuild Sayerne and rule their estates in wealth and harmony for decades. They would have every blessing and every joy.

Quinn could not wait. He rose from the bed with reluctance, knowing that they would sleep better with some minor alterations. He washed them both, then retrieved the lady's chemise and managed to tuck her into it without awakening her. He watched her sleep as he donned his own. He extinguished the lanterns, put a little more fuel on the brazier, then climbed back into the great bed. He pulled the covers over them both even as he tucked Melissande tightly against his side.

He did not miss that her lips curved in a smile.

He did not doubt that he was responsible for her satisfaction.

Before he slept, Quinn resolved to prompt her smile each and every night.

Against every expectation, he was the most fortunate man in all of Christendom and he would ensure Melissande never doubted his joy in that.

The blood on the linens was a rude awakening the next morning.

Melissande blinked but the incriminating red spots remained. She had awakened alone in the great bed and had peeked, guessing what she would find but startled at the brilliant red stain on the white linen.

Her maidenhead was gone.

She and Quinn were wed beyond any dispute.

What would happen to Annossy? Would this marriage lead to the destruction of all her family had built? Of all she had defended? What did her new husband know of administration? And how much would he take from Annossy to rebuild Sayerne?

She was not certain she wished to know.

Worse, she had broken her own pledge to await Arnaud. It was true that Tulley had compelled her to do as much, but she had not needed to meet Quinn abed with such enthusiasm. How could she have forgotten herself? How could she have heeded sensation and ignored all else of import? What manner of wanton was she becoming?

How much more base would she become in this man's company?

The possibilities were terrifying.

Quinn was already tending the fire, wearing only his chemise, the morning light picking out the glints in his hair. That he granted her a satisfied smile over one shoulder did naught to lessen Melissande's guilt.

Even now, she felt her blood simmer at Quinn's slow smile. Had she forgotten every virtue she had been taught to uphold?

What else would Jerome's son convince her to forget?

"Good morning, my lady." Quinn strolled back toward the bed, intent in his eyes, and Melissande was shocked that she warmed in anticipation of his touch.

"There is naught good about it!" she replied, hearing the fear in her own tone.

Quinn paused, watching her. Melissande knew it was unfair to blame him for her own failings—unless this had been his scheme. She pushed a hand through her hair, not surprised to find that it had tangled in the night since it had not been braided. She was a ruin and was surrounded by the scent of their mutual pleasure. She might as well have been a whore.

It would be easier to blame Quinn if she had not been so weak.

"I thought that last night's deeds would have made this morning a sunny one," he said, speaking with care.

"Last night's deeds are why all is in disarray," she said, feeling her tears rise. "I might have been at home at Annossy this morning. I might have slept with my hair braided and the linens unsoiled. I might not smell of...carnal union."

The corner of Quinn's mouth quirked before he sobered again. "Some might say that a woman is always at home with her husband beside her." He raised his brows. "And that the marriage bed should smell of carnal union."

"Some like Tulley, perhaps." She was no better than a tavern wench.

He sat on the side of the bed. "It seemed to me you enjoyed the fact that you were not alone last eve."

It was true and Melissande knew it. She tightened her lips. "I was seduced against my will. I was led astray."

"Nay, my lady." Quinn shook his head, his voice a low burr that made her blood simmer anew. "You might have been seduced, but you were willing."

Melissande could not argue otherwise.

He shook a finger at her. "I was not the only one who savored the consummation of our match. I strove to try to please you, but you met me halfway. We both enjoyed it. Do not deny that truth."

"Do you call me a wanton?"

"I do not." He was resolute. "I call you my wife. It is right and good that we should find satisfaction together."

"And the linens will provide the evidence." She knew she sounded bitter, but it was all so vulgar. To have every soul in Tulley know that her maidenhead had been claimed the night before was most troubling to her. She left the bed from the opposite side and went to the basin of water, then halted, modest again. How could she wash without Quinn seeing her nudity? Why did she care since he had seen her the night before? Melissande felt shaken and overwhelmed and she blinked back tears that would be of no aid.

It was folly to wish that all might be as it had been before. She was wed. She should accustom herself to that. How many would witness her nudity when she bore a child?

Melissande could not even think upon it.

Quinn, as she should have anticipated, came to stand behind her. His hands cupped her shoulders and he bent to drop a kiss on the top of her head. "Shall I remind you of your passion, my lady?" he whispered. "I am certain it can be awakened again."

He kissed her ear, arousing her desire with such ease that Melissande was dismayed.

"There is no need," she said. "I am no better than a harlot, it is clear."

He paused then turned her to face him. She kept her gaze downcast, but he placed that fingertip beneath her chin and compelled her to meet his gaze. She knew he saw her tears, for his expression turned serious. "You are dismayed that we found pleasure in intimacy? Would you rather it had been painful?"

"I cannot believe that I was so able to forget myself," she admitted. "I was taught to maintain my dignity in all circumstance."

Quinn smiled crookedly. "I think it fair that there be one exception."

"This is no jest!"

"I do not jest," he said, sobering. "I thought last night a fine omen for our future."

"I did not!"

His eyes narrowed, as though he suspected she might not say words he liked, but he waited and listened. Melissande already saw that was his inclination.

"It was the wine," she said. "The wine betrayed me and I forgot myself. I should never have accepted it from Berthe here. I indulged too much and that undermined my dignity." She frowned. "But I did not feel its effects so greatly until dinner." She remembering her enchanted cup, then looked at Quinn with newfound suspicion. "How curious that my cup was never empty."

He looked discomfited and she guessed the truth.

"You ensured as much," she said. "You wished me to be too besotted to avoid your touch."

Quinn colored. "I thought the wine might ease your fears," he said. "I thought you might be more at ease."

Already he chose for her, assuming he knew her desire and her need better than she. Melissande found that a terrifying portent. "You should have asked me. We should have discussed the matter together."

"You had already been drinking wine," he said. "I smelled it upon your breath. I did not think any discussion would be reasoned as a result."

"I saw my fears eased. It was not your responsibility to choose for me."

"Of course, it is my responsibility to choose for you," Quinn replied, his voice rising. "You are my wife!"

"I will not be your chattel!"

His eyes flashed and his voice rose higher. "Recall, my lady, that both of us had the same intent last eve, for we had both agreed to Tulley's terms."

Melissande retreated behind the table with the pitcher of water, hating how she wished to touch him even in this moment. She could just reach up and ease the crease from between his brows with a fingertip and perhaps dismiss his annoyance. That she wished to do as much was a treacherous indication of his power over her. "You thought the wine might grant you an easy conquest."

"There could be no easy conquest when you are bride," Quinn replied. He cast his hands skyward. "Zounds, woman, is any matter simple with you?"

"Of course!"

"You were concerned about the pain," he continued, then made a fist. "If you had clenched, the deed might well have hurt you. I tried to make matters right, Melissande!"

"You should have spoken to me."

"You should have spoken to me."

"How could I discuss such intimacy with you, a veritable stranger?" Melissande demanded.

"I am your husband!"

"And still there are matters that are delicate..."

"If you do not discuss carnal union with me, who will you discuss it with?" he demanded, his eyes blazing.

"There is naught amiss with decorum and dignity. There is

naught amiss with granting value to wit and intellect and skill..."

"There is naught amiss with passion between man and wife."

"You will not have my passion, sir!"

Quinn chuckled, curse him. "I already have it, my lady," he murmured in that low tone that still weakened her knees.

Melissande was more than halfway in his thrall already and she knew it, so she struck back. "Do you always ply women with wine to lure them to your bed?"

Quinn's eyes flashed fire again, his teasing mood banished. Indeed, he swore with a vehemence that made Melissande suddenly afraid. She feared she had pushed him too far and would see all too soon that he did resemble his father.

To her astonishment, though, he abruptly turned and crossed the room. He flung open the shutters, admitting a cold wind, and glared into the mist of the morning. Annossy's tower was obscured by the fog on this day and the air was chilly. Melissande did not dare complain, for she halfway feared he would fling her to the courtyard below. But Quinn folded his arms across his chest and tapped his toe, as if he counted.

"The wine cannot make you act as you would not," he said finally, without glancing her way. He bit off the words and spoke with precision, a sure sign that he was angry.

Melissande waited, warily, uncertain what to expect.

Quinn took a deep breath when she did not speak, then another. After the third such, he spoke again and his tone was remarkably temperate. "You have told me only half of the tale," he said with a perceptiveness that startled her. "Tell me what truly troubles you this morning."

Then he pivoted, his gaze locking upon her as if she was his prey. Melissande's mouth went dry, for she sensed that he would not abandon the quest for this truth very easily.

Even through her dismay, she noted that his tone was even, his words compelling in their demand. He had not struck her.

He had scarce shouted at her.

She locked her hands together before herself. If naught else, she owed him the truth.

"You know that I had no interest in this match."

Quinn snorted. "Yet I did?"

Melissande eyed him. "Why would you not be? I have a holding and some affluence. I am young enough to bear children and..." she faltered, unable to claim her own beauty as an asset. She was aware of it—how could she not be?—but she was not vain.

"And?" he prompted, teasing her as she blushed.

"You did express an admiration for my hair."

His smile was quick and when his gaze swept over her, she saw his gaze heat. She was surprised by how much it pleased her to have some influence over him.

"Make no mistake, my lady, you are fair to look upon, to be sure, but I had always hoped to choose my bride. I had hoped to make a match to suit both my heart and my lady's." Quinn raised his gaze to hers and the intensity of that look pierced Melissande's very soul. "I dared to hope last night that, despite the odds, we might have made such a match." He held her gaze for a long moment, his own searching. "Was I mistaken?"

Melissande turned abruptly away. "Aye, you were."

"Ah."

The chamber filled with silence, but it was not one of expectation or desire. Melissande found tears pricking at her eyes and felt that she had lost something precious, and that by her own folly.

It was all a trick, she reminded herself, a feint by Jerome's son to fulfill his father's fondest dream. How strange that each time she told herself such things, they seemed less plausible than they had before.

Was she falling under Quinn's spell, just as he planned?

"Tell me then, as you seem so inclined to do so," he said. "What was your objection to this match? Is my father's shadow so long that you cannot judge me in my own right? Or do you find me lacking so grievously that you would have chosen any other man in my stead?"

Melissande did not like to see this bitterness in Quinn and liked even less that she had provoked it. But he had to know the truth.

"I am pledged to another," she confessed.

"What madness is this?"

Melissande met his gaze. "You heard me."

"Pledged to another man?" Quinn ran one hand through his hair in his agitation. "Yet you did not imagine that this detail might interest me?"

"Tulley did not care."

His eyes flashed and Melissande braced herself for his fury. Already, though, she began to trust that the sum of it would be shouting.

"*I am not Tulley!*" he roared. "Do you think that I am such a selfish cur? Do you think that I would care naught for a pledge you had granted? Do you think that I would not have walked away if I had only known?"

His reaction chilled Melissande to her marrow. Was it true? "You would not have abandoned Sayerne," she insisted.

"I would not have willingly wed a woman sworn to another man. I would have told Tulley as much and insisted he change his terms."

"He would not change them for me."

"I might have been more persuasive," Quinn said grimly and she had a moment to wonder what he might have said or done. Then he pointed at her. "You owed me the truth before last evening and you know it well, my lady."

Melissande did not know what to say. He was right, of course.

Suddenly, Quinn's eyes narrowed and Melissande did not trust the abrupt change in the direction of his thoughts. He crossed the floor with angry steps to confront her. "What will you do when he comes for you?" he demanded. "Whose side will you choose?"

Melissande was astonished. She had not considered the possibility, though now that Quinn mentioned it, she wondered how likely it might be. Would Arnaud come to her?

What *would* she do?

"I cannot say," she admitted. "I had not considered the matter."

"Then you should do as much with all haste, my lady. Word of our match has undoubtedly flown from this keep already. If a woman was sworn to me, I would be quick to take vengeance upon any man who dared to claim what I knew to be my own."

"He would not," she protested, although she was not certain.

Their gazes locked and held for a moment, long enough to make her conviction fade.

"What is his name?" Quinn asked. There was a quiet precision in his tone that made Melissande shiver.

"Why?"

"Perhaps I am curious about the manner of man who captured your heart."

Melissande opened her mouth to correct his assumption, then closed it again. Her heart had naught to do with this matter. It was her word alone that stood compromised, though perhaps there was no need for Quinn to know that.

"You wish to be forewarned."

"Can you blame me?"

She could not. "I would have your pledge in exchange."

Quinn folded his arms across his chest and Melissande noted the sign of his rising impatience. She realized also that he had not hurt her or raised a hand toward her, no matter how much she had pressed him.

Was it possible that he was not like his father?

Or did he simply bide his time? How she wished she knew!

"What vow?"

"Not to touch me again," she said. "Our match is consummated. Both you and Tulley have what you desire. Now I would have what I desire."

Quinn dropped his voice low. "You would have me never touch you as I did last night? You would not feel such pleasure ever again as we shared just hours ago?"

Melissande blushed. "Nay."

Quinn placed that finger beneath her chin, then tipped her gaze up to hold his. His very touch sent a thrill through Melissande but she dared not let her gaze flicker. Some trace of her weakness must have shown in her expression, though, for suddenly Quinn smiled.

"You lie, my lady," he whispered. He waited, giving her time to recognize that he spoke the truth, then bent to kiss her.

He was making a point and Melissande knew it. She wanted to defy him to prove his assumption wrong. But Quinn had anticipated her and as before, her body seemed to be on his side.

She wanted his kiss and once his lips touched hers, she was lost anew. He was gentle, coaxing and tender. His kiss was beguiling and surrender was inevitable. It was frightening to Melissande how little difference the wine had made in her response.

She wanted him again.

Such weakness could not be borne. She must eradicate it before it became worse.

Melissande broke their kiss with an effort and stepped away from temptation. "Nay!" When Quinn did not retreat but merely stood watching her, eyes ablaze with desire, the very look of him tempting her again, Melissande flushed at her own weakness.

She could only make him retreat with harsh words.

"You will not force me to your bed again," she said with heat. "I will not become a slave to pleasure and forget all that I was raised to believe."

"I have never forced a lady in all my days."

"To be the first has no place of pride in this matter," Melissande said. "Make no mistake, sir. You will not so weaken me again. You are forbidden to cross the threshold of my chamber from this day forth, whether we be wedded or not."

There was a terse silence, but Melissande turned her back upon Quinn. She sat on a stool and donned her stockings, ensuring that he could not see her bare legs and wishing that she were not so aware of his watchful presence.

"We have need of a son, and there will be none this way," he said, his voice taut.

"You cannot know that. The feat might be accomplished."

"If not, you must invite me to your bed, my lady. To have no heir is a vulnerability that cannot be endured."

Melissande closed her eyes against this appeal, for she saw the good sense in it. Perhaps in time, she could meet him abed without losing her wits. Perhaps it was the novelty of this union and its pleasures that disarmed her.

"Promise me," she said instead and heard him growl beneath his breath.

He paced the width of the chamber, his frustration clear. She strove to ignore him and failed utterly.

"What is his name?" Quinn asked an eternity later.

"I do not have your vow."

"I will touch you only when you desire as much," he replied tersely.

Melissande turned to study him, surprised to have him concede this. Quinn looked more grim than ever she had seen him. Even in his chemise, he was evidently a warrior, and one who would undertake any risk for the sake of justice. He looked powerful, formidable even, yet he surrendered to her request.

Perhaps Quinn was precisely as he appeared.

"I will have you pledge that you will not tempt my desire."

"The pledge you have is the sole one I will grant, my lady," he said and his eyes flashed anew. "We are wed. I vow to let you decide the timing of our unions and will pledge no more."

Melissande dropped her gaze, knowing that she had won more than expected. It was not time to press for more.

"Now, tell me the name of the man who holds your heart captive forever."

"Arnaud de Privas." The name sounded hollow. Melissande tried to recall the face of the man to whom it belonged and could not.

It had been so long. In all honesty, giving her word was all she recalled of the matter.

And that glorious summer day. Her recollection of her father's delight was more clear than any memory she had of Arnaud.

Had Arnaud truly wed Marie or had Tulley lied? She did not know, so did not share that detail with Quinn.

"Privas borders Annossy and Sayerne."

"Aye."

"How is it that I do not recall meeting its ruling family?"

"It has been impoverished longer than Sayerne. Since the death of Arnaud's father, who was a great friend of my father."

"And your betrothed?"

"Left to seek his fortune, much as you did." She turned to watch him, curious about his reaction.

"Arnaud de Privas." Quinn repeated the name once more under his breath, as though committing it to memory, then met her gaze.

"I will keep my vow, but you will invite me to your chamber and soon, my lady."

"I will not!"

"Aye, you will, for there is a passion between us that even you cannot deny, even though you clearly would like to."

"I say not."

Quinn smiled slowly and she rose to her feet, aware of him yet again. He strolled closer, his gaze fixed upon her, his smile alluring, his confidence unassailable, then tugged his chemise over his head and cast it aside. "You shall invite me now, my lady," he murmured and Melissande's heart fluttered.

He was magnificent.

And he was aroused.

By the sight of her, in her chemise and stockings, her hair tangled about her shoulders.

Melissande caught her breath, astonished yet again by Quinn's effect upon her. It was a lie to leave him believing that Arnaud held her heart, but if it kept him at a distance, she could not afford to tell him the truth. The man had no lack of confidence in his own persuasive abilities—and his conviction was not without cause.

He reached her side and lifted her hair, letting his spill over his fingers. "You are glorious, my Melissande," he murmured and her breath caught when he said her name. He kissed the hair on his hand, his gaze rising to hers again. "As splendid as a goddess."

"I am not dressed," she protested. "My hair is not braided..."

He bent and grazed her cheek with his lips, then kissed her ear. She tingled at the brush of his whiskers and shivered at the heat emanating from him, thrilled by the power that he held in check. He was a man, such as she had never imagined a man might be. His breath fanned her throat and kindled her desire, and his hand rose to her nape again.

"Glorious," he whispered then kissed her ear. Her eyes closed in pleasure. When he grazed her earlobe with his teeth, Melissande heard herself moan with need. "With wine or not, you rise to my touch, just as I rise to yours," Quinn whispered into her ear and she felt the flick of his tongue. His kisses brushed down her throat and she tipped her head, granting him access to whatever he desired of her. "It is a fair promise for our shared future."

Melissande tugged herself from his embrace and hastened backward. "Aye?" she asked, ensuring her tone was sharp. "Did you not realize that I only pretended to share your pleasure, husband? I thought it a fitting choice for a bride on her nuptial night."

Quinn shook his head slowly. "You did not."

"You do not know," she said, then turned to choose a clean chemise. She kept her tone dismissive, though her heart was thundering. "It is done. And I have your vow."

"It is not done, my lady," Quinn said softly. "I will prove it to you, again and again, if necessary." She saw his hand rise and guessed his intent, knowing he would be proven right if he did touch her.

"Is your word worth so little, then?" she asked. "Does the pledge you have granted me mean naught at all?"

Quinn dropped his hand. She turned to find him glaring at her. "We will journey to Annossy together, and should you not invite me to your chamber, I will slumber outside your door."

"Like an obedient hound."

"Like a husband who knows his rightful place."

"You might find more comfort in the stables. Or at Sayerne."

"Nay," Quinn said with resolve. "You will not have the opportunity to forget about me, my lady." He shook a finger at her. "And rest assured, the next time that I am between your thighs—and I will be soon—I will have been *invited*."

"I do not share your confidence," Melissande said, but her husband only smiled that maddening smile, the one that made her catch her breath and...remember.

Their gazes locked and held once more across the chamber, the heat rising between them with an ease that Melissande despised. She wanted to look away but could not. She wanted to halt her own reaction, but she could not. She was powerless when this man simply looked upon her—when he smiled—and that sent terror through her veins.

Quinn took a step closer, his intent clear, and Melissande

fought her desire to flee. "Invite me now, my lady," he murmured. "I will ensure that you begin your day most joyously."

Melissande knew she would appear more resolute if she held her ground, but if Quinn touched her again...

He had no such chance, for someone rapped upon the door.

"I come for the linens," Tulley declared from the other side.

Melissande seized a robe and donned it over her chemise, her heart pounding. Quinn tugged on his own chemise and turned to face the door. Was it coincidence that he ensured Melissande was shielded from view?

God in heaven, this man would keep her emotions all a-tangle if she did not find a way to keep him at a distance.

What was she to do?

CHAPTER SIX

rnaud de Privas.

Quinn would never forget the name. He did have a vague recollection of his father hunting at Privas, but thought perhaps his father had not seen eye-to-eye with that holding's lord. That would have diminished contact between the estates and even mention of Privas. It would scarce be surprising for the lord whose son was to wed the daughter of Annossy to have conflict with Jerome.

To his own dismay, Quinn was irked, yet again, in the presence of his wife. Oh, he had wanted to convince her to invite him, and he knew he could have done as much—but the flash of fear in her eyes had been his undoing. How could she both fear him and provoke him? And how could Tulley have ignored her betrothal? Now, Quinn was caught between the fat and the fire, all to suit Tulley's dictate.

Indeed, Quinn had greater sympathy for Melissande now that he knew this detail. He could already see the importance she attached to vows, perhaps a trait learned from her father, and could understand how the situation would trouble her. Of course, she felt guilt over her reaction to his touch. Of course, she believed that she was disloyal to her betrothed. He understood all of this, and yet, he found it hard to believe that lovemaking could be so potent if they were not meant each for the other.

Perhaps he was a romantic fool like his mother, just as his father had oft sneered.

"Do I interrupt?" Tulley asked, with no care for the reply. His gaze flicked to the bed and back to Quinn. He smiled, the wily old lord, and Quinn's irritation found its rightful target. "Is there perhaps an estate—or two—falling forfeit this morn?"

Aye, Tulley would welcome that outcome. "The truth is evident, I believe." Quinn gestured to the bed, then paced to the window. He dared not trust himself to say more.

He tried to consider how he might take his lady's cause as his own. He stole a glance at her to find her gaze downcast.

Perhaps they had annoyance with their liege lord in common. The notion was almost sufficient to make Quinn smile.

"Ah! Very good!" Tulley declared. "It is a pleasure to be mistaken on occasion." He snapped his fingers and his châtelain hastened to gather the linens. Would they be washed or preserved as evidence? Quinn did not know.

The silence grew in the chamber, until Tulley coughed in his precise manner. "It seems to me that all is not rosy this morn."

No one responded.

"In fact," Tulley continued. "I could not help but overhear your...discussion."

At that, Quinn looked up, as did Melissande. There was alarm in her eyes, which Quinn took as a warning. She knew Tulley far better than he did.

"Perhaps I have not adequately emphasized the importance of this match." Tulley looked between the two of them, his expression forbidding.

Melissande blinked rapidly but did not speak.

Quinn took that as a warning.

Still, Tulley watched him, his manner expectant.

"I understand our union is a matter of some interest to you," Quinn managed to say.

"This is more than a matter of interest!" Tulley said. "It is of the utmost import that this marriage be seen as unassailable." He drove his fist into his palm, his emphatic gesture startling Quinn.

"The match is made and consummated," he reminded the older man. "As you have seen."

"Yet already there will be talk in the kitchens about the arguments between the pair of you," Tulley replied. He paced the width of the chamber and back, so clearly agitated that Quinn wondered what he would say next. "Such chatter will travel like the wind. You *will* share your bedchamber—you must!—and to ensure as much, I insist upon an heir within the year."

Quinn saw Melissande's hands tighten into fists and knew that she too was fighting her impulse to argue with Tulley. He moved closer to her side, feeling that they should battle as one.

"That allows but three months for conception," Quinn said, knowing he sounded more mild than he felt.

"Indeed!" Tulley agreed. "What deterrent to these raids is a crusading knight taking the title of Lord of Annossy if you, Quinn, do not express your claim in every possible way?"

Melissande's head snapped up. "Lord of Annossy?" she echoed. "Naught was said of Quinn becoming Lord of Annossy! I understood that this match was to assure his claim to Sayerne!"

"Surely you understood that the two estates will be merged with this match?"

Melissande paled.

Quinn did not appreciate Tulley's manner with her, for the older man spoke as if she were a witless child. Quinn knew that his wife was keen of intellect, and even he had not made what Tulley assumed was an obvious conclusion.

Tulley had not made his intention clear.

No doubt on purpose.

He was to be lord of both estates? Quinn was astounded. For the first time, he wondered whether he was adequately trained to administer a manor. Surely such a fact as the merging of the estates would have been obvious to him otherwise?

"Merged?" Melissande repeated. "I never agreed for Annossy to merge with any other estate. My father would have forbidden as much..."

"Your father is dead," Tulley said, interrupting her. "And the choice is mine to make."

"Had that always been your intent, you should have made the matter clear from the outset," Melissande dared to say.

Tulley's lips thinned. "The seal of Annossy has never been granted to you, Melissande. It is yet mine." Indeed, he produced the seal in that moment, and Quinn realized the lord had been holding it in his hand. "Annossy is mine to rule and its seal is mine to grant."

Melissande, with a pride that Quinn could only admire, extended her hand in obvious expectation. She might have been a queen, or even a goddess.

But Tulley shook his head. "Throughout all of Christendom, a woman cedes her property to her spouse upon her nuptials and you should not imagine that Annossy or you would be treated differently." Tulley offered the seal to Quinn. "Annossy will be your sole holding for the time being," he said when Quinn had accepted its slight burden.

Melissande gasped and Quinn frowned.

"I beg your pardon, my lord?" he asked. "I returned at your summons to govern Sayerne."

"You returned at my summons that your father had died," Tulley corrected. "I do not intend to grant Sayerne to you as of yet." He turned to leave the chamber. "I expect you both at the board shortly."

"What is this?" Quinn demanded, following his liege lord. "The entire point of this match was to bring Sayerne to my hand! I journeyed from Palestine at your summons!"

"You cannot do this!" Melissande charged and Quinn was glad to see that she took his cause. "You gave Quinn this expectation, whether you declared it outright or not."

"I can do whatsoever I see fit to do," Tulley replied, pivoting in the doorway to survey them. "And I will see this match made in truth before I grant Sayerne to anyone." His gaze narrowed as he eyed them. "I would strongly suggest that you never challenge me thus again."

Quinn's heart sank. He had been used by this wily lord, tricked into taking a wife who would drive him mad, and all for naught. Melissande had been compelled to break her vow, only to have

Annossy surrendered to him. And now, Tulley was insulted, as well. The future could bode no darker fate for him than this.

Sayerne was not to be his, ever if at all.

Perhaps it would have been better if he had gone to his grave with Bayard at that fateful battle at Acre. He would have been spared the burden of this disappointment.

Of course, then he would never have spent the night just past with a bride more fetching and passionate than he had ever expected to take to his side. Surely that match was worth a battle or two, even some sacrifice?

If only Melissande would meet him halfway.

"But mercifully for the two of you, I am not without compassion." Tulley held up a finger. "You have one year to produce a legitimate heir and when you do—" he nodded to Quinn "—Sayerne will be yours."

Melissande's lips twisted, her doubt clear, but she held her tongue.

"But, my lord..." Quinn began to protest, only to have Tulley interrupt.

"But naught!" the older man said with force. "This matter is serious beyond all. My holdings are at risk due to the vulnerability of Annossy. I will not tolerate such a risk!"

"But..." Melissande began, but Tulley glared at her until she fell silent again.

"Understand this," he said to Quinn. "It is beyond gracious of me to hold your estate in trust for an entire year and considerably more than your due. You should thank me for the opportunity to prove yourself. See that you do not disappoint me again." With that, Tulley spun on his heel and left the room.

"If naught else, he ensures that we know what is at stake," Melissande said.

"Is he always so irksome?"

She smiled with obvious reluctance. "He is a warrior and a man who knows his desire. I would wager you have known many of his ilk."

"Aye, but I have not had the misfortune to be required to please many of them."

Melissande clearly fought her urge to laugh at his grumpy confession. Their gazes met and he found hers twinkling, and he was glad to have amused her in this moment.

"You will have to invite me," he noted and her laughter faded.

She inclined her head to Quinn, her composure restored. "I would suggest, husband, that we ride to Annossy as soon as might be, before the Lord de Tulley feels compelled to make more demands."

"Aye, my lady, you speak the truth in that." Quinn reached for his chausses and boots, well aware that she had not agreed with him. "I will send your maid to assist you."

She nodded agreement, her lips tight, and he doubted he would see the fire in her eyes anytime soon.

He might hold Annossy's seal, but he had lost all favor with its lady.

Tulley was a fool.

Melissande could not believe Tulley's choice.

How could her liege lord surrender the seal of Annossy to Quinn, and so readily as this? She as yet knew little of her lord husband—yet he held the greatest prize in Christendom within his grasp, by her accounting. Five years she had administered Annossy, and so flawlessly that Tulley had been fulsome in his praise.

And now he gave the holding away.

Worse, with that surrender, she had become no more than Quinn's possession. She had no standing, no legal rights beyond his own, no argument to make in her own favor. Oh, Tulley's choice burned.

Their agreement was moot, as well. She would be compelled to invite Quinn to her bed, for she had to conceive a son to protect even this position of weakness. Melissande felt cornered and filled with a new fear, one she had never hoped to experience. All depended upon her womb—not her wits, not her talents, not her experience. How she hated to have her future dependent upon Fate and whim and her husband's inclination.

Melissande had Berthe draw her hair back tightly, choosing to look stern and cold. She could not bear for Quinn to touch her and reduce her to a wanton, not on this day. She had need of solitude to accept the change in her stature and fortify herself for the challenge ahead. She donned a thick gown of deep blue wool and a sturdy wimple, blaming the cold for her desire to hide herself away. She descended to the hall and broke her fast in silence.

She could not even look at Quinn in her consternation.

Did her father weep in his grave? She could imagine so. Sayerne had begun to devour Annossy, after all.

They departed immediately after breaking their fast, though Quinn had a short conference with Tulley. Of course, Melissande was not privy to the discussion. She fought her sense of injustice and kept her gaze downcast even as she seethed.

Her mare was saddled and waiting in the bailey, and Quinn lifted her to the saddle. She avoided his gaze, for she knew that if he smiled at her, she might forget herself. A company of Tulley's men escorted their party down the winding road to the gates of Tulley's town. At the gates, they were left to their own, and took the road that led east and slightly north.

Tulley's holding filled the valley between two ranges of mountains. At the lowest point of the valley ran the river Helva, its headwaters far ahead of their party. The peaks of the mountains defined the boundaries of the territory on three sides, the slope on the northern side cultivated in tiers that basked in summer's sunlight. The southern slope was thick with trees, which were mostly conifers. The distant end was lost in rocky outcroppings and jagged peaks. On this day, the river was glazed with ice in areas, and both trees and fields were covered with snow. From its position at the widest and lowest point of the valley, the keep of Tulley defended the entire valley.

Annossy lay ahead and to the left of the main road that followed the river's course. It perched on higher land, that vantage point offering a view toward Tulley and to distant Sayerne. Sayerne was beyond Annossy and had once been larger, but in these days, it was Annossy that prospered. Melissande's family holding's most valuable crop was wine. Privas was larger, perhaps larger than Annossy and Sayerne together, but it was almost completely forested, being on the south side of the road, opposite Annossy and Sayerne. There were more holdings further up the valley, and indeed, more between Tulley's keep and Martinach, but this was the part of the valley Melissande knew best. She could see those three keeps if she narrowed her eyes against the winter sunlight, in their various states of repair, though a banner flew only from Annossy's tower. Indeed, it was the only tower of the three that stood whole, with a roof. From this distance, the banner's silver and blue hues could not be distinguished but she could see its flicker against the snow of the fields.

Behind them, the road and valley continued to descend toward the junction with the river Darke at Martinach, a town administered by Tulley but plagued with flooding in the springs. The crops were rich there, though. Melissande knew it only as the place to turn south to take the road to the Beauvoir Pass, beyond which lay the Italian states, Rome, and sunshine. She had never journeyed through that pass. Beauvoir, too, was governed by Tulley and she did not doubt that its tolls contributed significantly to Tulley's treasury. Following the Darke River north led to Geneva and thence to Paris and the lands of the French kings. Perricault lay in that direction, sheltered in the next valley to the north, and she wondered anew if Tulley's tale of Arnaud was truth. Again, she had not travelled that road. Tulley had been the limit of her journeys. Beyond the mountains to the north and end of the Helva valley was the domain of the Holy Roman Emperor and his courts. Tulley answered to him, but as he had suggested to Melissande, neither king nor emperor looked closely at this corner of Christendom.

The air was already cold, and Melissande knew that as they continued, it would become colder yet. The valley rose toward the headwaters of the Helva and the mountains there were difficult to cross even in summer. The sunlight was fiercely bright on this day, the sky clear and the wind wicked. She was dressed for the weather, though she doubted that the cloaks of Quinn and his companion, Bayard, were thick enough.

Their blood must have thinned in Palestine and for a moment, she felt sympathy for them. She did not even know from whence Bayard had come.

She rode beside her husband in silence. Berthe was at her left and Bayard on Berthe's left, so that the men flanked the two of them. The four squires in service to both knights followed behind. Quinn made several attempts at conversation, but it seemed that his words froze in the air before him.

"You are vexed with me," he murmured finally and Melissande knew that only she could hear the softly-uttered words.

"I am disappointed in the Lord de Tulley's choice," she confessed, keeping her tone even with an effort. "But as a mere woman, my opinion is of no import."

He slanted her a glance and his eyes glowed gold, as she already knew they did when he was intent upon some matter. "I shall have need of your counsel, wife."

"Will you, sir? I should think a man would only be granted the seal to a holding when his own skills were such that he could administer it in his own right." Her voice had risen and she was aware that Bayard was watching her. Berthe's lips had thinned.

Quinn exhaled, evidently aware of the same. "We shall speak of this in privacy, my lady."

Melissande did not reply. She could well imagine how he would convince her to be of aid to him. She liked to believe that she would be able to resist his touch, but already knew that battle to be lost.

It was unfair!

It was approaching noon when a party of riders appeared on the road before them. Melissande caught her breath and felt Quinn glance her way.

"A party from Annossy?" he asked and she shook her head.

"We are too far as yet. And no soul lives at Sayerne any longer. It is too early for anyone to have ridden this far from one of the further keeps."

"A supplicant, coming to Annossy?" Quinn suggested.

"They may be thieves. There is no reason to be on this road in this time of year." Melissande swallowed. "If so, they can only be desperate."

The knight's destriers immediately eased closer to the women's palfreys and Melissande seized the reins of Berthe's horse. The two women exchanged grim glances and Berthe began to unlace the sides of her kirtle.

"Time it is that I am with child again," the maid muttered.

"What madness is this?" Bayard asked but the women ignored him.

"Thieves so close to Tulley's own holding? In daylight?" Quinn asked Melissande, his eyes narrowed as he studied the party. "Are they so bold as this?"

"I have never heard tell of them here, but that does not mean they do not ride through the valley at will. The road is to be governed by Sayerne's lord from that last marker, and there has been none of late." Melissande bit her tongue lest she say that his father had nigh encouraged lawlessness within his boundaries.

Naught would be aided by provoking an argument when her husband held all assets.

Berthe meanwhile had taken the small pack of valuables from Melissande's saddle and shoved it beneath her chemise and kirtle. Her hands disappeared inside her kirtle and Melissande knew she bound her belt beneath her chemise to keep the bundle in place. Satisfied with her knots, Berthe then laced the sides of her kirtle again, and looked for all the world as if she was six months into a pregnancy.

Bayard gave a low whistle. "That is quick work," he said with admiration. "You could have three babes by the Yule at this rate."

Berthe laughed at his jest, but Melissande did not. "Only the most depraved ruffian would look there for riches," she explained.

"I feel most depraved in this moment," Bayard said with mock solemnity. He winked at Berthe and she swatted his shoulder.

"You are a scoundrel and a ne'er-do-well, that much is clear. A gentleman would never make so lewd a comment to a lady..."

"But is a maid a lady?" Bayard countered.

"A man of merit treats all women, regardless of station, with honor," Berthe informed him. "Sir Rogue."

"I have been taught a lesson this day, Quinn," Bayard said and bowed to Berthe. "I thank you kindly for the instruction."

"How did you win your spurs, sir? In a game of draughts?" Berthe demanded and Bayard laughed.

"This is no jest!" Melissande snapped. "We are to be robbed, sir."

"We are not to be robbed," Quinn said with resolve and she had time to fear what he might do to defend them.

Then the other party urged their steeds to a gallop and charged closer. Quinn gave his destrier his spurs and the beast surged forward, leaving the women and Bayard behind. Melissande's heart skipped a beat that they were to be abandoned to Bayard's defense. Then Bayard gave a shout of delight and raced after Quinn. The squires hooted and galloped their palfreys toward the party as well, leaving Melissande and Berthe to stare at each other in astonishment.

"Faithless wretches," Melissande muttered and pulled her small eating knife.

"Of what merit are knights who leave us undefended?" Berthe demanded, her outrage equal to Melissande's own. "And this is the new Lord d'Annossy. Much changes, my lady, that much is certain, and the changes are not welcome..."

It was then that Melissande realized the men ahead were laughing.

All of them.

Quinn, Bayard, and each man in the approaching company laughed as if they celebrated a feast. Quinn leaped from his saddle, as did the man leading the approaching party. They embraced and patted each other on the back, shook hands and embraced again. There was no disguising the merriment of a company of friends well met: though Melissande could not have anticipated it, in hindsight, it made sense.

"Their companions aimed to meet them at Sayerne," she guessed and Berthe nodded. They had ridden to Sayerne, found it vacant, and retraced their course.

"More of them," the maid said wearily. She rolled her eyes and both women sighed.

The women walked their horses closer, in no rush to encounter the party of rough-looking men. Melissande assumed that the three most heavily armed men must be knights, despite their humble garb, which meant the other five riders were squires. She had no doubt her husband would invite them to Annossy, for truly, they could not be expected to take comfort at Sayerne.

She was reviewing inventories in Annossy's stores when she reached her husband's side. Quinn glanced up, his eyes alight with joy such as she had never seen before and she was struck anew by how very handsome he was.

"My lady wife," he said, gesturing to her as he claimed her palfrey's reins. "Melissande, I would have you meet three of our comrades. We battled together in the Holy Land and had been journeying home together."

"Until Amaury took ill in Venice," a fair-haired rogue said to her with a wicked smile. "He has a feeble constitution for a knight." He bowed low before her. "Niall MacGillivray, at your humble service, my lady." He had an accent that compelled Melissande to concentrate in order to understand his French, but his smile was ready.

And he knew well enough that he was handsome, to be sure.

"She is *my* lady, Niall, and you had best recall as much," Quinn said and that man grinned. Niall even had the audacity to wink at Melissande and she imagined that he found many a maid to appreciate his charms. Berthe already sat straighter in her saddle, though Bayard glowered at his companion when Niall took note of her.

The next man was dark of hair and blue of eye, a strikingly regal man with a steady gaze. "Amaury de Montvieux," he said, also bowing low before her. "Who might have imagined that our Quinn would make such a fortunate alliance?" His French was more readily understood.

"It is not the fortune of the alliance that makes it admirable," Quinn protested gruffly. "But the charm of my lady wife."

Melissande found herself blushing, but the men nudged each other companionably. Quinn gestured to the third knight in the party, a very tall and blond man with a quelling gaze. "Lothair is a talented healer," Quinn said. "He remained in Venice to ensure Amaury's complete recovery."

Lothair bowed but did not speak.

"As Niall certainly would not," Amaury said.

"Not if there was any company more interesting than yours," Niall agreed.

"And there were women aplenty in Venice," Bayard added. "However did you choose?"

Berthe inhaled sharply at this.

"Choose? Where is it writ that a man must choose only one?" Niall protested. They laughed easily together, obviously at ease with each other's natures.

Berthe glared at them all. "Sir Rogue, it seems your companions share your views," she said and the men laughed.

"Sir Rogue," Niall echoed and his brows rose. "This lady has taken your measure."

"I have taken no measure of him," Berthe snapped and Niall was quick to apologize.

Melissande felt the weight of Quinn's gaze upon her and knew what she had to do. "You must have invited your companions to visit you at Sayerne," she said quietly to him.

"Aye. We would have arrived together, had Amaury not fallen ill. I could not have known that Sayerne was a ruin, for Tulley did not tell me as such in his missive." His lips pursed. "It seems that his brevity meant that many details were omitted."

Melissande prayed silently that there would be enough food in Annossy's storerooms, but smiled as if unconcerned. Hospitality could not be compromised. Her father had been adamant about that. "Have you invited them to Annossy?"

"I await your blessing, my lady," he replied, a smile in his eyes.

"You do not need my blessing, sir," she reminded him gently.

Quinn frowned briefly, but did not avert his gaze. "Yet I still desire it," he confessed in an undertone. His hand fell to her knee and just the weight of it there made Melissande catch her breath. She stared into his eyes and realized that she would have to welcome him abed this very night, lest his friends suspect the truth, even as she knew in her heart that she did not entirely dread it.

"My home is now yours and you know it well, sir," she replied. Quinn studied her for a moment, then cleared his throat when she looked away.

"Friends and comrades!" he cried, interrupting their conversation. "I invite you all to Annossy."

"Annossy?" Niall echoed. "Where is that?"

"Just ahead of us, before Sayerne. It is the ancestral holding of my lady wife. You see the pennant flying from its tower."

"You are Lord d'Annossy as well?" Lothair demanded, his surprise more than clear. His French was spoken with a clipped accent and Melissande guessed that he hailed from the more eastern territories held by the Emperor.

"Aye, I am," Quinn admitted.

"That holding?" Amaury asked, pointing to Annossy's keep. Melissande nodded and he bowed again. "Quinn, you have made a wondrous alliance. We already admired the obvious prosperity and good administration of that holding."

"Amaury admired it, to be sure," Lothair said.

"Aye, Amaury was most fulsome in his praise of the management of the fields," Niall said. "While I would know naught of such matters."

"To be sure, it was impossible to see the charms of Annossy's women from such a distance, which would be your sole concern," Amaury said and Niall grinned.

"Though the lady herself is most beautiful." Lothair bowed and Melissande flushed.

"Who has governed Annossy before this happy day for Quinn, my lady?" Amaury asked.

"Since my father's death five years ago, I have administered the holding."

Amaury nodded, his gaze flicking to Quinn in some silent communication. His admiration of her skills was clear, and Melissande wondered at his origins. The knights mounted their destriers again so the party could proceed and she turned to Amaury, intent upon being a good hostess. "From whence do you come, sir? You seem to know much of managing a holding."

"Montvieux is my family holding and my legacy," he admitted. "It lies to the east and south of Paris, in a valley of land most fertile. I have the greatest admiration for it, and a full understanding of my responsibilities. My father taught me from the cradle to watch each detail, to keep the books, to manage the inventories and the seed…"

"Aye, as did mine!"

"It is not common to find a lady with such expertise."

"I have no brother. My father rode to war when I was a child, and my mother administered Annossy in his absence. She began to teach me, for I asked."

"Did she administer the courts, as well?"

"Aye, in his absence. Annossy prospered beneath her hand, and so my father saw fit to continue my instruction upon his return."

Amaury was clearly impressed. "Do you find your responsibilities a chore to be endured?"

Melissande laughed at the notion. "Because they keep me from my needlework? Nay, sir, I find administration a most intriguing challenge and one that gives great satisfaction." She realized then that Quinn was attending their conversation and did not look to be pleased. She dropped her gaze. "Of course, it is all my husband's duty now and I shall hone my skills with embroidery."

Again, Amaury looked between Melissande and Quinn, but he said no more.

"Let us make haste to Annossy, then," Quinn said. "Where doubtless we shall find warmth and a hot meal." He gave a nod and all touched their heels to their horses' flanks. The entire party galloped toward Annossy, the horses' manes streaming, the sky vivid blue overhead and the wind as cold as ice.

A hot meal. Quinn might be overly confident in that expectation. Melissande counted as she rode. Eight newly arrived men—for the boys were tall enough to have the appetites of grown men—plus the four youths and one knight who journeyed with Quinn meant there would be fourteen more men at the board this night and for the foreseeable future.

In the dead of winter, when stores were at their lowest.

Melissande merely hoped there was yet a cask of wine in the cellar for that might distract them from the lack of meat. There would be no time to hunt by the time they arrived, so whatever was in the pantries on this day would have to suffice for the evening meal.

What would Quinn do if he believed his friends to be insulted or given less than their due? Melissande did not wish to know, although she was plagued by memories of each and every tale of Jerome's displeasure as they rode for Annossy.

Aye, his wife was stung by Tulley's decision and Quinn could not mistake that truth. He was not truly surprised when the lady of ice had descended to Tulley's hall to break her fast before their departure.

This was his reward for carrying Annossy's seal.

Quinn would have spoken to her and tried to reconcile her to their liege lord's choice, but she ignored him at the board as surely as if he had vanished from sight. And truly, it would have been a poor choice to discuss the matter frankly when Tulley might hear or be told of their words. Quinn knew that Tulley could not be defied, yet wished he and Melissande might yet form a good match.

It seemed a distant prospect.

They rode out that chilly morn, together but separate. His hope for a private moment upon reaching Annossy had been complicated by the discovery of his comrades on the road. His own confidence in the future had been shaken by Amaury's apparent understanding and appreciation of all Melissande had done. Quinn already had doubts about his abilities to administer a prosperous holding, for that was beyond his experience. The words of Amaury, who came from far greater wealth than Quinn, only added to that concern.

And then there was Annossy itself.

The richness of the holding became more clear with every step toward it. The keep was large, though not so large as Tulley. A formidable stone wall encircled the village and the keep itself, which he much admired for defense. As Amaury had noted, the fields were tilled in orderly terraces that were still visible beneath the snow. Amaury and Melissande talked about the growing of vines for the making of wine, and their lively discussion made Quinn feel at a disadvantage.

He had so much to learn.

The keep perched on a slight rise and as they approached, it was bathed in sunlight. There was a square tower in the middle of the enclosure, with a pennant snapping in the wind at its summit. Quinn counted four floors in the tower, which was of considerable breadth. The gates were armed but opened to the lady with a cheer of welcome from the sentries. The men in the employ of the holding were garbed in the blue and silver of Annossy and bowed low as the lady rode through the gates.

One whose armor was more lavish bowed low before the lady and kissed her hand. He was handsome and his gaze assessing, his age slightly less than Quinn's.

"Gaultier, the Captain of the Guard," Melissande said to Quinn. "You will need to swear fealty to my husband, the Lord d'Annossy," she said to Gaultier, whose surprise at this was evident. Before he could ask any questions, she urged her horse onward and Quinn wondered when they two would speak in private.

And what they would say.

Bayard exchanged a glance with Quinn and he knew his old comrade shared his concern.

The villagers came forward to cheer Melissande's return and eye the new arrivals. They were garbed in clean but simple clothing, like that of Berthe, and appeared to be healthy. Quinn could smell fresh bread and the fire at the smithy. He turned back to consider the walls and their defense, and thought it good. Annossy was in good repair, to be sure, and strongly built. There were sufficient sentries and he saw more than a few men-at-arms within the walls. He was aware that Gaultier watched him. The villagers surrounded Melissande and their affection for her was obvious. She gave pennies from her purse and accepted small gifts. She might have been absent for a month. He would win their support by courting her favor, and in no other way. Amaury surveyed the tower and the walls when they dismounted, his approval clear. Bayard and Niall surveyed the women and Lothair gazed about himself in wonder.

The ostler bowed low, calling for boys to take the horses. Quinn's companions followed, for they were particular about the care of their steeds, and called for their own squires to be of aid.

Quinn saw with a glance that the stable was clean and well-tended, but he had greater concerns.

He knew Melissande feared him to be like his father, and Quinn could readily imagine what his father would have done in similar circumstance. Melissande might have found herself outside Annossy's walls with unwelcome speed, particularly if she did not conceive a child.

Even the pledge she had demanded of him might have seen her banished.

Quinn had to speak to his wife and calm her fears. Somehow, he had to convince her that he was different from Jerome in every way.

But the lady was out of her saddle and striding for the door to the keep with remarkable purpose. Quinn abandoned his comrades and hastened after her, ignoring the teasing of his friends and their comments about the desires of those newly wed.

He caught up to Melissande in the kitchens, still in her cloak and boots, conferring urgently with a short bald man. What was this? Quinn hung back, curious as to what his lady schemed. Did she intend to see to his demise with all haste? He could not believe it, but he wondered.

The little man laid books before her in rapid succession. "There is a keg of very new wine, my lady, and a small keg of older wine yet remaining from the Yule. Sadly, we sold a great deal of it this year and our stores are low."

"Aye, I recall as much." Melissande surveyed the accounts, as yet unaware of Quinn, and began to tug off her gloves. "What of ale?"

"We have little here, but I will send a boy to the village to buy whatever he can find. It is almost Lent so there will be little brewing, although that can be remedied in a few days."

"Aye, see that it is so, please, Louis."

"How long do they intend to linger?"

"I cannot say. It is possible their plans are not yet made. What of the meat?"

"There is a hind of venison in the larder and yet some salted pork..."

"The eels?"

"Gone, my lady. We finished them last eve."

Melissande winced. "Are there yet three roosters?"

"Aye, my lady."

"Kill two of them, please, Louis. We have need of more meat this night and George's chicken stew is fit for a king. Instruct him to make it with an abundance of dumplings, please."

"Aye, my lady." The little man snapped his fingers and whispered to a portly man who might have been the cook.

"And bread?" Melissande asked. She was as vigilant as the keeper of provisions for an army and Quinn had the sense she carried much of the inventory in her thoughts. She seemed to be verifying what she already knew to be true.

"I have already sent to the village for the baker's stores," the cook said. "I heard the party arriving, my lady, and knew we would need more bread."

"You are a marvel as ever, George," she said, sparing that man a smile. She blinked when she noticed Quinn in the doorway and her face paled. "My lord," she said and dropped to a curtsey. The two men—Quinn guessed châtelain and cook—glanced at him and bowed deeply. "Louis and George, this is my husband, your lord Quinn, a bold knight and crusader who is now Lord d'Annossy."

Quinn noted that she omitted to mention his home estate.

That might have been a prudent choice, for all would know of his father here.

"Sir!" the two men exclaimed in unison and others in the kitchen turned to look at him.

Melissande nodded. "Aye, we will need to ensure that the entire household and the guard pledge fealty to my lord husband before the evening meal, Louis, so we can eat as allies and comrades. It is not long past noon, so we should be able to manage as much."

"Of course, my lady. I shall see to it," Louis said. "The hall will be arranged and all the household summoned..." His gaze flicked to Quinn and his words faltered as he bowed again. "If my lord desires it to be thus, of course," he added with haste.

Quinn nodded approval and smiled. "My lady wife, as ever, shows wondrous good sense." He offered his hand to Melissande.

"She is a rare treasure. I shall rely heavily upon her expertise with regards to Annossy. If fact, you may assume that her every command is as mine own."

Melissande's eyes widened at that even as she put her hand in his, but the two men smiled as they bowed again. They turned to hasten about their duties but Melissande lingered on the threshold of the kitchens. "Eggs, George," she said. "We shall start the meal with eggs, and a broth soup if you can manage as much."

"With ease, my lady."

"Have you some fruit that can be stewed? Louis, you may open the spice box to ensure that all is at its best for our guests."

"Aye, my lady."

Melissande looked as if she would like to flee his side, but Quinn caught her shoulders in his hands, compelling her to look at him. She regarded him warily. "I fear it will be a meager meal," she said quickly. "We do not customarily have guests in winter at Annossy and the stores are low..."

"Melissande, it is not the king himself come calling."

"But we have guests," she said. "And hospitality must always be upheld..."

"These are my comrades from war."

"It matters little how you know them or even if you know them at all. They are guests in the hall, and must be granted every consideration for the honor of Annossy..."

"Consider, Melissande, that we rode to war together," Quinn said, giving her a little shake. "There were days aplenty that we had no bread, and more on which we had no meat. We seldom had wine, and oft made do with water from a well."

She eyed him, still not understanding.

And truly, he was glad that she did not know what it was to be famished.

He smiled. "If you took that one loaf of bread there to the hall and told them it would be the sum of our meal, they would divide it and thank you for it and savor every morsel." He shook his head. "They would not complain. They would be glad of your generosity."

The lady frowned. "But they are your guests."

"They are my friends," Quinn corrected. "They will have shelter and they will have good company. Their horses will have fodder and they will be able to sleep, knowing the walls are defended around them. It is remarkable how much a man can endure with those gifts. Indeed, they will be grateful for it." She still looked to be unconvinced. "Fear not. They will be awed by the hospitality of Annossy, however meager you might think it to be." He bent then and touched his lips to her brow.

She closed her eyes and caught her breath and he dared to hold her for a moment. "I would ensure that there are provisions made for your guests' comfort this night," she said and he knew that she wanted to flee.

"They will be glad to sleep in hall or stables," Quinn said but he lifted his hands away and Melissande strode from the kitchens. He watched her go, then looked up to find the châtelain, Louis, watching him. Affection was clear in the older man's expression and Quinn recognized that it was for the lady. Quinn smiled and nodded, and was glad when Louis smiled back.

"Welcome, sir," he said then bowed again. Quinn was encouraged to know that there were other souls who worried about the lady left to defend Annossy alone.

"I thank you, Louis, and would entreat your patience in my early days here. I have much to learn of Annossy."

"Aye, sir. I am certain that the Lord de Tulley chose well."

Quinn cleared his throat, recalling why Tulley had chosen him. "Louis, I wonder if you might arrange for any who know about the raids on Annossy's borders to come and speak with me? I am charged by the Lord de Tulley to see these attacks ended, and I see no cause for delay."

The little man bowed crisply, a light of approval bright in his eyes. "I shall see to it, my lord. Perhaps in the morning, after you break your fast?"

"That, Louis, is an excellent suggestion. I can see why my lady wife so relies upon you."

CHAPTER SEVEN

Quinn won over the entire household within moments.

Melissande had never seen the like. He might have known everyone at Annossy all of his life and simply been encountering old friends. By the time the evening meal was served, every soul at Annossy seemed to be enraptured with its new lord—save Gaultier. That knight watched Quinn steadily, as if he suspected him of being less than he appeared to be.

Melissande wondered whether her Captain of the Guard knew some detail about her new husband, and resolved to find out.

She was keenly aware that her hired warriors were nigh matched in number by Quinn's party, and certainly so if the boys who rode as squires with Quinn and his comrades were counted as warriors themselves. She did not doubt that they were each and every one adept with a blade.

She could not help her sense that Annossy had been besieged and over-run by her new husband and his fellows.

But the villeins seemed to welcome the arrival of a lord to administer the holding, even without knowing much of Quinn. Once again, Melissande regretted her gender. He was a stranger, a man whose history and skills were unknown to them, but because he was a man, they greeted him with enthusiasm. The truth of it was sufficient to make her seethe, but she smiled, not wanting to hint that she was not the ally of Annossy's new lord.

They came and knelt before Quinn, kissed his hand and pledged their fealty. The women smiled at him. The men watched him with admiration. The village boys followed him. The sentries and men-at-arms expressed pleasure to have a knight and crusader of his experience leading them and Melissande heard their relief at his arrival. She wondered at that, as well. He reviewed the guard on the walls and jested with the men and she saw how they stood taller after his words. At the evening meal, the servants in the hall saw that every course was served to him first. That was how it should be, but still Melissande found it irksome. She felt as if she had ceased to exist. All the labor she had done in this hall was as naught. All the sacrifices she had made for Annossy were forgotten, as was her lineage.

She had not done that badly, had she?

Their ready loyalty to a knight and stranger along with her uncertainty of how Quinn would use his advantage combined to leave Melissande concerned. She had not shared the detail of his paternity because she wanted Louis and George to accept him. In hindsight, she wondered if her whim had been foolish. It had seemed churlish to taint his arrival at Annossy with that truth, since he seemed to be different from his father, but now it would be more churlish to blurt out the truth.

Indeed, Quinn was polite beyond every expectation. He was the one who brought her into every conversation. He was the one who consulted with her about Annossy's traditions. He was the one who ensured she was not forgotten, which left her feeling both grateful and unsettled. She did not wish to owe him more than marriage dictated she did. Each time she glanced his way, he granted her the engaging, crooked smile that made her heart lurch.

She feared that this was but a game to him and she was naught but a pawn.

A pawn who had to conceive his son with all haste.

Perhaps that explained Quinn's charm. He knew what had to be done, and he but waited for her to make the invitation. Perhaps he meant to soften the blow to her pride. Melissande no longer knew what to think.

It was after the evening meal that Gaultier came to her. He bowed low and Quinn watched him, his eyes narrowed slightly. Indeed, there was a crackle of animosity between the pair. It was only in noting Gaultier's obvious displeasure that Melissande wondered at his own objectives at Annossy. It was true that Gaultier was tall and straight, a fine figure of a man and a knight often watched by the maidens of Annossy. His hair was so dark as to be almost black and his eyes were a striking hue of green. She knew he was a younger son with no hope of inheritance himself and she had been glad when Tulley had sent a man of such abilities to her gates the year before. Gaultier flicked a glance at Quinn that was markedly hostile and Melissande wondered again if there was a root to their seemingly immediate dislike.

"My lady, I would confer with you," Gaultier said.

"Surely whatever you would confide in my wife can be told before me, as well," Quinn said, a thread of steel in his voice. He reached out and took Melissande's hand, and Gaultier watched the gesture, his expression impassive. His eyes darkened, though.

"Before her departure, my lady granted me an assignment," Gaultier said, keeping his tone formal. "Since it was the lady's task, I would tell her of the result."

"And what task was that?" Quinn asked Melissande. Truly, the Captain of the Guard had an insulting manner, and she believed that Quinn was striving to be fair. Gaultier should not have tried to urge her away from Quinn's side to confer, after Quinn had bidden him to speak.

She was wed. She was chattel.

"There was a raid at the mill," Melissande told Quinn. "We heard of it in the morning and I intended to ride there to confer with the miller as to the damage, but Tulley's messenger arrived before I could do so. He insisted that I must ride with haste to Tulley, so Gaultier went to the mill, at my dictate."

"A raid?" Quinn asked and she saw Bayard glance over. The other knight's attention was avid and his charm dismissed. "By these same villains who harry Annossy's borders?"

"I believe so," Melissande said.

"And what did you discover?" Quinn asked Gaultier.

"I would speak with the lady," Gaultier said, his tone stubborn. "She granted me the task and the tidings are due to her."

The two men glared at each other, but Melissande spoke with quiet resolve. She knew her duty, even if she disliked the truth of it. "Gaultier, you have pledged your fealty to Quinn de Sayerne, Lord d'Annossy, and this report is thus owed to him." It was her responsibility to ensure that her lord husband was not insulted and she hoped she managed the feat well. She had never been much of a diplomat.

Quinn's features might have been set to stone, and she feared she had not been sufficiently fulsome.

"Sayerne?" Gaultier echoed and Melissande realized what she had said. "You hail from Sayerne?" he asked Quinn, his opinion of that more than clear. His voice rose slightly and the name of Quinn's home estate began to be repeated in the hall. The villeins and servants stared at their new lord in surprise.

"My father was Jerome de Sayerne, it is true," Quinn said, not flinching from the truth. He stood to address them all, his voice ringing over the company. "He and I parted ways twenty years ago, for we argued, and Lord de Tulley took me under his protection. I was only a boy, but Tulley sponsored me that I might train for my spurs. He found me employ to ensure that I gained experience at war, then suggested I take the cross when the pope called for the crusade. He sent word to me a year ago in Palestine, summoning me home, for my father had died. I had thought to rebuild Sayerne, but Lord de Tulley, in his generosity, granted me a bride instead." Quinn took Melissande's hand and lifted it to his lips, kissing the back of it as he smiled down at her. His smile was tight and she knew he was not pleased by the timing of her revelation, though she had not intended either to hide his lineage or suddenly reveal it.

"And Annossy," Gaultier said, his tone silky.

"And Annossy," Quinn agreed, their gazes locking again.

"What splendid good fortune for you," Gaultier continued, and it was clear he thought otherwise.

Quinn took his seat beside Melissande again, her hand securely captive in the breadth of his own. "And what did you discover while the lady was at Tulley?"

Gaultier's gaze flicked to Melissande, his dissatisfaction clear, then to her hand within Quinn's. She smiled with a serenity she did not feel, for she could not fathom Quinn's thoughts. He seemed harder and more resolute in this discussion, more a man of war, and her fears of his intentions were renewed.

She would be alone with him again this night, and his comrades filled the hall. How curious and troubling it was to consider that she would be outnumbered in her own abode.

"I have asked you a question, sir," Quinn said softly and color rose on Gaultier's neck.

The Captain of the Guard faced Melissande, making his true loyalty clear. "There was a theft, my lady. The miller and his wife were unharmed but frightened, and their coin was taken. The villains crossed the river at the ford, just below the mill, for I found the tracks from their horses there."

"They ride horses?" Quinn asked. "Where would they stable their steeds?"

"If I knew that, sir, I should know where to apprehend them," Gaultier snapped.

"You might be able to see their haven from the mill," Quinn replied.

Gaultier straightened and Melissande raised a hand to silence him. She turned to Quinn. "The mill, sir, is not on the river Helva, but on a mountain stream that flows into it. We did not pass close to the mill on this day, but on the other side of that stream, the forest is dense. I would wager that in twenty paces, the sight of a horse would be lost in the undergrowth."

"Thank you, my lady," Quinn said, his voice a low rumble of approval. His eyes glowed as he smiled at her. "I appreciate your summary of the site and its traits, and will ride there on the morrow to see it myself."

"But Gaultier has done as much already..."

"I would meet the miller myself, as well as hear his testimony," Quinn said, interrupting her smoothly. He granted Gaultier a look. "Do you have more detail to share?"

"No, my lord." Gaultier bowed again.

"You did not determine where the tracks led from the river?"

"They led toward the forest, but could be followed no further."

Quinn sat back, his dissatisfaction clear. "I look forward to seeing it on the morrow."

"I shall accompany you, sir."

"Nay," Quinn said firmly. "You will remain here at Annossy and ensure that the keep is secured."

Gaultier opened his mouth and closed it again.

"Aye," Quinn said, his voice silky yet stern. "We shall see if I learn more than you did on your quest. Upon my return from the mill, do not let me hear that you or any other men in the employ of Annossy have ridden through its gates since my arrival on this day with my lady wife. The tidings of my assumption of Annossy's seal shall remain here for the moment."

"If it was your desire to close the gates, sir, you should have told me as much."

"I summoned all of you to the hall to pledge fealty, which should have been sufficient to ensure that none departed."

Gaultier looked disgruntled and there was a gleam in his eyes that Melissande had never noticed before. "Of course, my lord," he said, his tone cold, and bowed once more. Then he took his leave, striding across the hall and calling to some of the other sentries.

"Was it wise to provoke him so?" Melissande asked, unable to remain silent any longer.

Quinn arched a brow. "I cannot say as yet. I am intrigued that he could be provoked, in truth."

"Why?"

"How long has he been here?" he asked instead of replying.

"A little over a year. Tulley sent him after the death of the Captain of the Guard who had served my father."

Quinn nodded and lifted his cup to her. "This is the wine of Annossy?"

"The last of it, I fear, sir."

"It is most fine."

"And this is the worst of it."

His brows rose as he sipped.

Melissande shrugged. "We sold far more than usual in the fall, so have little for ourselves now."

Quinn watched her. "You had need of the coin?"

Melissande nodded. "I had Gaultier hire four more men-at-arms, because of the attacks. The treasury was low as a result."

Quinn sipped, his expression thoughtful and his hand still locked over her own.

"You evade my questions, sir."

"I but think upon them, my lady, the better to give you a full response."

Melissande sipped her ale and waited, suspecting that her impatience showed.

"He does not like me," Quinn said finally.

"You do not like him," she felt obliged to note and he smiled, though there was no humor in his gaze.

"I invite you, my lady, to give me a plausible reason for his dislike."

Melissande was surprised to be asked her view, but then she knew more of Gaultier than Quinn. "He distrusts change, perhaps."

Quinn nodded. "And perhaps he, like you, disliked my father."

Melissande frowned. "I cannot think how he would have known Jerome."

"Perhaps I shall ask him," Quinn mused. "Still, his reaction is vehement. I am intrigued by that."

Melissande eyed her husband. "Why do you think he dislikes you?"

"I think he cannot dislike me so quickly as that. He knows naught of me. I suspect he dislikes what I represent."

"I do not understand."

Quinn's gaze met her own steadily. "He might not wish to have someone look closely upon his choices and actions."

"Gaultier has served me well..."

"Has he? I hope as much, my lady, but you have admitted yourself that you know little of warfare."

Melissande nodded in concession. "But surely, he would not

deceive me."

"I hope not," Quinn said mildly, then sipped again of the wine. "There are other possibilities, of course. He might think I have claimed a prize he desired for himself." He was watching her closely so he must have seen her surprise at his implication.

"I would not give myself to the Captain of the Guard!"

"That does not mean he had no such aspirations."

Melissande was outraged. "What advantage would there be to me in such a liaison? There could be no match. He has naught to call his own..."

"I have little to call my own," Quinn whispered, his eyes gleaming.

"You have Tulley's favor and that is more than sufficient."

"You told me he had Tulley's favor." His tone was not adversarial and Melissande had the sense that they strove to solve a riddle together, each contributing what they knew. It reminded her of how her parents used to confer and she found the discussion most seductive for all of that.

Melissande's gaze flicked across the hall but Gaultier was gone. Had he aspired to claim her hand himself? She had certainly given him no encouragement in that pursuit.

To her surprise, she felt Quinn brush his lips across her knuckles. "I like that you are startled by the notion, my lady," he murmured. "It reassures me about our shared future."

"How so, sir?" Although Melissande might have agreed with his conclusion, she had not expected him to utter such words aloud. Truly, this man defied her every expectation. She simply wished she could know that his words were honest.

Jerome had been a polished liar, to be sure.

"You have but one betrothed, not a line of suitors."

"Surely one betrothed is sufficient."

"Surely, it is, but you cannot blame me for failing to know what neither you nor Tulley confided in me."

Melissande could not. She smiled at Quinn and he blinked as if astonished. "You are right, of course." She bowed her head then, wondering if he wished for her to simply agree with him every time. How dull her life would become! But there were men who believed women had no place beyond the bed chamber.

Quinn leaned closer and dropped his voice to a whisper. "If you do not wish to invite me on this night, I will stay away."

Melissande met his gaze with surprise. "Your friends will notice."

"I can concoct a tale."

The very fact that he offered to do as much gave Melissande the confidence to make the offer she knew she should. "But I would not have you deceive your comrades on my account." She took a deep breath to bolster her confidence, then leaned close, touching her lips to his ear. "You are invited to my bed this night, my lord husband. We have but three months to see Tulley's objective achieved and I would not sacrifice an opportunity."

Quinn's pleasure was more than clear. Indeed, his eyes flashed so brightly that Melissande thought he might kiss her senseless before the entire company. "I am at your command, my lady," he vowed in a heated whisper and kissed her palm, his gaze locked with hers as he folded her hand over the burning imprint of his kiss.

Melissande shivered, right to her marrow, her gaze snared by his own.

Then that treacherous heat unfurled in her belly, filling her thoughts with memories of all they had done the night before.

That was even before the slow smile began to claim Quinn's lips. She watched, spellbound, and could not even take a breath.

Oh, she was lost for certain.

And already, she cared less than she should.

"And what of your fair sister?" Niall asked when the wine was gone and they were at ease in the hall. The villagers had returned to their homes and many of the torches had been extinguished. The hall was warm and Quinn's comrades were not only present, but hale and hearty. It was good to be amongst friends again and in such comfort. Melissande remained by his side, and he knew that she was listening to the conversation.

He held the seal of Annossy, a rich prize by any accounting, and had a beautiful clever wife by his side. Annossy's hall was gracious and the furnishings were fine. The meal had been delicious and the meat plentiful. The ale was good and the wine better, the bread fresh and the villeins of Annossy robust in their welcome.

Even more, his lady had invited him to her bed this night. Quinn's characteristic optimism was reviving.

Truly, he might make a home here.

"What of her?" Quinn asked. "I have had no chance to learn of her situation." Indeed, he had been surprised by Tulley's confession in one missive that he even had a sister. When Quinn had left Sayerne, he had been his father's only child. He refused to recall his last discussion with his mother, for her refusal to accompany him was still troubling. He could not bear to imagine what had happened to her in his absence. Tulley had only written to tell him of her demise, but had offered no details.

Did Melissande know?

Was that tale at the root of her dislike for Jerome? Quinn could believe as much. He doubted that his mother's life had ended well.

He turned to Melissande and asked only one of his many questions. "Do you know of my sister Annelise?"

She shook her head. "I heard of her but have never met her."

"Despite the proximity to Sayerne?" Amaury asked, his surprise clear.

"She did not live there so long as I recall. She was at the convent of Ste. Radegunde from a young age, from the time of the death of Jerome's lady wife."

Quinn did not ask how his mother had died. He dared not do so before the company, though he saw that Melissande's expression was bland.

Perhaps she did not know the full extent of his father's villainy.

That would be a blessing.

"I see the hand of Lord de Tulley," Quinn said lightly and Melissande spared him a quick smile.

"No doubt he had a part in that choice."

"He is a most vigilant liege lord," Amaury said and Melissande only nodded. Her tact was admirable.

"And after the lord of Sayerne died?" Niall asked. "What happened to his daughter?"

"Yves took her to Tulley, of course," Melissande said. "It was in December a year ago. She must have been sent elsewhere for she is not there now. Perhaps back to the convent. Heloise would have had a companion, if not."

"Yves?" Quinn asked.

She gave him a considering glance. "You must have known of Yves."

"I know of no one named Yves."

Melissande licked her lips, as if she feared he would not like what she had to say. "Yves is Jerome's younger son, his bastard."

Quinn blinked.

Bayard chuckled.

Melissande took a breath. "Yves earned his spurs with Tulley's sponsorship and returned to serve his father at Sayerne. Matters improved somewhat: Yves could be relied upon to keep his word, although his father oft broke the pledges made in his name." She straightened primly. "I was sorry to hear that he had left, but then, Jerome did not acknowledge him and Tulley must have made it clear that there would be naught for him at Sayerne or Tulley."

"But where did he go?" Quinn asked. He still could not make sense of the news that he had a brother.

"He escorted Annelise away from Sayerne and that was the last I heard of either of them. Neither are at Tulley and no one spoke of them there. I assume they were dispatched together but know not where."

He had a brother.

And his sister was gone, although Tulley had not seen fit to confide the truth of her situation to Quinn.

Although, to be sure, he had sufficient to keep him occupied.

Perhaps he should be glad that his siblings were absent.

A brother. Quinn could not help but think that another knight's strength would have been welcome in the task of rebuilding Sayerne.

"But why did Annelise leave the convent at all?" he asked, fearing that his sister had experienced abuse similar to what Jerome showered upon his mother.

Melissande shrugged. "Perhaps she was summoned. Perhaps

there was to be a match made for her. I was not privy to the dealings of Sayerne."

"And clearly you do not know all that the Lord de Tulley considers beneath his influence," Amaury noted quietly, then changed the subject. "I must say that your concern about the Beauvoir Pass in winter was well deserved, Quinn."

Quinn smiled. He was aware of Melissande's curiosity and explained to her. "When I rode to crusade, I went through the Beauvoir Pass in the winter. The snow was so deep that I feared we should never see the other side. The wind was fiercely cold and I was determined never to repeat that journey again."

"But you did?"

"Aye. On our return, we rode from Jerusalem to Constantinople, intending to travel by land into the Holy Roman Empire. Our scheme was to approach Tulley from the north, following the path of Godfroi de Bouillon, but we did not manage to make Constantinople."

"It was besieged," Amaury informed Melissande, clearly noting her confusion.

"And we chose not to join another battle," Bayard said. "I had no desire to see a Saracen prison again, though Quinn might have risked it."

Quinn could feel his lady's surprise.

"And I had no desire to tend another injury," Lothair noted to Quinn's dismay.

Melissande looked between them and Lothair indicated Quinn. "He healed well enough, for he is large and stubborn, but still, it was not easily done. An injury so fierce and untended so long required all my skill. Perhaps even an increment more."

"You were injured?" she asked Quinn and he dared to hope she felt some concern.

"And imprisoned at Acre," he confessed, noting the flicker in her gaze. "Bayard fought at my back, and chose not to abandon me when I fell, for which I am eternally grateful."

"And I shall haunt him for all his days and nights in return," Bayard said, prompting the other knights to laugh.

"We were imprisoned together," Quinn admitted. "Another

feat that saved my sorry hide, and all thanks to Bayard's quick thinking. He convinced the enemy that we could be ransomed, and otherwise, we would never have left that battlefield alive."

The lady had paled and Quinn folded his hand around hers once more. Did she tremble?

"Clearly, the rumor of Quinn's manners had preceded us, though," Bayard jested. "For there were no offers of ransom for these two sorry knights."

"You were a sorry sight when you were freed," Lothair agreed. "Sores and pustules."

"Lice and fleas," Amaury said with a shudder.

"And filth beyond measure," Niall said.

"But all is well that ends well," Quinn concluded, not seeing the merit of sharing more of this truth with his lady, and drank a tribute to that with his comrades.

"You were right about that pass, though," Amaury said again. "I was certain the guides led us astray and that the road could have no summit. The snow!"

"The cold!" Lothair agreed.

"The supposed hospitality of Beauvoir keep," Niall said and rolled his eyes. "Has ever there been a more forbidding and cold tower as that one? And the welcome was scarce warmer."

"Never mind the price of a simple repast and a night's lodging," Lothair noted. "I thought the horses were to be bedded down in gold!" The knights laughed together.

"Praise be we had only to stay the one night," Niall said.

"Lord de Tulley knows his advantage, to be sure," Amaury said. "I would wager his treasury overflows, simply from the tolls at Beauvoir."

Niall shook a finger at Quinn and Bayard. "But it was worth every penny when he confessed that, in the past fortnight, only two other knights had dared to climb the pass."

Amaury laughed. "And that they had four squires, one of whom had never seen snow before."

"Michel!" the knights crowed in unison and the boy bowed before them, his ears glowing red. He carried a pitcher of ale and brought it to the high table, pouring into the proffered cups.

"Michel was born in the Holy Land," Quinn told Melissande.

"And yet he is in your service." She smiled at the boy. "How is this so, Michel?"

"I am an orphan, my lady," the boy confessed, bowing deeply to her. "When my parents were killed, the bishop meant to surrender me to a monastery as an oblate, but I ran away. I wanted to go to Jerusalem to serve the knights and become one myself."

"You did not wish to become a priest or a monk?" she asked.

He shook his head. "I would wield a sword, my lady, for God is better served by deeds than prayers."

"I am not certain of that. We each have our roles to play in His scheme."

"My parents farmed in the Latin Kingdoms, my lady. My father had no sword and when the war came, he died." The boy's eyes shone with a conviction that Quinn had noted before. "I will not die so easily, my lady."

"I see," she said softly and Quinn watched her smile at Michel. The boy bowed again and continued to serve the ale, though Quinn indicated that he would have none.

"The hour draws late, my lady," he murmured and her gaze flicked to him with some wariness.

She nodded and stood, her agitation clear to him and more than a little disappointing. He must convince her that he would not be a husband like his father.

"Louis has prepared the chamber above this one for you all," she informed the knights and Quinn saw the châtelain in the portal, listening. "And you are welcome to retire there at your leisure. There is yet ale and I would not curtail your enjoyment of it. If you have any need, please ask it of Louis, as you are the guests of Annossy."

There were fulsome thanks all around then both Lothair and Amaury went to the stables to check upon their steeds. Quinn stood and offered Melissande his hand, bending to murmur to her. "I will see that the gates are secured and the sentries at their labor," he said to her. "And will come to you shortly, my lady."

She nodded, pale again, but did not flinch from his touch.

Perhaps he could make progress in this campaign on this night.

Perhaps ensuring the safety of Annossy, which she clearly held dear, would gain him some credibility. Tulley had commanded him to end the raids, and truly, warfare and defense were details he understood well. This would be the advantage he brought to Annossy, and Quinn knew already that his lady was sufficiently keen of wit that she would see his merit when it was done.

Berthe was gone and Melissande was alone in her chemise, her hair brushed, when she heard Quinn's voice in the hall. The low rumble both reassured her and troubled her. She turned to watch the door, her hands knotted together.

Would she always dread his appearance at night? She had claimed the solar of Annossy after her father's death and it was a fine chamber. It was at the summit of the tower with views in all directions. There was a great pillared bed in the middle of the room, with heavy drapes in silken velvet, woven in the blue of Annossy with silver embroidery along the hems. The wooden pillars rose to join the beams that held up the roof of the lofty chamber, and Melissande had always thought it looked like a crown in the midst of a treasury. Now that Tulley had commanded an heir, the import of the bed was unmistakable.

She had been born in this bed, and her parents had consummated their own marriage within it. In a way, her marriage would seem more real when she and Quinn had coupled in this bed, and more unassailable when she delivered a child here.

She heard him speak to his fellows, then the sound of his boots on the stairs. He dismissed a squire by the sound of it, tapped on the wooden door, then entered the chamber alone. He nodded to her, his eyes gleaming, then closed the portal to survey the chamber. "Now this is a fine refuge," he said, his admiration clear. He considered the iron latch, which was formidable, and secured the door, then went to the window that looked toward Tulley. He leaned out of it, confirming how much he could see from its vantage point, then closed the shutters over the opening. He went to each window in turn, repeating his movement, and she thought he lingered at the one that faced Sayerne. He completed his survey with the window that faced the gates. When it was shuttered, he turned to nod at Melissande. "Most clever. I assume one of your forebears built the keep?"

"My grandfather, although my family was in possession of Annossy before that. He was the one who built the tower."

"With considerable thought toward its defense."

"The tale was that he had fought to protect Annossy from others who wished to seize it. Tulley's line was not yet ascendant, so the valley was filled with warring factions."

Quinn nodded and set his sword aside. He removed his belt. "And the mill that was attacked two nights past? Where is it?"

Melissande went to the window that faced the northern slope and opened it again. Quinn came to stand beside her, and she jumped when his hand landed on the back of her waist. "There," she said, pointing to a faint light.

"It is solitary."

"But not previously believed to be vulnerable. It is a hard path up from the main road."

"And escape would be hampered by both snow and forest," he mused. "And there is no abode in the forest beyond?"

She shook her head. "I do not know of one."

"Is there a pass through the mountains where they rise above it?"

Melissande shook her head again. "It is steep. I remember goatherds appearing once, but it was midsummer. They were pursuing the goats and had followed a narrow path as I recall."

Quinn nodded and latched the shutters again. "Raids and battles are matters I understand, Melissande. I will see this resolved and Annossy secure." His voice dropped low. "I accept the challenge of proving to you that both of Jerome's sons are as different from their father as might be."

He had been stung by her endorsement of Yves' character, she realized that, yet the words had also encouraged him to believe that he could undermine her expectations. When he spoke with such conviction, as if he swore an oath to her, Melissande found herself yearning to believe him. That frightened her, for she knew so little of him, but before she could dismiss her response, he leaned toward her.

"What is it that you fear, wife of mine?" His gaze was piercing, those golden eyes seeming to see her deepest secrets.

"Why would you ask as much?"

"Because I wish to know. I cannot dismiss your uncertainty without knowing its precise root."

Melissande could not think of a short reply, much less one that would not reveal her own vulnerability. He needed no ideas of how to compromise her in her own home. "I expect events of this night may dismiss it," she said, then felt her cheeks burn.

Quinn nodded once and did not seem to be in haste to retire to bed. Indeed, the man possessed patience in rare abundance. He crossed the chamber, removing the seal of Annossy from his purse, and set it upon the largest table. Melissande could not help but stare at it, and she guessed her desire showed, for he smiled at her. "Have you never touched it?"

"Not since my father died. Tulley claimed it then." She took a breath. "As was his right."

"You sound as if you remind yourself of that."

"Perhaps I do."

Quinn picked up the seal and offered it to her on the flat of his hand.

Melissande met his gaze in surprise, then went to his side. She took the familiar seal and turned it in her grasp, well aware that Quinn watched her closely. It seemed impossibly intimate to be standing beside him in this chamber, the great bed behind her, the lantern's light flickering over both of them. The fire crackled in the brazier and she shivered a little at the sound of the wind in the shutters.

"When was that?" he asked in that gentle tone.

"Five years ago. It will be six in the autumn." Melissande did not look up for she felt her tears rising. "He died at the board, in the middle of his meal. One moment, he was laughing at a jest, and the next, he was dead."

"It must have been a shock to you."

"In more ways than one." She handed him the seal again.

"And your mother?" he asked again.

"When I was nine summers of age. My father had ridden to war and she had administered Annossy in his stead. When he returned, she conceived again." Melissande shook her head. "They were overjoyed, for they had hoped for years to have a son." She took a deep breath and nodded toward the bed. "She died there, bringing that boy to light, my father at her side. The babe died two days later."

"No son."

"No son." She looked up at him, and knew the tumult of her emotions showed. "Only me."

Quinn shook his head. "Do not discount your measure, Melissande. The state of Annossy five years after your father's passing, after five years of your administration, must be the surest measure of your skills. I am easy to impress in such matters, for I do not share your expertise, but my comrade, Amaury, is awed by your administrative talents. You learned your lessons well."

Her mouth was dry, her heart full of his praise even as she feared its import. "Thank you, my lord."

"Will you not call me by my name?" he asked. He gestured. "Especially in this chamber?"

Melissande met his gaze again. She swallowed, then licked her lips. "Quinn," she whispered and he smiled with pleasure.

His fingertip landed on her lips and she froze, shaken by the tumult of her heart. "I like how you say it," he murmured, then bent to touch his lips to her cheek. "Will you say it again, my lady?" he whispered in her ear.

"Quinn," she said with greater confidence, her voice more sure.

"I thank you," Quinn murmured and touched his lips to her ear, sending shivers over her flesh.

She stepped back and might have turned away, but Quinn caught her hand in his and she froze again. "What do you fear, Melissande? Tell me."

She swallowed and confessed the truth. "Only one thing. That you truly are your father's son."

"Is that all?"

"Is it not sufficient?" she asked, a challenge in her tone and the flash of Quinn's eyes made her wonder if she knew all of the tale.

Or if the fullness of the truth was even worse than she feared.

"Why did you leave Sayerne?" she asked and he bowed his head. "What drove you away from your home? Why did Tulley see fit to take you beneath his care?"

CHAPTER EIGHT

uinn was snared. He wished to confess all to his new wife, but was not at all certain that the truth would gain her support. Filling any gaps in Melissande's knowledge might cast his own merit in doubt. "What did my father do to make you despise him so?"

"You must know."

"I have my suspicions. Let us tell each other the truth this night, my lady, and for each day and night after this."

Their gazes held for a moment and there was uncertainty in her fine eyes. How Quinn wished he could dispel it forever.

Then she took a breath, squaring her shoulders, her stance becoming regal. He already recognized that she stood thus when she felt obliged to do something she would rather not, and he admired her strength of will.

She was much stronger than his mother had been.

The realization was startling, but true.

"While my parents were alive, Jerome abused his vassals by taxing them too much, feeding them too little and working them too hard." Melissande spoke without inflection, as if reciting an inventory. "He bedded every woman he could catch and when those women conceived, he cast them out to starve."

"And you know this by experience or rumor?"

She flicked a glance at him but Quinn remained silent. He would wager upon experience, given that look. Melissande's lips tightened before the words spilled from her lips. "Jerome spotted a maid of mine on a visit to my father, a nobleman's daughter lent to our service, and seized her. We searched for her, but she was well-hidden, and he lied to my father's man when asked if she was at Sayerne. In truth, she had been abducted by your father, hidden at Sayerne, and cruelly used for his pleasure." She touched her fingers to her brow. "Perhaps your father would have said she was savored."

Quinn winced.

"She returned two months later in rags and tears, with bruises upon her body and a child in her belly. Indeed, my mother said she scarce recognized her. She would not name the abuser, for she was afraid, but my parents gave her shelter and care." Melissande swallowed. "She had been my nursemaid when I was a child and was much loved here at Annossy." She looked across the chamber. "She was never the same. I remember her being a merry soul and the sound of her laughter, but there was none after her return."

"What happened to her?" Quinn asked, thinking she might have been wed to a man in service to the estate.

Melissande caught her breath and shook her head as though she could not speak. Quinn did not know what to do to ease the hurt of her recollection, but wished that he did. He waited in silence, despising his father anew.

"She died in labor," she admitted finally, and Quinn's heart clenched. "Your father never acknowledged the child or provided for it. He sent no regrets for her loss, either. The child sickened and died the next winter, despite all efforts. And that was the end of her tale." She raised her gaze. "Because she had the misfortune to be pretty and merry of heart and to have caught Jerome's attention, she was injured and died too young."

"It was unjust."

"You are not surprised."

Quinn shook his head. "Tell me more," he invited, knowing there had to be.

Melissande cleared her throat and spoke with greater vigor.

"When my parents died, your father began his campaign to forcibly join our two estates. When Tulley protested, Jerome became more subtle. He moved border markers. He stole the harvest and seed for sowing from our barns. He stole livestock, though it could not be proven beyond doubt, and he hunted in Annossy's forests without my consent." She shook her head. "I thought my woes over at last when he died, but the attacks on Annossy still continue."

"Though on a different border."

She flicked a glance at him. "Aye, closer to the mountains. The ford near the mill seems to be where the brigands cross into Annossy." She eyed him. "But Jerome is dead. Annossy remains plagued. I know that if Yves has secretly returned, he would not do these deeds. He is honorable. If he was starving, he would come to Annossy's gates and offer his service in exchange for food and shelter. But now you have returned to claim your father's land and legacy." She took a breath. "And I do not know precisely when you returned to Tulley."

"My comrades told of our coming through the pass a fortnight before them."

"*Your* comrades."

Their gazes locked for a long moment. There was accusation in her eyes that Quinn longed to erase. It burned within him that she thought he was like his father.

It was irksome that she accepted that his brother Yves was not.

"I am different," he said. "Give me the chance to show you."

Her expression turned weary. "I have known you less than a day, Quinn de Sayerne. I have been commanded to wed you. I have been bedded by you. You have been granted the seal to my family holding and you stand this night within my chamber, invited by me." She sighed. "It is as if my days and nights of labor here, for the good of this place, never occurred. And now my sole merit will rest upon whether or not I bear you a son, within a year. I am irrelevant, as irrelevant as my history, my hopes and my dreams, and I fear that my womb might be too reluctant for Tulley's satisfaction. My parents were wed three years before my birth, and their match was merry. Their lack of conception cannot be due to a lack of conviviality." She frowned and looked much less formidable than she had. "Would you not be discontent in my place?"

"You are not irrelevant! You are my wife and the heiress of Annossy..."

"Do not pretend to be a fool, Quinn," she said, interrupting him with a bitterness that surprised him. "Should I not bear you a son within a year, Tulley will support your desire to put me aside in favor of a more fertile wife."

Quinn could make no sense of that. "But he insisted on seeing the linens."

"And he kept them," Melissande reminded him. "All the better that he could see them destroyed if there was cause to have this match annulled."

Quinn stared at her in shock. He had never imagined such treachery.

Melissande shook her head. "Do not imagine that Tulley does not see to his own advantage above all else." She plucked at the ends of her veil. "So, do as you must, this night and every other. Naught is left for me to decide any longer. I am at the whim of Dame Fortune, though I cannot like it."

Quinn had never seen Melissande despondent and he did not care for the sight. She had battled him and defied him and matched wits with him. She had challenged him and she had met his passion with her own. He could not bear to see her so defeated.

Perhaps it was exhaustion.

Indeed, he felt sympathy for her for there was truth in her accusations. Much had changed for both of them in the past day, and the changes were to his advantage. He believed that they would both share in that good fortune, but his father's legacy was that she did not.

He disliked the tale of her beloved nursemaid and wished it had surprised him. Did she expect him to strike her? Quinn could not imagine doing so, but he respected that his lady wife—who had infuriated him already—might have her doubts.

She thought his half-brother had merit. Could he convince her that he did, as well?

To change Melissande's thinking, he had to challenge her expectations.

He had to surprise her.

"Shall I send Berthe for you?" he asked, tucking the seal back into the pouch at his belt. Melissande glanced his way with obvious surprise. The sound of laughter carried from the hall below and Quinn pretended to be enticed by it. "I would rejoin my comrades and hear of their adventures since we parted, but I would not insult you with my absence."

"What is this?"

"Choose," Quinn said deliberately. "Choose, my lady, whether I stay with you in this moment or leave you alone. You say you have no decisions to make, so I will grant you one."

"Just one," she said.

"Just one, for the moment. But when you have none, one is a bounty."

She smiled reluctantly, as if she could not stop herself. "It is indeed."

"And Berthe?"

She held up two fingers and that smile gained power. "Another choice?"

"A veritable feast of opportunity," Quinn said solemnly and her eyes sparkled.

"Aye, Berthe, if you please, sir."

"A bath?"

Melissande laughed a little. "A plethora of decisions," she said and Quinn chuckled, glad of a moment of accord. "Aye, a bath would be most welcome," she said. "I am sorry, my lord husband. It is not like me to lose hope."

He cleared his throat and lifted a brow, inviting her to use his name again.

"I am sorry, Quinn," she said softly and he smiled.

"But you have lost much in this, a mere day, and I should be surprised if you did not notice the lack. Annossy is fine beyond all expectation. I would have you sleep well, my lady wife, for I shall have need of your counsel to see all administered well here."

She considered him again. "I thought you simply said as much for Louis' benefit."

"I said as much because it is true. I did not even think of what our guests should eat or drink, never mind where they would sleep. I have much to learn from you, Melissande, and I would hope that you would see your way clear to granting instruction."

Their gazes locked once more, the chamber seeming warmer than it had. "You try to beguile me," she said quietly.

"If only that feat could be so easily done," Quinn replied. He bowed, then turned to the door, only to find Melissande by his side, her hand upon his arm.

"I do not know whether to trust you or not," she confessed. "I do not know what my place or my fate with be, but I thank you, Quinn, for the kindness of choices on this night." With that, she stretched up and touched her lips all too briefly to his. Quinn caught his breath at her fleeting touch, amazed that she had kissed him of her own volition, but she had already stepped away. He watched her retreat and dared to hope for their future.

Then he left the chamber, shouting for Berthe from the corridor.

It seemed he had found a way to gain some increment of his wife's affection and Quinn could only consider that a victory of the first order. No doubt the fire would be back in her eyes by the morning, but truly, he looked forward to that moment.

"A bath for your lady, if you please," he said to the maid when she came bustling up the stairs. "She is tired from the journey this day."

"And one for you, sir?" Berthe demanded.

"I will share the company of our guests for a while." Quinn nodded once, noting the assessment in the maid's eyes, then returned to his fellows. His appearance was greeted with a cheer and some teasing, but he called for a cup of ale and settled at the board again, most content.

Not every triumph could be achieved with haste, and in Quinn's view, the richer prizes took time and strategy to conquer. Winning his lady's heart and her trust would be the greatest victory of all and he was prepared to labor for it.

☙❧

Quinn had left.

He had given her a choice.

Melissande was astonished, but then, he had surprised her before. She heard the roar of greeting from his companions in the hall below, and smiled that he was held in such affection, then Berthe was at the door.

"My lord Quinn says you desire a bath, my lady."

"Indeed, I do."

Berthe sniffed. "Yet he does not so indulge." She shook her head as she untied the laces on the sides of Melissande's kirtle. "It is not right. A man should be clean when he comes to his wife's bed as a sign of respect..."

"I am not certain he comes to me this night," Melissande said, a statement so shocking that it silenced her maid momentarily. She smiled at the younger woman. "I confessed myself to be tired, and he made to resolve the matter, by summoning you and a bath."

"And joining his companions," Berthe said.

"He wished to learn of their adventures, as well," Melissande said mildly. She took off her boots and her stockings, then Berthe ushered her toward the bed.

"Be warm, my lady, while I make all ready for you." She bustled around the chamber, stirring up the coals in the brazier, then hurried away. Melissande unbound her hair and combed it out, thinking of the heated glow of Quinn's amber eyes.

She thought of his resolve to defeat the brigands and realized that she trusted him to accomplish that. Then she considered how she might be of aid to him.

What if she took him at his word?

Melissande found herself straining for the sound of Quinn's voice when the door opened anew. The tub was brought into the chamber and filled with steaming water. Berthe added herbs and soon the solar was warm with steam and the scent of lavender. "It will ensure that you sleep, my lady," Berthe said.

"My lord will ride out to the mill on the morrow," Melissande said as she stepped into the bath water. "It is possible that he will leave early, Berthe. Please ensure that I am awakened in time to offer him a stirrup cup."

"He does not ride far, my lady. It is not necessary."

"Aye, but I think it is. I would have all at Annossy see that I support him as lord."

"Aye, my lady. It shall be so."

Melissande settled into the bath with a sigh of contentment and wondered at her new spouse. She smiled as he laughed at some jest in the hall, the rich sound of his merriment making her warm inside.

Perhaps she softened too much, for it was merely a night's sleep and a bath he offered. Melissande felt her resistance to her new husband crumble even so.

Then she realized that he had ensured she could not talk to Gaultier this night.

Melissande's eyes flew open and she almost sat up in the bath. Had that been Quinn's intent? Had he been right about Gaultier's reaction? Or had the two knights met before?

Was there some detail that Quinn did not wish her to learn?

Once she had the thought that Quinn might have been trying to steer her thoughts in his favor, Melissande could not dismiss it.

How irksome that she had to wait until morning to confer with Annossy's Captain of the Guard.

But once Quinn rode to the mill, she would have ample opportunity for a private discussion with Gaultier.

By this time on the morrow, she would know the truth.

Berthe descended to the hall on her quest for her lady. It was strange to see so many knights in Annossy's hall, and she did not like the change. It would have been one matter if she could have been certain of their intentions, but they were strangers, as well as allied with the new lord. Berthe could not dismiss a very similar suspicion to that held by her lady, that these knights might take from Annossy to see Sayerne enriched.

While Lord Quinn and his companions seemed merry, Berthe noted the resolve that often touched their gazes. They were men of war, men who would not hesitate to mete justice with their blades.

She hoped against hope that she would never have to battle with any of them.

Especially that Bayard. He was trouble to be sure.

Even as she arrived, he was teasing Lord Quinn.

"Surely you do not forgo your marital due on your first night at Annossy?" that knight demanded with a conviviality born of good ale.

Berthe bristled. Lord Quinn had been considerate of her lady and she admired him for that.

"Ah, I just wanted to taste the ale," Lord Quinn said as Michel placed a filled tankard before him. "I had not the fortune to do so earlier."

"For you drank Annossy's wine instead," one of the knights, Amaury, teased.

"And it was fine indeed. I have high hopes for the ale." Lord Quinn lifted the tankard to his lips.

"Surely you do not choose our company over your lady's charms," insisted Bayard.

"My lady has need of her rest this night," Lord Quinn said firmly. He raised his tankard to Berthe to salute her. "And the attentions of her loyal maid."

The men turned to look at her and Berthe bowed for Annossy's new lord even as she felt her cheeks heat. "I think this a fine acknowledgment for a man to make for his wife," she said and granted Lord Quinn an approving smile. "I'm glad to see that some men understand how to treat a lady with respect."

"I should think a lady charged to bear an heir with all haste would welcome her lord husband to her bed to ensure that goal was accomplished," Bayard said.

"And you, Sir Rogue, would indulge in that quest?" she demanded.

He grinned, more handsome than should be permitted. "Aye! I would plunder my lady's charms and leave her smiling in the morn."

"And what of the child?" Berthe demanded. "I suspect that a man of your ilk cares only for his pleasure. You would like be gone in the morn."

"And why should he not be?" the fair knight demanded. Niall was his name, Berthe believed, and she thought him much enamored of his own charms. "A night of pleasure is well and good in itself."

"A rogue and a scoundrel," Berthe scoffed. "I expect naught better from the likes of you."

"And you shall find you better, my pretty maid," Niall said, lifting his tankard to her. He winked and Berthe turned away from him. "You know where to find me if your curiosity has the better of you."

"I shall not!" Berthe fired a glance at Bayard and their gazes held for a long moment. He was most serious and if she had not known better, she might have thought him insulted by his companion's words to her. "Nor will I seek you, Sir Rogue," she added with disapproval and that knight smiled just a little before he developed a keen interest in his ale.

Berthe told herself that she did not care if the newly arrived knights bedded all the maidens in Annossy.

Although she hoped Sir Rogue did not.

"My lord, my lady would offer you a stirrup cup on the morrow when you depart," she said to Lord Quinn. "I would ask that you see me roused when you prepare to ride out, that I might summon her."

Lord Quinn blinked, as if surprised, and seemed to bite back a smile. "It is not necessary."

"My lady says it is, sir."

"I will see you roused," Niall whispered, but Berthe stood straighter as the other knights chuckled. "Or better yet, awake all the night long." She felt her cheeks heat but she would not so much as glance at that man.

Bayard said something and began to rise to his feet, and the others teased him.

Lord Quinn looked between them, quelling them with a glance, then shook his head. "I will not, Berthe. It will be too early, for I mean to ride out early. Louis will bring those with tales to share after I break my fast, then we shall visit the mill."

"But my lady requests..."

"And your lord commands," he said with such quiet force that she fell silent. He held her gaze. "You know as well as I that dawn will be too early to rouse her. These past days have been a challenge for her."

Berthe hesitated. She knew that Lady Melissande did not like to have her commands questioned, yet she was herself bound to obey the Lord d'Annossy.

"I will tell her of my command, Berthe," he said, clearly seeing her uncertainty. "You will not be left to face my lady's wrath alone."

"My lady knows her mind, sir."

"And I know mine. As my wife, she is my responsibility. I would see her linger abed on the morrow."

There was such resolve in his tone that Berthe knew he would not be shaken.

"She will not be pleased, sir," she dared to say.

Against all expectation, he smiled. "I shall welcome the discussion, Berthe."

She marveled at that, then thought of the arguments she had already overheard between the pair. It seemed that he was untroubled that her lady had views of her own, and indeed, she had seen him invite Lady Melissande's council.

She bowed low, knowing she had no choice but to do as instructed, and hoped that he truly did have his lady's best interests at heart. It would not be all bad for Annossy to have a happily wed lord and lady, much less children in the hall.

"Do not tell her, Berthe. Not this night."

"She may ask, my lord."

His gaze was steely. "And you will not tell her of my plan. I will do so."

"Aye, my lord."

"Perhaps it is wise for a man to keep his lady wife abed," Niall murmured when Berthe passed him and she paused to glare at him. "Especially when he has need of a son with all haste. They say that any woman can be tamed with pleasure." He was watching her, his eyes dancing with devilry.

"You may rest assured that it is not unnatural, but *civilized* for a man to show a care for his lady wife," she informed him haughtily. "Should you heed your companion instead of your lust, you might learn something of merit."

"I have no need to learn of proper treatment of a wife," Bayard contributed. "For I do not have one."

"Nor will you, if you continue to listen to that one, and a fine thing that will be for women everywhere," Berthe informed him.

Bayard blinked in surprise at that, but she turned away, marching to the kitchens. The sound of his companions' laughter echoed behind her but Berthe did not smile.

She was thinking of a knight who was less of a rogue than his fellow.

Did that still make Sir Rogue too much of a rogue for her?

Berthe reminded herself that she had no need of any man, but felt disgruntled with her situation as she seldom was. She knew what was right. She knew what men such as these desired of women like her and had little doubt of what would happen after pleasure had been claimed. She was neither innocent nor a fool.

Still, she felt the lack of a man in her life as never she had before.

That was the fault of Sir Rogue, as well, and all the more reason to avoid him.

Melissande slept deeply.

She awakened when the solar was still dark and rolled to her back with satisfaction, feeling restored. The keep was quiet as the household slept on and the shadows were deep in the corners. Melissande heard no sounds of activity from kitchen or village and guessed that even the animals had not been tended yet. It was not yet dawn and the brazier had burned down to cold embers.

She should rise, if she meant to offer that cup to Quinn, although the bed was so wondrously warm that she was reluctant to abandon it.

She stretched, savoring her situation, and her hand brushed against warm muscled flesh.

A man's chest.

Her fingertips had brushed a tangle of curly hair in its midst that she knew must be russet.

Melissande's mouth went dry and she pulled her hand back in

alarm. Quinn had come to bed after all? There could be no doubt of it for he was beside her, his breath deep and even. She had assumed he would remain in the hall, but he had not said as much.

Of course, the lord slept in the lord's solar. Of course, Quinn had joined her abed, for there was but one bed.

She had slept with her lord husband by her side. He had not seized her in the night, much less demanded the marital due. Nay, he had let her sleep, as he had vowed.

Melissande turned to study his profile in the shadows. She could barely discern it, but then that seemed a perfect echo of her view of her husband's truth. When would she be certain that she had married a man of merit or a deceptive villain intent upon claiming all advantage at Annossy? How could she be certain whether he told her the truth? Quinn had thus far, as far as Melissande could determine, but they had not even been wed two days. That was not long to pretend.

She wished she could read his thoughts and intentions as readily as he seemed to be able to read her own. She listened to his breathing, and knew that he was yet asleep.

His scent surrounded her like a cocoon. There was something reassuring about his size and his presence, and Melissande knew she could easily come to rely upon Quinn, should she allow herself to do as much.

Should she?

The man had a power over her, even in sleep, for she doubted her choices with vigor. She might have found that vexing, but at this hour, in this place, she could not be irked. His presence beside her, so large and warm, awakened her curiosity—and more.

Aye. The hum of desire he had stirred on their wedding night reawakened, turning Melissande's thoughts to their need for a son. She could reach out and touch him again. Stroke him. Awaken him with a kiss, like an enchanted prince in an old tale. The notion made her smile a little. Would he greet her with pleasure? Or would he spurn her?

Melissande was quite certain that his eyes would glow with satisfaction and he would touch her with all the persuasive power of two nights before.

That made her yearn.

His chest and shoulders were bare, as evidently he wore no chemise to bed. Was he completely nude? Melissande had a desire to look upon him. The truth was she had seen very little on their wedding night, admittedly because she had been too frightened. Yet her fear of Quinn was vastly diminished and it was true that she knew little of men's bodies. Surely it could not hurt to peek now, before he awakened? Curiosity, her mother had always said, was a healthy attribute.

She took a deep breath, half certain the sound of her heart would awaken him, then reached out. Her gaze flew to Quinn's face, her hand hesitating above his shoulder. He lay on his side, facing her, one arm folded beneath his head, the other lying between them. He looked less imposing in sleep with his hair tousled and his lips twisted in a half smile. She wondered what delights filled his dreams to make him smile so. She reached up on impulse and touched one fingertip to his lips, just as he had touched his finger to her mouth.

His lips were soft, like her own, despite the hardness of the life he had lived.

But there any similarity between them ended. Quinn had seen the world while she had stayed home and administered Annossy with breathtaking predictability, from one season to the next.

That awareness made Melissande feel very sheltered.

Her finger strayed through the prickly stubble of beard on Quinn's chin, across his cheek and traced the outline of his jaw. His skin seemed heavier than her own, more robust, as well as tanned by a southern sun. He was even more handsome to her than the day before and she admitted his appeal in the privacy of her thoughts. Her other fingertips joined the first as she let her hand trail down the strength of his neck.

They encountered the puckered end of a scar.

Her fingers halted uncertainly, hovering above the heat of his flesh. She had not noticed this on their wedding night, but then, she had been overwhelmed. The wound was old and long-healed, although its mark still marred his shoulder. It was lengthy, extending down his chest, and she guessed the wound had been deep. She recalled his tale of being injured and imprisoned with Bayard, and Lothair's comments upon the challenge of healing his injury.

She could not doubt it, now that she studied the scar.

It was impressive that he had survived.

This was vivid evidence of how different Quinn's life had been from hers, and how vigorous he was.

Her gaze flicked to his face, but he still slept.

She tentatively touched the scar. She could not imagine what it would be like to be injured and imprisoned far from home. His comrades had spoken of dirt and darkness and she guessed that he might have felt despair. She could not imagine that this powerful and resolute man would take kindly to being at less than his full capabilities. She traced the length of the scar, knowing the injury and his recovery must have been an ordeal.

Praise be that Bayard had been with him.

No wonder they had such a close bond.

Melissande knew that she would have been hard-pressed to endure such an ailment away from everyone and everything she knew. The discovery gave her a new appreciation of the strength of Quinn's character, and of the gentleness he had shown her thus far. Misfortune had not made him cruel and she respected that.

This was a man who had seen and done much. Melissande knew that she could never have been bold enough to walk away from everything she knew to seek her fortune abroad, even if Tulley had advised it.

What had happened between him and Jerome? Quinn had evaded the question, inviting her own tale of Jerome, and she wondered why. Did that truth show Quinn in poor light. Just two days after meeting him, Melissande wondered if that could be so.

Perhaps he and Yves were both men of honor, despite their father's nature.

His chest was hard with muscle, and she let the flat of her hand slide over him, looking and feeling. He radiated warmth and she knew why the bed had become so cozy in the middle of the night. If she thought upon it, she might be able to name the very moment he had joined her.

Quinn grunted and frowned suddenly, stirring in his sleep. His hand brushed at hers as it might at a troubling fly. Melissande pulled her hand back and regarded him with wide eyes, certain she would be caught looking.

But Quinn merely rolled to his back, apparently satisfied that the "fly" was gone. He folded his hands upon his belly and his breathing deepened again. Melissande propped herself up on her elbow to study him as the chamber became lighter. Had his nose been broken once? The angle of it made her wonder. And there was a small scar on his cheek, as well as a few more on his hands. Doubtless, he thought them of little import. They were marks of his trade as much as his destrier and his mail.

Quinn's continued slumber made her even more bold. There was a great deal that she had not truly seen. Carefully, Melissande drew the linens even lower. Even in the shadowed light, the sight of him made her mouth go dry.

He was a warrior and his body showed the evidence. His muscles were developed to hard curves, there were more small nicks and scars all over his flesh. His flesh was darker than her hand, tanned to a bronze hue that still lingered.

Melissande's overwhelming impression was one of power. Here was a man who had earned his way with his hands and his blade. That choice hinted at a code of honor she could admire and Melissande found herself intrigued with her spouse.

Her fingers fell to his flesh again and she touched the dark circle of his nipple, surprised to find it like her own. Her hand followed the trail of hair that led toward his navel. Below his navel, a matching russet arrow swept upward from his masculinity.

She had not dared to look at that part of him, for only a wanton or a whore would do as much. She did as much in this moment, confident that no one would know of her curiosity. She lifted the linens and her eyes widened in surprise at his arousal.

Was he always like this? The recollection of his strength within her prompted Melissande to explore further. Was the surrounding hair wiry or soft? Was the flesh truly as hard as it appeared? Amazed by her own audacity, she touched him.

That part of him lifted to her hand, as though welcoming her touch.

She pulled back her hand, certain he had caught her looking. Melissande eyed Quinn but his chest merely rose and fell as he slept peacefully.

Surely she had been mistaken. Surely he had just moved in his sleep.

Surely there was no harm in knowing for certain.

She swallowed and reached out once more. As soon as her fingertips brushed against Quinn's hardness, it rose slightly.

This time she did not pull away. Melissande laid her hand across him and felt the slight swell beneath her touch. The skin was smooth and he was hard. Her fingers closed gently and quite naturally around Quinn's strength. Shocked at her own audacity and uncertain how to proceed, Melissande flicked a glance at Quinn.

Only to find his amber gaze locked upon her.

He smiled, looking wicked, and Melissande knew she flushed scarlet.

"I am sorry," she began in a fluster.

When she might have pulled away her hand, the weight of Quinn's hand landed atop hers, capturing it there.

"Do not apologize," he said with reassuring calm. "Curiosity is only natural."

"I do not mean to give offense," Melissande began.

Quinn chuckled. "And none is taken, my lady. Rest assured of that." His thumb slid across the back of her hand and the hue of his eyes deepened to a rich amber.

Melissande pulled her hand abruptly out from under Quinn's, feeling her face burn.

"You mock me," she accused and could no longer hold his gaze.

"I do no such thing," Quinn countered. "I welcome you to continue your exploration."

Melissande dared to look at him again and he smiled slowly at her. He caught her hand again and held it captive over his heart. She felt its steady beat beneath her palm. It seemed she could not take a breath, not when he watched her so steadily.

"I thought you did not mean to come to my bed last night."

"I came to *our* bed, but hope I did not disturb your sleep."

Melissande exhaled and sat up, but Quinn did not release her hand. Indeed, his thumb began to move slowly across her palm and she found it as seductive a caress as when he had traced circles on her back at their wedding feast. She stared at him and swallowed.

"Did you sleep well, my lady?"

"Aye. And you, sir?"

His smile disarmed her. "Aye! I have never known such comfort as this." He lifted a brow and stretched his arms over his head. Despite herself, Melissande could not resist the opportunity to look upon him again. His smile did not waver and he did not complain, merely claimed her hand again and placed it on his chest, covering it with his own. "I shall have to ensure that I am not completely seduced."

Melissande found herself flushing even more.

"There were comments, my lady," he added in an undertone. "As you anticipated. I thought we had best ensure rumor found no footing in our hall."

She had to concede the wisdom of that, and nodded once.

He still did not release her hand. She tugged a little, to no avail.

"Where do you mean to go so early when the hall is cold?" he murmured. "Stay and be warm, my lady."

He lifted the bedlinens in invitation and smiled. There was a dangerous seduction in his voice, yet Melissande was tempted all the same.

"We should, perhaps, endeavor to create a son," she said, knowing that she sounded breathless. "To secure the future for both of us."

"Indeed."

Their gazes held for a moment, then Melissande slipped beneath the bedcovers. She left a distinct distance between herself and Quinn.

"You will be too cold there," he said. "And we surely must touch to create that son."

"Aye," she agreed, then Quinn's arm locked around her waist, pulling her against his side. Melissande gasped at his quick move. He was wondrously warm, though, and she dared to release the breath she had been holding. It was quite comfortable to be nestled against his strength.

And thrilling, as well.

Then his hand lifted from her waist and his fingertip dropped unerringly to her lips. He could not have been awake when she touched him, she told herself. It was only a coincidence that he touched her where she had first touched him.

But Quinn's finger retraced the precise path her own had taken, though across her flesh instead of his.

Melissande felt his finger's warmth slide across her cheek, around her ear, down the length of her jawline. She swallowed when his other fingertips joined the first in sliding down the length of her neck.

She caught her breath when his fingers eased beneath her chemise and gently traced the silhouette of her collarbone.

"You mock me again," she whispered, mortified. She felt Quinn lean over her and reluctantly opened her eyes to find his eyes gleaming with intent.

"Nay, my lady," he murmured. "I would simply know you as you now know me."

Melissande might have protested, but she could not find the words when Quinn cupped her breast in one hand. His thumb slid across her nipple and she gasped as it tightened to a peak.

All she saw was Quinn's easy smile.

"This does not lie," he whispered. "You like this caress." Before she could argue, he bent to touch his lips to that taut peak. Melissande found her fingers in his hair as he gently suckled and teased her nipple. It was potent to be touched with such gentleness, knowing that he was so strong. He could have injured her easily, but he marveled at her instead.

And he gave her pleasure. He had to realize as much. His tongue flicked against her and Melissande was filled with a heat that left her trembling.

"Too much?" Quinn lifted his head and smiled at her, his expression seductive.

She shook her head, mutely. "So much but not too much," she whispered.

The warmth of his fingers slid around her breast and she saw his throat work as he watched his own hand. "You are beautiful," he murmured, and the awe in his voice could not have been contrived. "It astounds me that you should be my wife."

"Tulley willed it."

"Tulley could have chosen a crone."

"Not if he wanted you to have a son."

Quinn nodded agreement, his gaze fixed upon his fingertips. "He could have chosen a maiden whose wits were not so keen as yours."

Melissande opened her mouth and closed it again, uncertain what to say.

"It is your nature that crowns your beauty, Melissande," Quinn said softly. "The way you speak, the way you walk, the way you plan and think." He shook his head. "It is more, far more, than the shape of you that beguiles me."

He met her gaze, his eyes filled with a wonder that she realized was an echo of her own.

"It seems too much for chance alone to have brought us together."

Melissande smiled. "Will you tell me a tale of romance and destined love?" she asked lightly.

Quinn smiled. "My mother believed in it. She told me many such tales."

She bit her tongue, lest she note that such a conviction must have led his mother astray if it had brought her to Jerome.

Quinn must have noticed for he shook his head. "She loved another man," he confessed, again watching his fingers stroke her breast. "But they were not allowed to wed. Her father arranged her match with my father, and though she was unhappy, she endeavored to be a dutiful wife."

Melissande watched his throat work. "What happened?" she whispered.

Quinn shook his head. "I cannot think of it, even now," he admitted, his voice husky and she reached to touch his cheek. He turned his head and planted a kiss against her palm, his gaze locked with hers for a potent moment.

Then he smiled and she knew he would make a jest. "But we have an injustice to address, my lady," he said.

"An injustice?"

"Aye. You were able to look without restraint, while I do not have that privilege. Should we not be fair?" He indicated her chemise. It was unlaced at the neck and her breast exposed to his view, but the fine cloth covered her to her knees.

"You would look upon me? Again?"

He lifted a brow. "Surely you do not imagine that I am much more familiar with the makings of ladies than you were with that of knights?"

He was teasing her. Melissande tore her gaze away, her hands rising to the tie of her chemise. It felt uncommonly bold to expose herself to his view, yet he was her spouse.

Quinn retreated to his side of the bed. "The choice is yours," he assured her, and she knew he would turn away, or even leave, if she so asked.

And that made her decision so simple that it might have been inevitable.

CHAPTER NINE

elissande nodded then sat up beside Quinn, filled with resolve. She seized the hem of her chemise and lifted it over her head, casting it toward the foot of the bed before she could change her thinking. She looked away from Quinn, uncertain what he would say or do.

She was nude. Exposed. Vulnerable. Her heart fluttered at her throat and she took a quick breath, hoping her instinct had been right. She feared otherwise when silence filled the solar.

"Beautiful," Quinn breathed finally.

Melissande dared to look, only to find his eyes glowing. His hand moved slowly from her waist and she knew she did not imagine that his fingers quivered.

His uncertainty reassured her as naught else could, and Melissande rolled toward him. Quinn's other hand rose to her cheek and she reveled in the strength of his fingers tangling in her hair. His hand swept lower in an endless caress, his attention diverted from her face as he avidly watched its progress.

Melissande looked at his lips and considered how she would kiss him. She would take his strong jaw in her hands, just once, just to see how it felt, and press her lips resolutely against his. She would arch her back so that her breasts rubbed in that tangle of russet hair and Quinn would open his mouth to her.

The audacity of the impulse stole her breath away.

Then Quinn flicked a glance to her and grinned mischievously. Melissande did not know what to expect, but suddenly he wriggled his thumb within her navel.

It tickled. She laughed, even as she writhed to escape him. Quinn chuckled and his other hand joined the fray.

"Quinn!"

"Ticklish, my lady?" he demanded, his eyes dancing.

"Oh, Aye! Oh, stop!" Melissande could barely catch her breath from laughing. She twisted desperately, pushing at Quinn's hands in an effort to escape. "Nay! Stop, please! I beg of you!"

Quinn stopped suddenly, his hands locked around her waist, his fingertips too close to her ticklish spot for her to relax. He loomed over her and Melissande did not trust the unruly twinkle in his eyes.

"I will stop for a kiss," he whispered.

Melissande's heart leapt. "You are a devil," she protested lightly, more because she thought she should than because she had any particular objections.

Quinn laughed and the merry sound tempted Melissande to join him. "A devil?" he demanded with an arch of his brow. "Only a saint would demand so little from such a wife."

Though he jested, it was clear the compliment was meant honestly.

"One kiss will not make a son," she reminded him.

Quinn's grin broadened. "I am at your service, my lady. Take of me what you will."

The breath abandoned Melissande in a rush. "You do not mind if I make demands?"

"Far from it. I would encourage as much."

He wished her to be bold? There could be no doubt of it, not when he watched her with such anticipation. Melissande dared to indulge her notion. She reached up, framing his face in her hands. Quinn smiled, just a little, and waited.

The man's patience made it simple to follow her urge. She leaned closer, brushing her lips softly against his own. She felt his breath and her nipples barely touched the hair upon his chest. His grip upon her waist tightened. She saw him close his eyes, his expression so rapturous that she wanted to tempt him more.

She angled her mouth over his, just as he had kissed her, and deepened her kiss. Quinn moaned, the sound apparently coming from the depths of his soul, and Melissande felt triumphant in her seduction. She touched the tip of her tongue to his lips and closed her own eyes when he shuddered, then he rolled her to her back. His mouth locked over hers, even as he braced his weight above her and Melissande welcomed his touch. Her fingers fanned out of their own accord, sliding over his shoulders to pull him closer.

It was blessedly simple to welcome him. Indeed, it seemed both natural and right.

Quinn's groan made her smile, for it reassured her that he was as powerfully affected as she. His kiss was everything Melissande had longed for just moments before. His arms enfolded her and he eased his thigh between her legs. His tongue explored and Melissande greeted it with hers. She mimicked him, learning from him, feeling the heat rise to a crescendo between them. That she had the power to entice him, even to satisfy him, was a marvel. His hands slipped from her waist to spread behind her, one at her nape again and one cupping her buttocks.

Still she wanted more of him.

This time, they seduced each other, and Melissande felt the difference. It was a hundred times more potent, each caress sending her to new heights and tempting her to respond in kind. Melissande wound her fingers into Quinn's hair; she arched against his strength; she let her hands rove over him; she loved how gently he touched her. She wanted to know him, to touch him, to taste him as she had never before. She wanted to feel his strength within her with a ferocity that astonished her.

Quinn dragged his lips from hers, and Melissande was aware of the evidence of his arousal. She instinctively rubbed the softness of her belly against him.

"My lady," he gasped. "You must choose now if it will be a kiss or more. Any more and I will not be able to stop."

But Melissande did not want to stop.

She stretched up and rolled her tongue in Quinn's ear, savoring her power over him. He shivered, much as she did beneath his touch, and that evidence of his vulnerability emboldened her to new heights. She wanted to disarm him, she wanted to see this supremely self-controlled man surrender to her.

She wanted to feel him explode within her again.

She pushed him to his back and straddled him, capturing his face in her hands again and bending to taste him. "The lady desires another kiss," she whispered against his mouth, then she kissed him again. She was more demanding this time, echoing his moves when he had kissed and seduced her. Quinn clutched her buttocks with his hands and moaned.

"My lady, test me no further," he murmured, and the strain of maintaining his control was evident in his voice.

Melissande did not intend to give him any quarter. She was relentless. Her hands moved over him, savoring the warm satin of his skin beneath her touch, until her fingers landed upon that part of him. She shifted to one side and looked up to his face as she closed her hand around him. He was larger and harder than he had been before.

Quinn's eyes closed and Melissande marveled that he could be so affected by her touch.

"I want you," she confided.

Quinn's eyes flew open, his expression rapt as he scanned her face. "Truly?" he asked in evident surprise.

Melissande smiled. "Aye. You are invited, sir."

It took no more than that.

Quinn pulled her lips down for his impassioned kiss. Melissande felt his restraint fall away like a tangible thing and reveled in the surety of his touch. She tried to change positions, moving toward the bed, but Quinn's strong hands locked around her waist and held her in place, astride him.

"I would see you," he murmured, his voice rough with demand. Melissande did not understand until he moved her forward. Her knees were on either side of his waist and his erection nudged against her softness.

"Oh!" Melissande's eyes widened as he eased within her. There was no twinge this time, just a curious sense of satisfaction. She trembled deep inside and she felt her pulse quicken.

Quinn chuckled. "Oh!" he mimicked good-naturedly. His eyes glinted with a warmth that fed Melissande's confidence. "It is all up to you this time," he informed her. "I am your willing victim."

Melissande recalled Quinn's rhythmic movement from their wedding night, so she lifted herself tentatively above him, then down again. Quinn's little gasp of pleasure told her that she had guessed aright. She sat up and unbound her hair, recalling his admiration of it, and watched him swallow as she spread it over her shoulders. It fell to her hips, touching his thighs and resting upon his belly. It was curious and marvelous to feel that she had the power in this encounter, that she could seduce this powerful man and hold him, even briefly, in her thrall. She moved again, rolling her hips sometimes, rubbing herself against him others, and it seemed she could do naught wrong. Quinn responded favorably to her every move, which only made her bolder yet.

The heat rose between them, desire galloping to new heights. Melissande could not catch her breath and she did not care. A fire burned in her belly, spreading throughout her body, demanding a satisfaction that she suspected only Quinn could give. His gaze was locked upon her, his eyes glittering, and he clutched a handful of her hair at her waist. She moved more quickly, sensing the urgency in him and unable to deny her own.

Quinn caught her close and moved with greater urgency. Their hearts pounded as one, and her breasts were crushed against his chest. Melissande felt the fire beneath her flesh. Quinn's breath was in her ear and she sensed that culmination of pleasure drawing near.

When the wave broke over her, she reared back and threw her arms toward the ceiling in ecstatic release. She heard Quinn gasp her name and felt his strength surge beneath her. She fell atop him as he panted and held her close, then watched him smile anew.

"Enchantress," he charged and Melissande laughed.

"Not me."

Quinn's glance slanted to meet hers, his eyes glowing gold. "Aye, you, my lady wife." He kissed her hand in that increasingly familiar gesture, closing her fingers over the burning imprint of his lips upon her palm. "And I am your most willing vassal."

Melissande laughed at his whimsy and savored this moment of accord. At his encouragement, she nestled against him, liking how he tucked them both beneath the linens. It was still not dawn and Melissande found herself dozing anew. She knew that she smiled, for she was cradled against the solid heat of Quinn as he pressed a kiss into her hair.

Perhaps they would make a good match, after all.

Quinn carefully eased out of Melissande's embrace.

He had erred.

He had no devious intent, but neither had he intended to seduce Melissande again so soon. He knew that she loved another and that she had a high code of ethics. He had planned to talk to her more about this Arnaud, and endeavor to prove his own merit before they coupled again.

But her exploration of his body had set him aflame. He should have stopped with one kiss, but her delight in her power over his body had given her such satisfaction. He had wanted to see her gain confidence in her own allure, and also to see her pleased. He had been unable to resist her. He stood by the bed, watching her sleep, and wondered in all honesty whether he could have stopped.

He frowned, considering that she had not called him by name in that moment.

Had she imagined herself in the embrace of her beloved, Arnaud?

The notion troubled Quinn deeply.

Doubtless she would regret their lovemaking. That prospect troubled him even more. He washed hastily in cold water and dressed, knowing he had much to accomplish this day. Perhaps a successful routing of the brigands would win her true favor.

He could only hope.

He left Melissande sleeping and descended to the hall. Louis met him at the foot of the stairs, and they conferred about the villeins who had tales of the brigands to share. True to his word, Louis had summoned them all and they awaited him in the bailey.

"There is bread and honey and ale and cheese, my lord," Louis said. "Unless you have other tastes for breaking your fast."

"That will be most welcome, Louis. I thank you. My lady wife sleeps yet, but perhaps Berthe should take hot water to her."

"Of course, my lord. Berthe is already awake." Louis hurried away and Quinn went to the board. Michel brought him a tankard of ale and he wished the boy a good morning. "I will ride out after speaking with the villeins," he told the boy. "If they are awake and willing, I would have Bayard, Niall, Lothair and Amaury accompany me."

"Aye, my lord." The boy bowed and hurried away with purpose.

"Aha!" Bayard's voice made Quinn jump.

"What possesses you to startle an old friend so early in the morning?" Quinn asked with a smile.

Bayard joined him at the board. "What kind of newly wedded man are you to avoid the pleasure of awakening with your lawful wife?" He nudged Quinn companionably. "I should not be so quick to abandon such pleasures." Michel hastily brought more ale and Bayard sipped of it with satisfaction. Then he dropped his voice low. "Does the lady resist your charms?"

"Nay." Quinn dropped to a seat and sipped his ale. It might clear his head, if naught else. "It is not so simple as that."

"Nay?"

Quinn spared his companion a suspicious eye. "What makes you so inquisitive this morn? What manner of mischief have you been making in this hall?"

"Surely, Quinn, you must jest. You should know that I have done naught but slumber in this marvel of a hall."

"Alone?"

Bayard choked slightly. "How could you think otherwise of me? I am as sober a companion as ever you have known."

"Aye, that is true enough."

The other knight lowered his voice. "It is another of our comrades who shares his charm with much generosity, to my thinking."

Quinn took a draft of ale watching his comrade all the while. "And you do not approve."

"It is not my place to approve or disapprove of another man's choices," he said, sounding remarkably prim. Before Quinn could comment, Bayard leaned forward, his eyes glinting with curiosity. "Truly, it is long since we have known such hospitality. You have landed upon your feet, Quinn, to be sure."

"The matter is not secured as yet."

Bayard studied him. "Do you not make progress in the courtship of your lady wife?"

"There is a complication."

"So, tell me the whole tale," the other knight urged. "Your secrets are safe with me. *Does* the lady spurn you?"

"Nay," Quinn said again. Perhaps Bayard could help him in this puzzle. "You see—" he leaned forward, dropped his voice and Bayard followed suit "—it seems the lady had pledged herself to another."

"Nay! It could not be so!"

"But it is so. She insists upon it."

Bayard looked as shocked as Quinn felt. "Are you certain the tale is true? Surely Tulley would not have forced her to break her word?"

"Apparently that is precisely what he did."

"*Aie.*" Bayard leaned back and ran his hand through his hair. "And when did she tell you of this?"

"When she wept, the morning after the match had been consummated," Quinn admitted grimly.

"This is not good," Bayard informed him.

Quinn arched a brow. "I thank you for that counsel."

"And so all rides upon one night," Bayard said. "Or upon one knight's ride."

Quinn shook his head. "Not quite." He sighed. "She seduced me this morn."

"Which surely is progress."

"I fear she will regret it and blame me."

Bayard shook his head and drained his ale. "But tell me this: does she have any regard for this other man?"

That was a reminder Quinn did not need. "She says she loves him."

Bayard gave a low whistle. "What do you intend to do?"

"I do not know." Quinn frowned. "What is worse, Tulley overheard our argument yesterday morning. He demands an heir within the year and that before he invests me with Sayerne."

"So, should you proceed with honor, you lose all."

"Aye."

"And should you claim your due, she may despise you for it."

"Aye."

Bayard pushed his tankard across the board. "Then, it seems to me that you have little choice." His voice was low and thoughtful, a tone that gave Quinn hope that he had a plan.

"Aye?"

Bayard looked directly into Quinn's eyes. "You must compel her to love you," he said. "You must make her forget this other man and see no one but you."

The plan was too like his own poorly formed idea to be reassuring. Quinn spread his hands out in frustration. "I do not know how to begin."

Bayard leaned forward intently. "Did you see her pleasured this morn?"

"Of course!"

"Has she ever called you by name in that moment?"

Quinn could not hold his friend's gaze. "Nay."

Bayard frowned and tapped his finger on the board. "It seems you have a daunting task before you," he mused. "But the prize is well worth the effort."

"Not to mention that of a marriage without strife."

His companion studied him. "You already care for this lady, unless I miss my guess."

Quinn did not meet his companion's perceptive gaze and when he spoke, his voice was gruff. "We have similar values," he said stiffly. "I like her wit. She surprises me. And it pleases me to see her smile."

"Aha!" Bayard was triumphant. "The truth will out!" His voice dropped. "That is an advantage unexpected. It is my understanding that women love to be adored. It flatters their vanity and I cannot imagine that your Melissande is different. Do not worry, Quinn, we shall see the lady enamored of you yet."

"My lord Quinn!" Berthe's voice echoed as she entered the hall with a steaming bucket of water. Her expression was grim and her attention fixed upon Bayard. "I should advise you strongly against taking the advice of this ruffian, for Sir Rogue knows naught of what pleases a lady in truth."

Quinn looked to his companion to find Bayard's ears glowing a dull red.

"Surely you did not try to make sport with my lady's maid last night?" he asked.

It was not reassuring that Bayard's ears turned an even brighter shade of red. Instead of responding to Quinn, he lowered his voice to a whisper, no doubt anticipating that Berthe would hear. He sighed in a most affected manner as she crossed the hall with her burden. "Ah, Quinn, the pleasure of avoiding this lady's sharp comments buoyed my spirits this morn, but now the day is lost."

"I heard that!" Berthe declared at the bottom of the stairs. She put down the bucket with such vehemence that the water sloshed over the side, then shook a finger at Bayard. "My mother warned me against your kind, sir! I was lucky to keep my wits about me right from the first, despite the gilding on your tongue."

Quinn's brows rose in surprise. "You have a gilded tongue?" he asked his companion.

Bayard shrugged. "It was cold last eve. I offered to keep her warm."

"You thought to give me more than warmth," Berthe accused and Bayard looked discomfited.

"You could have declined."

"I did decline, and then you tried to steal a kiss!"

"You did not," Quinn said, though he saw the truth in Bayard's chagrin. "Melissande will have much to say of the matter."

"And it is neither her business nor yours," the other knight retorted with vehemence.

"Next time, Sir Rogue, I will blacken your eye."

"I do not doubt it," Bayard replied, some admiration in his tone. "Someone taught you how to strike a blow. 'Twas only my own speed that saw me unbruised." He smiled. "Next time, I shall need to be faster."

"There will be no next time!" Berthe glared at Bayard, but Quinn noted that her gaze was snared once she dared to look.

"I think there might be," Bayard murmured. Berthe flushed and the other knight's eyes sparkled, then she seized the bucket and marched up the stairs.

"Ah, Berthe, surely you do not give this rogue more of your attention than he deserves?" Niall asked as he appeared on the stairs. He smiled at the maid with all his charm, blocking her progress. "I must advise you that if you mean to choose a companion, I will grant you a merrier time than my sorry comrade there."

"You, sir, may keep your counsel to yourself," the maid snapped and glared at Niall until he stepped to one side. He blew a kiss after her, but she ignored him.

"She is this close, despite her chatter," Niall murmured, holding his thumb and finger an increment apart.

Quinn might have smiled at his comrade's confidence but he noticed Bayard's dark glance. "I would place my wager upon the maid," he confessed.

"That is because you know so little of the seductive arts," Niall said, continuing down the stairs to the board. "Should you have need of advice, I could teach you tricks that ensure your lady wife will not permit you to leave the solar before noon."

That seemed unlikely to Quinn, but he left the matter be. His other comrades were descending to the hall and he conferred with them as they broke their fast together. He then indicated to Louis that he would welcome the villeins to hear what they knew of the raids.

The brigands had to be routed for Quinn to have any chance of a happy future with Melissande. Unlike the challenge of winning her heart, this task, mercifully, was within his skills.

Melissande could not believe she had been so wanton. There was something about Quinn that provoked both her trust and her desire. It made no sense that he should have such an ability to influence her when she knew so little of him. It made no sense that she could find herself so quick to abandon her concerns about his family.

It was troubling indeed how readily she forgot her pledge to Arnaud.

She rose with purpose, intending to be her usual disciplined self again. Quinn had agreed to seduce her only when invited: she would not invite him to do as much so quickly again. She wondered if he would turn to another woman for satisfaction, felt a twinge of dislike at the very notion, then knew he would not.

How curious that she should be so certain of his honorable nature in that matter at least.

Perhaps she had been misled. She would speak to Gaultier this very morn and learn what he knew or suspected of Quinn. She would take advantage of Quinn's absence to muster her few resources.

"Good morning, my lady!" Berthe said as she entered the solar. She had made the merest knock upon the door before entering. She threw open the shutters, making her way around the chamber, admitting both the chill of the wind and the sunlight.

"Your lord husband already breaks his fast, my lady."

"Aye." Melissande began to wash. "I will have the blue kirtle this day, the one wrought in the colors of Annossy."

"With the white veil and blue slippers," Berthe said, knowing her lady's taste well.

"And that silver girdle, if you please."

"Aye, my lady." The maid moved to the chest where Melissande's kirtles were stored, then hesitated. She turned. "Your lord husband does not have a tabard in the colors of Annossy."

"We can hardly be faulted for that, as we did not know he would be Lord d'Annossy but two days past," Melissande noted with a smile.

Berthe nodded. "Aye, but should one be made for him?"

Melissande had not truly considered Quinn would be a permanent resident of Annossy, but she supposed she should. She simply had not progressed so far in understanding the changes that resulted from her marriage. "We should," she said then, thinking of the stores of cloth. "Is there not a short length of deep blue wool?"

"I believe so, my lady," Berthe said, bringing the kirtle to her. "I will search for it today."

"Thank you, Berthe."

The maid frowned. "Does Lord Quinn intend to reside here or at Sayerne?"

Melissande paused. "What have you heard?"

"The knight Bayard was most eloquent in the kitchen last night about Sayerne and his comrade's intention of restoring it to its former glory."

Melissande refrained from making a skeptical sound. Sayerne had never been glorious, at least not in her lifetime.

"He vows he will live there."

"I thought you did not speak to Sir Rogue?"

The maid blushed. "He has a charm about him, to be sure. And I thought there could be little harm in talking to him in the kitchens last evening. Truly, there were others present."

Her kirtle laced, Melissande turned to survey her maid. She had never seen Berthe so determined to avoid her gaze. "Tell me you have not been seduced by my lord husband's companion?"

Berthe flushed crimson. "Bayard de Neuville," she said. "That is his name."

Melissande felt her brow rise. "You did not answer me."

Berthe sighed and slipped behind Melissande to braid her hair. The move also ensured that Melissande could not see the maid's features and she doubted that was mere coincidence. "Do you not think he is handsome beyond all?" she asked after a moment's silence. "A woman could readily lose her head when he fixed his attention upon her, no less when he endeavors to steal a kiss."

"He did not!"

"He did." Berthe sighed. "Already I wonder if it was folly to evade him."

Melissande blinked. "But you chide him so, as if you dislike him."

"It is all I can do to keep my wits about me." Berthe tugged Melissande's hair tightly. "If he ever guessed that I have any regard for him at all, he might be bent on seducing me then, and I might succumb."

"That would be most unwise."

Berthe nodded unhappy agreement. "He says himself that he has no inclination to wed."

"So, you think him a rogue."

Berthe winced. "I am not so certain, my lady. The other one, the fair one with the accent, now he is a rogue to be sure."

"Niall," Melissande said.

"Aye, and since his arrival, I can see that Bayard is not so selfish as I had thought him to be."

"I had no idea of your regard."

"And with any luck he does not, either."

Melissande nodded. She was uncertain of the intentions of Quinn's companions. Did Bayard have a holding? Without one, she doubted he intended to take a wife, although he might welcome a woman's attentions abed. She was not even certain if he planned to remain in Quinn's service, but she did not want Berthe to be seduced and abandoned. She would have to ask Quinn, though he might not welcome the discussion. Doubtless men of war were not accustomed to concerning themselves with all those beneath their hand, but he would have to learn to do as much as Lord d'Annossy.

For the first time, Melissande wondered if Quinn was also coming to terms with the implications of their hasty marriage.

"I would ask you to resist the advances of all my lord husband's companions," she said to Berthe. "At least until I can learn more of their natures and intentions."

"Do you not think that a knight who took the cross and rode to crusade must have a noble nature?" Berthe asked, her tone wistful.

"I would hope so, but he might only have learned to savor every pleasure while he could. Some men take the cross for the hope of plunder, since there is naught for them to inherit. Some take it out of genuine piety." Melissande reached out and laid her hand over the other woman's. "My concern is for you," she said. "Bayard might have no holding or fortune so that he might make a home for a bride. He might be the manner of man to pursue a woman with sweet words and empty promises. We do not know, and I would be more certain of your future." Berthe turned abruptly away and Melissande was afraid it was already too late. "Tell me that you have not yielded to him."

"I have not, my lady."

"I will speak to my lord husband about this matter."

"But he might tell Bayard of my regard!"

Melissande smiled to encourage Berthe, for the maid was clearly distraught at the prospect. "I have no doubt that my lord husband can be convinced to keep your secret," she said, before she realized that Quinn might have a very obvious price.

An invitation.

For he needed a son.

What would happen to their marriage if she conceived, bore a son, and Quinn was entrusted with the seal of Sayerne? Would he abandon her here at Annossy to rebuild his family holding? Did Bayard know more of Quinn's intentions than she? Melissande had not considered the possibility, not before Berthe's question, but as she descended to the hall, she wondered.

It might be expedient to bear that son, if she wished Quinn to leave Annossy.

Melissande found him at the board, surrounded by his companions, his attention fixed on a villein who spoke to him. Her heart leapt in a most unruly and unwelcome way at the sight of her husband, the man who coaxed her pleasure and seemed determined to win her trust.

He glanced up then and smiled, his pleasure at her appearance obvious, and Melissande could scarce take a breath.

She told herself that she was a fool, as much a fool as Berthe, who lifted her chin at Bayard's smile. They had lived without men for too long, it was clear.

She headed for the kitchen to review the inventory, curtseying to her husband as she passed through the hall, even as she strove to envision a menu for the coming days.

They had need of meat, to be sure.

Who could she send to hunt?

It was clear to Quinn that Melissande had become a lady of ice once again. Her gaze was steady and cool when she descended to the hall and he was struck by how little similarity there was between her composure outside of the marriage bed and her playful manner within it. He knew which version of his lady wife he preferred. When she responded to his touch, when her hair was unbound, she seemed more vividly alive and more honest to him. When her hair was braided back and hidden beneath her veil, her lips drawn to a resolute line, she might have been a stranger—a queen or an abbess—and her thoughts were impossible for him to read.

When she curtseyed before him, as she had this morning in the hall, he could scarce believe she was the same woman who met him touch for touch, much less that he might conquer her heart.

The villeins knew little of import, though it was clear they were glad to have the opportunity to speak with him. Quinn was reminded of the gathering of information before battles in foreign lands—one never knew when there might be a detail that provided some illumination.

He did not see Melissande again until he mounted Fortitude in the bailey and she appeared with a stirrup cup. It was filled to the brim with spiced wine and was in itself a fine vessel of silver. She brought it to him first and he bent from the saddle to sip of it.

'Twas then he saw the shadow in her gaze.

"What is amiss?" he murmured before touching his lips to the cup.

Her gaze flicked but she shook her head minutely. "I will see it resolved."

Quinn reached for the cup, closing his gloved hand over hers. "Tell me," he murmured.

She eyed him for a moment, then nodded. "We have need of meat," she confessed quietly. "I do not know who to send to hunt."

"No one," Quinn replied, more sharply than he had intended. He still was uncertain who could be trusted in the holding and who should not be. "I have ordered the gates to be kept closed."

Her eyes widened and he knew she had forgotten this detail. She frowned. "But your guests..."

Was she truly only concerned with the administration of Annossy and the welfare of his guests? Quinn was well aware that Gaultier lingered in the bailey and feared that his clever lady might have some scheme to be rid of him. More than one unwanted husband had met his demise at the hunt, presumably by accident. Surely she would not, but once he had the thought, it was not readily dismissed.

"I will see the matter resolved myself," he said, wondering how it might be done. "No one leaves Annossy in my absence, my lady." He let his gaze bore into hers. "No one."

She dropped her gaze and curtseyed, but not before he saw the flash of her eyes. "Aye, my lord," she said, apparently demure, but Quinn could not silence his newfound doubts.

Bayard, Lothair, Niall and Amaury all were in their saddles, ready to ride out with him to the mill. He wanted and needed their protection and expertise, though he wondered if one should remain behind. Annossy was well-defended, though—so long as the gates remained closed. And the boys were within the walls. He did not doubt they would keep their eyes open and bring any tales to him upon his return.

Still, he could not silence his doubts.

When they rode out, Quinn looked back to ensure that the gates were closed. His last glimpse was of Melissande, still holding the empty stirrup cup, with Gaultier close by her side.

It was not the most reassuring sight and his mood turned grim.

CHAPTER TEN

Melissande did not have to seek out Gaultier. He was at her elbow before Quinn and his party had even passed through the gates. She felt a twinge of guilt when Quinn glanced back, but reminded herself that she had done no improper deed. She had shown her husband the respect due to him as Lord d'Annossy.

He could not know the doubts in her heart.

Gaultier indicated that the gates should be secured, just as Quinn had decreed, then bent to murmur to her. "My lady, I would confer with you in private, at your leisure."

"In private?" Melissande echoed, turning to consider the knight.

He frowned, his gaze flicking over the bailey. "I would not have my meaning misconstrued, my lady, but I am concerned." He met her gaze steadily and she nodded.

"I wished to speak with you, as well, Gaultier." She indicated the hall. "Perhaps in my father's favored chamber, by the hall." Louis met her as soon as she entered the hall, a question in his eyes. "My lord husband has been told of the larder," she told him, for they had discussed the details that morning. "He insists that no one shall leave Annossy in his absence." She did not add that Quinn meant to try to solve the lack of meat, for she could not imagine how he would have the time to hunt. She also did not know of his skill in the pursuit of game. The hunt was somewhat different than war. She smiled for Louis when he looked skeptical. "He has told me, Louis, that his companions will be grateful of whatever is offered, for they have shared times of shortage together."

"Of course, my lady," Louis said with a bow, his skepticism remaining. "Perhaps a fortifying soup with each meal?"

"A most excellent suggestion, Louis." She gestured to the small room adjacent to the hall. "Gaultier and I will confer for a moment. Please see that we are not disturbed."

Louis, to her surprise, flicked a glance at the Captain of the Guard that was not filled with approval. Perhaps there was another soul whose counsel she should seek.

"I thank you, my lady, for your trust," Gaultier said when they were closeted together. Though Melissande retreated around the large table that nigh filled that chamber, she felt keenly aware that Gaultier was both larger than she and armed.

Quinn's suggestion that the other knight had harbored ambitions could not be pushed from her thoughts.

She remained standing herself, not wanting the further disadvantage of taking a seat. "I had the impression, Gaultier, that you might know something of my lord husband or his reputation when he arrived yesterday. If so, I would invite you to share it with me."

"In confidence?"

"Aye."

"I would not have the man made Lord d'Annossy think me disloyal," he said, some bitterness in his tone.

"He will not know of it. I give you my word."

Gaultier nodded. "I know naught of Quinn de Sayerne himself, my lady, though I found his arrival as your lord husband most astonishing."

"Aye?"

"Aye. Have you not always advised me that Jerome de Sayerne meant to unite Annossy with Sayerne? Annossy has been plagued by brigands upon her borders both before and after Jerome's death, which implies that Jerome himself was not the villain responsible—or not the sole one."

Melissande waited, for this thinking was much like her own.

"And who should be better allied with Jerome than his son and heir?" Gaultier raised a hand. "Here he is, returned. The timing cannot be a coincidence..."

"Tulley summoned him from the Holy Land," Melissande supplied.

Gaultier's eyes widened. "Then perhaps Jerome's ally was Tulley!"

"Nay!"

"Think of it, my lady. Your family has held Annossy for generations and are much respected in the region. And since your father's demise, Tulley has held Annossy's seal. Should Tulley wish to grant the holding to another, there would have been a hue and cry of the injustice of his choice. He could not so deny tradition, not without protest within his demesne." He tapped a fingertip upon the table. "So, he saw you wed to his choice to govern both Annossy and Sayerne. I fear this to be a scheme, my lady, one which will not end well for you or Annossy."

"Nay!" Melissande protested. "Tulley would not so betray me."

But would he not? She was not so certain of her overlord's support as she would like to be.

"Tulley will see his own advantage defended at any price," Gaultier insisted. "He said as much to me when he dispatched me here." He fell silent and took a deep breath. "To be sure, my lady, I feared that he had a scheme even then. Tulley would not share the details, but told me that my tenure at Annossy would not be a long one."

Melissande sat down then, recalling that Tulley had sent word to Quinn in the East. That must have been around the same time that Gaultier had been sent to her. That could only mean that the Captain of the Guard had been sent to protect the prize intended for Quinn upon his return.

"I see that you are startled, my lady, and I apologize for any responsibility for that on my part. Tulley bade me pledge not to tell you as much, and truly, it was simple to make such a vow when I had never met you or been to Annossy." He bowed his head. "But in my time here, I have come to respect you greatly as Lady d'Annossy and to feel great fondness for this holding." He lifted his gaze to hers and the heat in his gaze made Melissande swallow. "I would pledge my blade to you and you alone, my lady, and remain your loyal knight regardless of what Lord de Tulley—or even your lord husband—commands."

Although Melissande was touched by his words, she shook her head. "You must not so betray your own word, Gaultier," she said. "You have vowed to serve Tulley and my lord husband. Do not make a pledge that might compel you to break word with either of them." She managed to smile. "I, too, serve my lord husband."

"But should you, my lady?" Gaultier whispered. "Or does your passion for duty only lead you along the path that will serve them both best?"

"I must do my duty, Gaultier, as must you."

He shook his head, discontent. "You did not see them last night," he whispered. "His companions separated and went through all the keep, as if by design. Do you think it a coincidence that they all should arrive at the same time? It is as if they had a scheme. That dark-haired one, Amaury, was in the inventory and the stores, counting and assessing. If he could have gained access to the treasury, he would have tallied it all. I would wager that he could put a value upon all within these walls within a *denier* or two. He spoke to Louis as if to make an alliance with him. The other one, the closer companion, he was in the kitchens, talking to all the servants. He made friends with cook and saucier, and with your maid, my lady."

"Bayard," she whispered.

"He would either turn her against you or use her as his spy. No doubt she had tales to share with you this morn as a result of that conversation."

Melissande thought of Berthe's confession of admiration for Bayard—and her questions about them living at Sayerne. Her heart chilled.

"They are men of war, my lady, and they seek to learn your every weakness, so that when they attack, you have no chance to defend yourself."

"But why would my lord husband attack me?"

"To gain your prize. The foreign one—Niall, I think is his name—was in the armory. He reviewed the guard and their weapons, and spoke with the smith for a long time. The tall one, Lothair, walked the perimeter of the walls. He spoke to those in the village, apparently befriending them and advising them about the pledge of fealty, but he gathered tidings as well. And I thought it was all for naught, for the lord had retired to the solar with you." Gaultier's eyes narrowed and his voice dropped to a hiss. "But then he returned to the hall alone, my lady, and dismissed all but his comrades. They conferred together for long hours, whispering around the board, surrendering all they had learned to him that he might best create his plan."

It was true. Melissande had not expected Quinn to leave the solar.

Her mouth went dry that he had come to their bed so late that she had not heard him. She suspected that if she had not been so willing, she might have been seduced all the same. Tulley had set a price upon Sayerne of an heir, after all.

Gaultier pushed his hand through his hair. "And then this morning, he and all his fellows ride out to the mill, while we are forbidden to depart for any reason. I cannot even lead a hunt to ensure that there is meat at the board this night!" He stepped toward her, eyes blazing. "Why does he so fear your departure from your own abode, my lady? You are as good as a captive here, and I would know why. Does he fear you will deny him?"

"I cannot. We are wed and Tulley ensured the match was consummated." Melissande shook her head. "But the worst I might do is flee to Tulley, and you already say they are in league."

"He is Jerome's son, my lady. What if he means to cheat Tulley?"

"How?"

"I cannot say. Perhaps he has ambitions for all of Tulley." Gaultier wagged a finger at her. "And if there is any soul in this realm sufficiently clever to see the truth of his ambition, it would be you, my lady. Were I such a villain, I would see you confined as well." He took a deep breath as Melissande struggled with these assertions.

As much as she might have expected otherwise, she was inclined to take Quinn's side.

Was she a fool to trust him? Or were her instincts correct?

"I should watch my surroundings in your place, my lady," Gaultier said grimly. "I shall guard your person when I can, but in the solar, you must defend yourself."

"What is this?" Melissande asked in confusion.

"If you died, my lady, Annossy would remain your husband's holding and he would be free to wed whosoever he chose." He lifted a dark brow, his eyes gleaming. "Perhaps a man held so high in Tulley's favor might even wed Tulley's niece."

And upon Tulley's demise, the entire holding would fall to that man's hand.

Surely it could not be so.

Melissande felt suddenly cold. She forced herself to stand and to speak calmly. "I thank you for your counsel, Gaultier, and would suggest that you ensure the gates are kept closed, as instructed by my lord husband."

"Aye, my lady," he said and bowed before her. He placed a sheathed dagger on the table then and swallowed. "If you will permit me to grant you a small token of my esteem, my lady. This is a fine small blade, sharpened well. If you would keep it upon your person, I should be relieved."

Melissande eyed the weapon, which had a jeweled scabbard. The entirety of it was less than the length of her hand. "It is too rich..." she began to protest but he interrupted her.

"Of greater import, it was a gift from my aunt when my uncle bestowed my spurs and is a lady's blade," Gaultier said, smiling slightly in reminiscence. "She bade me surrender it to a lady I admired beyond all others, and said that it would serve the recipient well."

"I cannot accept such a gift, Gaultier. I am wedded."

"And I am fearful. Accept the loan of it, my lady, if you will not take it outright."

Melissande eyed the blade. In truth, she was troubled by Gaultier's confession and she carried only a small eating blade which was not very sharp. She knew she should not accept the token, but she appreciated that Gaultier showed such concern for her welfare.

He had pledged his service to her first, after all, and this choice was a reflection of that.

"I thank you, Gaultier," she said and took the blade, liking the weight of it in her hand. It was small enough that she could bind it to her garter by day, and hide it in the bed by night. "I will return it to you when all is well."

Quinn rode with Amaury beside him, having inviting his friend to share his observations and thoughts about Annossy and its administration. It was another fine clear day, though the wind had a bite. The path to the mill wound uphill from the gates of Annossy, away from the village and the fields.

"An interesting choice of site," Amaury said as they left the keep behind.

"Why would they choose such a distant location for the mill?" Quinn asked. "I had thought it would be much closer to the keep." Sayerne's mill was in the village itself.

"I would, as well," Amaury agreed. "I will guess that the river flows faster and more reliably where the mill is located."

"The stream that flows into Annossy's moat and around the village is on flatter ground," Quinn said, thinking of the one at Sayerne. "And it might freeze during some winters."

"Aye, if the ice is not broken. On the other hand, the land might be too rocky and the site of the mill too far from the main road to make a good location for the keep." Amaury shrugged. "If naught else, the placement of the mill at such a distance hints that the valley has been free of brigands in the past."

"True enough," Quinn said. He studied the forest as they went, noting how the path from keep to mill was wide enough for a cart. The trees grew close to the road, and their growth was dense, leaving the forest full of shadows. He glanced back and was glad the road was straight, at least. A party would be able to see trouble along its length, but not to anticipate bandits hidden in the forest close beside the road. "I think I will have the way widened in the summer," he said. "If the trees were cut back for even three paces on either side, the road would be safer."

"And there would be firewood aplenty," Amaury agreed.

"How would you see it done?" Quinn asked.

Amaury pursed his lips. "It is a good length of road and will require a fair measure of labor. I would wish for the villeins to see the merit of the task and undertake it willingly."

"Aye," Quinn agreed. "I expect it would be best to wait until the crops were planted in the spring and the fields tilled."

"Indeed. Then I would declare my desire to see the way widened and explain that it is for the safety of all, and invite those villeins who help in the endeavor to keep a share of the wood." Amaury nodded. "I would keep perhaps a third of it, for construction, repairs and firewood in the keep, then let them share the rest." He gave Quinn a nod. "With winters this cold, I would wager that they will be glad of such a store of fuel."

"Where would they get it now?" Quinn asked.

"They must forage for dead wood in the forest. The new wood will have to be left to dry for a year or two, but it will be welcome, all the same."

Quinn nodded agreement.

"It is good to verify tradition in a holding that is unfamiliar," Amaury advised. "Ask before you act. People can have curious customs, and tend to be most offended when they are not respected, even if it is inadvertent."

"You speak aright. I will ask Louis for his counsel."

Amaury gave him a quelling glance. "You have a closer source of local custom than that," he said and Quinn realized he had not considered asking Melissande.

"I do not wish to trouble my lady wife with such matters. It is my responsibility, is it not?"

Amaury shook his head. "But your lady is skilled in matters of administration, Quinn, and I have to think that she enjoys the challenge. If you do not join ways with her, she may feel slighted. I would not surrender such an ally readily."

Quinn recalled how Melissande had been surprised and then interested when they had speculated upon Gaultier's response to his own arrival. Was it possible that there was another path to her heart, through conversation about Annossy? Quinn was more than prepared to discover the truth of it.

They reached the mill quickly for it was not overly distant and the horses were well-rested.

Annossy's mill was a prosperous one, the building sufficiently extensive to reveal that truth. Its location was ideal for its work, for the stream that flowed down the mountain to join the Helva was lively, even at this time of year. The water splashed and raced, a fine mist rising above the water.

The forest was thick on both sides of the stream and Quinn eyed the imposing face of the mountain from which the water originated. The peaks were wreathed in mist from this vantage but what he could discern was still white with snow. There was a ford just downstream from the mill, where rocks were scattered across the river's width. The dividing of the waters for the mill widened the river and tamed it somewhat, making it more shallow. The forest, Quinn was certain, provided a haven for the bandits.

He surveyed the course down the stream to the Helva and the major road that could be found there. It would be difficult for the bandits to hide in the valley itself. He pivoted and looked at the mountain again, wondering if there was a path.

The men-at-arms assigned to defend the mill greeted Quinn and his party first. Jean and Robert they were, both dark-haired and dark-eyed, a little older and a little more plump that Quinn might have thought ideal. There was a complacency about them that displeased him, but he strove to overcome his first impression.

They told of how the bandits had assaulted them before the dawn, overcome them both in the stables and bound them. When they continued to battle, they were each struck on the head and left unconscious. By the time they awakened and freed themselves, the thieves were gone.

Quinn was skeptical of this tale and he saw a similar response in Bayard's eyes. Though his companion appeared to be impassive, his eyes flicked in a familiar way. "Kudon," he said to Quinn beneath his breath and Quinn nodded.

He had been reminded of that very deception. Kudon was a

small village they had been assigned to defend in the Latin Kingdoms, one plagued by thieves that were said to have come from outside—perhaps even from the Saracen enemy—but had proven to be knights charged with defending the village themselves.

When the horses had been tethered, Quinn proceeded to the mill itself, his companions fast behind him. The miller and his wife stood before the portal, and bowed deeply before him. They were older, their faces lined from sun and years, and clearly robust. The miller was a large man and muscled, while his wife was sturdy. The boy with them looked to be ten summers of age, though Quinn was not certain he could be their son given the wife's age. There was an integrity about them that Quinn recognized and welcomed.

"Our grandson," the miller's wife said, giving him a nudge so that he bowed before the new lord. "We had two sons, my lord, and the younger apprenticed to the smith in Annossy." She touched the boy's shoulder. "Our older son was injured in the first attack by the brigands and died of his wounds."

"And his wife?"

The miller's wife smiled sadly. "She died bringing her son to light."

"I am most sorry," Quinn said, feeling that his expression of sympathy was rough. Melissande would have known better what to say, but the miller's wife nodded and blinked back her tears. "Tell me your son's name and I will make his acquaintance in the village."

She smiled then. "He and his wife have a boy and a girl, my lord, but they are very young." Her husband nudged her then and she fell silent so suddenly that Quinn knew she tended to be fulsome in discussion of her grandchildren.

"I wager your pride in them is well-deserved," he said and she flushed pink. "Now tell me of this assault."

The miller told Quinn of how they had been awakened by the hooded thieves and their grandson had been secured in an empty sack from grain. He leaned forward to show Quinn the bump upon the back of his head and Lothair stepped forward to assess the damage. They had been bound, hand and foot, then the fiends had threatened to kill the wife if the miller did not reveal the location of the treasury.

The pair were still frightened, which was only reasonable. Lothair offered a salve for the torn flesh upon their wrists and ankles, as Quinn walked the site with the miller, listening to his tale.

"Were the villains not pursued?" he asked Jean and Robert.

"They had vanished by the time we freed ourselves," one insisted.

"And it is folly to ride into the forest alone," said the other.

Quinn was not impressed with their dedication to their task. Indeed, his sense of distrust was so strong that he wondered if they were in the employ of the thieves.

He had always trusted his instincts and would do as much in this matter, as well.

"How many were there?" he asked the miller.

That man grimaced. "I saw two, but I thought there might have been a third."

Quinn sent Lothair and Niall to search the surrounding area, despite the protest of the men-at-arms that it was too late to find any detail. He ignored that and spoke to the miller. "Would you show me the mill? It looks most fine."

He entered the mill with Bayard and Amaury, the two men-at-arms following behind. There was dust yet in the air and the millstone was grinding, sacks of grain still waiting to be ground. Quinn asked about the annual schedule, the volume of grain, the tithes, and the miller was clearly glad to explain. Quinn glanced periodically at Amaury who nodded approval of these details. Finally, the miller showed the damage done to the stores by the bandits. Both grain and flour had been spilled and fouled with mud. He also showed the hidden treasury that he had been compelled to reveal, and expressed his dismay at the loss of his coin.

This practice too, Quinn thought, showed that the area had been safe for many years. "Something must change if Annossy's border and interest is to be defended," he said. "It is unacceptable that you and your wife should be threatened in your own home."

"Aye, sir. I am glad that you agree." The miller bowed. "Although we are indebted to the Lady Melissande for sending us two guards."

"Was there a guard before?"

"My son, my lord, then no other."

Quinn did not approve of that. "Did the Captain of the Guard not see fit to ensure your defense?"

The miller dropped his gaze. "He believed that after we had been robbed once, there would not be another attack."

Bayard and Quinn exchanged a quick glance, and Quinn knew he was not alone in his suspicions.

"You have another treasury," Amaury suggested quietly and the miller's eyes widened with shock.

He stammered a protest, but Quinn could see the truth.

"Millers always do," Amaury continued, his conviction making Quinn aware yet again of how little he knew of such matters.

The miller bowed his head in silent agreement.

"Do the thieves know of it?" Quinn asked.

"Who can say, my lord?"

"They might guess, as Amaury did," Bayard noted.

"Indeed," Quinn said.

"You cannot think they will return?" the miller asked in dismay. "Surely not thrice in one season?"

"I see no reason why they would not," Quinn said, not wanting to deceive the miller. "But this time, we shall be prepared for them. If we are wrong, then I will not regret it."

"Nor I, sir."

"We must lay in stores for a great bonfire this day, and stack it that it might be lit on a whim. I will post a sentry at Annossy to watch for the fire, and if it burns, we will ride immediately to your defense."

Quinn gestured to Lothair and Niall as they returned. "These are my comrades, who fought by my side in Palestine against the infidels. I would trust them with my life, and so I often have." The miller and his wife eyed the two knights, who did look most formidable. "I leave them to defend you."

"But we are here to defend the mill," one of the men-at-arms protested.

"No longer," Quinn said with resolve. "You will return to Annossy."

"But the Captain of the Guard entrusted us with this task," protested the other.

"We take our orders only from Gaultier," said the first."

"That has changed," Quinn said with soft heat and the second man flushed. They both dropped their gazes. "I am now Lord d'Annossy. I instruct you to return to Annossy and serve in its defense now."

The first warrior's expression turned mutinous and he spoke tightly. "Aye, my lord."

Quinn turned to face him fully, removed his glove, and extended his hand. "I would have you pledge fealty now, before you return to Annossy."

The pair hesitated only a moment but did exchange a glance before stepping forward. Each dropped to one knee and bowing his head before Quinn. He took their vow of service but did not believe it was heartfelt. Perhaps they liked this assignment far from their superior's eye. Perhaps the miller's wife was a good cook. They both appeared to be a little more plump that Quinn thought a fighting man should be.

Or perhaps they knew more of the raids than they chose to admit. They might even be in league with the brigands. Quinn knew only that he could not dismiss his sense that they were deceptive.

He gestured after they had made their pledge and Bayard led them to the task of laying the wood for the signal fire.

The miller took his wife's hand when they were gone, his agitation clear. "I pray you would ride quickly if that fire is lit, sir."

"Aye, with all haste. And now one choice is yours alone to make." Quinn dropped his voice as he conferred with the miller and his wife. "We would have greater chance of success if all believe that the sole change is the arrival of my men and the laid fire."

"Aye, sir."

"That would mean that you continue with your established

routine."

"And that I remain here, as well as our grandson," the miller's wife said, seeing his import before her husband.

"I cannot command you to do as much," Quinn said. "For there is peril in the choice. It must be your own."

"Did you kill infidels in Palestine, sir?" that woman demanded.

"Many of them, and I saw many of our own killed, as well."

"I would expect you saw much courage there."

Quinn smiled. "And fear, too. Such a war brings out the best and the worst in all involved, I suspect."

"We are at war here, sir," she said. "The stakes are not so high as the recapture of Jerusalem, but I would see these villains caught and put to justice."

"As would I."

"Your scheme would be more likely to succeed if I remained?"

"I believe as much."

Her lips tightened. "Then I will stay, my lord. And I will stand vigil with my husband."

Quinn smiled. "I thank you for such courage."

"This is our home, sir. We defend what is our own." She nodded at Lothair. "If you are willing to teach me, sir, I would learn some of your skill while you are here."

Lothair nodded. "That distance to Annossy can be too much if there is illness. We shall talk about the healing plants and their uses."

The miller's wife beamed with satisfaction. "I knew all would be well when the Lady Melissande took a husband," she said with a nod. "There were others who said she should choose with greater haste, but her family have always ensured the welfare of those beneath their hand."

"And I will see that tradition continued," Quinn vowed, to their obvious satisfaction. "And what of your grandson? Would you keep him here or have us escort him back to Annossy?"

"He could remain with Xavier in the village," the miller said.

"Let him choose," his wife said. "He knows the risk and I would be glad of his companionship, but the choice must be his. Our new lord is wise in this matter."

Quinn turned to the boy who nodded with a resolve that showed his resemblance to his grandmother. "I will stay, sir."

Quinn nodded approval of that. "Have you a knife?"

The boy nodded and produced it. It was a better blade than Quinn had feared it might be.

"Niall will instruct you in its use for defense while he is here," he offered.

"Like a knight's training, sir!"

Quinn smiled. "Not quite, but such skill as he can teach you will be of use no matter what your trade."

The miller nodded approval, then took his wife's hand and dropped to his knees.

"Let us pledge our fealty to the new Lord d'Annossy," he said. His wife nodded and followed suit, and Quinn looked up in time to see Amaury's nod of approval.

He would master this responsibility yet.

Niall had found tracks at the ford, hoof prints embedded in the frozen mud on the far bank. After the wood for the fire was laid and the miller supplied with tinder, Quinn made to take his leave. The knights conferred over the tracks and agreed that there was evidence of two or perhaps three palfreys. Two tracks were distinctive, one showing a nick from the shoe and a second in which a nail from the shoe made a larger impression. The tracks led into the forest on the far bank, then were lost in the undergrowth there.

"You see?" one of the men-at-arms said. "They escaped and, with horses, they could be in Rome by now."

Quinn doubted that this man had been through the Beauvoir pass of late, but he merely nodded agreement and surveyed the surroundings. There was no place within any proximity for horses to be stabled or bandits to be hidden.

Save the mill itself.

Kudon, indeed.

"I would ask you two to take the road back to Annossy, and seek any signs of horses on either side of that path," Quinn instructed the two men-at-arms. "Bayard will ride with you and explain my orders to Gaultier once you arrive at Annossy."

The pair exchanged glances, their suspicion clear.

Quinn kept his expression bland. "The day is so fine that I would hunt before returning to Annossy. Such a forest as this must be thick with game!"

"Deer and pheasant abound, sir," supplied Robert.

"Ah! How I have missed the hunt," Quinn lied. "We have neither beaters nor dogs, Amaury, but I say we shall make a fine day of it all the same."

"Indeed," Amaury agreed with enthusiasm and they laughed together as if carefree.

Bayard led the pair toward Annossy, and Quinn spoke quickly to his fellows, telling them of Kudon.

"You think the villains might have circled back to the mill?" Amaury asked when they were alone.

"I cannot see where else three horses could hide."

"Nor I," Lothair said. "And that pair know more than they have confessed. You are wise to keep a closer eye upon them."

"Better yet, I may dismiss them from service, should I find an excuse," Quinn said. "I would be curious to know who they might tell of whatever they know."

"And what of that second treasury?" Niall asked.

"When they are long gone, we shall leave a token within it," Quinn said softly and Amaury laughed. "This task of administration is not so different from making war."

"Not when there is a villain or a spy at loose," Amaury agreed. Niall and Lothair returned to the mill, intent upon seeing all set to rights. Amaury gestured down the river toward the bridge. "Let us look for tracks."

"Then a deer, if we can manage it. I see you brought your crossbow."

Amaury smiled. "There is not so much meat in the larder. I thought to be a good guest, if my lord host were inclined to hunt."

"Melissande told me as much this morn, but it was when she brought the stirrup cup. I did not fetch a crossbow."

Amaury bowed and surrendered the weapon. "Your holding, Quinn, so you must loose the first bolt."

"More than that, I would be of aid in seeing Annossy well-supplied."

"You would win your lady's favor, whatever the price," Amaury teased.

"Can you blame me? She is my lady wife and her happiness is my sole goal."

"You should tell her as much," the other knight advised.

"I fear she would not believe me," Quinn said. "Nay, I would tempt her affection with deeds not words."

Amaury nodded and glanced back toward the mill. Bayard and the men-at-arms were out of sight. They two rode down the hill on opposite sides of the river, keeping their horses well back from the flowing water. "Here," Amaury said, pointing to the ground at the same time that Quinn pointed down on the mill side of the river.

The hoof prints were evident on both banks, the steeds having gone down the river on the far side and returned on the side where the mill stood. Amaury and Quinn followed the returning tracks into the forest, lost them again, then rode back toward the mill slowly. Quinn dismounted outside the small barn beside the mill and crouched down, considering the tracks left by the three horses that had left for Annossy. There was fresh mud there and new tracks from the palfreys of the men-at-arms.

He indicated a nick in the shoe of one horse and the mark of a protruding nail in another print, then met Amaury's gaze. The other knight nodded. The tracks were the same.

"You have your brigands," Amaury murmured.

"But not their leader," Quinn said. "There might well have been three. Let us speak to the miller for a moment before we ride to hunt."

CHAPTER ELEVEN

Melissande could not give credence to Gaultier's accusation.

She might not have wed Quinn of her own accord, but she could not believe that he would contrive such a wicked scheme. She was not even certain he had spoken to Heloise before the wedding feast, and he might not have even known that Tulley had a niece. As vexed as he had been with her, he had never injured her. Indeed, he had been gentle, and had introduced her to the marital debt with much patience. She could not imagine that he meant to ensure her demise.

It could have been readily done by now, if so.

It was curious that she already possessed such a strong conviction of Quinn's sense of honor and his reliability. Truly, if he had not been Jerome's son, she might have chosen him of her own accord.

There was a startling realization.

Melissande sat down hard in the great hall to consider how readily she abandoned the truths that she knew. Was she detecting the truth of her new husband, or was he deceiving her with great skill?

Berthe came bustling down the stairs in that moment, much her usual self in the knights' absence. "Look, my lady!" she cried, shaking out a length of blue cloth.

Melissande was glad to be sitting down for the realization of what her maid carried was like a knife to her heart.

It was her father's tabard, embroidered with the insignia of Annossy. The wool was blue of deepest sapphire and Melissande recalled her mother fussing over the hue in the market at Tulley, then choosing the deepest blue. Berthe came and spread it proudly on Melissande's lap and she fingered it, with tears in her eyes. Her mother had embroidered the insignia and Melissande had been entrusted with the hem.

She had seen the tabard last when her father had died at the board, not three paces from where she sat in this moment.

"I thought he was buried in it," she managed to say.

Berthe shook her head. "I remember the priest thought it wasteful for the cloth is good and he said there would be a new Lord d'Annossy. He ordered the tabard removed before the coffin was sealed."

"I do not recall that detail." Melissande looked up at her maid, who smiled.

"Because you did not know, my lady," she said gently. "Louis took charge of all in those few days when you mourned your father, as was good and right. You could not have found a better man to trust with your responsibilities." She shook out the tabard. "And there has not been a single moth! There is a sign that it was meant to be worn again."

"Or that the sweet woodruff has been placed in the trunk."

"Aye." Berthe held up the garment. "Do you think it broad enough for Lord Quinn's shoulders?"

"Perhaps," Melissande said. "There is but one way to know."

"Indeed!" Berthe beckoned toward the stairs and the small fair squire, Michel, came down, carrying another burden. "I asked for his aid and his counsel as to Lord Quinn's requirements. He is a good boy," she whispered to Melissande.

Michel carried another length of wool and Melissande recognized it as well. It was the fur-lined cloak that her father had worn, of generous cut and heavy wool. Its hue was deep blue, as well, and the fur lining was silver miniver.

"Still in good repair," Berthe said. "'Twould be a shame for Lord Quinn to be cold when there is no need."

"Indeed," Melissande said, though she felt as if the breath had been stolen from her lungs. "I suppose there are chemises and chausses, as well."

Michel nodded. "The chemises will be most welcome, my lady, if you can spare them. Lord Quinn possesses only two plus the one granted to him by Lord Tulley. It is a bit small and the other two are much mended."

"Then take them, of course."

"Aye, my lady." He bowed and smiled, then at Berthe's nod, returned to the solar.

And so, more of her father's possessions were claimed by Quinn. Melissande knew she should not place too much value on old garments that could be put to use. They were only cloth, though they carried many memories for her.

"The hem is torn," she said, fingering the tabard. "If you will fetch my sewing needles, I can mend it before my lord husband's return."

"Of course, my lady," Berthe said with approval.

Melissande's heart sank. This would be her life. Waiting for her husband, plying her needle and doing as she was bidden.

She supposed it would be worse if she did not conceive.

Gaultier could not be right about Quinn's intentions.

There was a sound of horses stamping in the bailey and the maid's head snapped up, her attention seized by the rumble of men's voices. Melissande watched as one voice became clear, then Bayard strode into the hall, his expression grim, with two men-at-arms fast behind him.

It was the two men that Gaultier had sent to defend the mill.

What was this?

Berthe's eyes lit and she remained at Melissande's side as the knight approached. He spared the maid no more than a glance, then bowed before Melissande. "My lady, my lord Quinn bids me tell you that all is well at the mill and he has ridden to hunt. He will return as soon as possible."

Melissande stood, her gaze flicking to the two men-at-arms

standing behind Bayard. "But how can all be well?" she asked. "These are the men assigned to guard the mill."

"My lord Quinn has chosen to leave two of his comrades there instead," Bayard said. "Niall and Lothair will see to the mill's defense now."

One of the men-at-arms inhaled sharply and the lips of the other had drawn to a thin line. It was clear that they did not approve of their lord's choice. She did not have to look for Gaultier: he had stepped into the hall, his expression dark and his arms folded across his chest. She met Bayard's gaze and found his attention locked upon her, his eyes seeming even darker than she knew them to be.

This was a test of her loyalty to her husband's command. She did not doubt that her response would be reported to Quinn in detail.

Melissande inclined her head, hiding the rebellion that rose hot within her. She would tell Quinn her opinion of this in private. "I am glad to hear that my lord husband has had such success on this day and eagerly await his return." She sat down, arranging her skirts, and picked up the tabard to mend it. "I can only assume that you have instructions for Gaultier regarding these men's duties now that they are returned to Annossy?"

"Aye, my lady," Bayard said with approval.

"Then I grant you leave to deliver them and thank you for the courtesy of bearing me tidings." It took all within Melissande not to ask more questions of Quinn's plans, but she reminded herself that the defense of the holding was the lord's responsibility.

Bayard bowed and retreated, the men behind him. Gaultier gave her an intent look, which she ignored, then spun to follow the three of them with quick steps.

"Audacity," Berthe whispered though Melissande did not know whether she meant Bayard's message to her or his refusal to acknowledge her presence. She was staring after the men, bright spots of color burning in her cheeks, and her fists were clenched at her sides.

Perhaps Melissande did know what infuriated her maid.

"Do you remember where I left my embroidery needles?" she

asked pointedly. "This hem should be mended before my lord's return."

Berthe spun away, then stamped up the stairs. Her passage was audible the entire way to the solar and back again, though her temper might have been slightly improved by her return.

"A lantern, if you please," Melissande said quietly when the maid might have said more. The hall was falling dark as it always did after noon, for the rays of the afternoon sun did not come through the few windows. Berthe hastened to fetch a lantern and had the boys stir up the fire as Melissande settled to her mending.

Quinn had replaced the men assigned by Gaultier with his own comrades. That was just as Gaultier had predicted. He might simply intend to push her aside and take her place in the administration of Annossy. That would be sufficiently harsh to trouble Melissande. She frowned and wondered what course she could possibly take that would both fulfill her obligations as her father's daughter and Quinn's wife.

All paths led back to the conception of a child.

But what would she sacrifice herself if she surrendered repeatedly to Quinn's touch? She had no desire to become an ornament or a brood mare or wanton who hungered for her husband's attention abed. She scowled at the cloth and worked fiercely, stabbing her finger more than once due to her lack of expertise.

If this was to be her life, she had best become accustomed to it.

She did not, however, have to like it.

The shadows were longer when there was a roar of greeting in the bailey and the sound of horses once more. Melissande rose to her feet and smoothed her skirt, her heart skipping at the sound of Quinn's voice. He laughed aloud and she found her lips curving, so complete was the spell he had cast upon her.

Intrigued by what might make her husband so merry, she left the board and went to the portal. Her breath caught at the sight of Quinn, his eyes flashing gold fire as he laughed. He had a deer slung over the back of his saddle, while Amaury had two bunches of pheasants bound to his. Both destriers' nostrils were flaring, but the creatures held their ground, more accustomed to the scent of blood than was often the case with horses. Louis was clapping his hands, calling for boys from the kitchen to take the kill, and it was clear that Quinn had secured his popularity with this deed. Someone jested at the size of the stag he had felled and Quinn turned to help remove it from behind the saddle.

He looked so vital and masculine, so at ease and powerful, that Melissande could not tear her gaze away from him. Indeed, her mouth went dry and she tingled anew in recollection of what they had done abed. She had become hungry for his touch and, worse, she could not regret it.

Amaury held up a hand. "I confess that I but followed behind and gathered the kill," he said to those who gathered around. "'Twas Quinn who hunted with such success this day."

"He is too modest," Quinn protested, then surrendered a crossbow to his companion. "His aim is true as might be expected of one carrying such a fine weapon." There was a joyous shout at that and Quinn shook hands with those who pushed close to congratulate him. He laughed at a word from the smith, then asked that man a question. The smith indicated the miller's son on the far side of the bailey, the one who had become his apprentice, and she guessed that Quinn had spoken to the miller about his family.

Then he turned, as if he had felt her gaze upon him.

Melissande might have been struck to stone as his gaze locked with hers. Then Quinn smiled, a slow potent smile that heated her blood to a simmer, and she felt as if they were alone in the bailey.

"What else could I do?" he asked those surrounding him without looking away. "My lady wife told me this morn that we had need of meat for the board. Her will is as my command." And he bowed to her, his gesture making her cheeks heat and the villeins laugh.

Melissande could not think of a single word to say.

Quinn strode to her side, doffing his gloves, and paused beside her on the threshold. His eyes glittered and she fairly sensed his anticipation. "All is well at the mill?" she asked quietly, recalling their responsibilities.

"I believe it will be," he replied in kind.

"You dismissed the guards that Gaultier assigned to defend the mill."

"I did not trust them."

Melissande parted her lips then closed them again.

Quinn smiled. "And you do not trust me. You need not say the words to make your concerns known to me, my lady."

She felt herself flushing but could not be silent. "I do not know your intentions or much of your history..."

"And I did not know theirs. I learned long ago, my lady, to trust my instincts when it came to entrusting other men." He shook his head as she watched him. "There was something amiss, though I cannot name it. For the sake of the miller and his kin, I chose to be cautious. They have lost a son already."

"Aye." Melissande could not fault him for that choice, or for the sympathy in his gaze.

"But I would seek your advice in this matter, my lady."

"Mine?"

"Yours." His gaze clung to hers. "You know Annossy as no other, my lady," he murmured, his voice no less intent that his expression. "Have you not discerned that this is a challenge we must conquer together?"

"And then what?" she dared to ask.

Quinn smiled. "And then, we shall conquer another." He caught her hand in his and bent over it, kissing its back with a flourish.

Melissande felt a tumult inside herself and stepped back, retreating from his persuasive touch. "Berthe found my father's tabard and cloak," she said, her words falling in an uncharacteristic rush. "Perhaps both will suit you. And Michel has taken some of my father's chemises for you."

"I thank you, even though you will not meet my gaze when you speak of these garments." He spoke in that thoughtful tone and she found her cheeks burning again. Quinn touched her chin, compelling her to look up. He studied her and she feared he could see all her doubts.

"I did not realize the tabard was yet here," she admitted. "I thought it buried with him. And I forgot about the cloak."

"And you do not wish me to claim them?" he asked, no judgment in his tone.

"That would be impractical. They go to waste, left in a trunk."

Quinn shook his head. "They are the root of fond memory, Melissande," he said with soft heat. "I would not influence that."

It was curious to have him be the one who understood her emotions so well, but Melissande had been taught to avoid sentimentality. "You should wear them," she found herself saying. "'Tis only right."

"If you truly believe as much," he said and touched his lips to her brow. She shivered to her toes, but with desire instead of cold. Quinn smiled as he looked down at her. "Your eyes have darkened, my lady," he said lightly. "Is it possible that you will have an invitation for me this night?"

Melissande caught her breath and turned away, despising her own weakness. A kiss, a murmured confidence, a little understanding, and she was prepared to grant him all.

Perhaps women truly were weaker.

Quinn was not readily deterred. He claimed her elbow and entered the hall with her. Melissande found it reassuring to have his heat so close behind her back and was belatedly aware of how many watched them together. She led him to the board, where she had finished her mending, his touch making her feel skittish.

"I think the tabard will fit you, for my father was broad of shoulder as well, and the insignia is already upon it. The cloak will keep you warmer than that worn one you have..."

As had so often been his wont, he silenced her with a fingertip. This time, he planted it upon the back of her hand, where she touched the tabard. "Who did this needlework?" he asked softly.

Melissande took a breath. "My mother."

"And your father wore it?"

She nodded, then felt Quinn's arm slide around her waist. He stood behind her and bent so that his lips were close to her ear.

"Tell me," he invited.

"There is naught to tell. They are garments, no longer used. You should wear them."

There was silence for a long moment. "You must feel as if

everything that belonged to your father now comes to me."

She straightened but did not speak.

"You must feel that to be unjust."

"It is not my place to feel it to be just or unjust," she said, her voice more sharp than she had intended. "I am only a daughter, a mere woman and a vessel. My sole merit lies in my womb."

"Nay." Quinn spoke with such conviction that she had to look up. She found him watching her, his gaze warm, a smile of admiration upon his lips. "You have so much merit, my lady wife, that I fear I do not deserve to have your hand in mine. I am pledged to earn your regard, no matter what the price, for I know that if we were truly allies, naught would obstruct our path."

She stared into his eyes, wanting to believe him, then called herself a fool and turned away. "You say that to encourage an invitation," she accused and he laughed heartily.

Despite herself, she loved the sound.

"If that were true, it would be no flaw," he said. "Each night, I am more in your thrall, and I cannot regret it."

Melissande looked back in surprise and Quinn smiled at her. Her resistance to him wavered anew and she feared that she would capitulate completely—in less than three days. What fortitude did she possess to withstand a siege? Not much in the end.

"I have my courses," she lied on impulse, marveling all the while that he could make her forget herself so readily. "I would sleep alone this night."

"But you will not bar the door against me," Quinn said with conviction.

"What is this?"

He leaned closer and she saw again that resolve in his gaze. "I will watch the mill from that vantage point. Success against these brigands may rely upon it." He gave her a hot look, and once again, she was reminded of his military experience. She nodded, surprised that she was disappointed that he cited no other reason, and he turned away, calling to Louis.

"I will have a bath, if you please, Louis, in the stables with my comrades. I would not offend my lady wife at the board." He bowed to her again then crossed the hall with long strides. The boy

Michel followed him, speaking of clean chemises, and he smiled with affection as he listened to the boy.

"And how shall we have the pheasants tonight?" Louis asked Melissande. "I recommend we hang the venison so it can be roasted in a week or so. The birds, though, we might stew for the evening meal. Perhaps with peppercorns? The last of the wine would make an excellent sauce..."

Melissande was shaken.

Quinn could understand that well enough. Her father's seal in his hand and now his tabard, the one made by her mother, would be on Quinn's back, as well as his other garments. Quinn was sharing her bed in the solar and directing the defense of Annossy. Her list of responsibilities was diminishing with every passing hour, or so it must seem to her, and he knew she took great pride in what she could do, rather than how she looked.

He waited in the kitchen for Louis' return, and saw that man's eyes widen in surprise at the sight of him there.

"Sir! I sent word for your bath..."

"I know, Louis. You are most busy in this moment, but I would confer with you."

"Of course, my lord." Louis bowed, his manner expectant and prim.

Quinn led the older man to a quiet corner of the bustling kitchen. "I wish to ask your advice with regards to my lady wife."

"Indeed, sir?"

"She has administered Annossy on her own for some time."

"Since her father's demise, sir, and to be sure, she did a great deal in his lifetime, as well."

"And so, my arrival brings many changes to her life and routine."

Understanding dawned in Louis' eyes but he did not speak. He merely waited.

Quinn cleared his throat. "I should like to know which tasks were her favored ones, the better that I might ensure she keeps those responsibilities as we govern Annossy together. It is a fine holding, and I would see it continue to prosper. For that, I desire my lady's expertise."

Louis smiled. "She does not like the court obligation," he said. "Though she is fair. Her knowledge of the law and tradition of Annossy is complete, but I believe her heart is too kind for those times when justice must be harsh."

"Then perhaps I might invite her to advise me on those days, until I know Annossy's traditions."

Louis nodded approval. "She has a rare talent for keeping the ledgers. Her hand is neat and her sums are always perfect. I know she takes pride in a well-formatted and complete ledger."

"While I would not know where to begin," Quinn said. "In my trade, tallies are kept in one's head." He tapped his temple.

Louis smiled and nodded. "I imagine so, my lord. My lady is frugal but not cruel. I have always admired her balance in managing the coin of the keep, as well as the inventory of spices and wine. She has a gift for making less seem like more."

"There is a rare talent, as well as one I much admire."

"She also anticipates matters with great cleverness. Her father was much concerned with hospitality and she has inherited that from him."

Quinn nodded, recalling her concern about the evening meal upon their return. "I thank you, Louis, for your insight. Now I will know what to suggest to my lady wife." He would have turned away, but the older man cleared his throat. "Aye, Louis?"

The châtelain looked quickly over his shoulder. "I do not wish to be a person who tells tales of others, my lord, but I am concerned that there is one in this household who does not welcome your arrival. He is one who my lady trusts, and I would not have her misled."

"Of course not," Quinn said. He raised a brow, inviting more.

"The Captain of the Guard conferred with my lady at length this morning. I do not know what was said, for he ensured they could not be overheard, and my lady gave no sign of her own reaction."

Quinn could believe that. Melissande could hide her thoughts behind that veneer of ice if she so chose.

The châtelain frowned. "I am simply troubled by the timing. He went to her side as you were departing, sir, and spoke with her immediately afterward. She was agitated this morn, perhaps as a result."

"I thank you for your warning, Louis."

"I trust that you, sir, as my lady's husband will see her defended, but I am not so convinced of the intentions of others in that regard."

"I appreciate your concern, and will say naught of it." Quinn bowed then smiled. "And now, I think, my bath does summon me."

Gaultier. Already Quinn despised the man, yet he knew little of him.

Though it did not help that on the way to the stables, he spotted the two men-at-arms who had returned from the mill conferring with Gaultier in the bailey. Their manner was urgent and furtive. When one spotted him, he spoke to the others and the group quickly parted ways.

Aye, Quinn's suspicions needed to be buttressed. Perhaps he would send Bayard to Tulley with a missive and ask for more detail about Gaultier.

Tulley had sent the man to Annossy, after all. He must know more of Gaultier's credentials and alliances.

Lost.

Melissande was utterly lost.

Quinn looked splendid in the colors of Annossy, and he was attentive at the board that night. He laid his hand upon the back of her waist as he spoke to his comrades at the board, and he ensured that her opinion was invited in every discussion. He fed her the choicest morsels of the delicious pheasant stew that he had ensured was on the board, and she felt the warm weight of his gaze upon her. He asked her about Annossy, about the histories of the holding, about the names of the villeins, about their histories. He credited her with urging him to think of the welfare of all beneath his hand and she saw that he would excel at the task.

This warrior, so powerful and yet so gentle, would claim not just her body but her heart forever, and even knowing it was folly to surrender so readily, Melissande could not resist him. A veritable champion courted her favor, attending to her concerns with such resolve that she could not imagine he would ever do aught else. If it was a deception, it was a most potent one.

If all he seemed to be was his truth, if she could be certain of that, then Melissande knew she could surrender her heart to him forever.

But she was not certain.

And it infuriated her that she fulfilled every expectation of a woman's weakness. She surrendered to Quinn's allure and his touch and his warrantees—even knowing they might be lies—with annoying ease. Indeed, what had become of her resolve? What had become of her good sense? How could two nights abed so addle her wits?

She sat at the board, fuming as Quinn charmed all at Annossy, resenting his easy conquest and despising her own weakness even more.

He offered his hand to her when the darkness had fallen and the conversation was fading, then escorted her to the stairs. Melissande could fairly feel his expectation that they would lie together again, and her own body betrayed her with its tingle of enthusiasm. Where would Annossy and she be if he took all they offered then abandoned them?

Berthe gave a sigh as she watched them and Bayard rolled his eyes at the maid's reaction. Melissande shook her head even as Niall moved to be closer to Berthe. Bayard's brow darkened but he did not follow.

Quinn leaned closer as they climbed the stairs. "What troubles you?" he asked, his voice a low rumble that made Melissande yearn for the weight of his hands upon her skin.

"That Berthe and Bayard so provoke each other. What is his intention, do you think?"

"Bayard? I expect he has none but pleasure," Quinn replied easily.

As if that were not a problem.

Melissande stopped on the top step and her husband halted beside her. "You cannot mean that he will seduce my maid and leave her unwedded?" She kept her tone even with an effort, and was not reassured that Quinn seemed perplexed by her concern.

"His actions are not mine to govern," he said easily.

"Though he is in your hall and eats at your board?" Melissande demanded, her voice rising.

Quinn's expression turned wary. "Bayard is my comrade, not my vassal. I have no right to command his behavior."

"But he is your friend! Surely he will act with honor!"

Quinn indicated that she should precede him into the solar. He gave Michel a nod, for the boy had followed them, and shut the door, leaning back against it to watch her. "And how would you define honor in this instance?" he asked.

That he could even ask such a question was no good sign. "Any man of merit would wed the woman he desires."

"Any man of merit would not wed without the means to support a wife and family," Quinn countered, his tone reasonable. "Bayard has no holding and no fortune. He may well intend to continue to earn his way as a mercenary, which is no fitting fate for any woman."

Melissande put her hands on her hips. Though she agreed with this assessment, she still wished to defend her maid's chastity. "Then you will look aside if he seduces her beneath the roof of Annossy?"

"Surely Berthe can choose for herself whether to be seduced or not?"

Melissande exhaled. She knew already how easily objections could be overcome by a man's persuasive touch. Could Quinn have seduced her if they had not been wedded? She feared he might have found success. "Surely, your comrade should not even try to entice her," she replied hotly.

"Surely Bayard's choices are his own to make!" Quinn countered, his voice rising.

"This is not a camp of war, where all the women are whores. Nor is it some paradise where men can take their pleasure without regard for the consequences."

"I scarce think that one maid's seduction could lead to such repute..."

"This is a holding where maidens can come to give service to the lord and lady without fearing for their chastity!"

"Berthe need have no fear for her chastity!" Quinn replied, his eyes flashing. "Surely she has the wits to say nay."

"Surely all women know that declining a man's touch is not sufficient to turn him aside."

"Do you suggest that my companion would see his desires sated with violence?" he demanded. "If so, you insult both me and my companion with your assumptions about his nature..."

"If he would seduce my maid without any thought of the future, your companion insults her with his assumptions about her nature."

Quinn flung out his hands. "Bayard's assignations are not my concern!"

"They *are* your concern," Melissande snapped. "You are Lord d'Annossy. You have an obligation to every soul who takes shelter in this keep, to see him or her defended from violence, to see him or her fed and clothed, to see him or her protected."

Quinn stepped back, his eyes narrowed. "I do not."

"You most certainly do. They are your vassals and your villeins. Do you think their pledges of fealty come with no price? Do you imagine that you owe them naught for their loyalty and service?" Melissande spun on her heel and stormed to the other side of the solar. "I cannot imagine why I feared Annossy being bled dry for the sake of Sayerne. You simply choose to turn Annossy into a new Sayerne."

"I do not!"

"What is the difference?" Melissande cried. "Your father's hall was one of ill-repute, and many of his villeins fled here to defend their daughters from the lusts indulged in his hall. Should Berthe be compromised by your companion, that deed will cast a long shadow."

Quinn rubbed his brow. "I see."

Melissande feared he still did not. She counted on her fingers. "We have scullery maids in the kitchen who aid George in the preparation of the meals. We have more who tend the potage garden and yet others who do the washing. There are three in the hall at any given time who ensure that lanterns are filled and rushes are changed and linens are washed for guests. We need that labor, Quinn, and it is an honor for those pledged to Annossy to send their daughters to the hall. Your friends and comrades will depart at some point and I would still have Annossy well-maintained. You should desire as much, as well, as Lord d'Annossy." She folded her arms across her chest. "Managing a holding is not solely about defending its borders."

He nodded and folded his arms across his chest as well, watching her. "I will speak with Bayard and express your concern."

"You will bid him leave Berthe alone unless he means to ask for her hand."

Quinn's lips tightened. "I cannot command him."

"Then he should leave."

She saw the flash of his eyes and heard the fury in his tone. "Is there more?"

Melissande took a breath and decided to share all of her concerns. Quinn was already annoyed and she perceived that she had little to lose. "I do not like that you brought the men-at-arms back to Annossy. It looks as if you push aside the traditions and people of Annossy in favor of your comrades."

"I can only solve the matter of the brigands with men I trust." His tone was harder and she knew he did not welcome her comments.

"Gaultier will be insulted."

"Then he may leave and I will welcome that."

"And you would insult Tulley, who sent him to Annossy!" Melissande retorted, flinging out her hands. "You must think of repercussions beyond your own whim!"

"Whim?" he roared. "I must be surrounded by men I trust!"

"Alas, I am not to have that luxury!" she replied before she could stop herself. "I am to stand aside while you claim every iota of affection and loyalty, while you push aside people chosen by me in favor of your own choices, while you turn Annossy into a hideous echo of Sayerne. I am to stand aside in silence while you make your father's fondest dream come true, even as you destroy all that my forebears and I worked to achieve."

"You scarcely stand in silence, my lady."

"I will scream at the injustice, should it be necessary!" she countered. "I will not cede all to you so willingly as you might wish, whether you be my lord husband or nay."

"I am your lord husband and this match is consummated!" Quinn bellowed.

"Nay." Melissande shook her head. "It can still be dissolved, because I had a previous betrothal."

Quinn growled beneath his breath and took a step closer, his eyes burning with fury. Melissande feared a moment too late that she had pushed him overmuch, but then he shoved a hand through his hair, pivoted and paced the width of the solar and back. When he spoke, his voice still thrummed with emotion, but he was more controlled. "Is that the root of it? You do not trust me and my comrades?"

"I do not know them, and I do not know you that well."

Quinn paced more quickly. "As opposed to Arnaud, the knight who holds your heart in thrall," he said with some heat. "What if he had been the one to change the guard at the mill for his comrades? Would you welcome that choice whether you knew them or nay, simply because he is your beloved?"

Arnaud. The mention of that man's name stopped Melissande cold. What manner of woman was she that she had forgotten all about him so quickly as this? She turned her back upon her husband. "Berthe thinks you intend to abandon Annossy for Sayerne," she said, not having intended to breach that topic at all.

"Does she? I suppose that would suit you well enough," he said, his voice a low growl of dissatisfaction.

"Is that what will happen if we have a son? You will leave?"

What would happen if they did not have a son?

He did not reply. Melissande looked over her shoulder to find him watching her intently, his lips set. The air fairly crackled between them and when he spoke, his low words surprised her. "You would rather I had never returned from Palestine."

"I would rather I had not been compelled to wed you," she replied curtly. "Beyond that, I have no concern for your survival or location."

Quinn averted his gaze and she saw a muscle work in his jaw. She feared anew that she had said too much, especially when his hand clenched into a fist at his side, then relaxed again. He took a breath and lifted the fur-lined cloak, swinging it over his shoulders and wrapping it around himself. "Now this is a fine garment. I thank you for it."

Melissande watched warily as Quinn strode around the perimeter of the solar. What did he mean to do? She could not imagine that her blunt speech would create no repercussions. He closed all of the shutters across the windows, save the one that faced the mill, then drew a chair beside it. Wrapped in the cloak, he sat there, watching over the forest to the distant mill.

As if she did not exist.

As if she had been forgotten.

Melissande knew she should not have been surprised that Quinn did precisely as he had said he would. She had told him not to come to her bed. He had said he would watch the mill.

She was surprised by her own annoyance with the situation. Their dispute had made her keenly aware of him, as arguments had done before. That he could ignore her so completely indicated that he was not so powerfully affected by their lovemaking. It was a warning of what might be, and she told herself to be glad to have seen the truth of it so early.

Berthe knocked on the door then and came with hot water. She spared a glance at Quinn, but she did not speak to him and he never glanced her way. It might have been Melissande's forbidding expression that silenced any question that might have fallen from the maid's lips, and she was quick about aiding her lady to prepare for bed. Still, Quinn did not change his posture or look her way. Melissande laid abed after the maid was gone, watching him, but he might have been alone for all the attention he showed her.

She was a fool to feel its lack.

Melissande did not think she would sleep, but to her surprise, she did.

CHAPTER TWELVE

he moon was riding high when Quinn heard Melissande roll over in the great bed. She sighed, as if her dreams saddened her, and the sound tore at his heart. Her breathing remained slow and deep, though, and he knew she had not awakened.

The most vexing thing about his wife was not that she was inclined to be outspoken. It was not that she challenged him, for Quinn welcomed that. The most irksome thing was that he lost his composure in her presence, like some brute, and then, invariably, had to acknowledge that she was right.

If only she did not set his blood afire. If only the sight of her— eyes flashing, color high—did not make him yearn to kiss her to silence, seduce her, tickle her and coax her laughter. If only every exchange did not make him yearn for a true marriage in every sense.

She loved Arnaud. He could not believe her to be inconstant, so her heart, once surrendered, would be Arnaud's forevermore. Quinn did not have to like it, but he had to accept that truth.

His marriage was doomed to be unhappy, for the lady was right. A betrothal was as good as a marriage in terms of being an obstacle to wedding another.

He needed to talk to Tulley.

Quinn was not looking forward to that.

He was chilled to his marrow, despite the cloak, but he had given his word. He dared not stamp his feet to warm them for fear of awakening Melissande, so turned back to stare out at the night. He had sat vigil before and doubtless he would do so again. He reminded himself that he had gone days without sleep and that he had lived all his life without the comfort of a great bed like the one his wife occupied.

Never mind the sweetness of Melissande tucked against his side. Even if she did not wish to be intimate, he could have been content to hold her. How long did a woman's courses last? He had no notion, but he did know that her courses meant she was not with child.

It could all be put aside so easily, if Tulley could be convinced to see reason.

Quinn shivered and wrapped the cloak more tightly around himself, watching the night in the direction of the mill. It was not the cold that left him feeling hollow and alone. It was the knowledge that if he did right and defended his lady, he would be left with naught at all. Though he had possessed naught until just days ago, he knew that this time, he would keenly feel the lack.

Then something fell.

It hit to the floor behind him, the sound muffled. It must have fallen to the rug by the side of the bed. Quinn looked and could see the glint of some item on the floor there. He rose and moved silently to retrieve it. If it had fallen from Melissande's grasp, she did not miss it, for she slept on.

'Twas a knife in a jewelled scabbard and Quinn was certain he had never seen it before.

He spared a glance at Melissande, her braid cast across the linens, her skin as fair as ivory in the darkness. He took the knife to the window and examined it in the moonlight. The sheath was fine, etched with an elaborate design and studded with gems, and there was another larger gem in the hilt. He drew the blade, noting that it was in excellent care, and drew the blade gently across his hand. Honed to perfection.

A lethal weapon.

Why did she have such a knife?

Why did she take it to bed—on the very night that she had told him not to join her? Surely she could not imagine that he would force his affections upon her?

He made to sheath the weapon again and the moonlight caught something on the blade. It was inscribed. Quinn held it higher and turned it in the moonlight.

> *To Gaultier—*
> *With affection*
> *upon the presentation of your spurs*
> *—Marie*

Gaultier.

Could there be two men with such name in Melissande's acquaintance, both of whom were inclined to see her armed against her husband? Quinn suspected not. He had never believed in coincidence and his years at crusade had only confirmed his view.

He sheathed the weapon and silently replaced it on the rug, as if he had not seen it. Then he returned to the window, standing now as he looked into the night. Resolve filled him with new purpose, despite his exhaustion.

There were two questions for which he needed a reply and only one man could answer them. Why had Tulley ignored Melissande's betrothal to Arnaud? And what was known of Gaultier, Captain of the Guard, that he had been recommended for such a post?

Quinn would ride to Tulley and have the truth of it from his wily overlord.

The sun would not set upon Annossy again without Quinn knowing both the location of his lady wife's beloved and the allegiance of Annossy's Captain of the Guard.

It might not set again with Quinn still in possession of Annossy's seal, but that was a risk he had to take.

Bayard was awake when he heard quiet footsteps on the stairs. His hand fell to his blade hilt by force of habit but otherwise he remained still, listening. To his relief, the sound came from above, not below, and he recognized Quinn's silhouette as that man descended from the solar. Bayard and Amaury still slept on the second floor of Annossy's tower, and there was room for the younger squires now that Lothair and Niall remained at the mill.

To his surprise, Quinn moved quietly across the chamber to his side instead of continuing down the stairs. He seemed to expect that Bayard would be awake, for he looked down upon him, his features lost in shadows, and nodded once. Then he returned to the stairs and went down the stairs to the hall.

Bayard understood that he had been summoned. He tugged on his chausses and boots, but otherwise wore only his chemise. By force of habit, he took his dagger in its scabbard.

He found Quinn at the board alone in the shadows before the dawn. The keep was yet quiet, although there was some activity in the kitchen. He sat down opposite his companion and friend, wondering what was amiss.

Quinn's expression was so serious that Bayard did not tease him about leaving his wife's bed or the lack of ale.

"You must choose," Quinn said softly. He was serious and his expression intent, as if he anticipated an argument from Bayard.

"Choose?"

"We are no longer at war, and no longer moving from place to place. We no longer need fear that we will not awaken on the morrow..."

"No man knows when he will breathe his last."

"But we do not battle for our survival each day," Quinn said with resolve. "And so we must choose."

Bayard sensed he would not like his options in this choice, whatever it was. He sat back, folding his arms across his chest, and waited.

Quinn traced a pattern in the wood with a fingertip. "I intend to remain in this place, to maintain my pledge as Lord d'Annossy and to rebuild Sayerne, if God wills it."

"You mean if Tulley wills it." Bayard earned a look for that. "It seems that he has more influence in this valley than any other."

Quinn frowned and continued. "And that means that we must look upon the others in this valley as our neighbors, villeins and even friends, not as resources."

"This is about the maid," Bayard guessed, irked that his comrade would attempt to govern his behavior.

"'Tis."

"This is about your wife. She will see you gelded, if you allow it, and then if Annossy is attacked, where will you be? Timid at her feet, like a dog well-trained..."

Quinn cleared his throat and Bayard fell silent. "My lady makes a fair point. Women must be treated with courtesy, maidens in particular, when we have need of their services in the hall. Fathers will not entrust them to such service if they are to be abused or left with child."

"But a man must have his pleasures!"

"Must he? Is it not a consequence of war that a man takes no responsibility, that he pays for his pleasure and moves on?"

"We have been chaste while on crusade, Quinn," Bayard reminded his friend with impatience. "It was a choice but it is done. A man must satisfy his base needs..."

"Is such behavior not the mark of a mercenary who does not know if he will live another day? And if he does, he is unlikely to be in the same keep or town. By virtue of his trade, he chooses to abide in the moment." Quinn held up a finger when Bayard might have protested. "But we are no longer on crusade or at war. I vowed that I would give you a home, Bayard, and I will keep that pledge. I will grant you honest employ, as a man I trust above all others. I will have need of you and would not see us part. You may labor here or at Sayerne, but I will ensure that you do not lack, except if you seduce the maidens who serve in the hall."

"But..."

"Should you have need of such pleasures, then journey to Tulley or even beyond, but you will not so indulge in my holdings. I know you are more temperate than you would have others believe, but you may not indulge here."

Bayard heaved a sigh and attempted a jest, hoping that he might convince Quinn to soften. "You have been tamed by your lady, indeed," he began but Quinn interrupted him.

"I have been tutored by her, and she speaks good sense in this.

My father's repute was fed by his tendency to treat women as whores. I must be different. I must choose differently to convince all in this valley that I *am* different. And that means that you, and all men in my service, must do the same."

"Or?" Bayard invited, feeling rebellious before this demand.

Quinn gave him an intent look, one that Bayard knew meant his companion's decision was made. Quinn did not reply, but gestured to the portal. Beyond it were the gates, the valley, Tulley and the Beauvoir Pass.

Or he could leave.

Bayard frowned. "It is unnatural for a man to be chaste."

"But not for a man to pledge to one woman."

"Now I am to wed as well? You push me overmuch, Quinn!"

"Why not wed?" Quinn sat back and raised his hands. "It might please you well."

"You and your lady wife argue with fervor!"

"There is much at stake and all has changed for my lady." Quinn's expression turned rueful before Bayard could ask for details. "What of the maid? You watch her as keenly as she watches you, and you match wits with her. There is more than a pretty smile prompting all of this."

Bayard dropped his gaze, unwilling to share his secrets. "It has been too long since I savored a woman. She is here and she is pretty. It is no more than that." He scowled when Quinn cleared his throat and ceded another increment. "I like that she is keen of wit, and fearless."

"She does not fear you, that is for certain. Perhaps she sees your truth."

"Yet she calls me a rogue," Bayard retorted. "She might be disappointed to know that I am nigh as chaste as you have been."

"Perhaps not. You do not like when Niall talks to her."

Bayard frowned, feeling disgruntled. "Perhaps you make much of little."

"Perhaps you have forgotten the gift that Marcus granted to you."

Bayard fairly growled that Quinn spoke of it. He had hoped that his comrade might have forgotten. "*A perfume that will win the heart of the most reluctant maiden,*" he said, repeating the innkeeper's words. "I have not forgotten."

"Then think upon which maiden it shall be." Quinn made to rise, evidently believing the matter to be concluded.

Aye, they knew each other well.

"Where do you go so early in the morn?" Bayard demanded. "All are yet asleep."

"I mean to ride to Tulley. There are matters I would discuss with my overlord."

"Details he neglected to share?" Bayard raised his brows but Quinn did not confide in him. "And you will ride alone?"

"Aye. I intend to return this day, although the hour will be late." Quinn nodded as Amaury came down the stairs, as neatly attired as if he had risen hours before. Bayard immediately felt as if he looked to be a mercenary of no repute, perhaps one who ravished maidens and abandoned them with his seed ripening in their bellies. "I would ask you two to ensure that the gates are not opened in my absence. Until I know more, I would have all at Annossy remain at Annossy."

"You cannot ride alone when there are brigands abroad," Amaury protested.

"I carry neither coin nor treasure, and Fortitude is swift." Quinn was adamant. "I will arm myself and none shall trouble me. I will not wait for any other rider to join me."

Bayard and Amaury exchanged a glance. "I will go with you," Bayard said, but Quinn shook his head.

"I do not like how we are divided," Amaury noted. "Quinn, think of it. Solitude makes you vulnerable."

Quinn shook his head. "Not so much as you fear. So long as the gates are closed, there will be no peril to me. See that it is so. And I will grant you a task for this day."

"Any deed!" Amaury said.

"You have but to name it," Bayard agreed.

Quinn tapped his fingertip on the board, even as he lowered his voice. "I would know every way in and out of this keep, even if it is only a passage of sufficient size for a rat."

"Not all rats are small," Amaury murmured as the men

exchanged glances.

"There must be more than the gate itself," Quinn said. "And there may be breaches in the wall."

"The sewer," Amaury mused.

"The kitchens," Bayard said and the others looked at him. "The keep itself may have more entries than you realize. Any soul in the village might be able to reach the solar."

"Aye. I would know them all." Without allowing for further discussion, Quinn left them there, walking to the kitchen with purpose.

"I never knew him to be impetuous," Amaury said.

"I never knew his confidence to be misplaced," Bayard agreed. "Until, of course, we reached Tulley."

The pair exchanged a glance. "I might ride after him," Amaury said.

"I think you will only earn his ire," Bayard said. "Mind that the gate is closed after him and secured. I will join you there as soon as I am dressed. I will not fail to provide that list on his return."

Amaury nodded and left the great hall. Bayard returned to the chamber above and donned his mail tunic and tabard, dressing quickly. He heard the echo of hoof beats even as he buckled on his sword, then took his gloves and helm. He eyed his saddlebag, then opened it on impulse, removing the glass vial that was carefully packed within it. The liquid was still trapped in the bottle, for he had taken care with the gift.

Marcus had been the first in many years to grant Bayard a gift. Now, Quinn offered him another, a much greater one, if only he would cede to Quinn's desire. Was the price truly so high as he argued? A home was a dream beyond all else. A home and a wife, a hearth of his own, honest labor, and perhaps a son. 'Twas enough to steal his breath away—especially if that wife had flashing eyes and no compunction in telling him when he erred.

Bayard turned the bottle so that it caught the light and wondered if Marcus had spoken aright. If he could only claim one woman, he rather thought the maid Berthe might do well.

He tucked the bottle into his purse and strode to meet Amaury, wondering how he might put Marcus' gift to best use.

❧

"Gone?" Melissande repeated when Berthe brought hot water. "How can my lord husband be gone?"

Where had Quinn gone?

And why?

Yet the foremost question in Melissande's thoughts was why had he not told her of his plan.

Of course, she had been shrewish the night before and she was troubled that she could not apologize to him this morn. The dagger given to her by Gaultier was on the rug beside the bed, as if it had fallen from beneath her pillow, and she feared that Quinn might have seen it. She still wore his ring, but Melissande was afraid.

"He rode out before the dawn, my lady. Doubtless his men know his destination, but they do not share it. The gates are secured and they will allow no one to enter or to leave until my lord Quinn's return."

What madness was this?

Melissande dressed in haste and swept down the stairs to the great hall with purpose. She found no one there but the maids who swept the rushes, for it was the day that they should be changed. Berthe hustled behind her. Melissande did not pause in the kitchen but went straight through the bailey to the gates, where she found Bayard and Amaury. The two knights were fully armed and stood before the barred gates to Annossy, arms folded across their chests. They looked formidable and somber.

The skies were overcast and she could smell the difference in the wind. The rains would begin soon, perhaps even before midday. Soon it would be time to sow. Would Quinn abandon Annossy for Sayerne? The fields had always been more fertile there.

Gaultier came to her side in the bailey, following her to the gates when she did not pause. "It is unreasonable, my lady. No one is permitted to leave, and this for another day. Your lord husband is a tyrant..."

Melissande held up a hand for his silence. She addressed Amaury. "Is it true that my lord husband has left Annossy?"

The knight inclined his head. "But not for long, my lady. He had an errand."

An errand.

"Did he ride to Sayerne?" she asked, thinking Quinn might have wished to look upon it.

"I cannot say, my lady," Amaury said, but Bayard's quick look made Melissande doubt that had been Quinn's destination.

"Did you not visit that holding upon your arrival?" she asked him, remembering how Quinn's party had been behind her own on her ride to Tulley. They had come from further down the valley and as there was no access, they must have visited Sayerne.

And likely found it inhospitable.

"Aye, my lady." Bayard bowed slightly and his gaze flicked to Berthe.

"And?"

"It was in need of much repair, my lady."

Why would Quinn return to Sayerne so soon? Melissande could not imagine. Sayerne was a ruin and that could not have changed in these few days. She could not imagine him to be sentimental, or in need of a plan for restoring that holding. Every single task had to be done and every shelter rebuilt.

The only other destination he might have had—unless he intended to abandon her completely—was Tulley.

But why? Quinn could not seek an annulment. Tulley had ensured that. Melissande had told him that she had her courses, though, which meant that he would conclude that she was not with child, even after two nights together. The truth, of course, was that she might be.

Curse her impulse to deceive him! Her father had always said that lies only bred more lies, and Melissande wished that had not proven so very true.

Surely he did not mean to question Tulley about her betrothal to Arnaud? He had been vexed by those tidings, to be sure, as a man of honor might be. She could not fully explain the fear that rose within her at the possibility that Quinn might succeed in putting her aside.

She would be neither wife nor widow, yet not a maiden either.

What if she became a mother? By her own word to him, that child could not be his. She might be called a harlot, as a result of her own claim.

Her wits were addled, to be sure. What was it about this man that gave him such power to put her emotions in turmoil? Was it the same ability that made her body respond to the very sight of him and rise so quickly to his touch?

"Did he give any indication of when he would return?" she asked Amaury.

That knight nodded. "He vowed it would be this day, my lady, but guessed that the hour would be late."

He could ride to Tulley and back in that time, if he rode with purpose.

She supposed she should be relieved that his scheme was to return.

"But there are brigands in the valley," she said to Bayard. "Surely, he did not ride out alone?"

"He did, my lady." The knight, to his credit, looked discomfited by this and Melissande guessed that he and Quinn had disagreed about this course. Why would he take such a risk? She already knew that Quinn tended to be prudent.

Unless he was angry.

How much had she vexed him with her sharp tongue the night before? God in Heaven, but she hoped that her words had not prompted him to be careless.

"He also insisted that the gate be kept closed in his absence," Amaury added.

"It is unreasonable," Gaultier began to argue, but Melissande glared at him.

"It is not your place, Gaultier, to challenge the command of the Lord d'Annossy," she said coldly. "My lord husband must have good reason for his decision and his order, and so his command shall be obeyed." She turned and nodded to the two knights. "I thank you for these tidings. Please ensure that my lord husband's will is done."

"Aye, my lady," they said in unison and she could not miss the satisfaction both showed.

She also did not miss that Gaultier was displeased.

Tulley was at the board when Quinn arrived, and invited the arriving knight to join him with a gesture. "Your timing is superb. There is a boar stew this day and some of the wine of Annossy." Tulley's niece was seated by his left hand and smiled at Quinn but did not speak.

"In truth, sir, I come for tidings, not sustenance."

"Tidings?" Tulley's brows rose. "Of what?"

"I would know more of Gaultier, the Captain of the Guard at Annossy."

Tulley blinked. "I know naught of him. The one before him, Millard, he I knew for many years." He nodded, though Quinn did not know if his approval was of that knight or the wine poured into his cup. He sipped the wine and nodded again. "A good man from the king's own demesne in Paris, but a younger son. Well-trained and well-bred, but lacking in coin and opportunity. He served me for a decade then Annossy for another thirty. A most excellent warrior. I deeply regretted his loss. 'Twas just over a year ago."

"My lady wife told me that you sent her current Captain of the Guard to her, to replace the warrior who passed."

"I did not!"

Quinn was taken aback. "Then from whence did he come?"

"How am I to say? She employs him. Try the meat, Heloise. It is most fine this day. This piece, not that one."

"Aye, Uncle. I thank you."

Quinn cleared his throat. "But she employs him because he came at your recommendation."

"Well, she has erred in that, as women are like to do. I did not send him." Tulley savored his stew with satisfaction. "You must join us. This is a fine meal."

He waved to the châtelain, who set another place, while a squire took Quinn's cloak. He was brought a bowl of water to wash his hands and his stomach grumbled as he took his place at Tulley's right hand.

"What was his name?" Tulley asked when they were all eating.

"Gaultier."

"Gaultier," Tulley repeated, then shook his head. "Has he no holding of origin or town or family name?"

Quinn shook his head. "If so, I do not know it."

"Lonvaux," Heloise said and both men turned to look at her. She flushed a little. "His name is Gaultier de Lonvaux. I remember him."

"Remember him?" Tulley repeated, his tone cross. "How could you remember him? And when did you see him?"

"Last year, in the autumn. It must have been just before he went to Annossy. He was here, at Tulley, lodged in the inn in the town."

Quinn saw Tulley's brows rise and was surprised that the older man had missed this detail.

Heloise continued. "I saw him when I arrived, for he stood outside the inn, on the road, as my party passed. He spoke to me." She blushed a little.

"Audacity," Tulley muttered.

"Nay, Uncle. We had met before my parents died. There was a notion that we might become betrothed, but I was glad that my father was much against it."

"Why was he?" Tulley demanded.

"He said that Gaultier had no hope of inheritance, not since his aunt had wed again."

"Marie," Quinn said almost to himself, recalling the inscription on the blade in Melissande's possession.

"Indeed!" Heloise agreed with pleasure. "Marie de Perricault is his aunt and her former husband trained Gaultier for his spurs. She was said to be fond of him and sponsored him even after her husband's death. People said the most wicked things." She shook her head and her expression turned prim.

"What wicked things?" Tulley asked.

"Uncle!"

"Tell me. We seek news of this man and even rumor may hold a germ of truth."

Heloise blushed crimson. "That Marie would have wed him if he had not been her own kin. They said, they said, that their relations were most improper." She looked disapproving after confessing this much.

Tulley sipped his wine, then nodded slowly. "I remember this," he said. "It was most scandalous, but I did not know the young man's name." He snapped his fingers. "And then Marie did wed again, so the rumors fell silent. I suppose that might have been when Gaultier had to leave Perricault to find his fortune." He nodded, well content with this version of events and returned to his meal. "It is most fine, is it not? I tell the gamekeeper to take a boar whenever he can. It is by far the finest meat."

"Where is Perricault?" Quinn asked for he did not know of it.

"To the north," Tulley said. "En route to Paris. It lies on the other side of the mountains that mark the north side of this valley." He lowered his voice. "Not quite so well favored by the sun and so less prosperous as a result, but still fine territory. They make a passable wine."

Quinn leaned forward so that he could see Heloise. "Why were you glad that your father had objections to Gaultier, if I might be so bold as to ask?"

Tulley looked at his niece as if also interested in her reply.

She blushed again. "He was called Gaultier le Beau by some, because he was handsome to look upon. But I neither liked nor trusted him. There was something in his gaze that made me shiver."

Quinn nodded understanding. "I do not like him either, my demoiselle, though I cannot say precisely why."

"That is why you came to ask Uncle about him, for you knew that Uncle would not recommend a man who was untrustworthy."

"Indeed," Quinn agreed, though he was not so certain as that. He was convinced only that Tulley would not make a choice that might adversely affect his own situation, which was not the same matter at all. He frowned and cleared his throat. "My lord, my lady has mentioned that she was betrothed to another before our vows were exchanged..."

"Arnaud de Privas," Tulley said with disdain. "Another wastrel, I am sad to say. She is well rid of him, to be sure."

"But surely their betrothal has weight as an earlier bond..."

Tulley surveyed him, his gaze cool. "It would, if Arnaud had not wed another woman first."

Quinn was startled. "Does my lady wife know of this?"

"I told her, but she chose to believe me mistaken." Tulley sipped his wine and his lips tightened. "I am never mistaken about matters of such import." He glared at Quinn and Quinn dropped his gaze.

Relief surged through him. His match was legitimate and he was sufficiently honest with himself to be glad. There was no legal impediment—the sole obstacles remained his lady wife's affection and the conception of a child. These were not small obstacles, but Quinn found his heart lightened.

Tulley, meanwhile, shook a finger at him. "And I am reminded that I meant to speak to you about seeing Sayerne's fields tilled this year. They have lain fallow too long and we have need of the grain..."

"But I am not to take the seal of Sayerne for another year," Quinn felt obliged to note.

Tulley smiled. "Then you shall ensure the fields are tilled for me."

Quinn cleared his throat, recalling Melissande's practical questions, and strove to ask some of his own. She did not wish to see Annossy pillaged for Sayerne's sake, and he did not wish to see either plundered for Tulley's sole benefit. "If you are to claim the harvest, my lord, then who shall pay for the seed?"

Tulley harrumphed. "I could command that you do as much."

"But that would scarcely be fair, my lord, and you are known for your justice. Surely you know that Sayerne no longer has any villeins to do the labor, either." Quinn shook his head. "I recall that the fields were fertile, but they have not been tilled in recent years. This is a considerable labor to undertake, particularly with no promise of gain."

Tulley glared. Quinn held his gaze, ensuring that his own expression was bland. He was well aware that Heloise was endeavoring to hide her smile.

"I will send the seed," Tulley said finally. "But the villeins must come from Annossy."

"But where shall they live, my lord?" Quinn asked. "It is too far for them to journey back and forth each day, unless they are to labor for no more than an hour." He nodded. "And I visited Sayerne just this week. You may not be aware that there is not a single structure of integrity there, save the old grain barn on the border where we spent that night. The hall is not bad, but the roof of the solar is damaged..."

"I know the state of Sayerne," Tulley fairly growled.

"I cannot ask the villeins to abandon the comfort of their homes to labor without shelter. 'Twould be most irresponsible."

Tulley's lips tightened. "I will send men to help with the building, after the rain stops." He pointed at Quinn. "But you shall see that all is defended."

Quinn inclined his head. "They will need provisions, as well, for it will be months before the harvest. Although if you intend to claim it all, then they will still be hungry then. And there must be knights for the defense, who will also need shelter and provisions, as well as their steeds and squires."

"You would have me pay to rebuild all of Sayerne!"

"I would not impoverish Annossy to rebuild Sayerne, particularly when I do not hold the seal of Sayerne."

Their gazes locked for a potent moment and Quinn did not dare to take a breath. He was aware of Heloise's keen interest and Tulley's vexation, but did not blink.

"Half," Tulley snapped, casting his napkin upon the board. "I desire half. The rest you may divide for seed for next year and flour for your villeins." He sighed with annoyance "And I will send provisions for all when the ploughing begins, along with men to build. Are you satisfied?"

"I should think a third might be more fitting," Quinn said mildly. "For a tenth must go to the church."

Tulley inhaled.

Tulley exhaled.

Tulley glared.

And then he ceded. "You drive a hard bargain, Quinn de Sayerne. A third it will be then. Now are you satisfied?"

"I am certain I will have more questions, my lord," Quinn said.

"Such tasks of administration are new to me, after all."

Heloise giggled.

Tulley cleared his throat. "That is as may be. On this day, however, you *will* undertake an enquiry for me."

"But I intend to ride for Annossy, my lord, that I might be gone but a day."

"Nonsense. You will remain here in Tulley this night, for it is the only sensible course."

"But..."

"The rains will begin shortly, Quinn. I smelled as much in the air this morn as soon as I rose. Indeed, they might have begun already. And when the first spring rain falls in Tulley, it is no time for man or horse to be on the road. There will be a veritable deluge. The river Helva will swell its banks by the dawn, and tomorrow, after noon, the sun will reappear." He nodded with confidence. "It is always thus. The snow will have vanished within a week."

"All of it?" Quinn asked, skeptical. He recalled violent rains in Sayerne in his boyhood, but could not believe the entire valley experienced such a rapid thaw.

"All of it," Tulley said. He wiped his mouth on his napkin. "And so this day, instead of riding forth in such inclement weather, you will undertake a small task for me." There was steel in his tone.

"But my wife will expect me to return to Annossy, sir."

"Did you leave the holding secured?"

"Aye, sir. The gates were to be kept closed in my absence."

"And there is no reason for any to leave Annossy in such weather as there will shortly be."

"But the brigands..."

"Will undoubtedly also keep to their shelter. Perhaps they will be too foolish to do as much and will drown." Tulley waved off Quinn's objections. "Far better for you to earn my favor with the rapid fulfillment of this task."

"I would not have Melissande concerned."

"Would you not?" Tulley laughed. "You have a reluctant bride, Quinn, and I see the truth of it well enough. Let her miss you a little." He leaned closer and winked. "Court the favor of the lord you have just irked instead."

Quinn noticed that Heloise's eyes were sparkling and she seemed to be fighting the urge to laugh. He realized that she must have been confronted by Tulley's firm opinions before. "Of course, my lord," Quinn said, inclining his head. "What would you have me do?"

"A party arrived last evening. They crossed the Beauvoir Pass and are armed. I would know who they are and why they arrive in Tulley. They take their rest at the inn in the village." Tulley gave Quinn a look. "At least, I assume they remain there, and possess the wits to keep to shelter when foul weather arrives."

Quinn thought Tulley could have sent a messenger, but did not say as much. It would be unwise to provoke his overlord before the seal of Sayerne was in his hand. "Aye, my lord."

"I do not like parties of armed men arriving without announcement," Tulley complained. "And this is the third party to come through the pass in little more than a week. First, there was your party, then the others who proved to be your comrades."

Quinn was startled that Tulley knew this.

The older man nodded. "Aye, they were watched as they rode up the valley and when you greeted them upon their return." He gave Quinn a look.

"They are three of my companion knights, met on crusade. We had parted ways for the journey home and agreed to meet at Sayerne in the spring."

"And were there more of you?"

"Aye."

"Then perhaps these men are more of your fellows. One, I understand, is missing an eye."

"Luc," Quinn said softly and Tulley eyed him. "I cannot say, my lord, but one of the knights whose arrival I yet anticipate, Luc Douglas, lost an eye in battle."

"I suspect my instincts are right, then. Go, find their names and their reason for entering my lands, and return for the evening meal to tell me of them." Tulley rose then and gestured to Heloise to follow him. Quinn also rose and bowed, then retrieved his gloves and cloak. The twins, Thierry and Luc Douglas, had ridden separately from Palestine with Rolfe de Viandin. Quinn hoped this was their party, for he would be glad to see his comrades again.

As he left the stables and stepped onto the road that wound down the hill, passing through the village en route to the gates, he saw that it had started to rain. He looked up at the darkening sky as the onslaught became heavier and smiled.

Even the weather obeyed the command of the Lord de Tulley.

As he walked, he thought of Gaultier and his scheme to wed a rich woman. 'Twas not a bad plan, and he was hardly the first man to pursue it. But Quinn did not like that after Marie's marriage, Gaultier had come to Annossy. He had lied about Tulley dispatching him, and Quinn took that as a very good assurance that his original guess about the intentions of Annossy's Captain of the Guard was exactly right.

If naught else, the man had no right to such an exalted position at Annossy, and Quinn would see that remedied immediately upon his return.

CHAPTER THIRTEEN

It did indeed prove to be Luc and Thierry Douglas who had taken shelter at Tulley's inn. Both knights had dark hair and rode chestnut destriers that were also brothers. Quinn had smiled at the sight of Emperor and Dragon in the stables, knowing the truth before he even entered the common room of the inn. Their squires, Baird and Thorne, each standing behind his knight, grinned at the sight of him, and he was certain both boys had grown several inches in height. To Quinn's surprise, though, Rolfe de Viandin was not with them.

After greetings were exchanged and Quinn had shaken the rain out of his cloak, he joined them at the board. Baird hastened to fetch him a cup of ale.

"Rolfe rode on ahead. He wished to be home before the Yule, though we thought there would be too much snow on the pass," Thierry said.

"Aye, we recalled your tale of it well enough and were cautious as a result," Luc said, nudging Quinn.

"I never thought to ask if there had been others of our party when we came through the pass," Quinn said. "I thought you all behind us."

"And they are not so welcoming there," Thierry said with a grimace. "Truly, it is more than the wind that is chilly at Beauvoir."

They laughed together at that as Baird returned with another pitcher of ale and a cup for Quinn. He poured and the comrades saluted each other. It was good cold ale.

"Did you ask about Rolfe?" Quinn asked.

"Aye," Luc said and exchanged a merry glance with his brother. Quinn could not guess what amused them so. "Though I feared they might recall that beast of his more readily than Rolfe himself."

"Mephistopheles," Thierry said with a smile of affection. "What manner of fool would give the largest blackest destrier such a name? It would invite trouble."

"Though Rolfe has found fortune, not trouble," Luc observed and his brother nodded agreement.

"Aye?" Quinn asked. "How so?"

"You will never believe it," Luc said, dropping his voice low in confidence as he leaned over the board. His eye twinkled merrily. "Rolfe was wed at Beauvoir keep."

"Wed? Rolfe de Viandin? What madness is this?" Quinn demanded with a smile. He could not imagine Rolfe taking a wife at all, and certainly couldn't think of a reason for the ceremony to occur at that fortress. "He is the one of us who will be last to marry, to be sure!"

Luc wagged a finger at him. "Not so. Rolfe arrived at the pass with a maiden. Evidently, he had rescued her or was escorting her for some reason or another."

"A maiden?" Quinn asked.

"A maiden," Luc confirmed.

"She *was* very pretty, by all accounts," Thierry whispered and they all chuckled together.

"And Rolfe's mother was seeking him out, for she knew he returned home," Luc continued. "His father had been a comrade of Bertrand, Lord of Beauvoir, so she had paused there on her way south to find Rolfe, then was compelled to remain because of the snow. Evidently, she had appealed to Tulley to find Rolfe a bride, for his older brother died last fall."

"Rolfe inherited Viandin?" Quinn said with surprise.

Thierry nodded. "And was wed at the Yule, at Beauvoir, to the maiden with whom he traveled, at Tulley's dictate. When there was a thaw in January, he rode on to Viandin with bride and mother."

"These are fine tidings indeed," Quinn said and raised his cup to toast Rolfe's good fortune. They drank to their comrade's health and Quinn guessed that he was not the sole one to be amazed. "Are you certain it is true?"

"So they say," Thierry said.

"We thought to see if you had returned to Sayerne or not, then continue to Viandin to confirm the tale for ourselves," Luc said. "It lies on the path to Paris, does it not?"

Quinn nodded.

"Unless Rolfe comes to Sayerne in May, as we all vowed to do," Thierry added.

"He might not choose to make the journey if his lady wife is with child," Quinn said. They agreed on this, then the brothers looked expectantly at Quinn.

"And how did you find Sayerne?" Luc asked.

"In ruin," Quinn admitted ruefully and they expressed dismay. He held up a hand. "And I, too, am wed at Tulley's command, by strange coincidence, and am now Lord d'Annossy. It has been but days."

"Annossy?" the brothers asked in unison.

"A neighboring holding to Sayerne, and one that is in better repair." Quinn leaned forward and lowered his voice. "Annossy's borders are under attack from brigands, and the holding administered by a daughter alone. Tulley insisted upon the match and charged me to rout the villains."

"And a wife in the bargain, never mind one with a prosperous holding. Rolfe is not the sole one of us blessed by Dame Fortune," Thierry said, toasting Quinn.

"Not necessarily so," Luc said in a teasing tone. "Is the lady young? Is she a beauty?"

"Aye, she is both. Clever, as well, and well experienced in matters of administration." Quinn sighed. "I have much to learn from my lady wife."

The brothers studied him, perhaps hearing more than he confessed.

Quinn forced a smile. "Perhaps that is Tulley's scheme, for I am not to be granted Sayerne's seal for a year, and only then if we conceive a son." He thought of Melissande's concerns for her own future and wondered yet again how he could reassure her of his intentions.

Not by delaying his return on this day, that was for certain. He frowned, disliking that Tulley again dictated his fate.

"Have you heard tell of the others?" Thierry asked after a moment of silence.

"Aye! Bayard is at Annossy, of course, and Amaury ensures the gates are defended in my absence. Lothair and Niall arrived with Amaury just after me, and they guard the mill, which has been attacked twice."

"Brigands! What manner of coward attacks those who are not trained in the arts of war? I wager you have need of more men you can trust," Thierry said, a predictable gleam in his eyes. He never had any sympathy for those who preyed upon the weak.

"I do and I welcome you both, but this night, I am summoned to the board of the Lord de Tulley."

"Invite us," Thierry said with a grin, then nudged his brother. "He might grant one of us a bride, as that seems to be his habit."

"He has a niece close by his side, and I should not be fool enough to smile at her," Quinn advised and they laughed together. "I will ask him, to be sure," he vowed and they drank together to the success of that scheme.

'Twas strange to be without Lord Quinn at Annossy. Berthe felt his absence keenly, though she had met him only a few days before. There was a reassuring effect of his presence that Berthe noticed in his absence. She knew her reaction was naught compared to that of her lady. Though Lady Melissande strove to remain occupied and acted as if she scarce noticed her husband's absence, Berthe thought her lady too watchful. She jumped if any soul entered the hall and glanced frequently toward the gates. Berthe could fairly see her listening for the sound of a destrier's hoof beats.

But there was no such sound. The day dragged long, the shadows lengthened in the hall and finally the lanterns were lit.

Still, Lord Quinn did not return. The rain drummed in the bailey and on the roof of the keep. The dampness of spring filled the air along with the smell of the thaw. There were already a few trickles of water on the floor of the great hall and the moat was filled high. The guard changed on the curtain wall and in the bailey, and Gaultier came into the hall, his expression sour with disapproval.

Lady Melissande scarcely looked up. She was working upon the accounts for Annossy, having told Louis that very morning that she must ensure they were complete to date before surrendering them to her lord husband. She had labored upon them all the day long, seated by the fire in the great hall.

Berthe shivered, knowing she would find it hard to stay warm on this night, and hoped she could find a second straw pallet to put beneath her own. The very stone emanated a dampness in the spring that she felt more keenly than winter's chill. She wore a cloak, even though she was in the hall, and went to the kitchen to get a cup of mulled cider for her lady.

She was heating the cider over the fire when the door to the gardens was opened. Bayard entered the kitchen, shaking rain out of his cloak and hood. His eyes glinted when his gaze danced over her, but he did not speak to her.

Berthe straightened and turned her back upon Sir Rogue.

"Is it always so foul here?" he asked the cook.

"Only in the spring," George said. "You will see. It will rain and rain, until you think we have need of an ark. The snow will melt and the river will over-run its banks. The mud will be plentiful and deep, and just when you think you cannot bear to see another drop of rain, the sun will appear." He snapped his fingers.

"The air will turn warm, immediately," Louis confirmed. "The birds will sing and the valley will turn lush and green." He shook his head. "It seems to change in the blink of an eye, and then there is labor to be done in truth."

"So either there is rain or work," Bayard said. "I see little merry in that combination."

"But then the growing begins," the cook said with enthusiasm. "I will be very happy to have the first wild leeks of the season, perhaps for the sauce of a venison stew."

"We are all well and done with potage vegetables by the spring," Louis agreed.

"Is there any food sweeter than the first berry?" George demanded and soon everyone in the kitchen was talking of summer's bounty.

Berthe smiled as she listened, and swirled the cider.

A man's hand appeared in the periphery of her vision and she jumped, colliding with Bayard who stood directly behind her and spilling a measure of cider. "You startled me, Sir Rogue," she chided, keenly aware of his proximity. "Though I anticipate that was your scheme."

She halfway expected him to wrap his other arm around her waist or bend down to whisper in her ear—indeed, she hoped for as much, but he stepped back and disappointment made her irritable. Was she not sufficiently desirable for this knight even to flirt with her?

"I wished to ask you something of Annossy," he said and she glanced his way. "My lord Quinn would know every way in and out of both keep and solar. Do you know of any that are secret?"

Berthe looked down at the cider. "Have you asked my lady?"

"Should I?"

"I doubt she would tell you," she said, turning to meet his steady gaze. "If indeed she knew of one."

Bayard eyed her for a long moment, then nodded. "I wanted also to ask you what you thought of this." He spoke quietly, as if for her ears alone, and she found his expression unexpectedly serious. In his hand, he held a small dark bottle that looked to have some liquid within it.

"What is that?"

"A token of the East," he said. "It was given to me as a gift."

"By a lady?" Berthe could not keep suspicion from her tone.

Bayard shook his head. "Nay, a keeper whose tavern we favored. We were eight and when we said we rode for home, I think he knew he would miss our custom. He gave each of us a gift." He held up the bottle so that it caught the light. It was not black glass, as Berthe had originally thought, but glass of a very deep blue. "This was mine." His gaze met hers and his eyes seemed even darker than she knew them to be.

"What was it like?" she asked on impulse. "In Palestine?"

Bayard exhaled. "I do not think you truly want to know."

"Aye, I do. The priest talks of it as if it is a paradise..."

"It is no paradise, to my thinking." His voice was grim.

"Then tell me."

"It is different from all I knew before," Bayard admitted, his gaze fixed on the glass bottle. He turned it in his hand, apparently fascinated by the way it caught the light. Berthe guessed that he was sorting his memories and choosing which to share with her. She wondered how many horrors he had witnessed. "Because it is hot and dusty, and I was thirsty all the time I was there. We fought nigh all the time we were there, unless we were idle and waiting for the call to battle. Either I was fighting for my life and that of my comrades or we played endless games of draughts." He lifted his gaze to hers again. "Men died on all sides, yet I have never felt that any endeavor was so futile."

"But you must have won battles and regained territory."

"Aye, and like as not, lost them again afterward. It is, in its way, another endless game of draughts, save that men die when they lose." Bayard frowned and took a deep breath. "And yet it is familiar, because there are people tilling the fields and harvesting crops, cooking and praying, and living."

"Then you did not like it at all."

"I liked that I met my comrades, like Quinn," he said. "I saw places that I had only heard the priests talk about, places I had never been certain were real. I tasted foods that were unknown to me, and I was glad of all that." He smiled at the little bottle and her heart twisted at the sight.

God in heaven, but he was an alluring man. If he spoke to her thus all the time, she would lose her heart in moments.

It had to be a ploy to get beneath her skirts, and Berthe tried to remember that.

"But what is best of all is the gift that my comrade Quinn gives to me," he said solemnly. "For it is both unexpected and my heart's desire."

"What is that?"

"He asks me to remain here with him, at Annossy or Sayerne, to serve him."

"How is that a gift?" Berthe asked, confused. "You served together, but now you will pledge fealty to your friend?"

"And willingly, for Quinn grants to me a home." His eyes shone then and Berthe's heart skipped. "I have been without a home for many years, and indeed, that is why I went on crusade. I hoped to find some measure of fortune, but I found better. I came to this place and have been offered a home and a position—and better yet, I met the most intriguing maiden."

"Here comes the tale!" Berthe scoffed but Bayard shook his head.

"There is no tale." He offered her the bottle. "And as a token of my intentions, I give this bottle to you."

Berthe frowned in confusion.

Bayard took her hand and placed the small bottle within it. The glass was warm from his hand, and his hand was warmer as he folded her fingers around it. He leaned closer. "Open it and think of me." Then he smiled, nodded, and strode away.

Berthe opened her hand and looked at the bottle. Was this a tale he told to all the maidens he desired? Did he tell her this tale because he did not desire her? What an irksome man. She could not fathom what he desired of her at all.

She put down the pot of cider and gently removed the stopper from the glass bottle. It was tight, but then, she supposed it had been sealed all the way from Palestine. She took a sniff of the contents and blinked.

It was scent.

A wondrous, exotic, glorious scent. Berthe could not name it, but it made her toes curl. It made her feel warm and alert. It filled her with anticipation, and desire. She took a deeper breath of it, closing her eyes as the beguiling scent slid through her. It loosed her inhibitions, which should not have surprised her in the least.

She put the stopper back and dropped the bottle into her purse, its weight there a reminder of the intensity of Bayard's expression. It was when she was pouring the cider into the cup for her lady that she realized the import of what he had confided in her.

He meant to remain at Annossy.

He meant to make a home here or at Sayerne, in service to Lord Quinn.

She did not need to fear that he would tempt her affection and then disappear.

And he had given her a gift, given it to her and no other. She looked but he had left the kitchen, perhaps returning to either stable or hall.

Berthe considered the import of that.

What if Sir Rogue was not such a rogue after all?

She left the cider, asking a scullery maid to tend it for a moment, and ran after Bayard. She found him outside the stables, conferring with the ostler, but he turned as if he had guessed she would follow.

Or hoped she had. For his eyes lit with a pleasure that told Berthe her instinct was right.

"I think it wondrous," she told him, then stretched up to whisper in his ear. "It is said that a man can climb the tower on the side furthest from the gates, that there are handholds and footholds hidden in the stone, and that the solar can be gained that way."

"Why would anyone allow such a course to exist?" Bayard asked.

"It is said that the lord could retake the solar thus, if it was held against him." She smiled and shrugged. "I do not know if it is true, but the grey stone is said to be the place to begin."

Bayard smiled then and bent down so quickly for a kiss that she had no chance to evade him.

Or so she told herself.

"I thank you," he whispered, then touched his lips to hers again. Before he could have more ideas, Berthe pivoted and hastened back to the kitchen, her cheeks burning and her heart racing. She was well aware that Bayard watched her all the way and that there was something new in his expression.

He meant to stay.

The night fell like a black cloak over the valley and the rain drummed upon the roof of Annossy. Melissande moved from window to window in the solar, seeking some sign of Quinn's return. There was only darkness in every direction and the gleam of water on every surface.

She stood with her cloak wrapped tightly around herself and considered the myriad possibilities. He could have been injured. He could have been thrown from his steed and be lying in need of aid. He could have been attacked by brigands and left to die. He could have forded the river in a poor location and been swept away, taken by surprise by the rising water.

He could have abandoned her.

But no man of sense would surrender a holding so rich as Annossy. Quinn had taken the seal, though.

Perhaps he only left *her*.

The fact remained that he had vowed to return this very night. Melissande reminded herself that Quinn kept his pledges and feared that something had gone awry.

It made no sense to worry about Quinn. The man had been all the way to Palestine and back. He had fought in crusade, been imprisoned and wounded, and survived it all. He was clearly strong, but the longer he was gone, the more Melissande worried.

There was naught that she could do and Melissande did not like that truth a whit.

Nay, there was one thing she *could* do, one deed that Quinn did not fulfill this night.

She donned her heaviest cloak and settled herself beside the window that faced the mill. Quinn was not at home to watch for the fire that would signal an attack on the mill, so Melissande would watch in his stead.

'Twas the duty of a wife and lady of the keep and she would not disappoint her lord husband.

The rain fell incessantly once it started, continuing through the night. The river rose ever higher and the mist was so close to the ground the next morning that it felt as if Annossy had been swallowed by the clouds. Sound was both muffled and amplified and Melissande was tired, having sat at the window all the night long. Gaultier was in a sour mood, and tempers were short in the great hall. She returned to the books and Berthe brought her mending to sit beside her. Melissande wondered if she was the only one listening for hoof beats.

When she heard them, it was late afternoon. She looked up, scarcely daring to believe, then rose to her feet when there was a shout from the curtain wall.

"My lord Quinn returns!" cried a man and there was cheer from the villagers.

Melissande put away the ledgers, leaving Louis to secure them, then hurried to the bailey. The gates were open by the time she reached it, and a party rode through. She recognized Quinn's destrier immediately, that beast stamping and snorting as he was reined in to a halt. Quinn doffed his helmet and tossed it to Michel, then grinned at her. "My lady!" he said and swung from the saddle, bowing before her with such powerful grace that her mouth went dry.

"My lord," she said and curtseyed to him. "I am glad to see you returned."

"Are you?" he murmured, his smile widening as she blushed a little. He caught her hand in his and pressed a kiss to her palm, then spun her to face the two men who rode with him. "I would introduce two more of my comrades from Palestine, Luc and Thierry Douglas."

God in heaven, how many of them would there be? Despite her concerns, Melissande smiled and greeted the knights, glad beyond all that they each had only a single squire.

Four more horses, though.

Quinn bent down to whisper to her, the heat of his breath stirring her hair and disrupting her calculations. To her surprise, there was humor in his tone and she found herself glad when the weight of his hand landed on the back of her waist. "And as I have learned much from my lady already, I brought smoked eels from Tulley as well as more wine."

Melissande's lips parted as a cart came into view behind the knights and their steeds. It was pulled by a sturdy mare and laden with barrels.

"How did you afford it?" she whispered.

Quinn smiled. "My lord Tulley was inclined to grant me a gift, and I had the wits, thanks to you, to name something of use."

"Why did he give you a gift?" she whispered, and he laughed.

"I see we share a view of Lord de Tulley and his intentions," Quinn said. "Come, my lady, to the hall. I have tidings to share with the people of Annossy."

What was this?

"But our guests..."

"Louis!" Quinn called and that man appeared immediately. The older man surrendered a key to Melissande as soon as he had bowed to Quinn.

"Welcome home, my lord."

"And I am well met. Louis, could you see to the welfare of my guests? I fear, like all of my companions arriving from the East, they would give much for a hot bath."

Gaultier folded his arms across his chest to watch, but Melissande turned away from him. She was keenly aware of the weight of his dagger, hidden beneath her skirts.

"Of course, my lord. I shall see the arrangements made immediately, my lord." Louis bowed again, then whistled for the ostler, setting half the household to running.

Quinn looked down at the key, then met Melissande's gaze.

"It is for the trunk that secures the ledgers," she said, then realizing his import, offered the key to Quinn.

His smile was blindingly bright and the sight dazzled her.

His words startled her even more. "I would ask you to hold it in trust for me, my lady. Louis has told me that you have a great talent with the books and take pride in their clarity."

"I do."

"Then perhaps you might continue that labor, for sums are not my strength."

Melissande was astonished again and could only nod agreement. Her fingers closed around the key and she felt gratitude for this responsibility.

"I hope that you will explain them to me, at your leisure."

"Of course."

"And now I bring tidings from Tulley," Quinn said, raising his voice and addressing the villagers who had gathered in the bailey. "Lord de Tulley wishes the fields at Sayerne to be tilled this year, for he desires the grain of the harvest. Many of you will know that I do not hold the seal of my father's holding and have no chance of gaining it before my lady and I have been wedded a year and been delivered of a son." There was whispering at this, for not all had heard the details or been assured of their truth. Melissande wondered why Quinn confided this to the villagers.

How like Tulley to insist that the fields be tilled so he could claim the harvest. She folded her arms across her chest, unable to hide her disapproval of this notion.

But Quinn smiled, against all expectation. "No doubt he thought me a simple knight and crusader, one who knew little of practicalities. Already Lord de Tulley has forgotten the measure of the wife he himself granted to me." Quinn turned his smile upon Melissande and she found herself blushing. He shook a finger. "I know that seed is not found free of charge and I doubt that fields that have been left untilled will be easy to sow. I know that it is a goodly ride to Sayerne from Annossy, too far to journey there and back each day to work the fields. I have been to Sayerne of late and seen that there is no place to abide and naught to eat. I know also that my lady wishes to defend the prosperity of Annossy, and rightly so, even against the needs of Sayerne."

Melissande watched and listened, intrigued.

"And so I said unto Lord de Tulley that his will could not be done."

The company gasped.

"Unless, of course, he was inclined to be of aid in the pursuit of his goal."

The villagers laughed at this and jostled each other, their expressions expectant.

"And so I offer to you a choice. Lord de Tulley declares that he will send seed, that he will send food and materials and men to rebuild Sayerne, and that he will do all of this in exchange for one third of the harvested grain."

Melissande blinked in surprise. The villagers murmured to each other and conversations began in the crowd.

Quinn had to raise his voice to finish. "And so I ask, for you are pledged to me and my service, and I know that many of you came to Annossy from Sayerne. If you would choose to return to Sayerne, come and tell me of your desire. We shall decide how many can be supported, sheltered and defended, and begin to rebuild Sayerne." He took Melissande's hand. "In the hope that my lady and I will welcome a son before the year is out and the seal of that holding will be ours as well."

There was a cheer at this notion, and Melissande could not evade the truth of how pleased many of the villeins were. Home was home, she wagered, and she guessed that they would prefer to return to the place of their memories.

"You go too far in this, sir," Gaultier said, stepping to Melissande's side. "You cannot take villeins from Annossy to Sayerne, not without the approval of Lady Melissande."

Quinn's eyes narrowed and he held fast to Melissande's hand. "Your understanding of the law is limited, Gaultier," he said.

"Aye," Melissande agreed. "It is perfectly legal for any lord to invite those pledged to his hand to move to another of his holdings. In this, I believe my lord husband fulfills the hopes and dreams of many who fled Sayerne in the past."

"You cannot concur with him!" Gaultier said.

Melissande nodded. "But I do. They were offered shelter and have prospered here, but I know how a place can hold fast to one's heart."

"I still believe, my lady, that your lord husband should have asked your approval before he spoke."

Melissande took a breath, knowing that she had to prove to Quinn and all those who listened that she accepted his authority. "My husband is Lord d'Annossy. He holds the seal. He wears my father's garments. My approval is not required when he acts within the law."

The air fairly crackled between the three of them, then Quinn spoke with his usual calm. "I would ask my lady's counsel in one matter," he said and she looked at him. His gaze was hard, and locked upon Gaultier. "What fate would you decree for a man who gained a post in your service because he lied?"

"What is this?" Melissande asked. She looked at Gaultier, for Quinn was studying him, and found his expression furious.

"Lord de Tulley did not dispatch Gaultier de Lonvaux to Annossy, nor did he recommend that this man become Annossy's Captain of Arms."

"That is not true!" Gaultier said.

"The sole tale that Lord de Tulley knows of Gaultier is a rumor of his unnatural relations with his aunt after the demise of the uncle who trained him for his spurs. It seemed the knight had hopes of a fortuitous marriage, which were shattered when the aunt wed another. Oddly enough, that occurred just before Gaultier appeared at Annossy's gates."

Gaultier's eyes flashed. "You know naught of it," he spat at Quinn.

"I know sufficient to dismiss you from the service of this holding," Quinn replied with resolve and his voice rose as he made his pronouncement. "You will take your possessions. You will leave in this moment. And you will take the men-at-arms you hired to defend the mill with you. Your shadow is cast over all of them, and none of you will ever enter these gates again."

"You cannot do this to me!" Gaultier cried.

"I most certainly can," Quinn replied.

"My lady!" Gaultier appealed to her.

"I am no longer your lady," she said, her hand upon Quinn's. "You should never have deceived me, Gaultier."

"I have served you!" he roared. "I have defended you! I have earned more of a hearing than this!"

"There is another choice," Quinn said mildly. "You may prefer to be charged with treason, confined in Annossy's dungeon and heard when next we hold court. When will that be, my lady?"

"On the day after full moon. Three weeks hence."

"I am a knight," Gaultier fumed. "I am a man of honor and I shall not be treated with such indignity..."

"You are a liar," Quinn said. "And the opportunity to depart with your steed and weapons is far more than you deserve."

Gaultier clearly saw the merit of this argument. He spun and marched to the stables, only to discover that the ostler met him there with his stabled horse. The villagers watched in silence as he mounted, glared at Quinn, then rode out the gates with the men-at-arms behind.

"You have made an enemy this day, my lord," Melissande said, unable to silence her feeling of dread.

"Nay. I already had an enemy, and I would rather he was outside the walls than within my own hall."

There was, Melissande had to admit, good sense in that, though still she was uneasy.

CHAPTER FOURTEEN

uinn felt as if he had won a great victory. It had been bold to issue his invitation to the villeins without discussing the matter with Melissande first, but he had not thought it through. The moment had seemed ripe and he had followed his impulse. He was glad she had neither rebuked or challenged him, but he knew all was not yet resolved.

The storm might come in private.

Or not at all.

One thing he admired most about his wife was that she was clever. She knew of things he did not, and so he could not always anticipate her. She had a keen sense of justice, though, and he liked that she was not weak or fearful. She was a beauty, like his mother, but she did not possess his mother's frailty and Quinn was glad of that.

He was glad to be wed to a woman who would tell him if he was wrong.

He was determined never again to fail a woman who relied upon him, as he had failed his mother.

Trusting his wife completely was another matter, though. Did Melissande still possess Gaultier's dagger? What was between them? How could he discover that truth?

"You will be most relieved," Quinn said to her as they crossed the hall. "Lord de Tulley confirms that your betrothed wed another before we exchanged our vows."

Melissande frowned. "He told me as much, but I find myself skeptical."

Quinn arched a brow. "Indeed?"

"Do you not think Tulley would say whatever was necessary to win his desire?"

"Nay, I do not." He halted beside her and met her gaze. It was time to dismiss her concerns about her betrothal once and for all. "He is tough but honorable and not deceptive. You must accept, my lady, that your betrothed wed another. It is our future that is of import."

She studied him warily. "And your need for a son."

"*We* have need of a son," he reminded her.

"Sayerne's seal hangs in the balance, and I have no desire for it. *You* desire a son, sir."

Her emphasis made Quinn wonder. "And what do you desire?"

She met his gaze. "My desire is of no import, as we have seen already this day."

Ah, she was annoyed. "Your desire is of import to me."

"Indeed?" she said mildly, a thrum of anger beneath her words.

"Indeed." He put his hand beneath her elbow and guided her to the stairs.

"Your desire is pressing?" she asked.

"I would speak to you in private," Quinn said. "That you might share the truth of your thoughts."

She exhaled and shook her head, even as she accompanied him to the stairs. "You challenge my every expectation."

"As you defy mine. Is that not a good omen for our match?"

Melissande pivoted to face him. She was two steps above him and their gazes were level. "On the contrary, I think it a sign that we are poorly matched."

"I think otherwise. What drudgery it would be to find oneself wed to a person who offered neither surprise nor challenge. A lifetime together would feel like an eternity."

She eyed him. "I thought you wished a compliant wife."

"So did I," Quinn confessed, noting how she seemed puzzled

by his smile. "Until I was wedded to you, my lady."

Melissande's eyes lit with humor for a heartbeat, then she spun away. "You attempt to charm me, sir," she said as she marched up the stairs.

"That cannot be. I have been informed by a most reliable source that I am utterly devoid of charm."

She pivoted, glared at him, then continued up the stairs.

"What ails you?" she demanded as she entered the solar, spinning to face him. "Why are you so calm yet persistent on this day?"

Quinn shut the door and leaned back against it. "Because I am home, and I am glad of it. Because I am wedded and I am grateful for it." He pointed to the floor. "Because this is where we will build our future, Melissande, and I intend to do whatever is necessary to see that done."

"You dismiss my Captain of Arms," she said, flinging out a hand. "And I am to smile sweetly. You invite my villeins to abandon Annossy and I am to nod approval. You fill my hall with your comrades of war and I am to both welcome them and see them fed. You scheme with Tulley to rebuild Sayerne at his expense—"

"I thought you would be pleased by that," Quinn interjected. "I should never have thought to negotiate with him, had I not learned so much already from you."

Again, he was granted a hot look for that comment. "And now you will plant your seed. What happens once you have your son?" She flung out her hands. "What happens to me once I have fulfilled that obligation? What happens to Annossy when you cast it aside for Sayerne? How long is this match of convenience to endure?"

"You wish to wed another."

"I wish to *choose* my future, not to be told how it will be!"

Quinn saw the fear flash in her eyes and guessed the truth. "You fear I will abandon you."

"I fear that I am useful, no more and no less, and that once my purpose is fulfilled, I may no longer be so. It is not the same for women, my lord. If I am cast aside by my husband after bearing him a son, then I will be a widow of no import. You already possess Annossy. Do not take my dignity and my future, as well." She straightened and held his gaze. "Tell me the worst of it, my lord. Tell me your plan."

It was infuriating that she always saw the worst possibility, and blamed him for it. Quinn strove to control his temper. "I am not my father," he said with force and Melissande lifted her chin. "I have done naught to earn your distrust. I have asked for your counsel. I have heeded your advice. I have defended your family holding as if it were my own."

"It *is* your own!" she cried.

"Just as you are my wife!" he roared. "That makes you Lady d'Annossy. We are bound together, Melissande, by our own pledges. I would have an honest and loving marriage of merit, but I cannot compel you to trust me. Indeed, I cannot win your trust, either, no matter what I do and how I defend your interests. It seems that you withhold it apurpose."

"There is naught else I can withhold," she countered with some bitterness, and he turned to face her.

"You are afraid."

"I am not afraid," she snapped, but her tone revealed the truth. Was it possible that she held him in some affection? Did she argue with such heat because she came to care for him? Quinn knew that he himself was utterly smitten, but he had learned to be wary of Melissande's quick wits. He would not hasten to claim any victory, but would proceed with caution, and let the lady come to him.

"What will you do when you have your son?" she demanded again.

Quinn held his ground, his mood much improved by his sense of the possibilities. "I will do what my lady wife commands. If she wishes to truly put her hand in mine and labor for a better future, then I will welcome her wisdom and her skills. But if she wishes to remain alone at Annossy, I will leave her."

"You will take another woman to your bed," she accused and his temper flared again.

"You cannot have the matter every which way!" Quinn roared. "You can be my wife in truth, or you can push me aside. I will honor your wish in this, but I will not sacrifice every advantage I hold to see you secure at Annossy without me. You cannot cast me aside yet decide who comes to my bed. We are *wed*, Melissande, and if you desire a match of merit, you must meet me halfway."

She folded her arms across her chest yet looked less formidable. "I did not wish to argue with you."

Quinn was relieved that she saw the sense of his appeal. "There would be a change," he dared to tease her and was rewarded with a fleeting smile.

"Let us begin this discussion again," Melissande said, her tone softer. "I owe you an apology, and I was disappointed that you had departed yesterday morn, for I could not surrender it to you."

"An apology?"

"I was too harsh. I said too much about the reputation of Annossy." Melissande flushed and dropped her gaze. A note of confusion claimed her voice and dismissed every bit of Quinn's vexation. She so seldom allowed him to glimpse her vulnerability and it affected him powerfully. If she could have guessed that he was hers to command for the price of a single tear, he did not doubt she would have been more prepared to share her true feelings with him.

That did not mean, however, that he could make such a sweet confession.

Now, she paced, her brows drawn together in annoyance. "I cannot fathom why you make me so angry, or why I lose my composure in your presence. It frightens me to so lose control of my own tongue. I feel uncertain of what will happen when we argue, and that troubles me." She fell silent then, and her color rose even more as she stole a glance at him.

Quinn could not help but chuckle in his relief. "We have this in common, my lady," he murmured. "I am known for my temperance yet you—" He took a breath as she watched, then shook his head. "You, my lady, set my very blood afire." He wagged a finger at her. "I want to shout with fury when you challenge me. I could shake you to make you see sense."

"Or your version of it," she countered, softening her words with a smile.

Quinn smiled, surprised into it. "I could kiss you to silence or seduce you until you have no argument to make."

She stared at him, eyes wide, and swallowed. "Is it not unnatural?" she whispered.

"I do not care. I think it most excellent. I like that we enflame each other, for it hints that this union is of import to both of us." He took a step closer and she did not retreat. Nor did she look away. "For when all is said and done, it seems we oft agree."

"Aye," she admitted, her gaze clinging to his. "And the simple truth of it is that even though you say I irk you, you have never raised a hand against me. You never have shaken me to see sense, or seduced me to silence me."

"And I never will."

Melissande nodded with welcome confidence in that. She swallowed, then impaled him with an intent glance. "Why did you leave Sayerne?"

Quinn was startled by the abrupt question, but knew he had to reply. "Because he beat her," he said, bowing his head at the ignoble truth of it. His throat tightened at the memory and he hated that he had been not able to defend his own mother. "He struck her until she bled and I could not bear it. I was only a child when I tried to defend her, then he beat me, as well." He swallowed and looked away from Melissande, glad that she had never known such horror. When he recalled his father's violence and hatred, he could understand her doubts about his nature.

She laid a hand upon his arm and he laid his hand atop it, grateful for this encouragement. His voice was husky when he continued. "I tried to convince her to flee with me, but she would not leave him. I could not persuade her."

"You tried, Quinn."

"It was insufficient. He learned of what he called my treachery. He beat me for it, then cast me out. It was the dead of winter and she cried out, but then she was silenced." His throat worked and he could not summon any words for a moment, so overcome was he by the awareness of his own weakness.

Melissande stepped closer. "You were only a boy," she whispered, giving him clemency that he could not give himself.

Quinn fought to compose himself. "I should have frozen to death outside the walls. But Tulley was at hunt and found me. He took me away and sent me to train for my spurs." He dared to meet Melissande's gaze. "I thought to learn to fight that I could defend her."

"But by the time you could do as much, she was dead," Melissande whispered, her words filled with welcome compassion.

"And Tulley dictated my course. I owe him my life, but I still regret that my mother would not come with me."

"She died there as a result," Melissande said. "She died for her loyalty to Jerome."

Quinn nodded and bowed his head. "I should never have left her."

"Then you would be dead, as well. Even I know that Jerome did not tolerate defiance." She leaned against him but he could not look at her. "You are not your father's son, Quinn, and I am most glad of it. You are a man of honor." Then to his astonishment, she placed her hand upon his cheek. "I feared you had abandoned me," she whispered. "I was shaken by how much I missed you. I am most glad of your return."

Quinn risked a glance at his lady, to find her eyes shining. His heart skipped. "No matter the terms?"

She smiled. "Apparently so."

Quinn could not summon a word to his lips. Desire raged through him, but he reminded himself of her courses and strove to keep his need in check.

"I watched for the flame at the mill last night, as you could not," she admitted, remaining close and speaking as if she knew he needed a moment to compose himself.

"Did you?" The confession pleased Quinn greatly, even though he knew that his comrades would have watched as well. He was filled with tension yet unwilling to move lest he frighten Melissande away. He watched her, nigh holding his breath, as she tipped her head back and trailed her fingertips down his cheek to his mouth. Her skin was soft and cool, and he felt like a rough warrior in comparison to her fine beauty.

Melissande was not weak like his mother.

She was a queen, a lady, and his wife.

Quinn would love her until the end of his days, and beyond.

"Come to bed, sir," she said with new urgency and he feared he had only imagined the words. She smiled at him and his chest squeezed with painful vigor. "We have a son to conceive."

Quinn grinned at her invitation, catching her in his arms and swinging her around. Melissande protested, but when he set her on her feet, he caught her close and kissed her with abandon. He finally broke their kiss, his arm locked still around her waist, holding her captive against his chest.

"Tell me now if you still have your courses," he growled and Melissande smiled up at him, her expression so playful that he guessed what she would say before she did.

"I never did," she admitted. "I was merely vexed with you."

Quinn laughed again and scooped her into his arms, then stole another kiss. "I will make you a wager, my Melissande," he said as he carried her toward the bed. "Whenever one of us is vexed with the other, I suggest we spend that passion abed."

She gasped. "That is a scandalous suggestion, sir."

"But one with appeal?"

Her eyes twinkled so merrily that Quinn dared to believe in their shared future. She flushed a little and smiled at him. "Indeed, sir. Though I fear you may start an argument apurpose in future."

"Nay," he said solemnly. "'Twill be you who do as much." She gasped again in mock outrage, then laughed. Quinn kissed her soundly, the time for words being well past.

Her husband was a sorcerer.

Or perhaps he was an elixir that once sampled, left a woman desperate for more.

Either way, Quinn kindled a need within Melissande, satisfied it, yet could readily make her yearn for his touch again. It was the reverence in his expression and his caress, as if he feared she might fade to naught before his very eyes. He was so gentle, despite his strength. The fact that he tempered himself in order to give her pleasure was a concession that fed her own confidence in this deed.

Indeed, their coupling was more pleasurable each and every time.

She indulged her impulses this time and surrendered completely to their lovemaking. She felt his surprise when she took the lead, but could not mistake his approval. How could their passion be more potent each time? It was a puzzle she could not explain, but Melissande did not care.

She wanted Quinn.

She did not mind that he knew the truth of it.

She met him touch for touch, demanding more and more, and they exhausted each other in their quest for pleasure. The culmination was a marvel beyond marvels and she collapsed atop him in the bed, wondering how many had heard their triumphant cries.

"I have a confession to make," Quinn said when they were entangled together and sated.

"Not another," Melissande teased and he chuckled.

He lifted a tendril of her hair and twisted it between finger and thumb, then wound it around his fingertip. "I like what you teach me," he said.

Melissande rolled to lie atop him. "It seems that in matters abed, you teach me, sir."

"Nay, it is not so simple as that, but that is not what I meant."

"What then?"

"I thought of your inventories."

"Which is why you brought fish and wine. That was most welcome. How many more comrades do you expect to arrive at our gates?"

"None. For there is only one more and he is said to be wed." Quinn lifted a finger. "But when Tulley insisted that Sayerne fields should be tilled this year, I thought of my practical wife and her ledgers."

"And you negotiated." She smiled as she watched him, liking his pride in his accomplishment. He should be proud to have won a concession from Tulley.

"Aye."

"You did not insult him, I hope."

Quinn shook his head. "I think he respected the novelty."

Melissande laughed and Quinn joined her merriment.

"He vowed that he will send the seed, and men to rebuild the homes of the villeins, and provisions for those who choose to go to Sayerne from Annossy to till the land."

Melissande pursed her lips. "Yet he will take only a third of the harvest. However did you win such a concession? I am certain he wished for more."

"Half," Quinn admitted and she winced. "I told him that Annossy should not be diminished for the sake of Sayerne."

"You say this to seduce me fully."

"I say this because it is good sense." Quinn kissed the tip of her nose then rose from the bed with purpose. "I have much to learn, Melissande. Will you teach me more? Louis says you find satisfaction in keeping the ledgers and I would be glad if you so continued, but I would like to learn of them myself."

"Aye, of course."

He granted her a look. "What do you know of Perricault?"

Melissande felt her eyes narrow. "It lies to the north and is the holding of the widow, Marie, said to have wed my betrothed, Arnaud de Privas."

Quinn in the act of donning a chemise spun to face her. "Marie?" he repeated. "The same Marie who wed Arnaud is of Perricault?"

"Aye." Melissande blinked. "Why is that of import?"

"I am not certain," he confessed with a frown. "But this is twice I have heard tell of Perricault in rapid succession." He crossed the room and drew the blade that Gaultier had entrusted to her, showing her the inscription.

Melissande frowned. "Marie is Gaultier's aunt?"

"And the woman Heloise said he courted after his uncle's death."

"I do not understand."

"Nor do I, but Gaultier is said to have come to your gates, without Tulley's recommendation, after Marie wed Arnaud de Privas."

"Thereby breaking my betrothal to him." Melissande shook her head. "If that were true, it would be a most curious coincidence."

"Nay. I do not believe in coincidence, not any longer. It is a hint of a scheme."

"But what manner of scheme?"

He met her gaze. "Surely you do not imagine that I am the sole one with the ambition to claim Annossy?"

Melissande's thoughts spun with the implications. This tale lent credence to the one of Arnaud wedding Marie, though she still had difficulties believing Gaultier to be so deceptive. "But if Arnaud is wed to Marie, he governs Perricault. Why would he send Gaultier here?"

"Naught says he did. Gaultier, however, might have sought another noblewoman of property in the hope of making a fortuitous match." Quinn handed her the sheathed dagger as she considered this possibility again. If Gaultier had intended to court her, she had never guessed as much. If she had done so, she would have seen that notion dismissed from his thoughts.

"You should keep this," Quinn advised. "For it is a good blade."

Melissande nodded.

"Though I hope you do not need to defend yourself, I am glad to see you armed." Quinn spoke with confidence and Melissande understood that he trusted her not to use the knife against him. She would not. "I shall see this matter resolved with as much haste as possible."

"But you dismissed Gaultier and his comrades."

He smiled with a confidence she did not share. "I do not think we have seen the last of him. Such a lofty ambition will not be readily abandoned."

"Then why dismiss him, never mind leaving him with both horse and weapons?"

"We have but baited the trap, my lady. I doubt it will be long before it is sprung." Quinn whistled to himself as he dressed, though Melissande stared at him for a long moment, the weight of the dagger in her hand.

"A trap?" she echoed. "God in Heaven, will you risk your own life to see Annossy rid of the brigands?" she whispered and he turned to survey her.

"Would you mourn my loss if I did?" he asked softly.

"Aye," she admitted. "I would."

"Well, then. That is something." He nodded once and turned his back upon her, whistling once more.

He did not mean to confide in her.

That choice filled Melissande with new doubts. 'Twas true Quinn had insisted she keep the blade and that he seduced her well abed, but on this day, he had also dismissed Annossy's Captain of the Guard and the men he had hired, without consulting Melissande. She felt control of the holding slip away and did not like it a whit.

Melissande hastened from the bed, thinking this was no cause for merriment. She crossed the chamber and took his arm. "Tell me of your scheme."

"What scheme, my lady?" Quinn asked lightly and she knew he would not share the details with her. Her heart chilled that he did not trust her fully. "My sole scheme is the defense of Annossy." He turned then to confront her. "Are there any other ways into the keep, beyond the gates and the sewers?"

This time, it was Melissande who turned her back. If he would keep his secrets, then she would keep hers as well. "I do not know of any," she said, keeping her tone even. "Perhaps Louis knows more."

Perhaps she would have to defend Annossy's solar against its new lord.

"Perhaps. I will ask him." Then Quinn left the solar, still whistling, while Melissande stood and wondered whether she had erred.

Ten nights after the departure of Gaultier and his comrades, Annossy's mill was attacked.

Quinn was more than ready.

The moon was new, the night darker than dark. He sat at the window of the solar, fully armed, well aware that Melissande watched him from the bed but did not sleep herself. Though they had worked together since his return from Tulley, and they were intimate each night, there was a barrier between them.

She had lied about ways in and out of the keep.

Quinn had guessed as much immediately, for her eyes revealed when she disguised the truth. His wife was not an accomplished liar, which he admired greatly—though it grieved him when she did mislead him. He had been disappointed to learn from Bayard shortly after leaving the solar that his impression had been correct. There was another way into the solar, designed to ensure that the lord could retake it after an assault, and it could even be reached from outside the walls, if one knew where to look for it.

Quinn was certain that Melissande did.

At its root, this was the same issue. She feared to trust him fully. She feared to lose her import at Annossy. Though Quinn understood her feelings, he could not do more to overcome her doubts than he had. He would prove himself in deeds, and could only hope that in time, when his lady's worst fears did not come to fruition, it would prove to be sufficient.

The compromise did not content him, but the lady had to make her own choice.

In the short term, however, he had a holding to defend.

In a way, it was a relief when the flame appeared in the distance. It flared orange, and flickered as Quinn rose to his feet. He could have no doubt of its import, though, for the fire raged higher as the wood caught and cast sparks into the sky. Niall and Lothair would already be fighting the brigands.

Quinn did not waste a moment. He spun from the window and strode for the stairs. "I shall return when I can, my lady."

Melissande rose from the bed and seized his sleeve. "You cannot mean to ride out yourself! I thought you would send your comrades and defend Annossy yourself."

"I ride with my comrades." Quinn chafed at the delay, though he could not be rude to her. He did not wish to spoil an accord that he feared was fragile. "The defense of all of Annossy is my responsibility."

"But you could be injured!"

"I have been injured before and lived to tell of it." He tugged his sleeve free of her grasp.

"But you could be killed," she said with a distress that appeared genuine. "Send another in your stead, Quinn!"

Her use of his name was like a blow to the heart, but Quinn knew what had to be done. "I gave my word to the miller that I would defend his abode as my own," he insisted with heat and turned away.

This night might change all between them. He prayed that it might and hurried to the portal, pausing to glance back.

Melissande said no more, but folded her arms across her chest, watching him go. She bit her lip as she watched him and he saw tears glisten in her eyes. As ever, the sight of her vulnerability affected him powerfully. He hoped with all his measure that she truly was concerned for him.

"Is there some detail you would tell me?" he asked and she shook her head, her tears flying.

Still she withheld the tale of the second entry.

That told Quinn all he needed to know.

It disappointed him deeply.

On impulse, he reached into his purse and removed the one item he knew Melissande desired above all else. He tossed it to her as if it were a trinket of far less value than it truly was. He saw her catch the seal, then look down. There was no doubting the moment that she realized what she held, for her eyes lit and then she frowned.

"You should not surrender this to me," she whispered even as her fist closed over it.

"I spare you the trouble of seeking it, should I not return," he said, disappointment in his tone. She only stared at him. That displeased him—he would rather have parted with a kiss—and he turned to march down the stairs. His cloak flared behind him and he found his comrades already on their feet, awaiting him in hall and bailey.

"Sir! You cannot mean to die this night!" Melissande called from behind him.

He pivoted to find her on the stairs, her hair unbound and her chemise more sheer than she realized, her gaze filled with concern. She was a vision of loveliness, one that made his throat tighten, and he knew he would always remember her thus.

But she had not used his name.

"Few men mean to die when they meet their end, my lady." He bowed then and continued to the stables, his comrades quick behind him.

He risked more than she knew this night and he wished he could have trusted her fully.

The plan was made and now Quinn could only hope for its success.

Quinn's sense of duty would be his undoing. The man was as vexing as the first day Melissande had met him—nay, more so, for now she cared about his survival and recognized that much was reliant upon him. Honor and duty. The very words made Melissande grit her teeth. As Lord d'Annossy, it was not his personal obligation to strike the killing blow against the brigands.

He should send his comrades or his men-at-arms.

He should delegate, not risk his own hide!

Melissande dressed in haste, lacing the sides of her kirtle and tugging on her boots without stockings. The keep was filled with activity, though no one raised their voice. All was being prepared in stealth. Despite her haste, by the time she reached the hall, Quinn and his men were gone. She raced into the bailey to see the rump of Quinn's destrier as he led the company through the gates.

Curse him. He even wore her father's tabard this night, making himself an easy target. She bit her fist, her fear rising high, and hoped that she would have the opportunity to chastise him, then welcome him abed.

Nigh all of his comrades rode with him. They were armed and helmeted, their dark cloaks hiding their mail from view. She spied the steeds of Luc and Thierry, right behind Fortitude, then Amaury touched his fingertip to his helmet in salute as his horse cantered past her. Melissande stared after the men as all the many squires on their palfreys, each and every one armed, rode around her and filed out the gates. They had been prepared this night, and likely all the nights of late, to ride out at Quinn's command with little notice.

A movement at the top of Annossy's wall, above the gates,

drew her eye. A knight was silhouetted on the balustrade, his helmet and his raised gloved hand catching a glimmer of light as he waved off Quinn's party. She realized it was Bayard by his green tabard and the shape of his helmet. She saw him gesture for the gates to be closed after Quinn's departure, then take up his stance above the gates.

One comrade left in Annossy's defense.

One.

Melissande's sense of foreboding grew at that, even though she knew Quinn's expertise with warfare was far beyond her own. She knew also that Bayard must be a competent warrior and a trusted one for Quinn to have assigned him this task. Quinn had said he set a trap and he must have allowed for all the possibilities. Still, she was fearful.

She compelled herself to think of practical matters. The company would return hungry, at the very least, if not injured. She went to the kitchens to rouse the cook and urge him to set soup upon the fire. She sent to the village for the healer, for she was uncertain whether Quinn's companion Lothair would return to the keep or not. She consulted with that woman to make preparations in the hall, and wished she knew what was happening. The hall was filled with quiet purpose, women and men working as silently as shadows, their expressions fearful.

Quinn had given her the seal instead of a kiss farewell. How could he believe that only the seal of Annossy was of importance to her?

Melissande wished she had thought more quickly and spoken the truth to him. She wished she had told him about the old pathway to the solar, even though she was not certain of its existence. She had been compelled to wed him, she had challenged him and fought him, and Quinn had countered her objections with persistence, patience and honor.

She could love him.

She feared again for his survival and knew she already did.

Melissande wished with all her heart that she would have the opportunity to tell him so.

CHAPTER FIFTEEN

hen all was made ready for the return of the knights, Melissande returned to the solar, hoping she could see something of what happened at the mill from the high windows. She bolted the door behind herself, leaving the solar in darkness as she crossed to the window. The new moon meant the night was dark and she wanted to see whatever could be discerned. There was no lantern lit in the solar and the brazier, which had been stirred up when she had first come to bed, was now nigh cold. Only a coal or two glowed faintly orange within it.

When she looked toward the mill, there was only the silence of the night. The bonfire had been doused. She could not hear a single sound of battle, but she did hear men's voices. She leaned out the window as she spotted lights on the road to the mill. A party was returning to Annossy, a large party by the sound of the horses. There were torches being carried alongside, and she guessed that the squires lit the way.

The men were singing and she leaned against the frame with relief. Quinn's men had triumphed. Doubtless, they returned to Annossy with the brigands captive or injured. She had to admit that Quinn had been right about leaving only one knight behind. Annossy had not been assaulted, much to her relief.

The challenge to Annossy's borders was resolved, and Quinn

had done it.

She stepped back from the window, intent upon ensuring the soup was hot for the returning party, then heard the stealthy sound of a boot on the floor behind her.

Melissande spun quickly, but not quickly enough. A man seized her from behind and shoved a cloth into her mouth. She struggled against him but he was more powerful than she. She was enraged by his audacity.

What travesty was this? Who dared to assault the Lady d'Annossy in her own chamber?

Even as she struggled, her heart chilled. Her assailant must have known of the other entry. Whoever assaulted her, he had scaled the tower in the darkness. Too late she wished she had confided in Quinn.

Her attacker kicked her feet out from beneath her and she fell hard to the floor. He was overwhelming Melissande easily, which terrified her. She could never defend herself, not with force, for her attacker was much stronger.

Panicking, she thought of Quinn and his experience at war. She thought of how he turned matters on their heads to gain the element of surprise and realized this man expected her to fight him to her last.

Instead, Melissande gasped and pretended to faint. She collapsed on the floor and heard her attacker grunt with satisfaction.

He bent over her, reaching to bind her wrists. She felt the heavy rope upon one wrist and she did not know whether he intended to capture her or violate her. She gave him the chance to do neither. With her other hand, she pulled Gaultier's dagger from its sheath in her garter. She stabbed upward, not bothering to cast back her skirts lest the knife blade shine in the dark. Her hand was beneath his mail hauberk, for it brushed the back of her wrist. She felt the blade sink home—into his thigh, perhaps—and warm blood run down her arm as her attacker swore.

"Deceptive whore!" he snarled and Melissande froze in recognition of his voice.

Gaultier!

She tried to stab him again, but he caught her wrist and twisted it backward. If she could have made a sound, she would have cried out in pain. She was compelled to drop the blade and heard it clatter to the floor. She could not see it in the darkness and wondered how she would retrieve it.

Gaultier meanwhile bound her wrists together with savage force. His breath was coming quickly and his anger was palpable. Melissande's heart raced with fear. How had she allowed this serpent to live within the walls of Annossy? How could she have failed to see his true nature?

But Quinn, Quinn had guessed it from the outset. Melissande could have wept that she had so misplaced her trust. Because of her own failure to confide in her lord husband, she might meet her end at the hands of this villain.

She stumbled when Gaultier dragged her to her feet and pushed her toward the bed. She inadvertently kicked the knife, but it was gone, dancing across the floor. Gaultier must have heard it, as well, for he bent to retrieve something even as he shoved her toward the bed.

"My own dagger," he muttered. While he was distracted, Melissande tried to twist out of his grip. He grabbed her, shook her, then struck her across the face. "Faithless bitch!"

Melissande fell backward and slipped so that she nearly collided with the pillar of the bed. She blinked, astonished that he had struck her, then felt new fear for her survival. She scrambled across the floor, trying to move around the bed even as she fought to recall every item in the solar. Had Berthe left the pail of water or the one for slops? If so, where were they? The last coal glowed in the brazier on the far side of the bed, but where were the tongs? How could she defend herself when her hands were bound?

And what was Gaultier's scheme?

She was a fool a hundred times over and if she survived this day, she would spend her life making amends for her mistake.

Melissande could only hope she had the chance to do as much.

"I hear you, my lady," he whispered, his tone taunting, and her heart fluttered like a caged bird. "You will not evade me. You can come quietly or not. The choice is yours."

What did he intend to do to her?

Melissande tried to quell her rising terror. She heard a rustle and Gaultier's boot on the floor again. She was sure he would find her by the erratic thunder of her heart, or the sound of her breath. She could smell him drawing closer. Why had she told Berthe to remain in the hall? She eased around the bed, trying to stay out of his reach. She reached the side of the bed with the brazier beside it and managed to hook her foot beneath it. It was weighty and top-heavy. Could she kick it with sufficient accuracy to injure Gaultier?

She would certainly try.

She huddled against the bed, trying to become one with it. She held her breath and remained motionless. She thought she could see Gaultier, just barely, a dark silhouette against the shadows. She heard his footstep and waited for what seemed like an eternity. She heard a distant cry and the creak of the gates, then the sound of horses in the bailey. Quinn and his party returned! There was a cheer from those awaiting him.

Gaultier made a low hiss. He took another step and she heard a rustle of cloth.

Could she stall until Quinn came to the solar? She feared not.

"Come here, my lady," Gaultier whispered as if she were so witless as to be enticed to her own doom. "We have not much time. I do not want to injure you. Trust me."

Trust him. The very suggestion sent fury through Melissande. What did this vermin know of trust? No man of merit kidnapped a woman or struck her. A knight vowed to defend those weaker than himself! She heard a faint sound of a boot on stone and knew it was too distant to be Gaultier.

Who else was in the solar? If he had an accomplice, she was lost.

But Gaultier froze and she thought he turned toward the sound.

He was surprised. Did someone come to her aid?

Melissande scratched her nail against the floor, trying to convince him that he had heard her and not another. He chuckled and took a step closer. "There you are," he murmured, and when he took the next step, Melissande kicked the brazier with all her might.

It fell with a thud, scattered coals and debris from the fire across the floor. Gaultier swore again and she hoped it had injured him. She saw one fiery coal began to smolder as it came to a rest on a carpet, but it was too far away to reach. The smoke rose immediately and the flame sparked to life shortly afterward.

In its light, Melissande saw Gaultier lunging toward her, rage in his eyes. She hurled herself under the great bed. She heard him roar then snatch after her, but she scurried to the opposite side to evade him. Her eyes widened when she saw a second pair of boots appear behind Gaultier.

He swore again and stood, then Melissande heard the clash of steel on steel. The two pairs of boots quickly becoming indistinguishable as the men circled and fought with increasing vigor.

Who had come to her assistance?

It was beyond infuriating that she could not see the battle. The flames grew brighter and she squirmed across the floor, emerging on the other side of the bed. Gaultier battled a knight in a green tabard who still wore his helmet.

Melissande shook in her relief.

Bayard had guessed her fate somehow and she was heartily glad of it. She hurried around the bed and began to stamp on the carpet to put out the flames. Now she could see the bucket of washing water, not far away. She hurried to it and kicked it over so that the carpet was doused.

The fire went out, plunging them into darkness again.

The helmeted knight swore with gusto and Melissande turned to stare at him in astonishment. Quinn? Surely she had not recognized his voice. The knight wore Bayard's tabard and helmet. He must have swung his blade, for she heard it whistle through the air, and she ducked, cowering against the wall. No doubt Gaultier would have been glad to seize her, and Melissande scarce dared to breathe. She heard blades clash and men grunt, then a heavy weight fell to the floor.

There was silence.

She feared the import of that. If it had been her benefactor who had fallen, she was at Gaultier's whim. A boot tread sounded on the floor and she closed her eyes in dread.

"Zounds, my lady, but you could have let another measure of the carpet burn," Quinn said with frustration. "I feared to miss the villain and there is no honor in an untidy execution."

It *was* Quinn! Melissande made a choked sound of relief and heard him cross the chamber. She heard his helmet land on the carpet. A flint was struck and a lantern lit. She glanced down at the fallen man and it was Gaultier. His eyes stared blankly at the ceiling, and his blood flowing with vigor from his wounds.

She wished she had given him more than one herself.

Then Quinn blocked her view, ushering her to the other side of the solar. He removed the cloth bound over her mouth and untied her hands, his own brow furrowed in concern as he examined the rising bruise on her temple. He touched the rope burns on her wrists, his hands roving over her as he checked for injuries.

"I am well enough," she said, hearing the quiver in her own voice. He met her gaze and she smiled at him. "I feared you trusted overmuch in your companion, but you never left Annossy."

He grinned and tucked a strand of hair behind her ear. "There is no advantage in leaving the prize undefended," he said and touched his lips to her brow. It was far less than she wanted of him in this moment.

"This was a trap you set," she whispered.

"That it was." He left her for a moment to open the portal and call for assistance from below, then stopped by the bed before he returned. He lifted Gaultier's unsheathed knife, which he had retrieved from the floor. "I am glad I returned it to you."

"I was surprised that you did."

"I think it is right and good for a woman to be able to defend herself against a man determined to take what is not his to claim," Quinn said, his voice a low rumble. "And I trusted you not to use it against me."

"A confident assumption, sir."

"One of us had to make a concession, if we were to establish a truce." He raised a hand, humor in his expression. "I wagered it would have to be me." He watched her, waiting.

Melissande nodded. "I think our truce is made. I am sorry again, Quinn, sorry that I have been too stubborn to appreciate your merit. I am sorry that I did not tell you of the second entry to the solar."

"But you feared you might have to defend the prize of Annossy against me." He eyed her. "Do you still?"

Melissande shook her head with vigor. "Nay, Quinn. Nay."

He crossed the chamber with undisguised satisfaction and folded her into his embrace once more. Melissande felt then that he was shaking as well and closed her eyes at the steady sound of his heart. She wanted to be no other place in the world, and smiled when she felt his kiss against the top of her head.

It would steady him to tell her what he had done, so she asked. "What of the mill? Was it attacked?"

"Aye, but we surprised them. The brigands have been escorted to Annossy's dungeon and I shall have the pleasure of seeing them again when first we hold court together."

"Three days after next full moon is too soon," Melissande said with heat. "Leave them wait until after the next one."

Quinn chuckled, his breath in her hair and his arms tightly wrapped around her. "We think alike in this matter, my lady."

She tipped back her head and found him smiling at her, that glint of lazy intent in his amber gaze. "We do," she agreed. "I feared I would not have the chance to tell you that I love you, my lord husband." She watched his brows rise and relief light his eyes.

"Surely you might call me by my name when you make such a declaration," he teased and Melissande smiled.

She reached up and framed his face in her hands. "I love you, Quinn de Sayerne. I am sorry that I did not see sooner how well matched we are." She shook his tabard a little. "Now, do what you must and do it quickly. I would have you come to bed that I might prove my love to you."

Melissande saw Quinn's eyes flash before he bent and captured her lips with his own, claiming her with another of his seductive and potent kisses. This time, however, she met him touch for touch, surrendering her all to him willingly.

She was well pleased when he groaned and lifted her against

him, his kiss tasting of relief and a passion that answered her own.

It was not done.

Quinn felt as much in his bones, but he pretended that the death of Gaultier and the arrest of the brigands saw all questions resolved at Annossy. To his dismay, he discovered that Melissande's confession of love did not set his final doubts to rest. Instead, he wondered if she strove to falsely win his confidence. How he hated his suspicions! But her confession had been timely, and she had not been the one to tell him of the way to enter the keep from the side opposite the gates. She also had not been able to recall the location of the path to Perricault, or so she insisted. As much as he wanted to believe her, Quinn feared he would regret granting his trust.

There had been one brigand who had escaped at the mill.

It was not done.

But in the meantime, Quinn and Melissande labored together so amiably that he wished their marriage had been made of their own choice, for then he could have trusted his wife. She taught him of ledgers and of Annossy's courts. He learned of measures and makers, while he taught her about arms and defense. At night, each night, they met abed in mutual pleasure. His men worked upon strengthening the defenses of Annossy and he came to better know the villagers.

By May, the execution of the brigands was a memory of another time. The coin he had placed in the miller's second treasury had not appeared. None of the caught brigands had it, and indeed, there was a discrepancy between the hoard in their possession and the miller's inventory. Quinn made light of it, but he wondered at the identity of that escaped rider. When he rode to hunt, he sought a path to Perricault through the mountains.

There were only two reasons in his estimation that Melissande would not have told him of it: either she truly did not know, or she was complicit with whoever used that path.

He knew which answer he preferred.

If it had not been for that detail, Quinn might have always been Lord d'Annossy, for he seemed to have been accepted by all.

There was a goodly company of villeins wishing to accompany him to Sayerne to till the fields, more than enough to see the work done. Most of them had come from Sayerne, fleeing his own father's abuse, and wished to rebuild the homes they had known. He was honored that they trusted him to govern them fairly—and truly, he had learned so much from Melissande about such matters that he had more confidence in his own ability to do so.

Something had gone awry between Bayard and Berthe, for it seemed that Niall was the one most often talking to the maid, while Bayard glowered at the pair from the board. Perhaps Bayard had chosen not to court Berthe. Perhaps she had spurned him. Quinn felt he had said more than enough.

His fellows had begun to watch for Rolfe, for none of them could imagine that he would miss the promised meeting. There was much jesting about Rolfe with a bride, and considerable curiosity about that lady's appearance and nature. His comrades made plans to continue north after the reunion, making their own progress home, and Quinn knew he would miss their companionship. He had offered them all employ, if they chose to stay, but thus far, only Bayard had indicated that he might do as much.

Three months to the day after his marriage to Melissande, Quinn awaited his lady wife in the bailey. He held the reins of her palfrey and as ever, his heart leapt at the sight of her as she appeared in the hall. She was more than a beauty. She was clever and just, protective of those beneath her hand and a competent administrator. Her passion had been awakened by their marriage and he thought that she was a little quicker to reveal her feelings to others than she had been.

She smiled at him as she reached his side. "I thank you for your patience, sir," she murmured. "And apologize for the delay."

"You know I would have waited until noon," he said gallantly and her smile broadened.

"Even though you wished to leave at dawn."

He lifted her into the saddle and she bent to whisper in his ear. "It is the child," she admitted softly. "I am ill in the mornings, because of the child."

Quinn blinked, astonished.

Melissande laughed, clearly pleased with his response.

"When?" he whispered to her, well aware that the company awaited them.

"Who can say? It has only just begun. I suspect the babe will arrive in January, well within Tulley's dictate of a year from our nuptials."

Sayerne would be his, if the child was a boy.

Quinn went to his own steed in a daze, realizing that he did not care as much as once he had about claiming the seal of Sayerne. He hoped that Tulley would surrender it to him in time, but his concern was for the welfare of Melissande and the health of the child, regardless of its gender. Was there a midwife in Annossy? There must be, and he must ensure her skill. He might wish to send to Tulley for one of greater experience.

They rode out as he marveled at these tidings, the company trailing behind them in a long ribbon. Quinn rode at the front, Michel carrying his standard before him, Melissande on his left. His comrades, Thierry and Bayard, rode behind them and on either side. Amaury and Luc remained at Annossy to ensure its defense in his absence. There, the villeins had begun to tend the vines, pruning away winter's damage. There were wagons aplenty in the party, burdened with palettes and linens, food and crockery for Quinn's stay at Sayerne. Louis accompanied them, as did George's apprentice and two serving maids from the kitchen, as did Berthe.

The villeins who had chosen to move followed the supplies, with their carts and children and horses. In many cases, they brought all their possessions. Lothair and Niall rode at the vanguard of the party with their squires. The party was filled with an optimism for the future, one that was fed by the bright sunlight and the greening of the meadows.

They would reach Sayerne by noon and then the work would begin.

A child!

Truly all goodness came to Quinn's hand. He smiled at Melissande and she smiled back at him, her eyes alight. He dared to wish that trust would blossom fully between them.

And soon.

Arnaud de Privas watched the procession leave Annossy's gates. Although he stayed under the shadow of trees that he might not be spied, he could still identify Melissande's figure.

His gaze lingered upon the man by her side. A champion and a knight, a crusader and her legal husband, as dictated by Lord de Tulley. Quinn de Sayerne was the obstacle to Arnaud gaining all that he desired—he had also dispatched Gaultier. Arnaud hoped that Marie's nephew had been loyal to the last and held his tongue.

It was unfortunate to have lost such an ally within the very walls of Annossy, but Arnaud had no doubt of his own success. Within days, his plans would come to culmination. He smiled in anticipation of delivering the death blow to Quinn himself. They would have to hunt to feed this company at the wasteland that was Sayerne, and accidents at hunt were so easily arranged.

Indeed, Arnaud had an affection for the hunt. This time, however, he would hunt neither boar nor stag. He would hunt the Lord d'Annossy himself but no one would ever convict him. He had done as much before, having dispatched the Lord de Perricault, and he would do it again.

It was so simple.

Arnaud was already Lord de Perricault and would be a widower before the day was out. He would wed Melissande after Quinn's demise, become Lord both of Annossy and Sayerne, and Tulley would be obliged to return Privas to his hand. Melissande could administer them for him, for she was skilled with such details— unlike Marie, who had proven to be only a demanding expense— and he could do whatsoever he chose for all the rest of his days and nights.

Perfect.

Or it would be, once Quinn was dead.

Arnaud could not wait.

Sayerne.

Melissande had not visited the holding ever in her recollection and she was uncertain of Quinn's ultimate plan. Did he mean to make his court at Annossy or Sayerne? Or had he not decided as yet? He had been vague when she asked, but perhaps he wished to assess his father's holding with a clear eye.

She could be of aid in that.

Melissande studied the holding as they rode closer, striving to see its merits instead of the taint of its history. Tulley wished the fields to be tilled and she could see by the furrows that the fields were extensive. The soil was dark and she eyed the angle of the sun.

"Well?" Quinn asked, evidently having taken note of her survey.

"It seems that the fields must enjoy many of the same advantages as those of Annossy," she said. "The crops will be in bright sunlight all the day long, and the soil is so dark that it must be most fertile." She nodded. "And most of it has lain fallow. You could till as much of it as you desire this year."

"As much of it as can be tilled," he agreed. "I spoke with one of the older villeins and he suggested a plan which was used with success in the past. There was a scheme as to which third was left fallow each year and I would follow with tradition." He gestured to the north. "He said the oats did best in those fields."

"Tradition oft is a good place to begin," she said.

"And he said the barley did best to the south."

"And the construction?"

"I will have them begin with the homes for the villeins and a rudimentary hall for our own use. The keep can be repaired and extended once the villagers have good shelter."

"The forests are thin here," Melissande noted. "Especially close to the keep itself."

"Aye. We will have to ride far to the south to hunt with success, I would wager."

"Do you mean to ride to hunt?"

"I thought to go on the morrow. Will you join me?"

Melissande touched her belly. "I think less time in the saddle might be better than more in these days."

He frowned immediately. "Are you in discomfort?"

"Nay, nay." She spoke quickly to reassure him. "But I find I prefer to have my feet on the ground."

He nodded and looked at Sayerne again, his anticipation clear. "There is much to be done and I welcome your assistance."

"Of course."

"What do you think of offering some of the wood from Annossy here, when the road is widened to the mill?" Quinn suggested. "The firewood would be most welcome next winter and the villeins will have much labor this summer already."

Melissande smiled agreement, liking his concern for those pledged to serve him. "It would be, and Annossy does not have need of it all." They smiled at each other. "And I have a gift for your villeins, from Annossy, as well."

Quinn turned to her with surprise.

"There is a collection of seeds from Annossy, so that they can begin their pottage gardens. They must eat before the crops are harvested."

"I shall decree that they can trap hares," Quinn said. "Doubtless there will be an abundance of them."

"And the swineherds vowed to bring piglets to Sayerne for those who wished one." She nodded as they entered the village, sobering at the condition of the homes. "It will be a hard summer, Quinn, but the Yule will be a merry one this year."

"They seem glad to return."

She nodded, glancing back to note their reactions. Some were in tears, joyful tears. "Many lived here for generations. Their kin are buried here. Their memories are here." She reached out and placed her gloved hand upon his. "You are not the only one coming home, sir."

Quinn turned his hand over so he could grasp her hand, and gave her fingers a squeeze. "I would not know where to begin without your tutelage these past months."

She could see that he was assessing the damage and choosing where best to begin.

"Keep Louis with you, for his counsel is most good," she advised and Quinn nodded. "And if you can hunt on the morrow, or send your companions to do as much, a feast in Sayerne's hall for those who have returned will be most welcome."

"Your counsel is good, as ever, my lady," Quinn said, lifting her hand and placing a kiss upon its back. "I am fortunate beyond all men in my bride." Their gazes met and held and she almost asked for his plans.

But there was a shout from the vanguard and Quinn looked over the company, his eyes narrowed.

"A party arrives!" Niall shouted, gesturing to the road. Sure enough, there was a cloud of dust on the road to Tulley, and a group of horses riding hard for Sayerne.

Melissande recognized Tulley's banner and caught her breath. "God in Heaven," she whispered. "I hope that he has brought provisions to aid in the feeding of his company."

Quinn laughed. "Ever practical," he teased.

"People who labor hard have strong appetites and hunger leads only to dissent." She lifted her chin. "If he has not seen fit to contribute, I shall speak to Lord Tulley."

"It looks to be a small party," Quinn mused. He was right, to Melissande's relief. Though they wore Tulley's colors, there looked to be only three of them.

"Perhaps a messenger warning of his pending arrival," she suggested.

"Perhaps." Quinn inclined his head to her, then turned Fortitude to gallop past the party and greet his liege lord's messenger.

Melissande watched him go, thinking of how he had never confessed to tender feelings for her. Surely, he would not insist that they live separately, one at Annossy and one at Sayerne? She had conceived his child and only God knew if it would be a boy. There was naught more she could do until the child was born to secure her husband's affection and perhaps not even then.

Surely, this would not be the end?

Quinn's first day in residence at Sayerne was a wondrous one. He saw the work begun and aided in many tasks himself, lending a hand to a wagon stuck in the mud, clearing debris from the bailey and carrying wood for the smith to light his fire. He carried seed and even led the ploughhorse for the first furrow, smiling at the cheers of his villeins. It was a long day of hard labor, but he welcomed it.

Meanwhile, Melissande had been busy in the hall with the help of Louis. The place looked a hundred times better than it had earlier that very day, and the change was welcome. The boys had patched the roof and lit fires in the great fireplaces. There were benches and tables set up and a cold meal for all who had accompanied them. There was a barrel of ale from Annossy, as well as bread and bacon and cheese. Quinn was certain no fare had ever tasted so fine.

Afterward, Niall raised his voice and gave them a song, and some of the villeins danced as the others clapped in time. Quinn slept before the fire on a straw pallet, Melissande tightly against his side, with her father's fur-lined cloak over them both.

No ghosts haunted his dreams that night, but perhaps he was too tired.

At first light, he rose with Niall to ride out to hunt, giving Melissande a kiss farewell. "Remember that Tulley himself comes this day," he reminded her with a smile.

"How could I forget?"

"We had best ensure a fine meal."

"He had best bring the wine if he wants it," she said, kissing him in return. "Good luck this day."

"And to you."

Louis arrived then, as crisp and efficient as ever. "Do not forget the small game, my lord," he said with a smile. "And George is always glad of eggs."

"Aye, for the meat must be hung and we have need of something for this night," Quinn replied with a smile. "I will take three of the boys with me in anticipation of success. They can seek nests while Niall and I hunt larger game."

He left the hall with purpose and a whistle on his lips, savoring his sense that all came together most well.

It was when Quinn was saddling Fortitude that Melissande first saw the lone rider. He remained under the cover of trees in the distance, close to the barn on the perimeter of Sayerne. Melissande narrowed her eyes, wondering if she had imagined him. He retreated into the shadow of the forest, disappearing as if he had never been, as Niall and Quinn rode toward the gates, and she feared that the light played tricks upon her.

And then there was too much to be done to think upon it.

Tulley arrived by midday, with more supplies than Melissande might have hoped. He brought a large party of men to rebuild the homes of the villeins and the keep itself, and vowed that there were stone masons en route to repair the walls. The smith fired his forge to see the gates repaired and to make nails for the workers, and seed was unloaded from wagons with much satisfaction.

Melissande saw horses stabled and palettes arranged, a place made for Tulley himself for that night, and an order of precedence established for the work. Quinn had discussed most of it with her, and she followed his instructions. To her delight, Heloise had accompanied her uncle, and was quick to offer her assistance with the kitchen garden of the keep itself. Melissande worked with her there, along with Berthe, to plant the seeds after the earth had been loosened by the villeins. There was so much to be done that no one could be idle—even the Lord de Tulley took a turn at casting seeds into the furrows, much to the delight of the villeins. Lothair was busy tending the inevitable minor injuries. To Melissande's surprise, Luc and Thierry showed great skill in guiding the ox that pulled the plough.

She even had the opportunity to confer with Tulley, a discussion that seemed to amuse her overlord greatly and one that she feared would yield no result.

Melissande was returning to the keep to confer with Louis and George about the preparations for the evening meal when she chose to climb to the summit of the wall. The stones had tumbled down, making almost a stairway, and she could not resist the impulse to look for Quinn.

What she saw instead was that lone rider again.

In the late afternoon light, she could see him more clearly. His was a fine horse, one richly caparisoned, and large enough to be a destrier. He sat tall in the saddle and she thought the light glinted off chain mail.

A knight.

But who?

She was inclined to alert Lothair, but the fact that the knight was alone gave her pause. He did not lead an army. He did not arrive as a guest, or travel with his entourage. Knights did not ride alone in her experience. It was most curious. From whence had he come and what was his destination? Perhaps he meant to return to some abode, but the day drew to an end and there was little within range.

Melissande could not stifle her dread, or her sense that he looked back at her. He turned the horse, the creature flicking its tail before stepping back into the shadows of the forest. She saw that the caparisons were golden with some black insignia.

Her mouth went dry.

Privas had a gold banner with a black hawk emblazoned on it.

There was only one son remaining of the family of Privas: Arnaud, her former betrothed.

Why would Arnaud come to the perimeter of Sayerne and gaze upon it? He must know that she had wed Quinn, but still.

Was he truly wedded to Marie de Perricault?

If so, it made no sense that he should be so far from Perricault.

If not, his presence made even less sense.

Then Melissande recalled something that had not seemed right, though she could not have said why at the time. Quinn had said that Gaultier had come from Perricault, that he had courted his aunt, Marie, until she wed another. Quinn believed that man to be Arnaud, but he did not know what Gaultier had told her when Quinn had ridden out to the mill. Indeed, Melissande had nigh forgotten the words of her former Captain of the Guard herself.

"Tulley told me that he had a plan, and that my tenure at Annossy would not be a long one."

But Gaultier had not been sent to Annossy by Tulley. Had someone else told him that his time at Annossy would be short?

Who had sent him?

Melissande bit her lip as she recalled more of Gaultier's words, from the morning he had warned her against Quinn.

"If you died, my lady, Annossy would remain your husband's holding and he would be free to wed whosoever he chose. Perhaps a man held so high in

Tulley's favor might even wed Tulley's niece."

And upon Tulley's demise, she had realized then, the entire valley would fall to that man's hand.

Melissande had to wonder how Gaultier had concocted such a scheme to explain Quinn's choices. What if Gaultier had heard the plan from another and twisted it, attributing the motives of that other man to Quinn? After all, she had been the one assaulted by Gaultier.

What if she had not been Gaultier's target in truth? What if he had intended to abduct her, not to kill her? For then, Quinn would follow to defend her, of that no man could have any doubt.

Perhaps it had been a scheme to ensure *Quinn's* demise.

For if Quinn were to die—especially if she carried Quinn's child—Sayerne might fall to Melissande as well as Annossy. She would be a widow and might be commanded to take a spouse again. Arnaud might see the old betrothal upheld, claim Annossy, Sayerne and perhaps Privas. If he had wed Marie, he might put her aside and annul their agreement. If he had not wed her, then there would be no obstacle.

Would Melissande meet her own end, if she protested? That would leave Arnaud available to court Heloise and her inheritance.

Gaultier had not invented the scheme himself. She was certain of it. He had heard it from another and the presence of a knight wearing Privas' colors gave credence to the notion.

If Arnaud had wed Marie, then he was the man who had wed Gaultier's rich widowed aunt and they would thus have been known to each other.

What if Gaultier had been sent to Annossy by Arnaud?

And now this rider, wearing the colors of Privas, lurked in the forest where Quinn hunted.

It could not be coincidence.

She must be right.

Melissande heard the hunting horn in the distance. She realized that Quinn would pass near to the place where the rider was hidden. Was he still with Niall or had they parted ways? She recalled with a chill that he had said he would send the boys in search of eggs.

If he perceived the presence of Arnaud and guessed the scheme, Quinn would send the others to safety and face his opponent alone. Melissande knew his protective nature well. But if he did not realize the threat, he might ride into a trap unawares.

If she was right, she could lose all of import this day.

Though she prayed she had leapt to conclusions, Melissande had to know for certain.

"My horse!" she cried, knowing she had to intervene.

Lothair considered her with alarm as she hastened from the vantage point, but she wanted him to remain at Sayerne.

"I hear the horns," she said with a smile. "I would ride out to see how the hunt has fared."

Lothair frowned, but Melissande hurried past him, urging the squires to hasten. The knight followed, protesting, but she reminded him of his responsibilities and climbed into the saddle with confidence.

"You can see the forest from here!" she chided. "I will be as safe as here by your side."

She was not nearly convinced of that, but she had to warn Quinn.

Lothair protested, but she turned the horse, ignoring him. She gave the palfrey her heels and trotted through gates and village, waved to the villagers, then urged the beast to a run. Quinn's horn sounded again and Melissande prayed that she would not arrive too late.

CHAPTER SIXTEEN

Quinn was not alone.

He was crouched beside the stag, ensuring it was dead, when he first heard the other horse. He thought perhaps it was Niall or one of the boys, but could not imagine why they would remain hidden in the underbrush. Anyone within earshot would have heard him pursue the stag, never mind his cry of triumph when the bolt struck home.

He moved with purpose, as if unaware, and listened. He gutted the stag, leaving the offal for other creatures in the forest, then slung it over the back of his saddle. Fortitude flared his nostrils and stamped a foot, but Quinn took his time ensuring that the deer was securely bound. He went all around Fortitude, scanning the forest as he moved.

He spied the rider's silhouette, then a flick of cloth.

A cloak?

Caparisons?

The hair prickled on the back of his neck with the awareness that he was watched. He swung into the saddle again and turned Fortitude back toward the path. He had planned to meet the others there and hoped they had been fortunate as well. He kept his hand on his crossbow and gave no indication that he heard the twig snap to his right. From the periphery of his vision, he glimpsed the rider again.

Caparisons.

Gold with a black insignia. How Quinn wished he recognized it.

He was considering the merit of raising his voice and greeting the other rider, when he heard galloping hoof beats from the path. He straightened and saw the flicker of the other horse moving through the undergrowth. The horse cantered and then galloped, but the arriving horse was turned in its course. Quinn quietly followed the sound of hoof beats.

"Arnaud!" Melissande cried and Quinn's heart stopped cold. He did not move. "Arnaud de Privas! I thought those were your colors!" Her tone was charming and light, as if she welcomed a guest to Annossy. He must hear this conversation.

He found his lady upon her palfrey in a stream, facing a knight on a dapple destrier with golden caparisons. Her palfrey stepped with agitation, as if disliking that they stood in the flow of water. Quinn wondered if it was aware of its rider's mood. Melissande rode the same palfrey often and though she smiled, he sensed a tension in her.

Because she feared discovery?

Or because she feared Arnaud? Quinn dismounted, left Fortitude, and eased closer. He circled around the pair to a better vantage point, glad of the sound of the water. He halted where he had a clear view of Arnaud.

He loaded a bolt into his crossbow, more than prepared to use it. He must strike Arnaud in the throat to ensure the blow was fatal, for the other knight wore his armor. Indeed, Arnaud had not even abandoned his helmet, which was vexing. It was a narrow target and Quinn could have done without the undergrowth in between them. He would have one shot and he would make it count.

He tried to ease closer in silence and still remain unseen.

"Whatever are you doing here?" Melissande asked lightly.

"And where is here?" her companion replied.

Melissande laughed lightly. "Sayerne, of course."

"But not so far from Privas, surely?"

"I suppose not, though surely that keep is abandoned."

"But my family legacy, all the same. I ride to hunt but have lost my party." He gave a little laugh. "The boar was doughty and I could not resist the chance to take him. I outran my entire party in the pursuit."

"By considerable distance, it appears," Melissande said, looking left and right.

"Aye, that it does."

"And yet, you have no boar," she noted.

"Alas, he escaped. They are most wily when cornered."

"How strange that I saw you hours ago, this morn, and you were close to this place and alone."

Arnaud chuckled but Quinn heard his displeasure. "Who can say how long I have wandered?"

"Surely you did not spend the night in the forest?"

"Surely there are matters of greater interest than that," Arnaud said, his tone steely.

"Surely not," Melissande said, almost in an undertone, but Arnaud ignored her.

Quinn also found it curious that the other man had been in the forest in the morning. What was his scheme?

And what was Melissande's?

Arnaud's voice warmed. "And you look hale, my lady. How many years has it been?"

"At least twenty," Melissande replied. "I should not have known you but I recognized your colors."

So, they had not spoken of late. Quinn was reassured.

Unless, of course, this conversation was for his benefit.

"Aye, dear beloved Privas." Arnaud sighed. "How fares wondrous Annossy?"

"Well enough. I suppose you have heard that I am wed."

"To the son of Jerome de Sayerne." Arnaud clicked his tongue. "A sad waste indeed."

Melissande said naught at all.

"That is, of course, why I sought you out," Arnaud continued.

"Here at Sayerne, but not at Annossy? How enterprising of you to surmise my location."

Arnaud laughed.

Quinn was glad that Melissande did not.

"I have a proposition for you, Melissande."

"I imagine that you do."

"You do not look surprised."

"I think I know your wager."

"Then tell me of it and I shall tell you if you are right."

"I think you mean to ensure the demise of my lord husband and thence to force me to become your wife."

"Melissande! Surely you do not have to be compelled to keep your sworn word?" Arnaud's tone was silky. "We were betrothed by our fathers' choice."

"And I was wed to Quinn by Tulley's command. I carry his child. Tulley will not tolerate your interference in this matter, nor will he entrust you with Annossy and Privas, as well. He distrusts you, Arnaud, and I am persuaded to take his view."

"You carry your husband's child?" Arnaud repeated.

"Aye." Melissande sat proudly and Quinn's heart swelled at the sight of her.

"Even better," Arnaud whispered. "Tulley will not be able to deny me Sayerne." He moved with lightning speed, drawing his sword and slashing at Melissande's palfrey. The horse, perhaps with Melissande's urging, retreated quickly, but stumbled on the rocks in the river bed. It fell and Melissande fell from the saddle, catching herself on the low branches of an overhanging tree. Arnaud slashed at the horse again and the palfrey ran, its reins trailing in the river.

Melissande was knee-deep in the water, watching Arnaud warily as her breath came quickly. Curse the woman, she was standing between Quinn and his target, ensuring that his shot was not clear.

"Join me," Arnaud invited, his sword pointed now at her.

"Never," she said with welcome heat. "Your scheme has failed, Arnaud. Quinn saw the truth of Gaultier's deception, but I am the one who guessed that your true target was my lord husband. I will never aid you in attacking Quinn." Now Melissande's tone was hard.

"How sad that you make this choice," he murmured.

"Just as you make yours. Recall your knightly vows, Arnaud,

and lower your blade."

"And is it a choice when a man must act against his own desire to survive?" Arnaud asked.

"You survived well enough."

"Survived?" Arnaud cried. "After Tulley seized Privas, I starved. After Tulley took every denier of my legacy, I had naught, not even a steed. I would have died if I had not had my wits. Even then, he spread poisonous lies about my nature, spilling them into every listening ear. I had to go far, nigh all the way to Paris, then come back slowly and with stealth."

"You did not have to come back at all."

"Privas is my legacy."

"Not when Tulley holds the seal."

"And I will hold it again," Arnaud snarled.

"Marie de Perricault was useful, then."

"She was rich and had a title." His tone was gloating. "And she admired me greatly, a sign of her exquisite taste."

"Sadly, she was wedded."

He smiled. "Not for long."

"I thought she had another suitor, Gaultier de Lonvaux."

"He was too young to appreciate her advantages. I lured him away from her with tales of Annossy and your beauty, my Melissande."

"Mine!"

Arnaud winced. "Marie, sad as it may be, was no beauty, although she had her passions."

"You speak of your lady wife as if she is no longer of this world."

Quinn could not believe that Melissande was speaking at such length with this villain—and then he realized that she must know of his presence. She must be ensuring that he learned the full extent of Arnaud's crimes.

She must guess that he would strike, and she wanted Quinn to have no doubts.

Zounds, but his lady wife knew him well.

"She might not be," Arnaud said. "I will be a widower before the sun sets this day. I might be one already."

"I do not understand."

"Marie was very fond of her wine. When I left Perricault three days ago, I left an allotment for her from my personal store. Quite special wine. You will appreciate that when I tell you it is from Annossy. I opened it to ensure its quality for my lady wife, then added an herbal augmentation for her pleasure."

"Poison," Melissande whispered. "Is that how her husband died?"

Arnaud laughed. "His time had come, unfortunately."

"But surely a physician will treat her?"

"Ah." Arnaud shook his head. "Tragically, the physician has gone to Lyons to acquire supplies and will not return for a fortnight. No one will remember that I suggested it would be a good time for him to go." He shrugged. "No one recalled that I made the suggestion he make a similar journey just before Marie's husband met his end."

"But twice in succession," Melissande said. "Surely, someone will suspect foul play?"

"Marie always has a sour stomach. It is likely a result of her continuous overindulgence. Even if there is suspicion, I am far away at hunt."

"You do not hunt boar," Melissande accused.

Arnaud chuckled. "Nay, I do not."

He leaned forward, eyes shining. "Take my wager, Melissande, for then you will live to see the morrow."

"Never!" she spat and ducked.

Quinn did not hesitate. He loosed the bolt.

And he was glad when it sank home.

One moment, Arnaud was taunting her.

The next, something whistled over her head, Arnaud's sword fell into the river and he made a gurgling sound. Melissande straightened to see a crossbow bolt in his throat and his blood flowing. He looked suitably horrified and reached for the shaft of the bolt but she knew he would never dislodge it. She retreated with haste.

Quinn came charging through the undergrowth behind her,

seized Arnaud from his saddle and hauled him down to the river. Arnaud fought him, but so ineffectually that he might have been wrought of straw. Quinn pulled his dagger and buried it in Arnaud's chest.

"Cut out his filthy black heart," Melissande said with fervor. She held on to the destrier's reins with trembling hands.

Arnaud glared at Quinn through half-closed eyes. "Curse you," he whispered, and the blood trickled from the corner of his mouth. "Without you, four estates would have been mine, if not more."

Quinn grimaced. "Without your own cursed greed, you would have had the finest bride in Christendom and that should have been more than sufficient for any man."

Arnaud gave a long low moan and his breathing halted. Quinn pulled out his knife and let the other man fall into the water. He shook his head and stepped away, then turned to study Melissande.

"I saw him. I feared he meant to kill you," she said when he did not speak. "I could not let that happen.

Quinn nodded ruefully. "And so you prove to me that I should not have withheld my trust. I think, my lady, that we are better allied than at odds."

She smiled, for their thoughts were as one. "Aye, Quinn, that we are."

"A veritable force to be reckoned with," he said, giving her that seductive slow smile. Melissande could not look away. He held out his hand to her and she seized it, so grateful for his constancy and strength. She clung to his fingers and Quinn must have felt her tremble. He swept off his cloak and wrapped it securely about her shoulders, then lifted her into his arms. "Are you hurt?"

"Cold and wet. No worse than that."

"And I shall see both resolved with all haste." Quinn carried her to Fortitude, then led the destrier back to the path. He found Niall and the boys there and sent them to load Arnaud's corpse onto his horse.

They returned to Sayerne in quiet triumph, a slow but successful procession, with rather more kill than had been expected. Niall had also taken a stag in addition to the one Quinn had felled, and between him and the boys, they had dozens of hares, pheasants and even a brace of eggs. The sun was setting when they approached the gates and Bayard led a party out to aid them.

Quinn carried Melissande to the solar where Berthe helped her to change to dry garb, and he himself was glad of a wash and a change. By the time he led her to the hall, he could smell roasted meat and hot soup. Tulley was at the board, with Heloise by his left hand, and had been apprised of the entire tale by Niall. The older man was nodding with satisfaction.

Quinn could not help but notice that Heloise was gazing at Niall with adoration.

He winced when he noted that Niall bowed and smiled at her.

"And so our champion returns in triumph!" Tulley said, standing to applaud Quinn. "Not only have you routed the brigands from Annossy's borders, and begun to rebuild Sayerne, but you have dispatched this villain." He seized his cup and held it high.

Michel hastened to bring a cup of ale to Quinn and another to Melissande. He felt a surge of heat when she smiled at him, her magnificent eyes filled with pride.

"All hail, Quinn de Sayerne, Lord d'Annossy," Tulley said, then chuckled before he continued. He lifted his cup a little higher. "And Lord de Sayerne."

Melissande lifted her glass to Quinn. "All hail," she said and sipped of it.

Quinn nearly choked. "But I am not Lord de Sayerne," he whispered to Melissande.

The lady's smile did not waver. Indeed, she looked most pleased with herself.

"Indeed, Quinn, you speak aright," Tulley said. He cleared his throat and removed a familiar item from his purse. "Your lady wife made a most ardent and persuasive argument on your behalf this day while you were at hunt. Indeed, if I did not already agree with her assessment of your abilities, I might have been insulted."

The company laughed lightly, though Quinn doubted it was a jest.

"As it stands, however, I do agree." Tulley waved the seal.

"Come here, Quinn, bend your knee and be endowed with your legacy and your heart's desire."

He still could not believe it, but Melissande squeezed his hand. "Go," she whispered. "Lest he change his mind."

They shared a smile before Quinn bowed before Tulley. Tears pricked at his eyes when the weight of the seal was in his hand, and he could scarce catch his breath. He felt as if his mother was watching him with pride, and that was potent, indeed. Then he turned to offer his hand to Melissande who crossed to his side with a smile that filled him with mingled pride and desire. He knew then that his wife possessed an even more potent sorcery, and his heart swelled with joy as he kissed her hand before the company.

"If only Rolfe were here," Thierry said. "Our company would be completely assembled in Tulley."

"Rolfe?" Tulley himself said. "Rolfe de Viandin?"

"Aye, the last of our comrades," Quinn confirmed.

"Of course, he is not here. He is Lord de Viandin and has returned home with his mother and his bride to administer his holding," Tulley huffed. "I saw them wed myself at Beauvoir at the Yule."

"You might say the match was of your doing, Uncle," Heloise contributed.

"It was the match I made, but not when I made it," Tulley complained. He shook his finger at Heloise. "And there is the evidence that people, particularly unwed people, should do as they are bidden from the outset."

Heloise eyed Niall and sighed. "Aye, Uncle."

"I do not understand," Quinn said.

"I matched them," Tulley admitted. "But Annelise would not wed a man she had not met, even though he was a knight. Truly, Quinn, your sister did not inherit your mother's obedient nature..."

"Praise be to God for that," Melissande murmured.

"Annelise?" Quinn repeated, unable to contain his incredulous response. "My sister, Annelise, is wedded to Rolfe de Viandin?"

"Aye," Tulley said easily. "First she intended to return to the convent and Yves was to escort her there before riding to Paris, but evidently, meeting Rolfe aided her in seeing the merit of my scheme."

"My sister is wedded to Rolfe?" Quinn repeated, his voice rising.

"You know him?" Melissande whispered.

"As the greatest rogue of all," he replied. "Your maid would not know where to begin, were she to chastise him."

"Oh!" Melissande replied.

"We should all have the good fortune to be rogues like Rolfe but well-wedded in the end, all the same," Niall said with merriment. He began to laugh, and his other companions soon followed.

Tulley looked between them all without comprehension. "It is a good match," he said, his tone insulted. "And I believe she is with child already."

Melissande leaned on Quinn's side and gave him a warning glance. Aye, it would not do to insult Tulley in this moment. Quinn bowed. "I thank you, sir, for ensuring my sister's welfare."

"I was most glad to do it," Tulley said.

"And I will kill Rolfe myself if he serves her poorly," Quinn growled, much to the amusement of his fellow knights.

"Oh, he will not," Tulley said. "His mother is most fierce in ensuring that women are treated with dignity."

"And what of my brother, Yves?" Quinn asked. "Do you know his location?"

"Nay. He intended to return to the tourneys near Paris. I have no doubt he will fare well and gain the attention of a pretty heiress." Tulley did not appear to be concerned, though Quinn had a hundred questions about his younger brother. The older lord sniffed the air with appreciation. "Is that the soup at last?"

There was naught more tragic, in Berthe's view, than catching the eye of a man of merit then losing it again. Since Bayard had given her the vial of perfume, she had been unable to think of any man other than him. If the scent within it was possessed of power, though, it was fickle. For Bayard appeared to have no further interest in her—indeed, he had scarce spoken to her since that evening—while his companion, Niall MacGillivray, could not be avoided. He taunted her in the kitchens, when she was en route to serve her lady, when she passed through the hall and when she was in the gardens. Each time she turned around, there was Sir Niall, always ready with a compliment or a pretty word, not a one of them worth the trouble of listening.

And she had thought Bayard a rogue. The word might have been invented to refer to this knight, with his seemingly endless appetite for charming women. Even when he seemed bent upon seducing her, Berthe saw his gaze drift over her shoulder when another maiden passed by. His fulsome praise was without merit. His flattery was as dust for its worth and nigh as plentiful.

If Bayard had deigned to speak with her, she might have granted him more encouragement than once she had. But he was always with Lord Quinn or taking an errand for him, following his lord's dictate or tending his steed. He seemed most serious since the arrival of their companions, and while Berthe appreciated this side of his nature, she would have liked more of his attention. It was no wonder his armor shone so brilliantly, for he was always polishing it, though she thought that was the task of a squire.

She had hoped to speak to him on the ride to Sayerne, but he had never so much as glanced her way in the bailey of Annossy. She had ridden alongside Sir Niall in the vanguard, hoping that might vex Bayard into speaking with her, but he did not appear to have noticed. And now, Sir Niall was encouraged that his pursuit of her might bear fruit. She had been glad when he had ridden to hunt with Lord Quinn at first light—though still Bayard had eluded her company all the day long.

To her surprise—and relief—Sir Niall had taken one look at the Lord de Tulley's niece and appeared to have forgotten all others in the hall. He even seemed to have forgotten how to speak, for no pretty compliments fell from his tongue. He simply stared at the maiden and it had only been the tale of the success of their companion in wedding Lord Quinn's sister that had recalled him to his senses.

A fellow rogue, apparently, but one Berthe hoped was reformed.

The men then went to wash before the meal, and Berthe

wondered if Lord de Tulley would consume it all before their return.

Lady Heloise could not seem to tear her gaze away from Sir Niall as he left. "Knights," she whispered to her maid.

Sir Niall for his part, turned in the portal to grant her a charming smile and a bow.

Berthe heard the lady's sigh of yearning.

She did not tell Tulley's niece that Sir Niall could never be the knight of her imagination. He would never be content with one woman for more than a night.

If even that long.

For her part, she watched Bayard, wishing he would glance her way again. She would not so waste the opportunity if it came once more.

But he was striding after Sir Niall, his brow dark.

Berthe followed, intrigued.

Sir Niall halted when Bayard tapped him on the shoulder. He pivoted to find Bayard in his path.

"You!" Bayard said, pointing at Niall with such annoyance that Berthe was intrigued.

"Me," Niall replied with a smile, gesturing to himself. He held up his hands, as if inviting all to admire him. "One glance and the lady is nigh mine. This will be a conquest of the heart to eclipse all others."

"Make no jest of this," Bayard fumed. "You treat a maiden with indignity and you think the matter no more than a moment's amusement."

Niall flicked a glance toward the hall. "I treat no lady with indignity," he began, but Bayard strode closer and shook a finger beneath his nose.

"I speak of Berthe," he growled and she felt her heart flutter.

"Berthe?" Sir Niall echoed, as if he had forgotten her existence.

"Aye, *Berthe*," Bayard said with force. "All these months, you have courted her and tried to seduce her. I stood back when she seemed to welcome your attention..."

"As well you should," Niall replied, folding his arms across his chest. "A wise man always cedes to greater expertise."

"Greater expertise?"

"Aye. All know that I am the champion on the field of love. You might have watched more closely and learned something." Sir Niall shook his head. "But that one, that maid, she is a frosty one. No man will ever slip between her thighs."

"While you think Tulley's niece will welcome you?" Bayard retorted.

Sir Niall smiled. "Perhaps I will wed her with Tulley's blessing. If Rolfe can win that man to his side, it clearly can be accomplished with charm and persistence. Rolfe has no more a measure of either than I do."

"And what of Berthe?"

"What of Berthe? She is pretty enough, but she is a maid not a noblewoman. She can give me little but a merry night, and she did not even give me that. Indeed, I have not had a kiss. It was well enough to amuse us both over the lonely winter months, but now there are better prospects. What of Berthe, indeed?"

Berthe gasped that he could be so callous, but neither man heard her for Bayard struck Sir Niall. The other knight swore as blood spurted from his nose then swung at Bayard. Within a moment, they were grappling for supremacy, but when Berthe stepped out of the shadows and cleared her throat, they froze and looked up.

"What a pair of ruffians you are," she said with disapproval. "Sir Rogue and your even more roguish companion. You ought both to be ashamed of yourselves, fighting like this in Lord Quinn's abode."

"Even more roguish," Sir Niall repeated, obviously affronted.

Bayard cast him aside and stepped forward with a smile. "I take it that you do not approve of rogues," he said, his voice low and his eyes dark.

If Berthe's heart had fluttered before, that had been but a precursor to its wild movement now.

"I do not approve of rogues," she said, bracing her hands upon her hips. "I do not approve of men who make promises they do not intend to keep, and I do not approve of men who take what they desire and grant naught in exchange."

"I give plenty in exchange," Sir Niall protested.

"Confide as much in Lady Heloise," Bayard scoffed.

"I will."

"Or better yet, to Lord de Tulley," Berthe added. "He will be most interested in what you intend to grant. The confession might see you hanged."

"Or gelded," Bayard added.

Niall had the grace to flush. "You know little of it..." he began but Berthe dismissed him with a wave.

Bayard's gaze locked with hers at that gesture. He took a step closer and she thought she might die of anticipation. She was vaguely aware that Sir Niall muttered something, then strode back to the hall.

She was keenly aware that Bayard stood before her, that the stars were appearing overhead, and that there was no one else worthy of consideration in the width of Christendom. When he looked at her with such intensity, she would do any deed for him.

"Then what manner of man meets with your approval?" he asked, his low words making her shiver.

"I like a man who is fair to look upon," she managed to say. "But I like one better who can speak the truth in his heart."

Bayard stepped closer, his expression filled with a hope that echoed her own. "And?"

"And I like a man who shares a confidence," she admitted. She pulled his perfume bottle from her purse and his eyes lit.

"You yet have it!"

"I am not such a fool as to discard a prize," she scoffed, then smiled at him. He closed the distance between them and looked down at her with fire in his eyes.

Berthe's toes curled.

"I thought you smitten," he murmured.

Berthe let her smile widen as she tipped back her head to hold his gaze. "You are right. I am utterly smitten, but not with your companion knight." She reached out and boldly offered her hand. "I know better, sir."

Bayard smiled as he captured her hand within his own, holding her gaze as he pressed a kiss to her palm. "Be mine?" he asked.

"Quinn has offered me a post and a home, either here or at Annossy. If you wed me, Berthe, I vow to do all within my power to bring you happiness."

"You already have, Sir Rogue," Berthe had time to confess before Bayard caught her close and granted her a most satisfactory kiss.

Quinn was glad to leave the hall later that evening, abandoning it for the privacy of the solar. It was past time that he made a sweet confession to Melissande, especially as she had risked her life for him this day. The solar seemed large and cool when they were there alone.

He did not release her hand. "I thank you for your endorsement to Tulley. I did not think he could be swayed in my favor."

"It is my duty to defend the interests of my lord husband."

"Is that the sole reason you did it?"

Color flared in her cheeks. "I spoke for you because it was right. Tulley was unjust in withholding the seal and he had to know it. I merely reminded him."

Quinn could not help but smile at her fearlessness. "You might have waited until I could watch."

She flushed more deeply and seemed discomfited. "It was an argument that had to be made in your absence, sir."

Sir. Again, she retreated from using his name. Quinn reached and took her hand in his, feeling that she trembled slightly.

"Is this the moment?" she asked, lifting her chin.

"Which moment would that be?"

"The one in which you declare that you mean to remain at Sayerne, and that I should return to Annossy alone. The one in which you tell me that we shall live apart instead of together, and to advise you whether I deliver of a son or not." She continued when he did not speak. "The one in which you divide the household as you see just, and request that I send word of the babe's gender when he or she is born."

"I thought that you wished to hold the seal of Annossy above all else."

"As did I." Melissande took a breath and held his gaze. "Until I came to love my lord husband. Now I desire above all else to be by your side and become your wife in truth."

Quinn nodded, his chest tight with emotion. He slid his thumb over her hand, awed that this lady should be his bride, his wife and his love. "It was in this chamber that my mother told me the tales shown in the tapestries she had brought as her dowry. They are all gone, of course, as is she, but I remember those tales."

Melissande remained silent, her gaze intent.

"In every one of them, a noble and gallant knight won the love of a beautiful lady. Quite often, she was clever, too, and the way my mother told the tales, the happy couple well deserved each other." He watched his thumb move across her hand. "They faced obstacles together, fearsome monsters, and dreadful trials, but their love for each other ensured both their success and their happiness."

"Yet your father..."

"Yet my father was the man he was," Quinn agreed with a sigh. "And I knew that she had loved another, but she did as bidden by her father. There was naught to be done about it, for to defy my father and her own would have been a rejection of every code of honor she knew. But she told me those tales, and she bade me find a lady deserving of my love, then do whatever was necessary to win her heart forevermore." He lifted his gaze to Melissande's and found himself snared by the vivid green of her eyes. "I believe I loved you from the first, my lady. My heart has been yours from before we exchanged our vows, and it is yours forevermore."

"You love me?"

"I love you."

Melissande flung herself toward him in her relief and Quinn smiled as he caught her close. "But you did not trust me," she accused after he had kissed her.

"You did not trust me," he countered, moving onto the pallet with her in his lap. "We are alike in so many matters, my Melissande."

She laughed and curled against him in contentment. "Aye, perhaps even in our desire for the great bed in Annossy's solar on this night of nights."

Quinn chuckled. "We shall have one here, as well."

"Aye. And a tapestry or two." She lifted her hand and his mother's ring glinted on her finger. "Oh, Quinn." She turned her hand to grip his. "I am so honored to wear your mother's ring."

"I could give you no other. It was a mark of my pledge to win your love at any cost." Quinn bent and captured her lips with his, loving how she rose to meet his embrace. His kiss soon turned incendiary and they might have surrendered to temptation, but Quinn had more to say. "Zounds, Melissande, who might have guessed that love could grow so strong so quickly? I cannot imagine my days without you."

"Aye," she whispered. "I love you as I never imagined I could love anyone. My only fear is that you will despise me for bringing Arnaud and his hate so close to your door."

"Hush, my lady." Quinn laid his fingertip across her lips. "Do not even utter his name. It was you indeed who saved me from him and that is no small thing. I am in your debt and I would take the remainder of our days to show you what that means."

By the way his lady wife smiled, and by the way she returned his kiss, Quinn knew that she had no complaint with that.

EPILOGUE

It was a year after their first journey to Sayerne that Melissande retired to the solar at Sayerne. She and Quinn had ridden to that holding to oversee to the ploughing and the planting. After the evening meal and much merriment, Melissande climbed to the solar with her son in her arms.

After the roof had been repaired and the rest of the hall restored, Quinn had ordered that a great bed be built at Sayerne, much like the one at Annossy. Melissande found it nigh filling the solar, just as she had envisioned it would be. It was hung with heavy draperies, as she had wished. The braziers had already been lit in the solar for it was still cool at night and the new tapestry she had requested from the Low Countries was already hung on the wall. Melissande touched it with wonder, thinking of the stories she would tell the infant in her arms. She settled then beside the fire to nurse him while she awaited Quinn, smiling at the sound of his deep voice rising from the hall below.

Could she ever have imagined she would be this content? Could she ever have imagined that it would be her joy to see Annossy and Sayerne united, and herself the beloved wife of Jerome's son? It defied belief, yet was so, all the same.

She and Quinn had settled into a pattern of living mostly at

Annossy, but holding court monthly—on the new moon—at Sayerne. Bayard commanded the garrison at Sayerne and managed the holding for Quinn in his absence, which had ultimately cost Melissande a maid. She had known that Berthe was smitten but Bayard had been determined to offer her a home. He had built his abode at Sayerne with his own hands, with Berthe's approval. The pair had married after Melissande was delivered of her son in January, and Berthe had moved to Sayerne then.

Melissande missed Berthe's companionship and her competence, but loved to see the younger woman so happy. Her former maid had greeted her at the gates to see little Bayard herself and make a fuss over him. Melissande did not think she imagined that Berthe's stomach was a little rounder than before.

Niall remained in Quinn's service, and was always prepared to take any message or errand to Tulley. Amaury, Luc, Thierry and Lothair had left for home the previous June, along with much goodwill and many invitations to return. They had intended to halt at Viandin en route to see Rolfe. Melissande and Quinn had ridden to Viandin to visit Rolfe in the autumn, and it had filled Melissande's heart with joy to see Quinn meet the younger sister he had never known. Annelise had been told foul lies about Quinn by Jerome but their reconciliation had been most potent.

And their infant son had been most handsome.

Tulley had developed a fierce cough during the winter and there had been concern for his welfare. To Melissande's surprise, it had been the wife of Annossy's miller who named a concoction that had proven to be of aid, for she had learned of it from Lothair. Tulley had taken the miller's grandson under his care and had vowed to see the boy trained for knighthood as compensation for their aid.

Melissande settled her son into his cradle, then went to the window that overlooked the keep. She could see the spring onions coming up in the kitchen garden to her right, but there was a new garden dug before her. The soil had been turned, but she was uncertain what would be planted in this space, which was outside the walls of the kitchen garden. No doubt Quinn had a plan. The rich smell of the earth rose to her nostrils. She leaned out the window and watched the stars appear one by one as the sky deepened from indigo to black. The warm spring wind stirred her hair and the silver crescent of the moon rode high in the sky.

Melissande was more content than she had guessed it was possible to be.

All because of Quinn.

She heard his footfalls and turned to watch his approach. He granted her a smile that heated her to her toes, then she noticed the small package he carried. "I have no need of a gift," she said, her tone teasing and he smiled.

"Nor I, but this is for both of us."

Melissande tipped back her head to hold his gaze and was lost in the warm amber glow of his eyes. By the saints above, she loved this man with every fiber of her being.

Then Quinn offered her the box.

"It is from the East," he said as she accepted its slight weight. "And the only thing I brought back from there besides my own hide."

Melissande held the box toward the moonlight, seeing that there was detail on the surface. The moonlight picked out the inlay on its lid and she ran one fingertip across the wood in appreciation of the fine craftsmanship. A vine of flowers was made of ivory on the lid, the leaves delicately traced and petals lovingly drawn.

Melissande looked questioningly to Quinn.

He cleared his throat, though still his voice was gruff when he spoke. "It was given to me by Marcus, the keeper of the tavern we frequented, when he learned that we intended to leave the Holy Land. He gave a gift to each of us, all different, all mysterious in their own way."

"Mysterious," Melissande echoed with a smile.

"I heard the news of Sayerne and Marcus knew of that."

"It is a lovely piece of work to grace your home."

"Perhaps it is that. I think it is more. He said 'When you have found the residence where you mean to remain forever, then open it and have your home blessed forevermore.' I have debated the merit of both Annossy and Sayerne, but the truth is that my home is with you."

She eyed him in uncertainty.

"So you must open it," he urged.

Melissande gave the box a shake and something rustled within it. Quinn merely lifted a brow at her glance. Carefully, she lifted the lid of the box.

"Seeds!" she said with delight. The wind stirred the contents then and she understood the keeper's instructions. She also understood why the soil had been turned below the window. "You knew!" she accused and Quinn smiled.

"I peeked, but only a week ago," he confessed.

Melissande turned and leaned out the window, letting the wind catch and sweep the pearly seeds from their sanctuary. She watched the seeds swirl in the air, then scatter onto the freshly turned soil. "What are they?" she asked.

Quinn shrugged. "We shall see soon enough."

"Whatever shall we do while we wait," she mused, smiling as Quinn's arms slipped around her waist. She leaned back against him, entwining her fingers with his. "I have an idea."

"Do you, my lady?" he murmured in her ear, the sound still giving her shivers.

"I think our second son should be conceived at Sayerne," she said, turning to look up at him in time to see his eyes light.

He scooped Melissande up in his arms and kissed her before he carried her to bed. It was the first night that they loved in the great bed in the solar of Sayerne.

Melissande knew it would not be the last, and that made her glad indeed.

AUTHOR'S NOTE

Duke Godfroi de Bouillon was one of the nobles who answered Pope Urban II's call for the First Crusade at the end of the eleventh century. Godfroi left his estates in what is now Belgium to fight in the Holy Land. Later he was elected ruler of the conquered city of Jerusalem and chose the title Defender of the Holy Sepulchre.

Godfroi died of a fever a year later, but there is an old story that on his deathbed, he gave a box to one of his knights. He bade the knight take the box home for him and open it there. The knight did so, only to find that the box was full of seeds, which were blown into the courtyard of Château Bouillon.

Every spring, wild pinks still bloom there and the story maintains that these are the descendants of the seeds Godfroi sent home from Jerusalem a thousand years ago.

Watch for

One Knight's Desire
Book #3 of Rogues & Angels

The *Rogues & Angels* series of medieval romances continues with the tale of Niall MacGillivray and Heloise von Idelstein—can a charming rogue reform his ways and win the heart of a beautiful heiress? Can Niall persuade the Lord de Tulley of his noble intent?

ABOUT THE AUTHOR

Bestselling and award-winning author Deborah Cooke has published over fifty novels and novellas, including historical romances, fantasy romances, fantasy novels with romantic elements, paranormal romances, contemporary romances, urban fantasy romances, time travel romances and paranormal young adult novels. She writes as herself, Deborah Cooke, as Claire Delacroix, and has written as Claire Cross. Her Claire Delacroix medieval romance, *The Beauty*, was her first book to land on the New York Times List of Bestselling Books.

Deborah was the writer-in-residence at the Toronto Public Library in 2009, the first time TPL hosted a residency focused on the romance genre, and she was honored to receive the Romance Writers of America PRO Mentor of the Year Award in 2012. She's a member of Romance Writers of America, and is on the RWA Honor Roll. She lives in Canada with her family.

To learn more about Deborah's books, please visit her websites at:
http://deborahcooke.com
http://www.delacroix.net